Half Crazy

HALF CRAZY

Dara Lebrun

Heliotrope Books

New York

Also by Dara Lebrun:

The Bunny Hop

SubRosa

Designed and Typeset by Heliotrope Books
Cover by Naomi Rosenblatt with Dara Lebrun

For

L

Lavishly

PRELUDE

And you know that she's half-crazy,
But that's why you want to be there.
—Leonard Cohen, *"Suzanne"*

AUGUST 2006

All of me—why not be a taker? The music goes down and around. Standing by the stone wall at Union Square Park, his lips on the mouthpiece and lungs feeding the horn, Jordan reeled tones to the sky to fall upon passers-by like gossamer. Even corporate types actually closed their cell phones to stand and listen, though Jordan doubted they would toss a bill into his saxophone case. At best they'd be good for a dime or quarter, and more likely they'd ramble on and barely notice that the music came from a live person.

A pretty girl in a shamelessly short skirt snapped her fingers—a girl whom Summer would say "Looks like she's wearing a lunch napkin," often adding, "Some women don't believe they're being seen unless the world sees everything." But these miniskirted coquettes tended to lure dudes with cash in their wallets.

Today even Jordan had cash in his wallet, from a party where the trio played last night. He owed most of it to his drummer and bass player, having drained his own cut into a late phone bill. He needed to earn more and swung his torso, taking the tenor sax along and letting tunes bellow through him. A small crowd gathered in the shade of a plane tree, shoppers from the green market with their cider and fresh tomatoes, tapping feet and bobbing heads. A woman with a baby stroller produced two dollars from a belly bag, and another snapped open her wallet. A tall guy in a straw fedora tossed in a few bills—what a happy contagion. Jordan's case would have enough cash for a mushroom and pepperoni pizza, a couple of beers for Summer and him, and lemonade for the little boy.

He would pick up Rashad from day camp later because Summer was auditioning for a TV commercial. Every now and then, her deadbeat manager called with a possible stint. After she got home, Jordan figured they'd order pizza. He felt hungry now, but he'd hold out, working the late lunch crowd and green market shoppers who seemed sweet on Gershwin and Porter. Then he'd head downtown to Rashad's camp at the Pitt Street pool.

As it happened, he was so ravenous after playing in Union Square for three hours that he indulged in a couple of street hotdogs heaped with sauerkraut—a dollar each, for which he used the dimes and quarters he'd just earned. When he arrived at camp, most of the kids were gone already. Rashad scurried around the gym with a limber little girl and a chubby boy while a counselor wearing headphones sat on a folding chair in the corner with a magazine.

"Daddy!" cried Rashad, running up to greet Jordan. Sometime last spring, the five-year-old had decided to call Jordan "Daddy." No one discouraged him, as Jordan planned to adopt the boy after Summer and he married.

"Could Gemma and Ryman come over?"

"Hmm, maybe another time," Jordan suggested.

"Please...?" Rashad grabbed Jordan's leg and tossed back his head.

"Not today." Jordan stroked the child's soft curly hair. Then, taking his hand, Jordan walked Rashad over to the counselor, who continued to read *Wired* magazine, nodding his head to the music. Jordan produced a laminated ID card from his wallet and stuck it under the guy's nose.

"I'm here for Rashad Summers," Jordan announced. "And maybe you'd like to keep your eyes and ears on our kids—why we pay you the big bucks."

The guy stared back as though there were something wrong with Jordan, not himself, and continued reading as Jordan and Rashad exited the gym. Through the corner of his eye, Jordan noted that a woman with long copper hair had grabbed her little girl, and she too was giving this punk counselor a piece of her mind.

"Is Mom on TV?" Rashad asked as they headed up the street.

"She might be," said Jordan. "We don't know yet. She's trying out."

"*Auditioning*," Rashad proudly corrected, as he often did when Jordan tried to simplify what was happening. "What show?"

"An ad for laundry bleach. They need someone who sings...you know Mom can do that." The boy grinned and they turned south, off Delancey Street, to walk by a vacant lot. Jordan wished it were a beach or a meadow in the late afternoon sunshine that spilled over the city, melding even dull brick buildings into appealing shades of pastel.

"Hey," he said to Rashad, "we'll be at the beach next week."

"With Mona and Capitano?"

"That's right." Rashad remembered Jordan's parents by the strange grandparent nicknames they had given themselves—and their visit to Fair Harbor last autumn. How nice that this kid could run again on grass and forget about sidewalks for a while. And maybe, Jordan mused, he could borrow some cash from Molly and take Summer and Rashad to Cape May in September so Summer could find that yellow house from her childhood…if it was still yellow.

Rashad wrapped his sticky little hand around Jordan's. In his other hand Jordan carried his saxophone. Usually he slung the case over his shoulder, but the long crumbling strap had finally broken, so now he had to carry it.

He began to ponder mending the strap with duct tape and barely noticed the shadows and footfalls. Then he was thrust forward into the lot, air out of his lungs and chin on fire from hitting the rubble. Before his eyes, big sneakers scuttled alongside steel-toed combat boots. Both Rashad and the instrument case were no longer in his hands.

Jordan got up and stumbled after the five men. He didn't care if there were rats in the lot or how his jaw stung. He didn't even care about his beloved Conn Lady Face—the first sax he'd ever been given—he would not let them get away with Rashad.

"Daddy!" Rashad screamed as Jordan gained on the guys when they stopped for street traffic. The one who carried Rashad was the biggest of the bunch, and the only one dressed in normal shorts and a T-shirt. The others were exactly the types Jordan didn't want them to be, with tattoos winding up their necks and spooky insignias on their shaved skulls, wearing spiked leather vests and black jeans. They were the kind of guys that could affront any passer-by who might have noticed this chase and thought to help Jordan.

Heart pounding as he choked on his inhales, Jordan sprinted after them, zigzagging under the Williamsburg Bridge at the eastern tip of Delancey Street. There they assembled amid flypaper, syringes, and condoms on the asphalt, with Rashad bawling and pleading, "Help!"

"Shut up!" snapped a gawky guy with a narrow face and long, lizard-like eyes. To Jordan's horror, he grabbed the big iron cross around his neck by its chain and swung at the child's forehead. Jordan recoiled as if he too had been struck. Rashad shrieked and the guy who held him, the muscle-bound guy in the normal shorts and T-shirt, shook him brutally until he stopped.

"This your kid?" the one with lizard eyes asked Jordan, ambling toward him. Jordan nodded, losing his saliva. He was too upset to say that Rashad was the son of Summer's previous boyfriend, who had abandoned them years before.

"Why's he black?" asked another, who wore a torn vest with hawks stenciled on it. "*She's* not black."

"Why do you think?" he wanted to scream, but all he said was "The father."

"You know him, Jordan?"

Jordan shook his head, wondering how the fuck they knew his name. Was it possible that they were friends of that asshole back at camp who was sitting around with *Wired* magazine? Might he have texted them to come harass him? But no, these assailants knew Summer wasn't black, so they must know her. What did they want from him? Cash? Was Rashad now their hostage?

The boy began to wail again, and Jordan saw a dark triangle appear at the crotch of his khaki shorts. His captors noticed too. With disgust, the big guy in the T-shirt let him down and shoved him over to Jordan.

Convulsing with relief, Rashad grabbed Jordan's leg. Jordan stroked the boy's hair with his own shaking hands and asked the guy with the iron cross, as conversationally as he could: "How do you know my name?"

"Your wife told us. We had a little chat last week when I asked her why she named her kid something Arab after they hit our city." He sauntered closer to Jordan and Rashad. "You a defector too?" The others watched righteously. Jordan felt he could hear each of them breathing, or was it cars and trucks passing on the bridge overhead? "You also believe it was an inside job?"

Shit. All of Summer's stupid buttons and pamphlets and ranting.

Without difficulty, Jordan said, "We disagree about that."

"She's your wife," said the skinhead who held his saxophone case.

She wasn't yet, but Jordan didn't feel inclined to correct anyone.

"Husbands and wives disagree. Summer can be opinionated," he continued.

"You mean Cathy," said the big guy in normal shorts and a T-shirt.

"Cathy, Summer, whatever." He shook his head, trying to find his saliva. "She doesn't know her own hair color this week. She can't remember where she put her keys. How the fuck does she know who did what on 9/11?"

The guys seemed vaguely pleased with his annoyance. He'd hooked them by talking about how nuts she was, like they were friends. He had to forge some kind of truce so he and Rashad would be released without a fight, because Jordan knew he couldn't win against them; he didn't have that Hollywood knack of kicking one guy in the groin, then whirling around to expertly cuff two others before lunging at a fourth. He surveyed the noxious strangers, desperate to rewind life ten minutes earlier and walk west rather than south.

"You think we 'had it coming to us?'" The muscle-bound guy in shorts asked.

"Of course not. Who'd we protect in Bosnia?" That reference may have eluded them, so Jordan added, "No way our government did it."

"You playing me?" The gawky guy and his iron cross stood so close to Jordan and Rashad that he could have stepped on their toes. He smelled foul, like mildewed clothing and sweat. "'Cause if you are," he continued, "we'll beat the shit out of you."

Rashad was squeezing Jordan's leg tighter.

Take all of me. But spare the kid. Please.

"Call up my ex-girlfriend," Jordan said, still stroking Rashad's warm head and lifting his cell phone from his pants with his other hand. "The first number"—he nearly choked with a surge of sentiment—"is Molly. A cabdriver told *her* a month before it happened. He actually said, 'You seem like a nice lady. You should leave New York 'cause something terrible will happen here soon.' If this was a government plot, how would a frigging cabdriver know it?"

He handed his phone to the guy with the iron cross, speed-dialing Molly.

"Molly," he said again, as if her name would save him and Rashad now.

The guy with lizard eyes cocked his shaved head, phone to ear.

"Voice mail," he said.

One of the others pointed out that Jordan was allowing the kid with piss-soaked pants to touch him, and the gawky guy waved him off, shutting Jordan's phone.

"It did say 'Molly' though. So long, Molly!"

He tossed Jordan's phone into the gutter.

"Fucking sand-nigger, danced when the towers fell," asserted the skinhead who held his saxophone case, turning sideways to spit amply on the street.

Jordan looked at the familiar instrument case with its broken strap in the guy's hand. He heard the J train rumble over the bridge and remembered arguing with Zikomo over a set list last week, en route to a gig in Ditmas Park.

Then the ugliest of the goons, streaked with dark green tattoos, took out his own phone and began texting. He could have been fifty, Jordan estimated. His stubble was going gray and his face looked like someone had chewed on it.

"Your wallet," said the lizard with the iron cross, making a buttery movement with his bony fingers and glancing around as if he expected someone.

Were they really after cash—for all this? Who was the other asshole texting? Jordan reached into his back pocket, glumly remembering the cash he planned to give Z and Bruce later…if he lived.

The gawky guy grabbed it, shook it open, and pulled at the fifty-dollar bills with mock awe. "Eyyy…looky here."

They huddled together, the tatted wonder stuffing his phone into a pocket, and the skinhead who held the saxophone spitting again.

Then a black sedan pulled up, followed by a cop van. In all Jordan's years of smoking and selling pot, and growing up with parents who smoked and sold pot, he had dreaded the sight. Now it could not have been more glorious.

"Scatter!" cried the gawky guy with the iron cross, and they took off in different directions. The skinhead who'd kept spitting still had Jordan's saxophone, and the gawky guy had his wallet. A couple of undercovers emerged from the sedan's back doors, slammed them shut, and ran after the thugs.

Only the big guy in shorts and a T-shirt remained stationary, looking stunned.

"Hello, Frankie." A young cop chewing gum waved from the driver's window of the cop van. "Three years of house arrest wasn't enough for you, eh?"

A woman about Molly's age, with long, copper hair, freckles, and brown eyes also got out of the van with a little girl. Jordan recognized them from camp.

"Gemma's in Rashad's group," she told Jordan. "We saw those guys push you down in the lot. Sorry it took us so long to get here."

The next night he played slow Ellington tunes in the living room as sunset tinted the sky outside pink and pale blue like an Easter egg. He had to play slowly because his chin and lips still hurt. The cops had returned his saxophone and his wallet with all the fifties—which he was glad he'd earned legitimately, when it came to filing the crime report. There was no property damage other than his lost cell phone, valued at thirty-five dollars. He didn't especially miss it, because he didn't especially want to speak with anyone.

Neither he nor Rashad had ventured out into the tauntingly bright August day. In the morning, Summer had suggested that they get doughnuts, but he refused. He was still shaky and didn't want to see anyone he didn't know. He'd spent the morning trying to make reeds, while Rashad watched TV and napped, then played video games and napped again. Jordan watched *Judge Judy* and the afternoon soaps, Rashad clinging to his chest.

"Daddy saved me," Rashad kept telling Summer.

"Those scumbuckets have it coming," she muttered, and Jordan assumed she meant that they would have no defense before a grand jury. The cops had seen Rashad's nicked forehead and Jordan's bleeding chin; they'd both been photographed before they were rushed to Downtown Hospital for tetanus shots. The cops had seen the injuries, and Gemma's mom had seen the rest. She could testify that they had pushed Jordan over and grabbed Rashad. She even had photos from a digital camera.

"And you know this white trash—*how*?" he asked Summer. "I assume they're not part of your '9/11 Truth' squad."

She explained that Frankie's brother, Geoff, had been her high school sweetheart.

"Geoff who stalked our gig last spring?"

"Geoff of the restraining order."

"Douchenozzle," Jordan mumbled. "It's been twenty fucking years, hasn't it?"

"Well, look at how long you've been hung up on Molly."

"I'm not hung up on Molly. You talk about her more than I do."

"Men fixate on one past and relive it ad infinitum. I figure it's a side effect of testosterone, 'cause every guy I know seems to—"

"Easy. I had a bad fall yesterday."

Jordan felt too achy for their usual bickering.

In the corner where Summer had tacked her 9/11 Was an Inside Job poster, he had taped a shopping bag over *9/11* and written *Summer Vale* on it.

It now read: *Summer Vale Was an Inside Job*—but inside what?

PART ONE

I don't know, don't really care.
Let there be songs to fill the air.
—Grateful Dead, "Ripple"

AUGUST 2004 – AUGUST 2006

Her name was Cathy Summers, but onstage she was Summer Vale. Jordan, Zikomo, and Bruce appeared at the Hotel Susquehanna, along with competing bands who must also have seen her ad in Craigslist. She sang in this historic hotel once a month, seemed to have amassed a following of neighborhood locals and hotel guests, and needed jazz backup for her vocals. Jordan sat with Z and Bruce at a round table with a long, white cloth near the stage and watched her perform with only a pianist.

The Victorian Ballroom smelled dizzyingly of lilies, as there was a large vase of them on a podium behind the Steinway. And her singing made them giddy. Z whispered to Jordan, "White girl, black pipes." She sang standards they knew well by Rogers and Hart, Porter, Gershwin—and then more obscure Bessie Smith and Muddy Waters blues. Not surprisingly, "Summertime" seemed to be her signature piece. She drew her voice out of her belly and snaked it around the room, over the octaves.

"'Over the Rainbow'—and over high C," Jordan whispered to his band members, who were all impressed by her range.

"Her phrasing…" Z began. Jordan too had noticed that she didn't sing anything as he'd heard it before. Each line was delivered with the wonder of a child just seeing a cake full of candles. She wasn't doing that rote thing at the mic and trying to sound torchy—quasi-screaming. She had her own voice, and she listened to it.

After this first set, Zikomo and guys from the other bands went up to introduce themselves, to hand her business cards and demo CDs. Z had always been their envoy since Jordan came off as pushy and Bruce was shy. But Z returned from his chat with Summer Vale shaking his head and saying, "We don't have this one." Still, unlike all their rivals, the Jordan Radfar Trio stayed for her second set. If the first was her warm-up—first sets tended to be—they wouldn't miss the crescendo.

Proving worth the wait, she started right in with "Mack the Knife," followed by: "*Oh show us the way to the next little boy. Oh don't ask why.*" And then husky, naughty, almost in a whisper: "*Oh don't ask why.*"

It made Jordan want to take out his horn and start riffing with her. He felt sorry they "didn't have this one," because that had been one of the few occasions, back then, when he'd entirely forgotten about Molly.

"I know you Europeans didn't come across the pond to hear songs from your own backyard, and I promise we'll get back to the U.S.," she said mellifluously into the mic. "I just couldn't resist Kurt Weill. And I don't think I can resist Edith Piaf or Sandy Denny…"

But when she returned from "Sous le ciel de Paris" to English and launched into "Who Knows Where the Time Goes?" tears pricked Jordan's eyes. "*For who knows where my love grows?*" Summer hit those high notes perfectly, almost aggressively. "*And who knows where the time goes?*"

"That was fun," Z said as they walked out into a clammy August night, leaving lilies and air-conditioning behind them. "We should keep her in mind if we get a theme bar mitzvah again. Barbra Streisand, move over. Otherwise, we didn't make the cut."

But the next afternoon he called Jordan to say, "Hey, I was wrong. We're rehearsing Thursday with Summer Vale."

"How much is she paying?"

"The hotel pays."

"No shit."

As a sideman, Jordan generally received payment from the band, not the venue. He knew that vocalists often didn't even get paid themselves and earned only tips.

"She's been working with them for a year," Z explained. "They upped her fee about a hundred bucks and said to go find a band. Guess she's been wanting that for a while. But she asked the hotel to pay us because she's too scatterbrained and felt she'd mess it up."

"So how much are we getting?"

"Thirty each, plus tips and food."

That meant another ten or twenty from the tip jar, and a meal with hotel wine.

"Cool," Jordan said. "Is there a P.A.?"

"She's got the amps. By the way, I told her we could rehearse late at my place because the neighbors don't care, and I've got my drums set up and a bass for Bruce. Well, she didn't seem fazed by my 'hood—just asked about the subway line. She's actually laid back on the phone. But you know what I say: they sing like angels and make your life hell."

Z held that most men couldn't sing, that they kind of whelped in interesting ways, like Tom Waits or Dylan. He ceded that Nat King Cole and Sinatra could carry a tune, "but men never bring tears to your eyes. Songs were meant for women. And when they have that gift, it's like fire—it'll burn everything in sight. I just hope she doesn't get all crazy about keys and micromanaging our arrangements. I told her that we were pretty improvisational. She liked your playing on the CD. A lot."

"Good," said Jordan.

"She asked who Molly Douglas is."

Molly, of course, had produced their CD and designed the cover. It had been one of her concessions when she'd broken up with Jordan.

"What did you say?" Jordan asked.

"I said, 'Molly's a long story. But not my long story.'"

Rehearsing with Summer Vale proved surprisingly painless for the Jordan Radfar Trio. Her song list was smart and eclectic, while she was punctual, focused, and not fussy. If they were off-tempo, she'd suggest, "Let's start again." After a melodic interval, she'd often giggle as if she were being tickled and say, "Ooh, I like that."

She was flirtatious in the most general way, with all of them at once. More often than not, she seemed guarded and mistrustful of men. When she wasn't onstage in a long, vampy gown, she wore shapeless pants and big cotton shirts or wrinkled thrift store dresses that fell below her knees. She was ample in a languorous way, like certain Balthus or Picasso women. As Jordan got to know her better, she would describe herself as "too fat," and he would counter her with: "No, you're not fat. You're here, baby."

She was also a mom, and there didn't seem to be a dad around. Instead, she always called someone named Betty when they rehearsed, to ask about "my kid. How's he doing?" and "Can he stay a little later with you? I should be home in an hour."

Summer tended to withdraw and get moody around midnight, often placing what Jordan called her Cinderella coach call. "Hey, it's Cathy," she'd say. "I need a car." Some friends of hers operated a cab service out of the airports in Newark and Queens, and they always seemed happy enough to send one her way.

"Would you like us to call you Cathy?" Z asked once.

"To people who know me through music, I'm Summer," she told him.

"What does your family call you?" Z asked.

"They call me nothing because we haven't spoken in years."

Neither Z nor Bruce had pushed for details, but Jordan asked, "How many years?"

She glanced back at him as though she enjoyed the attention but was not planning to reward it, her gray-blue eyes opaque.

"A while now," she said.

"Three years? Ten?"

"Somewhere in between."

He picked up the saxophone, heading straight into "Who Knows Where the Time Goes?" and she followed him, her voice streaming out like golden lava— that woman could hold a note as long as it needed to be held and never flew off-key. Bruce and Z picked a rhythm, but Summer and Jordan carried the tune into space.

They brought their open, driving sound to the Hotel Susquehanna cabaret. People clapped enthusiastically after each number, lined the tip jar with bills, and always called out for an encore. There was nothing more bolstering than a room full of strangers applauding with cries of "More! One more!"

The trio was doing what she'd requested by "making the act less about a lone woman singing to piano accompaniment, and more about music."

Z asked her, "What's wrong with a woman singing to piano? Your voice is great, and you blow people's minds."

"Yeah, but it can get too 'Mary Had a Little Lamb'—just me and my tinkling songs."

"I don't know what you're talking about," Z challenged. "I like it when you can't hide behind effects. I started drumming on buckets when I was a kid. I still do sometimes, in the subway. And I play mean cajón. It's simple, simple."

"There's nothing like ensemble," she insisted, and Jordan shared that appetite. He could make beautiful and interesting sounds by himself; he'd done it so many times. But the lure was infinitely deeper when piano chords mingled with plucked bass strings, horns harmonized or grew dissonant, and the human voice wavered through it, adding words and even more texture.

As the weeks rolled on, they began to get mentioned on travel websites. *Don't miss Summer Vale and the Jordan Radfar Trio,* someone had written. *Awesome and affordable night of oldies and blues at the Susquehanna Hotel.*

She should be famous! someone else added.

"Why aren't you famous?" Jordan asked at a rehearsal, when they'd come upon those reviews. She had shrugged and said, "Bad luck."

After three months, the trio raised their fee at the hotel to fifty dollars each, plus tips, and rehearsed with Summer less frequently. They had established "musical trust," as she put it. They could anticipate each other's interludes and intervals, had learned when to stand back and when to take the stage.

But on occasion, they still convened in Bed Stuy at Z's, to chat over beer and play into the night. Once or twice Fred, her piano man, had come along and enlisted the keyboard at Z's for his trills—they were practicing a Christmas set. Summer had recommended "a pocketful of Yankee holiday songs, to reinforce tourists' impressions of how corny and gullible we are." No one disagreed.

"'White Christmas,'" she'd elaborated. "Theme song for a racist society."

Summer's preference for black men had been made as explicit as her disdain for "dominant culture." One night she proclaimed that all white Americans were drunks. "It's in our DNA. You couldn't get Evian water in feudal times, in Europe—if you wanted to live, you drank wine. You still do. But black people know how to party. We know only how to get sloshed."

She promised them she'd "sing 'White Christmas' like an ice queen" and sipped her Beck's from the bottle. "I love that it was written by an immigrant Jew."

"That would be…Irving Berlin?"

Bruce had a way of saying everything as though it were an answer on *Jeopardy*, sometimes plucking a string or two of his bass to underscore it.

"You ever write songs?" Z asked, and Summer parried: "Nothing I could say hasn't been said by Irving Berlin or Cole Porter. And I'd rather sing exquisite lyrics than write crappy ones. Do you ever sing?" she asked them.

"I cry when I sing," Jordan explained. "But Z's range is awesome."

"Not so much anymore," Z admitted.

In those days, Jordan had wondered if Summer had a crush on Z, with his gangly, basketball player–like arms and legs, his moth-eaten sweaters and sphinxlike head of dreadlocks that whipped around when he hit those cymbals and high hats. He was older than the rest of them, but Z was eternally popular with women.

"What do you think?" Jordan had asked him once.

"I don't get that from her," Z said. "And If I were a betting man, I'd say she's sweet on you."

"It's a music thing," Jordan countered him, "not a man-woman thing with

Summer and me."

But Z advised, "Hold your hat."

After rehearsal, Jordan usually crashed at Z's—since Jordan wasn't sleeping with anyone, he didn't care where he slept. In fact, he was happy to avoid his apartment, which was littered with roommates' clothes and empty beer bottles, and he preferred the pile of pillows in Z's basement. But one night he planned to hook up with a girl who'd seen the trio open for an act at B. B. King's. She looked sultry and had given Jordan her card. He knew, however, that girls his age tended to idealize him onstage and abruptly lose interest when they learned that he was broke and aimless. Molly hadn't cared about that. She was thirteen years older than he and able to provide financial remedy.

He'd found women after Molly to be as anticlimactic as Impressionists after Monet. They couldn't relax, even when he performed acts that made Molly breathless. One of them had even stopped him right in the middle of making love and announced: "This isn't getting anywhere"—an assessment that didn't conform to Molly's rave reviews. But Jordan forced himself to go to parties and went on any date that came his way. So that night he asked if he might share Summer's "Cinderella" cab to Manhattan to meet the girl from B. B. King's.

"Where do you live again?" Summer asked when they sat side by side in the back seat, bumping their way over cobblestones and potholes.

"I share a place with some guys in Sunset Park. But I crash around at my friends." He felt awkward speaking with her. They said more to each other through music. "Got a date in the city tonight," he mumbled.

"Kinda late, isn't it?"

"Whatever."

"You don't sound thrilled, Jordan."

"I already know what's going to happen."

"Tell me." Summer peered at him through the darkness.

"Okay. We'll have a beer. She'll say she's some NYU student, and I'll tell her what I do. She'll smile and go, 'Uh-hmm,' but that's about the point she's deciding this is *not* a wrap. You know, what does some nursing or journalism student want with a guy that won't score half her income? But I'll try to kiss her, and she'll stop me and say she's not ready, and then I'll never hear from her again."

"Got it," said Summer. "Wanna hear my version?"

Did women have a version? "Sure."

"So, he'll come up to me after a gig with stars in his eyes. No one I even noticed."

"They never are," Jordan interrupted her. "You never see paparazzi 'til they blow into your face."

"Shaking my hand and telling me I'm off-the-charts, and he knows someone who can produce me, and we should go out to dinner. We'll trade numbers, and he'll call. But when Rashad starts crying in the background, he'll say, 'Oh. What's that?' and I'll say, 'My son.' He'll say, 'Oh. You married?' and I'll say, 'Nope.' And he'll say, 'Well, let me get back to you tomorrow to confirm.' And that's that."

"Guess a woman with a kid is as doomed as a guy without cash."

"Then I'm double trouble, with a kid and no money," she said.

"Look, a woman without money can get a date," Jordan told her. "Guys even like paying. And feeling superior."

"Not my type of guy. I don't do the control freaks. And it's not like I haven't had my chances. Right, Vali?" Summer called to the cabdriver: "Right?"

"Right what?" the driver replied with some kind of accent. "I don't listen to your conversations, Cath."

"Oh, don't be so respectful," she dismissed him with a laugh.

Jordan thought his date hadn't shown up, until she texted that she was too tired to wait any longer for him. He wrote back, *Understand* and left it at that. If she was tired now, she would be tired next week. He ended up in a bar on the Lower East Side until it closed, looking for a girl who liked walking after midnight but not finding her or anyone. He used to look forward to the sounds of nighttime, to its nip and shiver. At that restless point in his life, even sleep or getting high didn't help. Only playing music brought him peace. And sometimes it was too late and quiet, or too damn cold to sit outside with his horn.

He called Claudia and Dustin to see if he could crash with them, but no one answered. It was never easy for him to go there anyway because they still lived in Molly's old building near Gramercy Park. Every time he walked up that creaky, carpeted staircase he remembered his last night with Molly, which he had mistaken for a promise.

It crossed Jordan's mind to call Summer, but he instantly nixed that thought. What might he say? "My date blew me off, just like I told you in the cab. You got a sofa for me?" How tacky that would sound. Molly said she couldn't stand it when he "posed like the world owes you something." There was a protocol with women that Jordan seemed to be learning slower than most handsome young men. And without Molly, he might not have learned it at all.

So that night, like so many others, he'd ended up on the R train heading to the Brooklyn apartment to which he possessed a key. It was where he kept a mattress on the floor, contributed to monthly expenses, and scrawled his initials on six-packs in the fridge so his roommates wouldn't pilfer them. As the empty train bucked his thighs and the saxophone case beside him, he compared his life to Molly's, reviewing with familiar distress how hers had taken off in the four years since they'd split, while his had gotten ratty.

If someone like Z were to ask him, "Well, wouldn't you want her to be happy?" he would say, "Of course." She's a great woman. She'd done so much for him: producing the trio's CD, helping him pay down his student loan, landing him a part-time job—thanks to members of her co-op board—teaching music at an uptown private school for boys. He lived off these triumphs like light after a comet. Without Molly he'd be less than the orange rind he saw sliding across the floor as the subway car swayed.

But she didn't miss him. When she bought her apartment on Riverside Drive with windows overlooking the Hudson ("Sickeningly classy," Claudia had ranted), won awards for excellence in her ad campaigns (he had attended the ceremony only to realize that she'd invited him by mistake), or traveled to Rio ("At Carnival with Eugenia," Claudia had blurted) or Berlin ("They went to the film festival") or any other exotic destination, he understood she was just fine—too fine. He actually liked it when Claudia told him Molly was out of town, far enough away that he didn't have to feel her loving this other person and carrying on quite gloriously without him.

At one point it had gotten back to him that Molly and Eugenia seemed rocky. This third-hand rumor had Eugenia advocating friendship—because she felt so fond of Molly but feared their romance wouldn't last because Molly wasn't really gay. "Friends last forever," she'd apparently said. "Girlfriends tend not to."

But Jordan knew that Molly would set the goal of being the one who did last; she was as dogged and determined as he. Why couldn't they have teamed up in their unrelenting idealism? Why did she prefer someone who'd dismiss her as "a friend"?

"Look," Claudia had told Jordan back then, "Molly's been flying pretty close to the sun. Her wings will burn, and she'll fall hard."

"I'll be there for her," Jordan pledged, already imagining how tenderly he would comfort her.

"You'd better be. She'll need you," Claudia had assured him. "It's almost impossible for a woman to get over her first love affair with a woman. You basically never do."

Jordan had waited, weaving intricate fantasies of solace and an erotic reunion. But to everyone's surprise, the trouble blew over and he'd next heard from Claudia, "Those two are thick as thieves. I think Molly and Eugenia are business partners now. Eugenia's telling all the girls she's found the love of her life and that her days of 'binge-and-purge dating' are over."

He'd tried not to curse this fate, if it was what Molly wanted. But he sometimes felt too mashed up inside to breathe. Over the years Molly had unarguably been generous, throwing him a thousand dollars when he was in a pinch—she was that kind of friend. And she was the kind of ex-lover who gave lip service to their kisses: "Jordan, you saved me, after years in a sensory deprivation tank with Thomas."

Then why hadn't it lasted?

Sometimes he called or wrote to her, lamenting that he wasn't over her. She'd offered to pay for him to speak with a therapist: "At times we all need a referee. Eugenia and I wouldn't have lasted without some outside help."

"Tell me who the outside help is so I can box their ears," Jordan had grumbled.

"If you still feel so strongly," Molly had said, "it's not about me anymore."

"It will always be about you."

He had taken her up on the offer and met for a year with Barbara, a psychotherapist who specialized in treating artists. While he appreciated talking to Barbara, nothing changed much. Psychotherapy had simply reduced him, on occasion, to tears and cinders. He would never forget the session where Barbara had written the name *Molly* for him and changed it into *Mommy*, the word he'd not been encouraged to call his own mother. With Barbara's help he'd wrested about as much insight about himself as he could take. And for that he'd scribbled Molly a thank-you note in the Christmas card he sent her.

The holiday season that year had been particularly good for the trio. Z secured a bunch of office parties, and their cabarets with Summer Vale were so packed that the hotel booked a separate audience for each set. Jordan had first met Rashad during one of those crowded December gigs, with Summer singing—as promised—"White Christmas" in a long, red Santa Claus cap.

"There's a very special member of our audience tonight," she announced into the mic. "My son." Everyone clapped and shouted, "Yea!"

"You want to hold him up, Betty?"

In the crowd, a woman with long, dark hair stood up with a little boy in her arms, striking a Virgin and child pose. The room was too candlelit for Jordan, or anyone else, to descry the boy's darker skin. It was hard to see anything clearly except the stage. But applause thundered, and Z produced a grand drumroll.

"Betty is my personal patron saint," Summer confided to Jordan after their first set ended, and the band left the stage to mingle for a drink before the second set began. "She lives a couple of blocks from us—my kid is in preschool with her sons, who are twins and always fighting like Cain and Abel. But something about Rashad calms them down, maybe because he looks so different, you know, not another carbon copy. Even though they're fraternal twins, her little guys look madly alike."

Jordan tried to find them in the dark room but couldn't.

"It's all great for me, because Betty and Curtis like having Rashad around. They feed him well and treat him to movies and video games I couldn't swing on my wormy income and the pittance I get from his dad. Don't know what I'd do without good ole Betty."

When Jordan met the Wilcoxes, he couldn't imagine what Summer had in common with them, along with the even more sleek, conservative-looking couple who sat with them. Their aura of wealth didn't escape his notice, but they also all seemed strangely delighted with Summer, as though she were some mesmerizing and colorful fish in a tank.

It then hit him that they were rich in a more boring way than Molly. If these couples hadn't come to the cabaret to watch "their own Summer Vale" entertain a roomful of tourists, they'd be at a table ordering dessert wine and chatting about how to trade the NASDAQ. Being rich was hardly a guarantee of being interesting—Molly just happened to be both.

"Z, this is Ray and Angela Crawford." As Summer introduced everyone, hands were shaken, and Summer sauntered his way. "Curtis DeFreest Wilcox..." She presented a man who was neither tall nor short, with strands of brown hair that fell neatly over his forehead, and whispered into Jordan's ear, "Son of the American Revolution." Jordan quickly shook the guy's hand, and before he knew it, his wife, Betty, was passing Rashad to Summer. The jovial chanteuse squeezed her son in her arms and cooed, "How's my sweetie?"

Rashad smiled shyly, aware of being watched. He must have been three at the time, but he'd always radiated a sense of how the world received him. His skin was caramel, his brown hair springy. Jordan was struck by his dab of a nose, a tiny replica of Summer's, and his eyelashes, so long and black. Over at their table, the two Wilcox boys looked pale and pointy by comparison.

"Betty Wilcox." A slender and surprisingly cold hand slipped into Jordan's. But Betty's smile was self-effacing in an endearing way, and her large blue eyes were kind.

"Enjoyed your sound!" Curtis raved. They spoke about how long Jordan had been on sax. Curtis bought a couple of Jordan's CDs and asked him to sign them. "Christmas gifts for my nieces," he explained, saying their names so Jordan could include them with his autograph: "For Claire. For Jessamyn…Happy Holidays, Jordan."

"This is Z," Summer was saying to her little boy, and Z nodded at Rashad—he was not one to get overly involved with children, but he was nevertheless gracious. "And this mysterious man who plays the big stand-up bass is Bruce," she went on.

"Oh, I don't know about mysterious," Bruce demurred. He had a son, so he knew how to speak to Rashad. "How you doing there?" he asked warmly.

"Fine," said Rashad in his honeyed little voice.

Then Summer turned to Jordan: "And this yummy, adorable man is the one Mommy always talks to Betty about…Jordan."

Rashad smiled and held out a small hand.

"Nice to meet you," Jordan said flatly, disoriented by Summer's comment and by having to say anything social to someone so young.

The Wilcoxes left with all the children when the audience for the next set filtered in, which was just as well. The kids were sleepy, and one of the Wilcox boys was starting to whine.

The second set was a hit: Fred's fingers scampering over the keys with arpeggios, Bruce walking the bass in his meandering way that went everywhere, Jordan on fire with his sax after a hit of tea and Courvoisier. The audience loved Summer's Christmas medley as much as the first crowd had. But no one was prepared when, in the middle of "White Christmas," a man in the audience fell over his table.

The music stopped abruptly. Summer said into the mic: "Someone, please dial nine-one-one. We have a medical emergency." House lights went on, and waiters quickly began reshuffling tables so that there would be a clear path to the exit when the medics came. Now the man lay on the carpeted floor. Someone had taken off his shoes, and a small, hapless crowd gathered around him.

"Why doesn't anyone do CPR?" Summer whispered to the band.

"You know how?" Z asked. She shook her head.

"Too much to drink," she assessed, away from the mic. "Too much for his age. Maybe he's dehydrated. Let's hope he's not diabetic."

Finally three firefighters showed up in their high boots and black slickers. One of them strapped a blood pressure cuff around the fallen man's arm and seemed to pump consciousness back into him. Meanwhile, waiters offered free champagne to the patrons whose tables had been reshuffled, and the captain took notes and spoke into a walkie-talkie. He was the sort of broad-shouldered hero that instantly made Jordan feel inferior. Jordan even wondered if Summer was noticing the guy. But, of course, he wasn't black. And why was Jordan even thinking about guys Summer noticed?

The firemen led the fragile but revived man out of the lounge, his companions anxiously following. Once they left, Jordan played a long, slow C, and Summer began singing quietly: "*May your days be merry and bright.*" The house lights dimmed again, and everyone applauded.

For this display of showmanship, they were offered the Hotel Susquehanna's New Year's Eve party in the Victorian Ballroom—which paid a small windfall. Summer usually had to drag her amps and microphones out after her act, but the ballroom manager agreed to store her equipment for New Year's Eve. Looking back, Jordan could never recall how they decided to go smoke a joint in Central Park after the gig that nearly killed a guy.

Summer generally didn't smoke; it wasn't good for her voice. But this was a night of exceptions. In her big fake fur coat with Santa Claus cap, she linked her left arm into Z's and her right into Jordan's after bidding Bruce, the family man, good night.

"*Lions 'n' tigers 'n' bears, oh my*...I wouldn't scale this park without a couple of tall, strong escorts."

"Hate to disappoint you," Jordan countered, "but I'm neither."

At 5'9", he was aware that many women—like Molly's lover, Eugenia—were taller than he, and possibly stronger. Z, on the other hand, stood nearly 6'4". If Summer wanted her tall, strapping stud, she had him on her other arm.

"But you're part black, aren't you?" she asked Jordan, as they crossed Central Park West.

"What?"

Z burst out laughing.

"Where do you come up with these..."

"You saw my kid. I can always tell."

"You're wrong about me," said Jordan. "My ex, Molly, called me a Mediterranean Party Mix."

Z was still cracking up, and Jordan was gratified to have flustered Summer by this reference to another woman.

"Mediterranean Party Mix?" she asked coyly.

"My dad's family are Iranian Jews, and my mother's part Italian, and part Basque."

"So you're not Caucasian."

"What the—sure I am!"

Jordan had been mistaken for Greek, Lebanese, and Puerto Rican but never for African. His girlfriend in college had theorized that he resembled the historical Jesus.

Z doubled over with laughter, his breath steamy in the cold, clear air.

"Remember, Jordan—white is political," Summer continued. "Caucasian is anthropological."

"We haven't even smoked yet!" Z managed to say through his laughter.

"Are you fucking with my head?" Jordan asked Summer as they walked up Central Park West, parallel to the park.

"I'd prefer to fuck with more than your head," she whispered in his ear, "if I may be so blunt."

Then she flicked her tongue at his earlobe, sending an electrical shock to his toes—particularly hot on this damp night. Jordan knew that men were supposed to make the first move, but he so preferred women like Molly or Summer, who did a better job of it.

He turned to her grinning face in the Santa Claus cap.

"You're crazy," he whispered.

"Half-crazy. But that's why you wanna be there."

"I, uh…I actually do wanna be there, Summer. But you know the drill. Can't wine you and dine you."

"That's okay," she said. "Some people have oysters Rockefeller. I have oysters *on the* Rockefellers."

"Never tried those," said Z as they walked into the park at the 86th Street entrance.

"Jordan will love them," she insisted. "I always do."

"Raw bar?" he asked. "On my nonexistent dime? Like I was saying—"

"That's the whole idea," she explained with glee. "The restaurant is treating you. They just don't know it."

Arms still linked, the three musicians proceeded downhill on the winding path until Z indicated a grove of bare trees by a streetlamp. There they convened in the long, branchy shadows.

"So…you're talking about, like, a happy hour raid?" Z asked as he slipped off his drum case and fished through sticks and cymbal stands. Jordan shivered as Z tried to find the joint they'd rolled earlier.

"No, I'm talking about fine dining and disappearing like Houdini when the bill comes around. You can't do it every night of the week, of course. I pull it off two or three times a year."

Once he found the joint, Z stuck it between his lips and flicked the lighter. Jordan's nostrils tingled with the zesty scent. Z passed the joint to Summer, who drew in girlish, staccato gasps before giving it to Jordan, her fingers brushing his.

He took an expert drag and exhaled into her face.

"You're just one smokin' gun, Summer Vale," he said.

"Just one smokin' mirror," she replied with a smile that, in the shadows of a city night in the park, stunned him.

The next evening Jordan met Summer at a seafood bistro in the West 50s. Her method was to never patronize the same place twice, and Eddystone Light was new to her.

"Me father was the keeper of the Eddystone Light;
He married a mermaid one fine night..."

She sang the old sea shanty as they walked in. Lights were low, and the walls draped stylishly with nets that were held in place by starfish. Above the bar hung a large, framed photo of the actual Eddystone Lighthouse off the coast of Devon.

The hostess told them it would be a ten-minute wait, and Summer whispered to Jordan: "Excellent. It's so busy that a bunch of different waiters will serve us. Mind you, we'll leave a nice tip. We're not really stealing, we're just giving ourselves an artist's discount." Then she continued singing:

"From this union there came three,
A porpoise and a porgy and the other was me!
High ho, the wind blows free,
All for the life on the rolling sea."

The bartender, a burly guy with a white beard, grinned at them. "Been working here for three years," he said. "Never heard anyone sing our song."

Jordan began to boast about her great voice, but Summer stepped on his toe. He took the hint not to draw any more unnecessary attention than she already had. Luckily the bartender went off to other customers, and Jordan winked at Summer. Her straight hair was freshly tinted with copper henna, and she had pinned it up in a bun, with strands falling over her eyes and cheeks. Jordan noticed that she also wore a touch of rouge and mascara—all decked out for the occasion.

"You know Edgar Allan Poe's four conditions for happiness?" she asked him.

"Ponder a raven on a midnight dreary?"

"It's more cheerful, at least according to Camus: Condition number one is 'Life in the open air'—like *life on the rolling sea.* Two is 'The love of another being.' Three is 'Freedom from all ambition.' Four is 'Creation.'"

"Life in the open air," he repeated. But he forgot the second one, so she said again: "'The love of another being.' Notice Camus doesn't say human being. It could be a dog or a salamander."

"Wouldn't mind any of it," Jordan said. "Especially the salamander."

"People attribute this list to Camus, but he was interpretting Poe in his journal. Shows how closely we read these days."

Her scent was pleasant: shampoo and baby powder—so different from Molly's tinges of tea rose and eucalyptus. He touched the pearls around Summer's pale white neck.

"These 'on the Rockefellers' with the oysters?"

"On loan from Betty Wilcox. She did my hair today."

"Does she know about our dinner plan?"

"Not every aspect of it."

An earnest young hostess approached them.

"Your table's ready. Would you care to check your coats?"

"No thank you," said Summer easily. "We're okay."

Once they were seated across a candlelit table, she explained her rationale for stealing perishables. "If they don't serve it, they'll toss it all out, which is more of a crime." Jordan mentioned that Molly and Eugenia gave their extra food to soup kitchens, and Summer said, "Very philanthropic of them, but we're actually paying the waitstaff."

"Are we?" Jordan whispered. "I'm afraid these guys will get docked."

"You ever work in a restaurant?"

He shook his head no.

"Well, I've waitressed far and wide. You have your assigned tables, but everyone helps each other as the night goes on. Generally you pool tips and cut in the bartender and busboy. So when a bill ducks out, the owner or the manager eats it—and trust me, they can afford to."

Jordan glanced around at the scurrying men and women in black pants and white shirts.

"Look, Summer, I have a Visa card for the trio. Why don't we just put our tab tonight on here, and I'll write it off my taxes? We're actually earning money this year, so I need a write-off," he said proudly.

Molly had helped him to create an LLC and track the trio's expenses. She held that owning a small business could benefit an artist in an otherwise daunting system, but Summer was cackling.

"Why are handsome, young boys who play saxophone taxed? That is crazy."

"Well, I don't necessarily pay—I just file. Sometimes I even get money back."

"As you should," she said with a toss of her head. "The government should pay artists in this philistine country. Even the monarchs had jesters."

"Do you file?"

"Strange that you should ask." Across the finely set table with turquoise cloth napkins, blue candles, and carnations, she placed her head upon folded hands. "I dropped out of the system for a while. I'm just kind of…emerging again from the ashes."

"Did you owe big-time?"

"I make it my business to never *owe*. It's not a concept I enjoy."

"Got any tips about how to avoid it?"

"Plenty. But let's start with the task at hand. And in case you're wondering…" She leaned in toward him, and he leaned closer too. "I'd never lift wallets. That's just nasty. People have sentimental pictures and little phone numbers and things." She sat back again. "I stick with just stealing food, and sometimes toilet paper and dish towels. I think the gods forgive me that."

A tall, abnormally thin waiter with a white shirt and black pants appeared with a basket of warm bread and their menus. Summer thanked him graciously and put on reading glasses to peruse the selection.

"When did you start to need those?" Jordan asked.

"They're fake," she said. "They make me look legitimate."

She slid them down her nose like an old schoolteacher, and he laughed helplessly.

"Let's get a dozen oysters on the half shell, shall we?" she suggested.

"Whatever you say, darling."

And so they feasted on West Coast oysters, a fine bottle of Pinot Grigio, roasted red snapper with parsley and rosemary, and lobster ravioli, all the while conducting a lively debate about Sartre's moral imperatives. Their references grew more drunken and sloppy as they ordered chocolate hazelnut torte with brandied currants and orange for dessert, with a glass of ruby port and sparkling water for each of them.

Jordan quoted from *Existentialism Is a Humanism*, on which he'd written a term paper in college—he figured if Summer could quote Camus referencing Poe, then he'd quote Sartre referencing Kant and Socrates. "Sartre wrote somewhere that our essence is determined by our deeds. At least, that's what I thought he meant. So we'd have to ask ourselves, 'Can humanity guide itself by our actions now?' Like, if everyone did what we're doing, there wouldn't be restaurants."

"But we're not *always* doing it," she objected in her hushed voice. "That wouldn't work. This is a special occasion, and how dull life would be if everyone obeyed rules all the time. You know that Leonard Cohen line about how light gets through a crack that's in everything? That's my life."

They finished their port, and she flagged a waiter—not the one who'd been serving them—scribbling in the air just like Molly always did. But Molly had every intention of paying for a pricy meal, while Summer's plan was the opposite. When the bill came in its leather binder, Summer tore the top page off and stuffed it into her purse.

"In just a second we'll leave our tip," she instructed him. Breaking into a cold sweat, Jordan threw a ten into the binder with her. They even piled coins on the bottom part of the bill so it looked like they'd left a tip with their change.

"Hey listen, Summer, are you sure we shouldn't—"

"Hush," she said, rising slowly and putting on her coat. "We'll just mosey on out of here. *Goodbye, Ruby Port!*"

As they left, a busboy scrambled to clear their napkins, empty plates, and glasses for the next party that was waiting at the bar. Once outside they quickly flagged a cab, which they would ride for twenty blocks. Their plan was to then take the subway; Jordan wasn't sure where they'd go, but he had some theories. And if he wanted to land at her place, he would have to close that deal.

He glanced out the back window of the cab, but city traffic had safely engulfed them. "I can't fucking believe we scored this."

"It's possible that no one will notice our check's missing 'til the end of the shift," she posited. "Since it was a busy night and we left a good tip, everyone will think the runner took it to the station and someone lost it. *High ho, the wind blows free!*"

After their twenty-block ride, they got out of the cab as planned, her gloved hand in his. "*All for the life on the rolling sea!*" She sang again, slamming the cab door before it drove away.

Marveling at her ingenuity and buzzed from the port, Jordan stopped her from walking farther once they got to the curb. Brushing aside the strands of hair on her cheek, he began kissing her, his lips meeting hers gently, learning their shape. Her warm tongue melted deliciously into his mouth as she pressed her body in its fake fur coat against his—so aching, so wanting, just like a woman, not a thwarted, nervous girl like the many he'd met in Molly's wake. Summer pulled him closer, one arm around his back and the other around his neck. They surely appeared to passers-by as yet another festive couple in Christmas season.

"Jordan," she whispered, after they'd kissed fiercely for a while. "I'm not nearly good enough for you."

"Oh, come on."

"Just a beautiful, sweet boy."

She traced the hair around his forehead with her gloved hand. He shut his eyes.

"I figured out that I'm eight years older than you," she confessed.

"So?"

"Old lady."

He opened his eyes to her smirk.

"If it's any comfort, Molly was thirteen years older than me. In fact, she left me for someone more her own age."

"And more her own gender, I hear."

"Who've you been hearing from?"

"Our jazz cabaret world in New York is small."

He leaned in to kiss her more, and she put a finger to his chin.

"You should just meet some decent, uncomplicated girl. I'm indulging myself at your expense."

"No," he protested. "Stealing a two-hundred-dollar meal is indulgent. What you're doing with me is awesome."

By the time they rang in the happiest year of his life with song and champagne at the Hotel Susquehanna, Jordan had moved in with Summer and Rashad. Once Jordan had started sleeping with Summer, he didn't want to be away from her for long, and, happily, she shared his attachment. Neither of them called the other "clingy" or asked for time alone, as Molly had. They fell in together naturally—"*Mi casa es tu casa*," Summer declared. "*Mi dinero es tu dinero. Mi tiempo es tu tiempo.*" So he'd taken his instruments, music stand, CDs, and clothing from Brooklyn and left the mattress on a floor he hoped to never see again.

Summer had inherited a roomy apartment on the Lower East Side from a songwriter called Gus Granato. When a big royalty had come to him, Granato bought the two-bedroom apartment in Seward Park Cooperative with a terrace that faced east toward the river. The man had died when Rashad was a year old and, according to Summer, signed over his estate in gratitude for her care during the last year of his life. One of Gus' R&B songs had been adapted by a well-known Motown artist in the seventies, another had been used in a movie score. The estate still earned residuals that ranked significantly in Summer's annual budget.

"Some people tough it out on the meds and live on," she explained. "But Gus was hit hard by AIDS. He said it was penance for his years of partying and bathhouses."

There were still shelves of Gus' dusty, hardcover books and crates of his old vinyls and paperbacks all over the living room floor. In one corner Summer kept a sort of shrine to him, an urn of dried roses and a photograph of herself with this spritely, delicate-boned man wearing a plaid driver's cap.

"Gus looks over me," she told Jordan. "And he's glad you're here now too."

Jordan noticed that most of her mail, including phone and electrical bills, was addressed to G. Granato, and a lot of junk mail was simply for Resident, Apartment 16E. Virtually nothing came for Cathy Summers. And nothing for Jordan Radfar. They lived there week in and week out, but the ghost got more mail than they did.

Gus had also left them an old black Yamaha on which Summer banged for hours as she sang, with Jordan jamming on his sax. He would never, so long as he lived, forget those luscious Saturdays when Betty and Curtis Wilcox took Rashad for a day with the twins, leaving Summer and him free for hours of love and music. Rainy, misty afternoons had passed under the spell of Bessie Smith or Louis Armstrong and the warmth of each other's skin.

Summer, like Molly before her, was a fan of Jordan's abs. Molly had produced drawings and photos of his torso, while Summer would just run her face over his tummy and croon, "In a country of beer bellies, I've found the treasure of the Sierra Madre." But then she would dive beneath the sheets, condemning herself as "fat" or "klutzy," and they'd play an arousing game where he'd try to pull the sheet away.

They would make love and make coffee and make more love, and then make music. They cultivated different types of *embouchure* for kissing, and she teased him wickedly about how he licked his reeds before playing. They'd laugh about ridiculous things, like farting in the key of F—F-sharp was a bad one, "like a sick dog's," she would say. He called her "Dew" or "Summer Dew," and she called him

"Foo Boy," and they called Rashad "Roo" or "Root Beer."

Sometimes Jordan would wake up in the mornings to find little Roo wedged between them under the blankets. The boy got frightened in his room alone, which was across the living room from theirs.

"Did Gus die in that room?" Jordan once asked.

"He actually died in hospice in the Bronx," Summer told him. "But when we lived with him, that was his room."

On weekdays Jordan was in charge of waking up, even when Summer didn't, and getting Rashad to school. Summer picked him up in the afternoons. Often, waking up early and walking Rashad to school was the last thing Jordan cared to do, especially when his head felt like a canister of rock salt from being out late, playing music, and drinking the night before.

But he'd learned from Molly that quirky, brilliant women tended to hate getting up in the mornings, and they adored it when their guys actually helped them. He'd been such a jerk to Molly by not making coffee, even when she told him how much she would appreciate it. He'd just snore away while she yanked herself out of bed to go to her office. He wouldn't make that mistake again with his new love.

Precisely because he was diligent about it, Summer often joined Jordan when he took Rashad to school. On nice days they strolled beneath the plane trees, stopping for cappuccino at an Italian deli on the way back home. If they had time, he played sax and she sang in the messy little parks with pigeons and paper scraps. Now and then people threw them coins, though it wasn't their most lucrative spot for busking.

Once they'd stopped by a bench where a man lay on his back facing the sky. When Summer sang "In My Solitude," Jordan had caught the man's grateful glance before they walked on.

In rain and snow everything was more fraught—not only busking but getting Rashad to school. Rashad refused to get up, and Jordan had to bargain with him—a drama that could sap his willpower for the day. Still, he'd been raised by parents who were sometimes too distracted to care whether he and his sister got to school. A social worker had come and spoken to them. It had become important to him that Rashad not have that happen.

One spring evening, when Jordan had lived with them for half a year, he'd stopped by to pick Rashad up at the Wilcoxes' after dinner. Betty and Curtis had a duplex on Essex Street with a little roof garden, just a five-minute walk from Summer's place. The building had once been a brick tenement, like others around it, but in the nineties had been converted into a condominium with chic floor-to-ceiling windows. "Retro-futuristic, like the Jetsons," Summer had described it. When Jordan arrived, Rashad was absorbed in a TV show and lying back on the sofa with the twins, Ian and Archer. So Jordan chatted on the roof deck, over jasmine tea, with their parents.

"There's something I've wanted to show you," Betty said, surprising him as she pardoned herself to get it. She returned with a scribbly pencil drawing that she placed on the glass table before him. An adult had written *Rashad Summers* across the top. Jordan cocked his head in the twilight and tried to make sense of the picture. Curtis looked over his shoulder.

"It's Rashad." Betty pointed to a mass of scribbles that Jordan now saw had two arms and two legs. "And that's you," she said, regarding a taller mass, also with arms and legs, and beads around his neck—Jordan sometimes wore ebony and rosewood beads with cowrie shells. In Rashad's drawing, he even seemed to be carrying his saxophone case with its funny hump.

"He did it at school," Betty explained. "It fell in with some of Ian's and Archer's."

"Impressive," said Curtis, sitting back down.

Jordan looked at it again, seeing more details, like buttons on Rashad's shirt and loosely curled hair similar to theirs.

"He loves you," Betty volunteered. Jordan didn't disagree, but he wouldn't have used those words. "Of course we were all thrilled for Summer when you came into her life," she continued. "But I didn't know how it would play out with Rashad. He's so attached to her. And kids that age…"

Jordan shrugged, a little embarrassed.

"It's been pretty natural," he said. "Summer cares about him, so I care about him." *Tu hijo es mi hijo.*

"You've been so kind and patient," Betty emphasized. "And you don't talk down to him."

"Well, he's a good kid. He makes it easy."

"Very smart," Curtis commented, with an approving nod. "Sometimes he understands things quicker than our boys, who I like to think are keen."

"There's no question that it's meant the world to both of them to have another caregiver around."

"A daddy," added Curtis.

"Whether it's a daddy, auntie, or grandma, kids need more than one important grown-up," Betty affirmed.

"You know," said Curtis, "he was just getting to that age when he was starting to ask Summer, 'Where's my daddy? Do I have a daddy?'"

"Oh, I remember that." Betty glanced at her husband. "I felt so awful when I saw the look on her face."

"What was she supposed to say?" asked Curtis. "'Your daddy lives in California and doesn't want to know you'?"

They were quiet for a moment, realizing that they were skirting the terrain of gossip. Jordan sipped his jasmine tea, looking around at lights from the surrounding apartment buildings. Betty picked up her knitting again. She was always knitting sweaters or blankets with brightly colored yarn.

"I know this will sound weird," began Jordan, "but in some ways, it's better for me that Khalil is out of the picture."

"Except for the *humongous* check he sends every year," said Curtis, giving the final nod to gossip, if not sarcasm. "Of course it's to his credit that he gives her anything." Curtis turned to Jordan. "You know they were never married?"

"Yeah, he didn't divorce his wife. They were just separated."

"That's what we've been told too. We never met him," said Betty.

Curtis took a long sip of his tea. "Can you imagine cutting out on a wife and two little girls to go 'find yourself'? What are you expecting to find?"

Betty shook her head sadly as she knit, yarn slipping again and again from her finger to the long needle. "Summer always says that Khalil's not a bad guy. Just very confused."

Jordan looked at Rashad's scribbly self-portrait, sensing that he would know this boy for a long time, when Rashad would have broader shoulders and longer legs than his own. Betty's knitting needles tapped rhythmically. A shrill ambulance siren erupted from the street. Jordan glanced at Curtis' watch and decided that he'd take Rashad home in five minutes. But he was grateful to speak about his situation with people that knew it.

"She told me Khalil comes from a traditional Sunni family," Jordan confided, "who totally called the shots. And then he was dominated by his wife and her family."

Betty and Curtis seemed to know that already.

"A guy like Khalil grows up in L.A. and sees people taking liberties that his culture shuns…and when he found Summer, it was like he broke through the looking glass. That's how she says it," Betty reflected.

"It's fair to say he used her," Curtis commented.

"Well, they were in love," said Jordan—though saying it hurt him.

All the other stings of his and Summer's past loves had been neutralized, but not Khalil, and not Molly.

"She was onstage then, right?" asked Betty with a trace of excitement.

It was never clear whether Summer had met Khalil in Los Angeles and he'd followed her back to New York, when her manager at the time had booked her in the chorus of an off-Broadway show, or whether they'd met here in New York.

"It's all a little…" Jordan gestured with his hands.

"Sketchy?" asked Curtis. "Summer doesn't say much about her past to us.

She's kind of…our present-tense friend."

They seemed eager to see if Jordan knew more than they. In a way, he didn't.

Betty looked up from her knitting. "We met her in the park when the boys were about two. Back then, we were so…" She smiled at Curtis. "Remember that, honey? Just jonesing to get out of the house, even once a month for an evening alone. But we could never find a sitter who would take on the twins. So I was asking Summer if she knew anyone, and she said, 'I know a supermom who will look after your boys together with her own, in exchange for some good food.' I said, 'Great! Introduce her!' The rest is history."

"It worked out for everyone," said Curtis. "She'd come over with Rashad, and when we'd get back from a movie and dinner out, all three boys would be sleeping like angels, tucked into their beds."

"That's when we got a bed for Rashad here."

"His home away from home," Jordan eulogized. "And by the way, you're both awesome with him too."

"He's a great little guy," said Betty. "We love him."

"We just wish…" said Curtis. "We wish we could help her out more. Hun, should I tell him about Bill?"

"I don't think it could hurt," said Betty.

"You got a sec, Jordan?"

Music wafting from the open door implied that the boys' TV show was ending.

Apprehensive about Bill, Jordan said, "Let me just go check with him."

Jordan popped inside to tell Rashad to slip on his blue Croc sandals, that they'd be leaving in five minutes. Then he went back out to the deck. It was a comfortable spring night, when doors and windows were open and air conditioning wasn't necessary yet—as pleasant to be indoors as to be out.

"One of my colleagues, Bill, knows ASCAP attorneys and producers," Curtis told him with an air of discretion. "We took a bunch of them to one of Summer's shows, when she was singing with that swing band, what's-his-name?"

"Skip Harrington," said Betty.

Jordan made a quick, sour face. Skip Harrington had been as much of a disaster for Summer as for himself.

"Well, these producers loved Summer's style and voice. They were ready to record her, but the problem is that she doesn't have original songs. She does only standards and covers. You know, if someone wants to hear old Billie Holiday songs, they'll buy those recordings."

"Or find them on YouTube," said Betty.

"Summer did suggest an album reviving the Big Mama-type classic blues queens of the thirties—singers most people don't know."

"Oh yeah," said Jordan, who loved how well Summer did know them. "Bertha Idaho, Sweet Peas Spivey, Ida Cox, Sara Martin. We've been listening to them."

"Interesting idea, but it didn't pass muster," Curtis continued. "They said if she could come up with songs of her own, they'd lay down the cash. But she wasn't open to writing songs."

"At all," interjected Betty.

"You know," Jordan hazarded, tapping his foot on the flagstone for a couple of beats. "Maybe I could help her."

"I dunno," mumbled Curtis.

"Tread lightly," Betty added.

But treading lightly was not Jordan's way, especially when opportunity beckoned. It would behoove them to record Summer and have CDs to sell. At some trio gigs, they earned more by selling their CD than by collecting their meager fees. Since Molly had produced it as a gift, they made full profit on every sale.

Jordan walked home that night with Rashad, feeling lucky as the golden moon sat like a slice of brandied pear in the sky. He was happy in Manhattan, happy with springtime and his sweetheart. Rashad chattered about the TV show, explaining scenes in too much detail as they walked into their building. Jordan nodded at Johnny, the nighttime security guard at the front desk. Johnny seemed used to him by now. The situation was admittedly peculiar, with Summer inheriting the apartment and keeping Gus' name on the mailbox—and now Jordan living there too. But New York City was filled with peculiar situations.

At the sixteenth floor Jordan took the key from his pocket, thinking about how this apartment was the most home he'd had since he'd been a boy in Midwood. He walked in with Rashad to find Summer watching the evening news and painting her toenails. Little wads of cotton were propped between each toe as she applied the blue polish.

"We saw *Mulan*," Rashad blathered, and she smiled at both of them. Jordan kissed her forehead and whispered, "Dewdrop." She snuggled her head on his chest and said, "Sorry 'bout this stinky stuff."

It wasn't the right time to talk about writing songs—that would have to wait.

The nail polish emitted strong toxic fumes, and the room was jammed with amps and mike stands, electrical cords, the usual boxes of Gus' stuff and a big basket of laundry in the middle. But they had a romantic view of the East River, with its bridges and wavering lights from the barges, and Jordan felt as grand as any man with a woman and child who loved him.

Despite their comfort together, Summer intermittently suffered from what she called "trapdoor moods," because she "just fell into them." Anyone worth knowing would get into untouchable moods. Those really worth knowing would also find their way out.

Molly had referred to her angst as "the mean reds," quoting Holly Golightly from *Breakfast at Tiffany's*. Unlike Summer's trapdoors, Molly's mean reds came from menstrual cramps, a nasty day at the office, or a hostile phone call from her mother. Z didn't have a name for his blues, but he did for "the supreme human stupidity" that tested his usually placid nature—like being declined for a loan to buy equipment, or dealing with an unjustified run-in with neighborhood cops.

Jordan tended to be intense, but, like Molly and Z, he reacted to specific triggers and disappointments. Summer's despair came out of nowhere. She simply grew quiet, remote, and often sick to her stomach. He would have understood if she were worried about money—a big source of his own malaise—or Rashad's future. He would have understood if she just felt crappy the way Molly did before she got her period: "Like I don't belong in the world," Molly would say. "Like there's no place for me."

But Summer, for all her wit and cynicism, couldn't find words for her sorrow. Jordan knew to shepherd her through such spells carefully. He thought of those lines from *Macbeth* about how "grief that does not speak knits up the o'er wrought heart and bids it break." If Summer fell into the trapdoor at night, he would hold her in his arms beneath the covers, gently kiss her hair and cheeks, and she'd wake up feeling better. But if she tumbled in the afternoon, he stayed out of her way.

He once asked, when she was her normal, talkative self: "What's the best thing I can do when you fall through a trapdoor?"

She said, "Ignore me. Or bring me a glass of Diet Coke with ice. And please take care of Roo so he doesn't notice."

"Would weed help?"

No, she preferred inebriation when she was happy and horny—a predilection that seemed rather pure, since Jordan often reached for a joint when he felt out of sorts.

"Should I worry about you?" he asked another time, when she lay in bed after being quite ill. She'd shaken her head.

"Always had a sensitive tummy."

"Is it nerves, baby?"

"It's just..." She'd taken a while to speak. "Sadness has gathered in me like leaves in a gutter. Sometimes the winds blow them all there at once."

Jordan was never sad with her. He'd left sorrow on the empty R train and in after-hours bars. But he did get snappish when they couldn't find important things, like performance contracts, ATM cards, or paychecks, in the heaps of clothes and papers all over the apartment. He was especially finicky about the

Brooks Brothers suit Molly had bought him years back, which he wore to formal gigs like the Susquehanna.

"Where are my fucking pants?" he would cry, when he could find the double-breasted jacket but not the trousers. At those moments—usually just before they had to leave—he and Summer would toss shirts and socks and bathing suits and brassieres all over the place in a mad search. She'd say, "We just have to find the pieces of ourselves in this detritus," and they generally did, at the last minute. Or else Jordan would wear jeans with one of Gus' tweed jackets, which fit him excellently. He knew Summer liked seeing him in those jackets.

By the time they got anywhere, they were laughing and kidding around. If they were going to a party, they were the life of that party. If it was a gig, the show was now beginning because Jordan and Summer were there. Something about sweethearts who played music together absolutely thrilled the madding crowds. Jordan was acquainted with couples that were both painters or both writers, which was all very noble and conceptual. Couples who acted onstage could strangle each other's scenes like two golden pythons. But those who sang harmonies or blended voice and instrument, like Lester Young and Lady Day, stole the world's heart.

Now that Summer was on the scene, the Jordan Radfar Trio got twice as many bookings. Even if an audience didn't know that he and Summer were together, they felt romance from the music. People loved Summer at weddings, and she sang a great "Hava Nagila" at bar mitzvahs. In hospitals, they played oldies—carefully omitting tunes like "Don't Get Around Much Anymore," staying with pure cheer.

When her gig at the Hotel Susquehanna was nominated for Choice Cabaret of the Year, resentment smoldered into a blaze among their jazz compatriots in New York. Everyone loves the boy and girl who play music together except those who are still singing solo. When Jordan heard that the Skip Harrington Swing Band was a Choice Cabaret contender, he knew trouble was coming.

Word had gotten back to them that Summer's vanquished suitors—the men she'd blown off because they weren't sufficiently buff or because she was "still too heartbroken over Khalil"—wondered why they'd been bested by scrappy little Jordan, a penniless white boy so much her junior. Jordan didn't doubt that Skip Harrington was milking that mystery for whatever reprisal it held.

And Summer remarked that suddenly every pretty singer or flute player seemed sorry to have spurned Jordan's previous interest. Now that he appeared to be going places and taking Summer with him, they fluttered their eyes at him, hoping that one day he'd be the wind to fill their flutes.

Indeed, the only woman who'd rebuffed Jordan and seemed genuinely glad that he'd found Summer was Molly. Jordan had told Claudia at one point: "Make sure Molly knows how well it's working out with us."

When Claudia did so, she reported, "Molly's overjoyed for you."

Was she still with Eugenia? "More than ever. Hey, Eugenia's even got her training for the New York Marathon. Can you imagine our Molly in spandex running shorts? Well, she's doing new things, and that's why opposites attract." Including opposites of the same gender.

"I don't want Skip to get Choice Cabaret," Jordan announced as he bounded in the door one evening in May.

"Oh, who cares?" Summer replied. "These things are all gamed anyway."

"Says who?"

She sat on a stool folding their finally clean laundry and didn't answer.

"Maybe we should write some songs," he proposed, thinking of his recent chat with Betty and Curtis about their ASCAP contacts.

"You write them."

"Let's try together."

"It's not going to matter."

"You're so…expressive. You love singing. Haven't you ever wanted to write lyrics?"

She continued balling Rashad's light blue socks.

"Every American is writing a novel or a screenplay or some woo-woo about how to find God and lose weight. Doesn't matter if they can spell—they're writing the next best seller. And in Nashville they're writing the next hit song.

"You know, you can't fake drawing—you need some mimetic skill. You can't fake what we do—you can't play music with a tin ear. But words are up for grabs. There's no gold standard. Every idiot uses words regularly. But they don't use pliés or half notes or chiaroscuro …"

"Hey, my sister says there's enough crappy artwork to fuel a nation."

"Jordan, my point is you can tell it's crappy. You can tell if a figure drawing is out of proportion or foreshortened incorrectly. You can tell if someone's off-pitch. But purple prose isn't purple. People are fooled by words. Writing is the ultimate cop-out."

"Well, I'm glad Tolstoy and Paul McCartney didn't listen to you. Or look the hell at Gus."

"Gus wrote songs for the same reason I stole toilet paper from the Grand Union today—because we ran out. It was necessary. Did you ever see that Hitchcock movie *The Man Who Knew Too Much*? Doris Day sings for more than her supper. She's singing for her son's life. That's how Gus wrote songs."

Summer now held a pair of Rashad's little white socks in her hands.

"How did he start?" Jordan asked. "Did the songs just…"

"The words came first, and the tune would wrap itself around them. He'd have to tweak the bridges. Those didn't come so fast. But the idea was abracadabra." Summer began balling the socks. "He'd be chatting with a friend who'd say something like, 'These damn landlords are scamming everyone like there's no tomorrow.' Suddenly Gus had a song called 'Here Comes Tomorrow.' Or he'd walk down the street and see a newspaper headline about some creep carving his initials on his girlfriend's arm, and he's got a song called 'Branded by Your Love.'"

"But what am I supposed to write?" She looked up again and began mocking a folk singer they knew who called herself Golden Meadows and wrote about her mother, camping trips, and cookies. "Goldilocks says she's a songwriter, and that's accurate: she writes *one* song, over and over. 'Mommy, Mommy, you are my teddy bear…'"

After they finished laughing—and they laughed for quite a while because

Summer was a mean mimic, perfectly catching the woman's faltering style and shallow breath—he suggested, "So write about your own mother."

Summer looked as though she were eating foul mayonnaise. "My mother? I don't even talk about her."

"I've noticed," said Jordan. Realizing that he should lend a hand with the laundry, he took a pile of his own T-shirts to fold. They worked quietly for a while, and then Summer surprised him. Instead of changing the subject, as she often did after dropping hints about her family, she volunteered: "There's already a hit song for my mom: *what a draaaagg it is getting old!*' And for her, oh hell, it was more than a drag. My mother had this complex about turning forty. It's a rare strain of OCD: I think she's one of five Americans who's ever been hospitalized for phobia of turning a particular age—and trying her damndest not to."

Jordan didn't know what to say. Summer had described her mother as "a lush," cleaning up after a big party by drinking the remains of everyone's liquor. But he hadn't heard about this darker obsession.

"She's still alive—right, Dew?"

"Last I heard. As alive as you can be around my father."

"If either of them were to—I mean, if something happened to them, would anyone know how to find you?"

Summer shook her head no as she folded her own blue checkered blouse. "And it doesn't matter. We died to each other years ago, when my dad heard I was giving birth, out of wedlock, to a black man's child. I reminded him that Thomas Jefferson had done something similar, but it failed to console him. My father's not a believer in 'What's good for the gander is good for the goose,' especially when the goose is his gosling. Anyway"—she turned to Jordan with a fast smile—"not cheerful material for songs. None of it."

"So write about Gus."

"That would insult his memory."

"No, it would be an honor."

They both glanced at Gus' photo, by the urn of dried and crinkly roses.

"I do confess some…I don't know," Summer hazarded, laying the checkered blouse upon her knees. "Maybe I have songwriting envy, like the days before I had orgasms, which was pretty much throughout my twenties, and I'd see my boyfriends get so…exercised and relieved, but I felt outside it all. I never had penis envy especially, but I did have orgasm envy."

Jordan blushed. She had no such trouble now; she sputtered like a boiling pot in the most beautiful way. But he knew the envy of songwriting. Jordan had written only two long, wordless rhapsodies to Molly in a Coltrane vein, neither of which was as amazing as what Coltrane composed. So he too felt envy, and a little awe over how songwriters matched lyrics to music.

"Let's try writing a song."

"Jordan, I can't."

"Why not?"

"Don't push me. Please don't push me."

"Okay, but—"

"No 'but.' Look, when Deb and I were in high school, our father tore our writing to shreds. Literally. And he used to write all our term papers for us—which, weirdly, made us good writers. Deb was put into English Honors and was valedictorian of her class and all that. I was almost skipped up a grade. Because we had to learn how to write when he wasn't around, for essays on tests, and we had to learn fast, under miserable pressure."

Summer barely spoke about her family, so when a wealth of references like this leaked—and they often did when Rashad was not at home—Jordan paid attention. He'd determined that she was raised in central New Jersey and had an upper-class, suburban childhood like Molly's, with a backyard garden and swing set. He'd seen three photos of her and Deb in little sundresses with ponytails and bangs in their eyes. Deb, two years older than Summer, smiled fretfully with her crooked baby teeth in all three pictures, and Summer looked surly. She couldn't have been older than Rashad—but Roo wouldn't have begun to know how to look so depressed.

"You would cry too if it happened to you," was all she'd said when Jordan found those photographs.

"Do you have an address for Deb?" he now asked, folding back the sleeves of his T-shirt.

She shrugged and said, "Probably. Somewhere. But her husband doesn't allow us to talk. He's decided I'm a bad influence." Deb apparently had three children and lived in Orange County, California.

"So Roo has cousins out West," Jordan said.

"He's also got half sisters in L.A., from Khalil—but I don't think he'll meet any of them."

A few days later Jordan came back from teaching band at the boys' school, wearing his jeans and Gus' tweed jacket with elbow patches. As he fit his key into the lock of apartment 16E, he heard Summer tinkling out a ragtime tune on the piano that sounded like "Sun Showers" or "A-Tisket, A-Tasket." When he stepped inside she stopped playing and raced over to him, announcing that she was actually writing a song.

"It just started to come, after all our brouhaha the other day. Wanna hear it, so far?"

"Of course."

Jordan tossed down his briefcase overflowing with sheet music and sat eagerly on the cluttered sofa. She resumed her seat on the piano bench, swung into a cheery prelude, then began singing in a style reminiscent of Ella Fitzgerald.

Betty makes life better.
I think you'd see what I mean if you met her.
She's the friend who knit me this yellow sweater.
You can bet on Betty to make life better!
Betty, you won't forget her.
Take my word, or come 'round and vet her.

She'll put a smile on your face if you let her.
Bet on Betty to make life better!

Thrilled, Jordan took his sax out of the case and began adding his own licks while Summer hummed and jammed away on the piano.

When they finished, Summer got up from the piano bench and flew over to him, laughing. Jordan put down his sax, and they embraced in the middle of the floor as Gus Granato looked on from the wall.

"Look, I fucking love it," Jordan whispered, squeezing her in his arms, making her giggle. "I gotta say I'm just kinda jealous that it wasn't about me."

"Oh, I've got one coming for you," she said eagerly.

"Really? As good as this?"

"You'll hear it at our next Susquehanna. Hey, are your parents going to be there?"

"Still in Oregon. Not coming east 'til the end of June."

"They change plans a lot."

"You're telling me…"

But he was glad that they wouldn't be there for the debut of his song, because he wanted that for himself.

Before they performed "Betty" at the Susquehanna cabaret, Jordan worked with Summer on a bridge. Seated beside her on the piano bench, he'd asked: What about Betty can you say between the verses?

At first Summer had resisted him and jested: "We all need somebody to lean on… oh…isn't that original?" But then she'd come out with: "Everyone needs a friend who doesn't get scared no matter how scary you get."

"Great." Jordan laughed. "Rhymes with bet. What more can we say about her?"

"Well, she's not a fair-weather friend."

"So she's…like, a foul-weather friend?"

"That doesn't sound right."

By the time their gig rolled around, they had worked it through:

We all need a friend who never gets scared,
No matter how scary you get
We all need a friend who is fair in foul weather,
And in my case you can bet
That friend is Betty;
She makes life better.

Betty and Curtis came to the show and held hands at their round table with its candle—Jordan had told them they couldn't miss this one, even though finding a babysitter was tough since Summer was spoken for. He felt gratified when he noticed Betty wiping her eyes with a cocktail napkin as Summer took her bow and the audience heartily applauded her new song.

"Thank you," she said into the mic, which squeaked for a second. "And guess what? You're all my guinea pigs. I've been singing since I was a kid and I heard Doris Day warble "Que Sera, Sera" in a Hitchcock film. But I never wrote a song before last week…thanks to that delectable boy over there playing sax." She indicated Jordan with a sweep of her arm, stirring up a patter of applause. "My honey keeps me on my toes. And this one's for him. It's called 'A Lot I Don't Know.' I've rehearsed with Fred Quinn over here on piano. But for Bruce, Z, and Jordan—it's all new, so chime in when you want!"

She walked to center stage as though wading into fresh pond water, the spotlight blurring her silhouette at the edges. Jordan watched her lift the mic to her chin and throw the hair from her face. Fred played a brief lead-in, and she began:

"Falling in love again was Marlene's big mistake;
As for me, I'd written off the grief and heartache,
Locked my heart and threw away the key
But there's a lot about this world I didn't see.

Falling in love again was Elvis Presley's folly;
Then I met a sweet boy who was still obsessed with Molly.
Never dreamed we'd be a 'go'
But there's a lot about this world that I don't know.

Horatio! Horatio!
There are more things in heaven and earth
Than are dreamt of in your philosophizing;
But now I find the story inside my own heart
Most of all surprising.

Falling in love again, nobody wants to do it
I tried to stay outside the ring of fire, but I blew it
Now my honey keeps me on my toes
And there's a lot about this mixed up, muddled up, shook up world, Lola.
There's a lot about this sweet old world, Lucinda.
There's a lot about this wonderful world, Louis.
That I don't..."

Z rolled on his snare then hit his tom-toms, building to a cymbal crash as Summer sang an old Irish air a cappella.

"...*Do you love an apple; do you love a pear;*
Do you love a laddie with curly black hair?
Ah, but still I love him, I can't deny it.
I'll go with him wherever he goes
'Cause there's a lot about this world I don't know!"

Jordan jumped in with saxophone at the end as she held the note on *know* to a tremendous standing ovation.

After the houselights went on and Z and Bruce set about packing the amps, people flocked to Summer. Did she have a CD they could buy with "A Lot I Don't Know," a website, a MySpace page? Was she on iTunes? She smiled and shook her head no.

"We could get you booked in Amsterdam, or in Toronto. But we need to show something to the managers," someone said.

"I'm like someone who sings on the back porch," she explained. "Marketing's a headache."

"Are you on the run?" someone asked jokingly.

"Pretty much," she said.

At that point Jordan cut in with some copies of the trio's CD.

He sold some—he always did—but many refused it, saying they wanted *her*.

"You can be on our mailing list," he offered.

People signed on after Jordan explained that they listed their upcoming shows on the trio's site. He gave out business cards; he told people to keep in touch, but he knew they were losing many opportunities.

"So you're undiscovered," mumbled a thin, pale guy with a croaky voice.

"Maybe you've just discovered me," Summer replied blithely.

"I'm gonna send someone around," he mumbled again.

Jordan put his arm around her waist and kissed her warm, sweating forehead.

"Love it," he whispered. "Did I tell you that? I love our song!"

Summer's birthday fell on June 23, just after spring ceded to her eponymous season and Gemini the twins surrendered the night sky to Cancer the crab. The solstice magic of longest, lightest days graced their region with a cool front before the long burn of summer. Betty and Curtis had Jordan and Summer over for rum cake and lemonade on the roof deck. Earlier in the day, they'd sprung for a memory-foam mattress to help her sore back, and it had been delivered to apartment 16E with a card: *We've got your back.*

"Making life better," Jordan and Summer agreed, elated to see their worn, lumpy bedding dragged out the door.

The trio pitched in for an retro Super 55 mic with a stand. Z, who was forever refurbishing vintage mics and amps, knew exactly where to find choice specimens.

Jordan saved his special gift for when they were alone later: a simple, spiral-bound notebook with staff paper. He advised her to keep it by the piano so she'd always know where to find it—to write down her music and lyrics, and notes for new songs.

A couple of days later, he was pleased to peek in and see that she had transcribed his song and Betty's, and sketched some lines for several new ones. He chuckled to himself as he read the first title: "My Brooklyn Boy." That was clearly his story: *Raised on Ocean Parkway but he never learned to swim.* Another title came right from his description of Molly: "She Was That Kind of Friend."

A week later, Jordan saw she had crossed out *She was* and titled the song "That Kind of Friend." *Lip service to our kisses*, she had scrawled, *that's what you're good for now, baby... Lip service to our kisses, that and a check now and then maybe...* an ode to Molly, and to Khalil, to exorcise their haunted hearts.

♪

Summer wrapped her notebook and new mic into a bevy of T-shirts as they packed for a July week in Vermont with Betty's folks. Like Jordan's parents, Betty's father was Jewish and her mother gentile. But any resemblance between the two families stopped there. Eli Wolff was chair of the history department at a prestigious liberal arts college in the Champlain Valley, and Marjorie, Betty's mom, was partner in an antique and crafts store near the college. So their home, as Summer described it, was full of scholarly books but also apple crisps and gingerbread, wind chimes and lavender sachets. On the bus ride up, Summer told Jordan that Marjorie "came from money. Academia couldn't buy half of what you'll see." They owned an impeccably restored Victorian mansion in town and a cottage on Lake Champlain, about an hour north. The plan was to have dinner in town and then drive to the lake—so Jordan would see both of these splendid residences where Betty had spent her childhood.

Like most city kids, he was wary of the hinterlands, of bears, bats, spiders, and other imponderables of wooded life. But as he disembarked from the Adirondack Trailways coach with his saxophone case and took a first sweet breath away from bus stations and highways, Jordan felt eager to throw off his traveling shoes and wear shorts and flip-flops like Betty.

Her dad had joined her and the twins at the doughnut shop that served as their bus stop in the small Vermont town. When the twins saw Rashad they squealed, "You gotta see the boat!" and "Grandpa, take us on the boat!"

"What do we say?" asked Betty.

They knew, but they were going through a bratty phase.

"Please?" volunteered Rashad with a shy smile.

"Thank *you*, Rashad," said Betty. "You'll come on the clipper, and my boys will stay at home on a time-out."

They groaned and yanked at her shorts, screaming, "Please, please!" as she formally introduced Summer and Jordan to her father. Professor Wolff was tall and skinny, like Betty, with straight white hair, an equally white, clipped goatee, and a soothing, soft-spoken way about him.

"Curtis has been extolling your song for Betty," he said.

"Summer actually wrote it," Jordan explained as they got in the car.

"Oh, but you helped me."

"It was your inspiration, honey."

"It came from both of us," said Summer.

"I understand you're quite the duet." Professor Wolff started the engine.

"We'll play for you later," Jordan offered. He and Summer had known, before they left New York, that for a week of lakefront, fresh food, and wine between the Adirondacks and the Green Mountains, they would be the live entertainment.

And the trade proved more than fair. Jordan hadn't felt so relaxed in years, if ever in his life. After days in the hammock and porch swing, running around barefoot on the soft grass, playing badminton with Rashad and the twins, he began to let his guard down, to shed his frantic city self that chased this dollar and that gig.

Stealing time alone behind the guest cabin that he and Summer shared, which was down a dirt road from the main cottage, he puffed on a fat joint one afternoon after playing his horn. His exhale vanished into the diaphanous sky, the scritch of cicadas and piping sparrows. He shut his eyes, breathing in the musky ferns and fainter essence of pine needles in the sun, drawing in the joint with his head thrown back.

"Daddy!"

He snapped his eyes open and threw his head forward again. Rashad, in his khaki shorts and sneakers, dashed around from the front of the cabin. Jordan quickly hid the joint under his saxophone case.

"We're go-een on the boat!"

"I'm okay here, Roo," he said.

"No, come with us!"

Rashad pulled at his hand.

"Okay, okay..."

Jordan wobbled to his feet.

"Are you smoking cigarettes?" Rashad asked with a pout. Jordan put the sax into its case, sneaking the joint in too. "Because Miss Sharon—Miss Sharon says it makes you sick, and sometimes I hear you cough."

Summer was right about her Brooklyn boy. He hadn't learned to swim. Jordan dog-paddled around near the shore while she glided into the lake, one arm arching out of the water as the other came up behind it, a small spray trailing her legs as they kicked. It was becoming clear to him that Summer "came from money" as much as Betty and Curtis; Summer seemed to hail from a girlhood more white glove and cucumber sandwich than Molly's, with all its attendant skills of swimming, piano, riding. Summer played piano well enough to accompany herself—her style was not so dazzling as Fred's but perfectly adequate. At a stable the next day, she was the only of the four adults who confidently took the reins and cantered around on a mare. Betty and Jordan decided to "sit this one out if we don't have a seatbelt," while Curtis struggled to keep up with Summer.

She spoke and sang Parisian French, delighting French Canadians when she sang Piaf after dinner at a Quebecois bistro on the lake. On the sailboat she talked to Eli like an insider. Jordan knew how to appeal to a Jewish dad rhetorically over dinner, but Summer kept him busy on the lake, analyzing sails and wind patterns. Jordan didn't mind any of that; in fact, the mystery of it all aroused him. He was downright proud when they raced Curtis and Betty in a canoe—and won because Summer was steering. In the other boat Curtis navigated at the stern and seemed a bit flustered.

Once the boys went to bed that evening, Summer and Jordan curled up together on the porch swing, their arms pleasantly sore from paddling the canoe. Betty sat on an Adirondack chair across from them, thumbing through the local paper, and Curtis came out with a bottle of Chardonnay that he plunked on the wooden table between them. He went inside again and emerged with four wine glasses, the screen door slapping after him.

"Where'd you learn to paddle?" he asked Summer as he filled everyone's glass.

"Summer camps," she said vaguely.

"Like, where?"

"I don't know. They sent us away when we were tiny. I must have been five, and my sister was seven. We slept in tent cabins."

"Five?" Betty repeated. "That's awfully young for a sleep-away camp."

"My mother was going bats, and I guess they wanted to distract us. You know, I was starting to write a song about all that, about losing her so young."

"Doesn't sound happy," Curtis remarked.

"It doesn't have to," she said.

"I just mean it may not be very commercial."

That word sat in the sweet night air like a sudden stench of gasoline. Summer put down her wine glass and sank her head into Jordan's shoulder.

"Tsk, Curtis," Betty muttered.

"She's just writing now," Jordan explained, stroking Summer's sunburned shoulder very gently. "We're not thinking about production or profit."

"I'm not a trained seal," Summer added, lifting her head. "I can't do this on demand, Curtis."

"Well you did write two great ones in a week," Curtis reminded her.

"They just came. I have lots more in a holding pattern. Just little outlines."

"'Betty' is a brilliant song." Curtis sat on an Adirondack chair, holding his wine glass. "I want to record it. I want it around, just for myself."

"It's not brilliant," Summer retorted, sinking her head back into Jordan's arm. "It's fun, it's cute. You like it because you know Betty. I'm not sure how well it would stand on its own."

"Are you kidding me? Everyone loved it at the Susquehanna."

"Curtis!" Betty slammed down her newspaper and glared at him.

"Eli and Marjorie can't get enough of it," he continued.

"Of course they can't get enough—they're her parents," said Summer. "I'm sure if you came out with some ditty like *Cathy didn't turn out so trashy*, even my psycho folks would crack a smile."

"We've got to record it," insisted Curtis.

"Look, I don't give a rat's ass if I'm ever recorded," Summer snapped. "There were songs for centuries before there were sound studios."

"The offer has been made," said Curtis.

Summer turned restlessly in Jordan's arms. "I'm pooped," she whispered.

After saying good night to Betty and Curtis, they walked down the dirt path to the guest cabin. Jordan saw twigs, pinecones, pebbles, and roots of maple trees that snaked into the soil. Under this full moon, they didn't even need the flashlight Betty's mom had kindly given them.

"Nice to be here with you and the crickets, Foo." Summer took his hand.

"I smell the lake…"

"And cut grass."

Those aromas of earth at night combined with their private lodgings, away from Rashad and everyone else, inspired long nights of passion—pure, delightful fucking and Summer's generosity with her singing mouth. But she'd never allowed him to reciprocate until their stay on Lake Champlain.

In the city she confessed to feeling "unclean and grubby," claimed she found it "unnerving to think of a head burrowing around down there. Even yours."

"Women love it," he'd insisted.

"Yeah, the women you know," she'd rejoined. The previous night, he begged her to try, and she went along, resistant nonetheless to his intuitive, probing tongue. Finally she gave in, pushing her heels into the small of his back, and opened herself, moaning. "Now you know me too well."

As they approached the moonlit cabin, he wondered if tonight might warrant a repeat performance with his tongue. They climbed a few wooden stairs onto the porch, where his trunks, her bathing suit, and a series of beach towels hung on the railing. "Can I know you too well again tonight, baby?" he asked.

"Do we have an official lesbian relationship now? We share our feelings and perform cunnilingus."

He cracked up and said, "I'm sure last night wasn't your first time."

"You think Khalil ever did this, with his Sunni background? I'm amazed we made it to the missionary position. People assume I'm worldly."

"Unless we know you too well. Which I intend to."

"Jordan," she parried. But her tone was warm. "Can we not *plan*?"

"But it's like our set list. You know what's coming up, so you perform your best. How about it, you sweet *embroch-able* you?"

She dropped his hand and began gathering their bathing suits and towels "before they get all wet and dewy."

"Ummmm." He sighed. "Wet and dewy."

She gently swiped his face with her damp bathing suit.

"And you know...you don't have to protect me around Curtis. I can take him."

"Huh?"

In that mood, Jordan didn't want to think of her "taking" any other man.

"I can take his pressure about recording my songs."

"Listen, he means well. But he shouldn't preempt what's gonna be commercial. Write what you're interested in writing."

"And so I am."

She opened the cabin door and told him to get inside before the mosquitoes joined them.

"Reentry's a bitch," Curtis muttered at the wheel of his Corvette as Jordan and he headed back to the city the next morning. Betty, Summer, and the boys were staying on in Vermont a few more days. But Curtis had to return to work, and Jordan had gigs with the trio that week: a wedding and a retirement party.

"Always a bitch to leave the apple tarts and coffee by the lake," Curtis lamented.

"Awesome that she made us care packages."

Jordan and Curtis had each been given a bag of local corn, squash, tomatoes, and rhubarb pies and cookies.

"Marjorie always packs food for us. What a doll. I sure traded up with my in-laws—they're better than my parents." Curtis laughed nervously.

"How?" asked Jordan.

"They actually talk. To each other and everyone else."

Jordan laughed with Curtis. At first he'd wondered whether they'd have much to say without the women around, but they'd spoken freely as they whisked past dairy farms and cornfields on their southbound route. At Castleton, Curtis turned west toward New York.

"I'd get on the Thruway," he explained to Jordan, "but we've got to go through Defreestville—the town my Huguenot ancestors founded."

Jordan gazed at the mountains and then at Curtis, wind blowing through his brown hair, eyes squinty behind sunglasses.

"Not like I know anyone who lives there. But it's fun to feel like an ancestral son, or something. We stopped there with the boys on the way up. Hey, did I tell you Eli and Marjorie will take them for Labor Day so Betty and I can drive to Montreal? We've already booked a room."

"Sweet," said Jordan.

"Keep this under your hat, okay? We're hoping to end up with a daughter nine months later."

"Betty hopes that too?"

"Not as badly as I," Curtis admitted, facing the road ahead. They were on Route 4 now, slowing for a yellow light in Whitehall. "She's understandably tapped out, after bearing and raising the twins. But she knows how much it means to me to have a little girl, so she'll give it one more try. It's kinda now or never." He glanced Jordan's way as he checked for traffic. "Hey, you ever want a kid?"

"I have one."

"I mean your own kid?"

Jordan shrugged. "At this point, I'll be happy if we give ourselves and Rashad a decent life." He didn't want to remind Curtis that they were musicians, not equity researchers who drove Corvettes, with wealthy in-laws in Vermont.

"You talk like you have a future with her."

"I plan to," said Jordan.

"Think you'll marry her?"

"Yeah."

He would be thirty in November, and she had turned thirty-eight in June. It was time.

"She's lucky. A lot of guys wouldn't want to take on another man's kid. Look at me: I'm having trouble settling for only boys, even though they're mine. Guess it all started when the twins were in utero and we couldn't tell Ian's gender. I'd pinned my hopes on a son and a daughter. We even picked out the name, Isabella. Isn't that pretty? Isabella Wilcox."

"Suppose you have another boy?" Jordan asked.

"It will increase my chances for a granddaughter. And look, I don't wanna give you the wrong idea. I love the twins; I'm so grateful for them. But a daughter is the apple of her daddy's eye like nothing else—you know?"

Jordan had never thought about it and wriggled in his seat. Curtis was saying, "Maybe you and Summer can have a girl too, and our daughters could be friends, like our boys."

"We're broke!" Jordan suddenly exclaimed. "I don't have a teaching salary 'til September. She does the lunch shift now in that dive on Stanton Street, and we play weddings, but it's so unpredictable. Another kid would throw us over the top."

"What about Gus' residuals? She was coasting on that income when we first met her."

"Hasn't been great lately. You know, with downloads and online piracy, songs don't do so hot anymore."

"There must be a way to use the internet to your advantage."

Jordan poked his elbow out the window as Curtis accelerated them out of the next red brick, upstate town. Jordan noticed a sign for Defreestville. "Digital royalties pretty much suck," he said, half to Curtis and half to the wind. "You really need to work a lot of gigs, do session music, tour—which is another reason for Summer not to have a baby."

"I know investors who are looking away from real estate to the arts these days," Curtis mentioned.

"Yeah, to Madonna and Mariah Carey. Not unknowns like us."

"Hey, Madonna was just a weirdo from Detroit. You gotta start somewhere… if Summer wrote a bunch more songs—and for shit's sake, *not about her drunk mother*—like I've said, I could get backers for you guys, no problem. She's already in the running for Choice Cabaret. Even if she doesn't get it, the nomination is a boon."

"I'd like to think so, but there're a lot of good people out there," said Jordan firmly, his arm still out the window, wind blustering in his face.

"Then push faster than rest of them." Curtis exceeded the speed limit now, as if to underscore his point. "We should record 'Betty' and your song before

Summer changes her mind. Which she does, a lot. As I'm sure you've noticed. I'll book time in a studio. Whaddaya think? We can go little by little."

"Look, if you're game..."

Curtis extended his arm sideways from the steering wheel, and Jordan grabbed his hand, uncertain of what their shake meant.

Alone in the stuffy, cluttered apartment, Jordan felt blue. Z had disappointing news about the bank loans for which the trio had applied. Curtis could say what he might, but no one gave money to artists who didn't have it. Except Molly. She was that kind of friend.

Two messages awaited him on the old answering machine: Rashad had gotten into day camp, where he'd been wait-listed, in August with the twins—which was good news, except they'd have to figure how to swing it. The other message was Summer, singing:

"Raised on Ocean Parkway, but he never learned to swim, my Brooklyn Boy.
I wasn't very worldly before I hugged on him, my Brooklyn boy.
He shook my tree... he rang my bell.
We got to know each other... just a little too well.
But he comes from Midwood, and I come from hell, my Brooklyn Boy."

More than "Betty" and "A Lot I Don't Know," "Brooklyn Boy" had an R&B–type drive. Jordan took out his saxophone and called her with a refrain. She was probably in the lake or having supper, because she didn't answer, so he played it on her voice mail. "Love you, sweetheart," he said, before hanging up to contemplate his own sorry meal. "Love knowing you just a little too well. Miss you."

The rhubarb pie tempted him for dinner and involved no preparation. But he decided to be virtuous and at least roll out some tomatoes and corn while they were ripe. He had no idea how long corn should cook but figured he'd wing it. When he was young, he'd shucked ears with his mom and swept up sticky rays of corn silk from the kitchen floor. He remembered how messy it got and opened the door below the sink where a plastic trash bin was hinged.

Ready to rip the husk off his ear of corn, his eye fell upon a crumpled, handwritten envelope in last week's coffee grinds and eggshells that should have been dumped before they left for Vermont because it reeked to high hell. He extracted this envelope from the trash to read a series of addresses scrawled beneath an ink-stamped finger with the words *Please Forward*. First came Summer's old place on East 12th Street, then Khalil's post office box in Marina Del Rey, California. Khalil must have crossed out *Cathy Summers* and written, in the squared-off penmanship Jordan recognized: *Summer Vale, c/o G. Granato*, and the current address on East Broadway. The envelope, which originated from a D. Richardson, had gone across the country three times since March.

Jordan slid out a creased Hallmark card, a sappy watercolor of two little girls sitting side by side on a hill. *Sisters Are for Sharing*, read the inscription. Jordan opened the card:

Cath,

I hope you and your son are doing well.

Wanted you to know that Dad's health was dicey, but he's pulled through after a kidney transplant. He and Mom are now in a North Carolina retirement community. She's still in treatment but off lithium and doing Twelve Steps. We're talking again, and she wants to speak with you too. While I respect your decision about them, I thought you should know all this.

I miss you and feel especially sad every year at Christmas and in June around our birthdays. Sorry that Stewart has made it so hard to keep in touch. Feel free to use my cell number, if you ever want to call me during the day.

Love always to you and your little boy,

Deb

Jordan read Deb's note several times. He knew Summer just a little too well? All week she hadn't once mentioned this card.

He paced around the apartment, speaking aloud to her, in fragments: "Why didn't you…" "Summertime, how could you not have…" "I mean, I tell you everything…" "She's your only sister…"

He remembered the childhood photos with Deb smiling fretfully and Summer scowling. Maybe nothing in families ever changed much. And because Deb was family, he felt inclined to retain the record of her address and cell phone number.

Forgetting the corn, tomatoes, and pie, he called Z and asked, "Hey, can I come over?" And in another hour, he was lounging about Z's basement sound studio on the canvas director's chair, where he'd spent many stoned hours. Z read Deb's card, shook his head at Jordan, and advised, "Stay out of it."

"But why didn't she just fucking tell me?"

"She's keeping her lover out of family dramas," he said. "I get that."

But of course Z, with his standoffish ways, had broken his share of hearts. That was not Jordan's style.

"I'll file it," Z said, slipping Deb's card—envelope and all—into his Summer Vale folder. Z kept a file for everyone they played with and everywhere they worked. He proclaimed himself "disorganized," but Jordan found him formidably meticulous.

"Any internet hits on us this week?"

"Nah, nothing new," said Z. "July doldrums."

"You ever try anything on Cathy Summers?" Jordan asked suddenly.

"Just Summer Vale. There are a million women in this world named Cathy Summers. At least a million."

But Jordan settled himself at Z's laptop, keying *Cathy Summers* and the name of her hometown into the Google field. He'd never thought to do that before. At first he didn't find a thing but then stumbled upon a bonanza of commentary: Her high school class was planning a twentieth reunion after Labor Day. Summer was listed with other "AWOL" classmates on the site.

Anyone know what happened to Cathy Summers? someone had written—a Sue something-or-another. *She wasn't at our 10th reunion.*

My mom heard she sang in a Broadway chorus line a while back, under a dif-

ferent name, someone else had answered.

Others had swooned, in their chat room way: *Cool, wow!*

Remember her in Bye Bye Birdy *in 8th grade? The Ann-Margret of our class.*

Remember how she used to mimic Mrs. Sullivan? lol I wet my pants ☺

Let's find her! Sue had challenged. *She was my best friend in 3rd and 4th grade.*

Did she marry Geoff Ahlstrom? another woman asked.

I hope not, wrote Sue.

That was it for Cathy Summers. But Jordan learned even more when he typed in Deb's name and came upon her engagement announcement from fourteen years back, in the *Newark Star*:

Deborah Scott Summers, daughter of George and Vivian Summers, is engaged to Stewart Martin Richardson, son of Marilyn Richardson. Ms. Summers graduated with highest honors from Swarthmore College, where she was senior class speaker, and is now employed by McGraw-Hill. Her father is the Republican chairman of Monmouth County. Mr. Richardson, an industrial and systems engineer, is a graduate of Rutgers University. His mother serves as Democratic assemblywoman in New Jersey's 7th congressional district. The wedding is planned for September 15, 1991.

"Holy fuck!" cried Jordan. "Z—check this out!"

Looking over Jordan's shoulder onto the computer screen, Z whooped with laughter. "Talk about Montagues and Capulets—you landed in a hornet's nest. Republican chairman, Democratic assemblywoman. Oysters *on the* Rockefellers, anyone?"

"Why didn't she tell me?" Jordan kept asking Z and himself.

Around 10:30 p.m., Z reheated leftover arroz con pollo and diced some onions, peppers, ham, and pineapple, his knife practically driving six-eight time on the cutting board. Jordan gazed with envy upon his friend's broadly fanned shoulders as Z maneuvered around the counter. Summer claimed Z was "at least one point ten times the size of the average American," which was about right. When women saw Z, they looked dazed, as though he could carry them somewhere or protect them in his larger-than-life arms. When women saw Jordan, they wanted to stroke his face like a puppy's or run their fingers through his thick, dark ringlets like Molly always had.

"This is the first relationship I've actually worked at," Jordan ruminated as he sipped Rolling Rock from its green bottle. "I've had the benefit of past girlfriends and Barbara, my shrink…so I don't just knock around like an interpersonal illiterate. But will it just land me in the trash?"

"I don't follow." Z tossed pepper and onion pieces into the frying pan like confetti. "She hasn't trashed you. Hell, she's written another song about you."

"Yeah, but if we have a big fight or something…what's she going to do with me, if she can trash her sister's greeting card so quickly?"

"That's a hypothetical concern," said Z.

"I call it a red flag."

"Well, watcha gonna do about it?"

"I don't get why she doesn't trust me." Jordan set his bottle on the table. "We play music for hours, we sleep together, I take her kid to school."

"Do you trust her?"

"Now I don't."

"Oh come on, Jo-Jo, you're making a little much of nothing, aren't you?"

Jordan didn't answer but stared at the back of Z's head in his rainbow-knit Rasta tam. Above him, on the open pantry shelves, Jordan recognized some of his own mother's ceramic bowls and goblets and remembered giving them to Z one Christmas because he had nothing else. Miles Davis played softly over the speaker, something from *Blue Moods*.

"It's like her life began when she had Rashad. She tells me about all that—caring for Gus when he was dying from AIDS and his boyfriend ran out on him, meeting Betty and Curtis and other neighborhood friends.

"I'm caught up with everything from Rashad onward, but before that—all blank. She lived thirty-three years, longer than I've been alive, as old as Jesus was on the cross, and I know barely anything about it."

"You know more than you think."

"Yeah, but I learned half of it from finding Deb's card in the trash and getting on the internet now."

"That's sometimes how we learn about people," said Z.

"It's not right. Something's off."

Before sitting down across the table, Z ripped off a sheet of paper towel for each of them to use as a napkin. Then he slid sizeable helpings of his concoction onto two plates and passed one to Jordan. Jordan felt far away from the freshwater trout and roasted Cornish hen with Chardonnay that he'd savored in Vermont. He forked Z's farraginous food into his mouth, at once ravenous and queasy. He didn't remember the last time he'd eaten—probably Marjorie's warm apple tarts that morning, holding hands with Summer as they sat together brooding about their pending separation of three days.

"This is our first night apart in months," he explained to Z, his mouth full. "We do different things all day, but we're together at night. So I'm messed up as it is, but now I learn her dad was some Republican kingpin."

"My favorite part of it was 'Mom's off lithium and doing Twelve Steps.' Doesn't that say it all?" Z shook his head.

"You know," Jordan said between mouthfuls, "my sister makes me crazy sometimes, but I'd never throw a card from her into the trash. No way."

"Well, we don't know what happened," said Z, after swigging some beer. "Maybe she did call Deb and they had an altercation about an old issue. Or maybe they had a warm-and-fuzzy reunion and hubby got on and said, 'I've forbidden you to speak to your insane sister in New York. Get off immediately, or I will give you nine lashings!'"

If Summer had been really angry, Jordan thought, she would have ripped the card—her crumpling did suggest defeat more than rage. He tried to imagine her standing at the trash can with this nice note from her only sibling.

"They *never* just talk to me," Jordan whined, about the women he loved. "I'm always left guessing."

"Oh, my heart doesn't bleed for your misery at the hands of women. Molly was our grand patron, and Summer's our top-notch vocalist. Not bad for under thirty, Jo-Jo. At my obscene age, I have yet to find someone who doesn't compete with my drums for attention. Your women make our music even hotter, so you're doing something right."

"I'm in love," Jordan cried. "I've fallen in love with her." He stood up, woozy with nerves and a half bottle of Rolling Rock. "Gotta call her—I don't want her blindsiding me, like Molly did."

"Siddown, Jo-Jo. Just siddown for a second. Look at me." Sighing, Jordan sank back into his chair. Z's large brown eyes were full of entreaty. "I'm not goin' through that story about Molly again."

"*You're* not going through it. How 'bout me? If Summer can hide all this from me, what else won't she tell me? Until it's too fucking late, like Molly…"

"May I gently remind you that when you crashed with Molly, you were selling weed from her living room behind her back? So, who blindsided who?"

"Different kind of blindsiding," Jordan permitted.

"You were putting…" Z leaned back, giggling too much to even contemplate another forkful. "If I recall, you and Claudia were gutting rubber dildos and folding in bags of weed, then gluing them back again." He laughed so hard that he hiccupped, and despite himself, Jordan chuckled faintly. That had been Claudia's scheme for clearing customs when they sent prime Western Hemisphere dope to Paris and Geneva. The shipping method remained effective, and she was still earning. If Jordan had stayed in the business with Claudia, he'd be earning too. But Molly had warned him against it, if he wanted to get on the books and manage an LLC. In her way she looked out for him; she was that kind of friend.

"It was crap," Jordan ceded. "And I apologized to Molly."

"Well, she did more than apologize when you were bleating bloody murder 'cause she started seeing Eugenia—she produced our CD, paid off your student loan."

"She paid it *down*, not off. I'm still shelling out."

"...and you two weren't even together anymore."

"We were plenty together," Jordan countered, slamming his fork on the table. "She was two-timing me. People don't break up just once and it's all over. That's why she felt guilty enough to offer all this restitution."

"Your memory is melted, my dude."

Jordan lifted the Rolling Rock bottle to his lips. The beer had gotten warm, and it didn't help the clash of cooked pineapples and onions.

"Why the fuck did you put pineapples in here?"

"Why not?"

Z laughed again as though the question was incredibly funny.

"I'm tired of women blindsiding me!" Jordan roared, pushing his half-empty plate away. He hadn't worried about losing Summer since he'd moved in with her last Christmas. Their intensely moment-by-moment life precluded time for idle speculation. But away from her, he suddenly feared that lightning would strike twice.

"Jordan...go easy. Just for fun, let's look at the facts: you and Molly had post-breakup sex a couple of times. For maybe a week you didn't hear from her, and then she told you about Eugenia. I know. Ouch. But how 'bout when she walked in on you and Claudia weighing kilos on her coffee table? A little beyond ouch. And Summer? She's not telling you her father was some county bigwig? Who the fuck cares?"

"So where are you going with all this?"

"I'm going with *your* secrecy was the most damning of anyone's. You could've landed Molly in a shitload of trouble. Instead of pointing fingers, own up."

"What I did with Molly was damning, but it's in the past. I haven't kept secrets from Summer. Why's she keeping stuff from me?"

Z shook his head, clearly tired of the topic.

"Give her a little time. You haven't been together for even a year."

Jordan's heartbeat slowed back to a normal pace. He was getting carried away, and Z was right. The next thing he said was right too.

"Can I tell you, doing that roll at the Susquehanna for her song…I was breaking new ground, man. No drummer had done it before. Now look, I love playing the standards. Beats the hell out of delivering UPS and whatever else I've done for bread and butter. But there's nothing like new stuff. And Summer's just scratching the surface of what she can write, and sing, and hell, …she's fucking brilliant."

"I know," said Jordan.

"She'll get us back to that point of making our own sound…you know, when we were working on the CD and Molly told us to do our own stuff so we're not just another wedding jazz band. We should get back to writing, you know that? Even if we don't do lyrics. We should jam our own compositions, like we did for Molly."

"Helps to have a patron, doesn't it? Especially since she was also my muse."

"I saw her," said Z. "Last week."

"You *what*?"

"Don't go all crazy now. When you were up in Vermont, I was hanging in the Village with some friends, and I ran into her and Eugenia with some of their friends. We all ended up at an outdoor place on Grove Street, eating melon and strawberries and drinking champagne 'til two in the morning."

"I'm sure Molly paid for all of it," Jordan grumbled. "She'd drop hundreds on a night like that."

"She has it to drop, you know, like trees drop blossoms. We were their guests."

"Great. Now you're in with her. Now you can hit her up for cash."

"I wouldn't," said Z. "She even invited me to, but I can't. Doesn't feel right."

Jordan sighed angrily. "So was Eugenia an asshole to you?"

"She was chilly at first—we're on different sides of the Jordan Divide. But by the time the night was over, we were old friends. Her sense of humor is ruthless!" Z grinned in his starstruck way, and Jordan realized his friend had developed a little crush on Eugenia. Z fancied tall, even elongated-looking women with ridiculously beautiful faces, whether they came in the fair hues of Eugenia or were darker than French roast. But Z's women always presumed that you couldn't take your eyes off them, while Eugenia made it known that she was looking at you too.

"Maybe," Z continued, "we can invite Molly and Eugenia to Susquehanna and take it from there. They'd love the cabaret."

"Summer would never forgive me."

Z got up again and opened the door to the fridge. "Want any water?"

"Yeah."

Z poured each of them a glass and came back to the table.

"Look, you want me to invite her?" Jordan asked. "You think it would help us?"

"I don't know," said Z. "Couldn't hurt to revive some connection. Like I said, she seemed fine with it. And hell, one or two well-placed print ads or web banners could make all the difference in our bookings. Molly was always great with ads. Damn that bank loan. We really need a new van. If I restore that old engine once more, it'll give out on us in the middle of the highway."

"Fuck it. I'll shoot Molly an email right now."

And given Summer's secrecy and subterfuge, Jordan thought, let her not forgive him.

After Jordan hit *Send*, Z rolled a joint with which to polish off another beer, and Jordan's cell phone burbled.

"Girlfriend," Z guessed. "Key of G."

"Hey," said Jordan sleepily into his phone.

"Where have you been?"

Now that he knew her dad was a politician, he heard a stridence in her voice that took his breath away.

"I'm right here, answering the phone," he groused back.

"I've called home, called your cell for hours."

"Well, I'm at Z's. I think his air conditioner is too damn loud." Jordan walked over to the window and put the phone up against the snarling motor. "Hear that? Still don't believe me?"

Jordan handed his phone to Z, who passed Jordan the lit joint and crooned suavely: "Hey there, Summer. How you doing? Yeah, yeah, he's been here all evening. We're onto cheerful topics like cash flow or, in our case, cash drought. No, I haven't heard back about the antique car shows, but you up for some Maurice Chevalier? These are roaring twenties folks. The Gatsby set on the north shore…" Z grinned; Summer must have said something clever. "We'll know by the end of the week. I'll put him on again. Go easy; we really didn't hear the phone ring. And Summertime, it's too damn hot."

Z flung the phone, and it somersaulted and plopped on the pillows where they'd been sitting. Jordan retrieved it. Z recovered his joint, waved goodbye with it, and left the room.

"Rashad got into day camp," Jordan said, now that they were speaking alone. "We gotta score those car shows so we can frigging pay for it—"

"I miss you so something fierce," she interrupted him. "Betty and I were out on the dock watching that evening sun go down, both of us dog miserable. Curtis is pressuring her to have another kid, and I fell into more than a trapdoor."

"But why, baby? You should be happy up there."

"You left, and I couldn't hear music in my son's voice or the birds."

No one had ever told him anything like that. "Baby," he repeated warmly.

"We're getting too close." Her words and breath came out fast. "Too merged. And it's dangerous. It's starting to kill me."

"I'm fucked up too. Couldn't stay home without you and Rashad. I don't like even one night alone. You know, I missed you so damn much I Googled you." He swung back on the pillows, his legs tented.

"You *whated* me?"

"I typed your name and hometown into a search engine. Your high school class is having a twentieth reunion, and everyone's on the lookout for you."

"Whoa, nosey-buddy. My macho boyfriends never gave a damn about all that, even though I was always trying to interest them in my life."

"So I'm not macho?"

"You're 'expressive-artsy macho.' My default type is 'bottled-up macho.' They drove me to tantrums, but I knew who I was with them: I was the one who wanted more. That's why they needed me and never forgot me. But I see why they pushed me away. It can be too much…whoa, did I ever think I'd say that?"

"What are you saying?"

"You're creating a Frankenstein, and watch out. All these songs starting to whirlpool through me, phrases coming all the time, out of nowhere like bats in a bad movie…I hadn't fallen into a trapdoor since I wrote 'Betty,' and I thought maybe songwriting was my silver bullet. But who ever said silver bullets don't kill you? I'm in the most beautiful place in the world, with the nicest people, and ready to set the woods on fire."

"It's just a mood, Summer." He drew his legs in and sat up, slightly lightheaded. "Frankly, I'm in the same mood. It would be a problem if one of us felt this way and the other didn't. But since we both miss the hell out of each other, it's a good sign."

She was quiet for a moment. "It's more than a mood, Jordan. It's who I am."

"Maybe," he proposed, "a bad combination of both."

"Oh, sweetheart. Don't play me, 'cause you're playing with fire."

Summer came back to New York a day earlier than planned, with a spider bite on her leg and another verse of "Brooklyn Boy":

His daddy is a Persian Jew; his mama comes from Italy and Spain,
And he looks so exotic it drives me unbelievably insane,
He stole my peaches, he broke my bell.
I let him get to know me just a little too well,
But when I go to hell he'll get on the J train, my Brooklyn Boy.

The antique car shows came through, so she'd had to learn Maurice Chevalier songs as she lay in bed with an ice pack around her spider-bitten leg. Though she hobbled and cursed under her breath that there shouldn't be any such thing as a recluse spider in Vermont, that it must be due to global warming, she lit up the stage. North Fork tycoons with their Model T Fords and four-cylinder Fiats cheered her "Love Me Tonight" and "*Donnez moi la main.*" Even if she lay around all day saying nothing, behind a mic she cast her inexorable spell.

Rashad appeared taller and more surefooted since he'd returned from Vermont: cocking his head to take in the sensory world, narrowing his eyes to make sense of ideas, and pursuing questions that Summer didn't seem to appreciate.

As they drove back from the North Fork in Z's van, he asked, "But why can't we have a house with trees?"

"Because we live in the city," she said.

"Where's my grandma?"

Grandmas came with big houses, surrounded by grass and trees—like the twins' grandma, and also those of kids from camp who invited him to Long Island for day trips.

"Where's my grandma and grandpa?"

"They live very far away," Summer said, like a line from a picture book.

"But where?"

"North Carolina."

"Do they still have a boat? You told Marjorie they did."

"Not anymore. They're too old. My father's very sick now."

"Aren't you sad?" Rashad asked.

Summer looked to Jordan for help, and he said, "My mom and dad have a house by the ocean…on Fire Island."

"I know Fire Island," Rashad squealed. "That's where Miss Sharon went."

"They share the house with some other people." And to Summer he added: "They share all houses with other people. They're pretty serious socialists. And nomads."

It wasn't easy to explain his parents' eccentric life, and some of Jordan's friends never got it. After he and his sister had left for college, their Brooklyn apartment vanished. Weary of debt and possessions, his parents decided to sell everything and live with different constellations of friends and family throughout the year. They tried to make contributions wherever they went: His mother cooked and kept house for infirm relatives, and they looked after dogs, cats, and gardens. Eventually his dad inherited a modest sum of money so they could help their hosts with expenses. Sales of his mother's pottery in the United States and Britain splashed a little more income their way.

When they were east in the States, they shared a Fire Island cottage with artist friends from Brooklyn. Membership in a rural Oregon collective provided a home in the West. They spent the rest of the year in London, Bilbao, and Calabria with outposts of family, enjoying their dual citizenship and availing themselves of health care abroad.

They'd come to the East Coast soon but visited New York only when they could stay in a particular Morningside Heights apartment that held sentimental value for them. If that apartment wasn't open, they'd forego the city. Set in their ways but traipsing around with backpacks like college kids, they'd nevertheless become Rashad's most promising grandparent figures.

By September, they even made it to the Susquehanna show when Summer debuted "Brooklyn Boy." Not surprisingly, they loved the song with their cameo appearance. After the set, they praised her voice, her poise, and skill with lyrics.

"So what kind of trees is he shaking?" Jordan's father asked Summer with his most charming smile.

"She's implying that she adores it," said his mother, offering Summer a big hug when Jordan introduced them. In her embroidered shirt with long dark hair in a bun, his mom struck a familiar profile, both girlish and mature.

"I'm so happy to meet you, Mrs. Radfar," Summer gushed, her eyes twinkly.

"Mariana, please."

It seemed they'd all known each other more than three minutes because Jordan felt that he'd known each of them for centuries. He high-fived his dad, who continued to tease Summer: "So he's lambasting you, making trouble, and then getting on the J train when the shit hits the fan?" Because he retained a British cadence from his London childhood and had spoken Farsi with his family, Arman's odd accent could make an expression like "shit hits the fan" sound cute.

"I wrote it in an extreme state of mind," she admitted. "I can get into those."

"It's not an accurate portrait of our relationship," Jordan assured them.

"The housing details are right: Ocean Parkway, Midwood," Arman recounted. "And I guess we didn't teach him to swim. How foolish."

"It's not too late," said Mariana as Z and Bruce approached them, eager to be introduced. Jordan relished this blended world of music, friends, and family—and of course, Summer—that spilled over into the next day when they took Rashad on a picnic in Central Park.

Arman bought a purple soccer ball on that balmy afternoon and taught Rashad how to kick and throw. Jordan toggled between them and Summer, who was chatting on the picnic blanket with his mom. Mariana served Chianti in Dixie cups from a grape juice can, camouflage that delighted Summer.

"Rashad!" Arman called, tossing the ball.

With a deft catch, the boy cried, "Got it, Grandpa!" Jordan noticed his father jog over and then kneel beside him to confer. He could guess what was being said. Arman had never encouraged his son and daughter to call him Dad; he felt that "Mommy" and "Daddy" were infantilizing after a certain age. "Call us what our friends call us," he'd told Jordan and his sister around Rashad's age. And so Rashad must be hearing that too.

The season's last peaches and first apples were spread on a plastic plate and garnished with mint leaves. Alongside lay baguettes, a chunk of melty Camembert, and a bowl of salade Niçoise with tuna, olives, and blanched beans. As they ate salad, ripped the bread, and spread cheese, they spoke of Katrina and "the federal government's inept response," as Arman phrased it.

"I couldn't agree more," said Summer.

"The U.S. airlifted food into Somalia," Mariana pointed out. "We couldn't help our own?"

"This country has been a godsend for many people," said Arman. "But it has a big loose screw."

"…called the Republican party," Summer chirped, and they all laughed.

"Would that it could be reduced to only the old-boy's network," said Arman.

"Of which every country has its version," Mariana added. Her own father, for whom Jordan had been given a middle name, Eztebe, had been a Basque nationalist—a moderate, "pacifist against the odds," he'd liked to say—shunted between fascist Spain and the radical ETA. "When Americans rage about living in a fascist country," Mariana continued, "they don't know what they're saying."

Her husband agreed, reaching for a small, soft peach. "Because in a truly fascist country, they'd never speak that way in public. What we have here is corporate capitalism, and a different dilemma."

"What would you call McCarthyism?" Summer asked.

"A Faustian pact," replied Arman, eyeing her with respect. "The difference being that in this country, people were blacklisted for four years, while in others they're carted off to prisons or killed in their homes."

"Other countries whose dictatorships we've supported," Summer added.

"In some cases, yes," Arman ceded. "Other times, the United States has taken risks to oppose them."

"Sometimes both," commented Mariana. "Heaven knows—if you're looking for a country with no history of hypocrisy, don't look on earth."

"You sure seem to prefer the medical systems abroad," Jordan observed.

"Oh no, Jordie," said his father. "We dislike going to doctors anywhere."

"We can't choose our doctors on the road any more than we choose our toilets," said his mother, and they all laughed.

"Capitano!" sang Rashad, standing behind Arman and throwing his arms around the older man.

"Who?" asked Jordan. "Whahhh?"

"I don't wanna be called 'Grandpa,'" Arman explained, his hand clasping Rashad's cinnamon-brown arm. "So I gave him some alternatives."

Jordan began laughing but caught Rashad's dejected pout and stopped himself.

"What should he call you?" Summer asked Mariana reverently.

"Ohhh, goodness. We called my grandmother 'Amona'…call me Mona. That's nice, isn't it?"

In bed that night, Summer sidled up to Jordan and whispered, "Mona and Capitano are wonderful. That's why you're wonderful."

"Am I wonderful?" he asked. "You've been pulling away from me ever since Vermont."

"Not really."

"Yeah, really."

He kissed her on the mouth, like they hadn't in a while, their heads rolling, his hands sliding wildly over her curved body.

"Baby," she cried, interrupting the kiss, "I'm not pulling away—just trying to be careful so I don't fuck things up. I always fuck things up."

"You're not fucking anything up. My parents adore you. And they're fussy; they don't think highly of everyone."

"It's amazing I didn't fuck up Rashad's first four years. I'm so relieved. Do you realize, I didn't even drink a glass of wine 'til he was three?" Jordan had heard that from Betty too. "I didn't want to act remotely like my mother. Still don't. But if I screw up when he's ten or fifteen, at least he'll have that core that can't be shaken."

"You're not gonna screw up." Jordan kissed her soft forehead, her cheeks.

"Don't be so sure; I'm like that chair you think you've glued together that keeps collapsing when people sit on it. Why do you think Khalil bolted? Hell, I fucked up with my own sister, and she's the nicest person on earth."

"Do you miss Deb?" he asked, stroking her hair.

"All the time. Let's not talk about it."

"You can tell me stuff," he said. "I won't disappear on the J train."

"Well, you say that now. We haven't been together for even a year."

"Baby," he said with a sigh, nestling his head upon her collarbone. "No woman has ever given me such love. My gratitude won't change, if we're together for keeps or if we go up in smoke tomorrow."

"What about Molly? She was more uninhibited and sexually adventurous."

"I prefer the challenge of you."

"And filthy rich! She gave you a CD and a prestigious teaching job."

"She left me. I was just a station on her way…all my exes have been traveling ladies, Summer. You're my home." He felt hard in his boxer shorts, wanting her, savoring how the cotton silk stiffened with him. He wound his hand into hers.

"I want to have your child," she said suddenly, and a hot heartbeat jolted through him. "I love you and your parents. I want to bear their grandchild and make you a father. This child will be beautiful and strong, like your family—and like Rashad. I may be the weakest among you. But even a weak link is a link. My mother was a weak link."

"Summer," he whispered, caressing her breasts through her nightgown, his finger grazing the ridge of a nipple. "You're not weak, honey. That's so not true."

"One day you'll see how weak I am," she stammered, aroused. "And you'll recoil. But even if you do, your parents will be there for us. My children will have a family. I've never known that before."

He rolled her nightgown up to her belly, and she grasped him between her bare legs.

That autumn Summer practiced scales with diligence so she'd never hit a flat note. She stopped stealing because Jordan didn't want Rashad to start, and he promised that he would buy whatever she needed—his lady didn't need to filch. They spent a windy weekend with Mona and Capitano on Fire Island, walking by the sea in a drizzle at Fair Harbor. Summer now kept her song notebook private and went off with it to write. To Jordan's surprise, his capricious, mercurial parents seemed to stabilize her moods. Around them she never fell into trapdoors or worried about fucking up.

After they got back to the city, Jordan began to arrange a Christmas show for his students at the boys' school, giving private lessons, gigging almost every night. He'd landed a regular stint in a Tribeca pub with Eliot Waxmann, a cantankerous old leftie who played stellar blues guitar in the vein of Django Reinhardt.

Molly had sent a witty reply over email to Jordan's note last summer but still hadn't shown up at Susquehanna. The trio managed to get a monthly lease on a new van through Bruce's wife.

One sapphire October afternoon, Summer and Jordan sat with Rashad at an outdoor café at South Street Seaport with nearly fifty dollars from a morning of street music. As they sipped Cokes with lemon, they smiled at each other without needing to explain: Somehow, despite each of their trepidation, things were working out.

"How'd you like a little sister or brother?" Summer asked her son.

"Sure," he said as though they'd offered him a blueberry muffin. They didn't speak directly about marriage, but Jordan imagined an engagement announcement:

Catherine Jane Summers, aka Summer Vale, is engaged to Jordan Eztebe Radfar. Ms. Summers studied at Julliard and UCLA without earning a degree and sings in cabarets, clubs, and NYC subways. Her estranged father was Republican chairman of Monmouth County, New Jersey. Mr. Radfar holds a bachelor of music degree from Oberlin College, where he majored in performance. His parents live off an inheritance and the sales of his mother's pottery. The wedding is planned for whenever the couple can afford it.

Now Summer and Betty were talking about being pregnant together, but a month later they were each menstruating. It had been one cycle for Jordan and Summer, two for the Wilcoxes. Curtis, however, remained unvanquished: "Anything worthwhile is worth waiting for," he said.

"Even if it doesn't come to pass," Betty added, "we have incredible lives."

And so they focused on the next order of business. True to his word, Curtis had booked time in a sound studio in Long Island City, and they were preparing to record "Betty" and Summer's two songs for Jordan.

She'd also been working on "a song about my mother," she told them when they'd assembled at her piano to plan and rehearse. "Curtis didn't want me to write this one, so I was paralyzed for a while. But then I got moving. It's a little slower and mellower than my other ones. Bear with me—it's called 'Short Stick.'"

She sat at the piano bench, cleared her throat, and proceeded to play it for Jordan, Betty, Curtis, and Z. Jordan shut his eyes and listened as her lyrics yielded words she'd never said to him directly. Maybe it was best to hear it this way because what could he possibly have said? Jordan had seen shit go down as a kid but nothing like this.

"Drawing window shades against the sun,
I remember how Aunt Maegan said, 'You're scaring everyone.'
Now you see her, now you don't—
She loves me, loves me not—
The short end of the stick is what we got."

Summer spoke the song's last line and was quiet for a second before piping a vocal refrain, like a child, to gentle piano. Z spontaneously joined in, and their tone grew. He hadn't sung since his days with the Octane Furies, though he'd begun his career as a choirboy. Surprised by Z's passion, Jordan let the piano chords and vocals crest over him like waves.

When they stopped, before anyone could clap or comment, Curtis said: "Next!" and laughed uncomfortably.

Betty glanced at him as though someone had flicked paint in her eye.

"That was one of the most affecting songs I've ever heard."

"Hit home a little too hard, Curtis?" Summer asked, swiveling around on the piano bench.

Curtis didn't flinch. "Sorry—it was a downer. I knew it would be."

As Z addressed Curtis, he tried to catch Jordan's eye.

"Ever hear James Taylor's 'Fire and Rain'? Or Neil Young's 'The Damage Done'? Downers to boot, and hits—because they were real and people could tell."

"Here's the drill," said Summer as Curtis got up to pace, knowing he was outnumbered. "If you want to record 'Betty' and my two Jordan songs, this goes too."

"Look, I guess," said Curtis. "You guys know the business. I just smell a sinker."

Betty turned away from him, to the wall.

"Sorry I can't be light and breezy about my mom's suicide attempts," quipped Summer.

"Why do you have to write a song about it in the first place?" Curtis begged.

"I never thought I would when Jordan suggested the idea. But it wanted to come out," she said. "That's all I can tell you."

"What do you think, Jordan?" Curtis asked.

"This one will make her," Jordan responded, trying not to get emotional. "It's stunning and courageous, and I think Z should sing with her."

"Just at the end," said Z.

"Did your sister really do CPR?" Betty asked hesitantly.

Summer nodded. "Oh yeah."

"How old was she?"

"Sixteen, maybe seventeen. She had a date that night with a guy from town. I think it was her first date; she was getting all dolled up. I was in my room, hermetically practicing for our school musical that year, *Bye Bye Birdie*. So there I was, singing 'How Lovely to be a Woman,' and suddenly I stopped. Can't explain why. Sometimes you just know something's up. Then I heard screaming and opened my door, ran into my parent's room, where Deb was compressing Mom's chest, shouting for me to 'call nine-one-one; she isn't breathing!' You should've seen that rescue act, both of them dressed to the nines. I guess my mother wanted to die looking like Grace Kelly of Monaco or something."

Z again caught Jordan's eye; Summer was filling them in on those years before Rashad was born. Jordan took a seat beside her on the piano bench and cradled his arm around her. Summer took his other hand in her hot, sweaty one.

"Where was your dad?" Curtis asked her.

"Don't know, but he wasn't around."

"Did your sister actually go on the date?" asked Z.

"After EMS came with their defibrillators and all..." Summer glanced to the floor and back up at her friends. Jordan squeezed the hand he held then kissed her neck. "I remember a horn honking outside. Can you imagine their conversation? 'So, how was your day?' 'Oh, I mowed the lawn and played eighteen holes of golf. And your's, Debbie?' 'Just saved my mom from doing herself in.' But of course, we weren't supposed to say anything. My dad was in county politics, and he didn't want word getting out about his wife." Summer left it at that.

"You told us you didn't know CPR," Z reminded her, "when that guy went down at Susquehanna last Christmas."

"I don't. Deb got certified when she was a summer camp counselor, which I never did, 'cause I spent summers in music programs. I'd be too hysterical to pull off CPR anyway. My sister's more stable."

"The one in California?" Curtis asked.

"The only one I have."

"So your mom must have been our age when all this happened?" Betty asked.

"Hmm, let's see." Summer shut her eyes for a second. "She had Deb when she was twenty-two, so she must have been…shit, she was my age. Thirty-eight. Wow. I haven't thought about that, happy to say. But if it ever comes down to me hurting my son or anyone around me with that self-centered bullshit, I authorize any of you to shackle my arms and legs." Summer sounded both convincing and tentative. Slowly, she slipped her hand out of Jordan's.

Several days later, Jordan reminded Summer about her high school reunion, and she finally wrote on the website: *Cathy Summers here. Sorry to miss the party and hope you're all doing fine!* A flood of posts then ensued from her former classmates asking what was she up to and where did she live?

Easy on those details, Summer answered them.

Was she married? Kids? How was Debbie?

I'm engaged to a sizzling sax player, and I write love songs about him. Raising a four-year-old son. Deb's great—three kids, brainy husband, Orange County, CA.

We sent an invitation to your old address, and it got forwarded to North Carolina but came back to me. Your name was crossed out, and somebody wrote "addressee unknown," a classmate posted.

My dad probably did that. Long story.

Oh sorry. Would be great to see you and catch up.

Come to my cabaret, old chums. She posted a link to the Susquehanna.

A month later they'd secured a crowd of thirty, including spouses, who came from Philly, Trenton, the Jersey Shore, Queens, Poughkeepsie, and Boston. They came with digital cameras, and one asked if she could shoot video for the reunion site. Generally the hotel didn't permit recording and video, but they consented this time since Summer had asked so politely and procured so many guests. So they had a paparazzi night, cameras firing off like cherry bombs. Summer performed her standard set to profuse applause and shouting.

"I'm honored tonight by a grand turnout of high school friends here," she announced to the audience. "It's our twentieth reunion. Who knows where the time goes? I planned a special song for them—one I sang in our eighth grade play. 'Lovely to Be a Woman.' And a bunch of originals that my sweetheart has inspired, which some of you regulars have heard before."

Her classmates didn't want to let her off the stage after "Brooklyn Boy" and "A Lot I Don't Know." In unison, they screamed "Ca-THEE, Ca-THEE, Ca-TH-EE" and even "Jor-DAN, Jor-DAN!"—much to his satisfaction.

So the band had an encore. "Okay," she said into the mic. "I wasn't going to do this one, because I'm not big on airing dirty laundry. But my songs are personal, which is why I bother to write and sing them. This is about my mom… anyone remember her?" Jordan thought he saw one arm rise. "Who remembers my dad?" A forest of arms shot up. "Well, now you may learn why no one remembers her. The instrumentals are all improv; it's a work in progress," she forewarned. "It's good for me to share pieces that aren't so finished—or easy to hear."

Fred was at the piano, and she gave herself over to singing. Z joined in the last refrain, and Jordan performed a solo on his horn. Everyone clapped and hollered as if it would keep the show from ending.

Jordan gave up on Molly coming to the Susquehanna, but she emailed him one morning after he'd taken Rashad to school: *Hey, congrats on that* Labombar-humba *write-up! Tamara—you remember my sister-in-law?—happened to see it and send it my way. Guess I'm famous now. Will definitely come by the show.*

What write-up in that online zine of cool music-world chatter, informally known as *La-B*? And why would she be famous? Jordan clicked the link she sent.

Summer Vale: New Songs in Oldie Styles, read the review title, beside an image of Summer in the sequined gown she'd worn for her high school friends.

Some talents flash across the stage like aurora borealis—with rare and unforgivable luminosity. Summer Vale, whose loungey cadence will haunt you long after her singing stops, is now composing songs of equal range. The show-stopping vocalist was cast in off-Broadway choruses in the 1990s and appeared in Los Angeles cabaret clubs before stealing the stage from a twelve-piece New York City swing band when she came back east.

After vanishing for half a decade, she's reemerged with an outstanding cabaret act at the Susquehanna Hotel. With her she brings John "Zikomo" Saintcroix, former drummer and vocalist for Octane Furies, and new sweetheart Jordan Radfar, a promising young saxophonist who studied at the Oberlin Conservatory of Music. Radfar provides inspiration for her original songs, like "A Lot I Don't Know," a clever homage to him that references everything from Hamlet to Elvis Presely: Falling in love again was Elvis Presley's folly; I met me a sweet boy who was still obsessed with Molly; Never dreamed we'd be a go; But there's a lot about this world that I don't know.

"Betty," a carefree Hoagy Carmichaelesque ode to her best friend, comes right from the early thirties—the mouths of babes and blues mamas. Other numbers evoke her late mentor Gus Granato in their R&B swagger.

For that reference, a link was provided. When Jordan clicked on it, a video opened of Summer hamming it up. Clearly, this footage came from her high school pals.

With hair in her face, Summer had let the strap of her gown drop as she slinked out to a friend in the audience. "*He stole my peaches and he broke my bell...I let him get to know me just a little too well,*" she sang in a gravelly snarl. "*But when I go to hell he'll get on the J train, my Brooklyn Boy!*" The next cut showed Jordan himself playing away onstage in his wine-colored shirt.

The band also features Fred Quinn on piano and Bruce Roman on upright bass. A strong contender for Cabaret Choice of the Year, Summer Vale has once again turned eyeballs her way and should not be missed.

Jordan touched the screen where his and Summer's names appeared. So long and implacably he'd gone without a word of recognition; even on the web there were only brief show listings, some amateur videos of Z and him, and the same old MP3s they'd done with Molly years back. That's why Skip had purportedly dumped him. "I need people who are getting around," he'd claimed.

But there was no mention in this piece that either Jordan or Bruce had played for Skip Harrington. And in Summer's case, the reviewer had referenced only her "stealing the stage from a twelve-piece New York City swing band."

Eat that and your dirty socks for lunch, fuckwad! Jordan thought with glee.

He checked the byline: Leandro Gomez. Maybe Skip had swung it to him too.

Thanks for sending this along, he emailed Molly back. *I'm reeling.*

Didn't I always say your time would come?

U gave it more than lip service, Molly.

Have your girlfriend or Z seen it?

Both still sleeping ☺

She's intense and the show looks just fabu. We were all set to go (on the cal-endar, promise!), but Gene's nephew appeared on her stoop last month, a teenage refugee from Fire-and-Brimstone Texas. So we got derailed by him and his crack-er-barrel family, and by our fundraisers for hurricane victims.

Just as well. Summer's still jealous of you and may flip out if you show up.

Why jealous? You don't eulogize me all the time, do you?

She thinks so.

I'll take her word for it.

Would love to send you a new CD we're mixing.

Please do.

At that moment Z texted him: *Helium balloons! Check out Gomez in La-B... She'll get Choice Cabaret.*

At 11:30 a.m., Summer waddled into the living room in her slippers and blue bathrobe, her long, brown hair tangled, rubbing her eyes against the glare of her east-facing windows.

"You gotta see this!" Jordan cried. He had carefully deleted the email exchange with Molly.

"Rashad at school?"

"Check, sweetheart."

"I'd be a mess without you," she muttered. "They'd be coming to pack me up."

"Look at this," Jordan repeated, indicating their laptop on the wobbly table. Summer took a moment to read the review and nodded with a smile.

"Nice," she said.

"Yo, *nice*! This is the first real online hit we've had."

"I wouldn't exaggerate," said Summer. "It's no Grammy nomination."

"I wouldn't underplay. Next step could be the *Times*."

"Look, you met my old classmate, Sue? She does publicity for some designers or something," Summer told him through a yawn. She covered her mouth, mumbled, "Excuse me," and went on. "So she asked me some questions over email for the *Monmouth Gazette* or whatever the hell it's called. Then she found this guy at *Labombarhumba* who remembered my act with Skip. Sue has contacts all over. She's a media person."

"Just what we need, honey!"

"Jordan, you're a little younger than I am. This is sweet, but it's still a long way to Tipperary."

"Z thinks it's our ticket to the next echelon, and he's older than you."

"How old *is* Z?" she asked.

"Like forty-four or forty-five?"

"Oh, I think he's at least forty-eight," she said. "Black people don't age like we do. Or like I do. You're Moorish—you can hack ten years off your life and no one will know the difference. That's what Z does."

In her zeal about the write-up, Molly had forgotten that Jordan was turning thirty. Over the years, he and Molly had always remembered each other's birthdays—which wasn't difficult since his was November 1, and hers followed on the 6th. But that year she was distracted, and now it really didn't matter. Summer would take him to dinner in the Village ("No stealing!" he stipulated) and afterward they'd have champagne and dessert with the Wilcoxes.

"Aw, can't I come with you?" Rashad pleaded.

"No, honey," said Summer, brushing his nose with her finger. "You stay with the twins, and we'll see you later."

After Halloween, the city streets were always sprinkled with bright leaves and black and orange crepe paper. Jordan remembered his combined birthday and Halloween parties where Mariana filled buckets with water, and his little friends in their glittery costumes got soaked trying, with little success, to bob for apples.

The evening was brisk with newly minted chill. They wore jackets, and Summer had popped a small woolen beret on Rashad's head.

"Did you hear from Mona and Capitano today?" she asked Jordan as they trotted toward Essex Street.

"Of course." They'd called in the morning, full of cheer.

"C'we go to Fire Island again?" asked Rashad.

"Hmm, not for a while," said Jordan. "It's getting cold for the cottage."

"1975," Summer said with a sigh, shaking her head at him.

"I'm a damned antique already," he began.

"Not quite. But me, you can find me at bargain prices in the second-hand stores. I came out the year Nancy Sinatra sang 'Sugar Town.'" At that, she and Rashad launched into "Shu-shu-shu Sugar Town," swinging their arms.

Upstairs, Curtis opened the door eagerly, his hair combed back and face flushed. He slapped Jordan's shoulder. "'Ey my dude, welcome to your thirties!"

Behind Jordan the room was disconcertingly dark, and a well of voices arose in a single pitch: "Surprise!"

Someone undimmed the lights slowly. Jordan's gaze fell first upon his mother's dark eyes and pretty smile framed by black hair; then his beaming sister, Robin, who must have flown in from London; Z and some friends; Bruce with his family; Professor Wolff; guys from Midwood and Brooklyn public schools; a couple he'd known at Oberlin; and assorted musicians from different bands and gigs.

"Holy..." Jordan looked from face to grinning face, trying to fit these disparate parts of his life together. His father, clad in chinos and a long, embroidered white shirt began clapping and led everyone in a round of "For He's a Jolly Good Fellow."

♪

Jordan had no idea how Summer had pulled it off. She'd apparently been emailing his sister for weeks (his mother had put them in touch) and networking through Z. The only important people missing were Molly and his therapist, Barbara—which was fine.

Outside on the roof deck, Summer set up a mic and Z assembled his timbales for a brief tribute. People gathered around in their jackets and shawls.

First, Summer and Robin performed a poetry slam–style spoof of Jordan's life—clearly Robin had filled in the childhood references and Summer the current ones. Knocking hips together, Summer's voluptuous curves against Robin's bony frame, they chanted, "He sparkles, he bubbles, he rolls, he rocks; he spins the woodwinds, makes trouble…and never stops." Everyone laughed, toasting with champagne and hot cider.

Then Summer borrowed an acoustic guitar and sang a medley of love songs: "You Go to My Head," "Tenderly," and her own "A Lot I Don't Know." She sounded amorous with only her simple guitar strumming, even though Jordan loved Fred's shimmery piano. And Z tapped away on the timbales behind her, keeping the percussion low-key.

After that, Arman grabbed the mic, his large brown eyes shining. "Wow," he began, flashing a toothy smile at everyone from beneath his moustache. "So. My kid is thirty. I can't hide from anything now, can I? What I want to say is, our Jordan's a warrior. He doesn't let anything stop him, and never has. We don't know where he got that trait, because Mariana and I no sooner entertain an ambition than we've figured out why it will never work. But this boy doesn't know the meaning of doubt—or compromise. Now I see him playing music in all sorts of venues—recording, teaching—and finally getting the credit he deserves."

Everyone clapped. Everyone knew about *Labombarhumba*. Robin and Summer had printed out copies of the page and pasted them all over the wall behind the food table, interspersing childhood photos of Jordan with some from Vermont last summer.

After Arman's toast, various guests took out instruments and improvised with Z. Rashad, the twins, and Bruce's boy dashed around, giggling and spilling soda.

A friend of Z's sauntered over to Summer and Jordan to hint that Skip Harrington was furious about their glowing review. "Good," said Summer. "Let him be. He could've worked with all of us if he wasn't such a proud son of a suck."

Eliot Waxmann, the older jazz guitarist with whom Jordan gigged in Tribeca, straggled in late; he'd of course gone to some underground meeting and arrived regaled in buttons that said *9/11 Was an Inside Job*.

"You buy that rubbish?" Arman asked him casually.

Waxmann looked shocked. He assumed that everyone south of 14th Street with an instrument case or an embroidered shirt towed his line.

"The true American conceit," Arman continued, "believing that no one else is competent—that only America is capable of damaging America."

Jordan and Summer watched with fascination as Eliot shriveled from this challenge.

"You ever travel?" Arman continued to prod him. "Do you ever talk to people who live abroad?"

"I'm a guitarist!" he protested gruffly. "Lucky to make my rent, much less travel."

"So you walk from home to the bagel store, but you know everything about the world?"

"Am I not entitled to my opinions because I don't jet-set?"

"Well, is this an opinion? You present it like testimony. Fully unproven, and never will be proven. Just a wild goose chase."

"That's exactly how they keep you quiet," muttered Waxmann.

Arman traded an amused, patronizing glance with Professor Wolff, who had drifted over as well. "No," Arman countered. "That's exactly how they—whoever 'they' are—distract you from conditions you might actually stand a chance of changing."

For his candor, which seemed to embarrass ideologues of every stripe, Arman had been ousted from universities and denied tenure. But Summer whispered into Jordan's ear: "Your dad. Sharp cookie." He nodded, taking her hand. "And Betty," she continued to whisper, "not drinking."

After all the other guests left, they learned that Summer's hunch was correct.

Curtis poured the last glasses of champagne and offered sparkling water to his wife. "To Jordan!" he toasted. "To many happy returns in your preferred key of B-flat…but may your profits *not* be flat!"

They laughed, clinked glasses, and sipped.

"To Isabella!" Summer volunteered, raising her glass again. Curtis and Betty smiled bashfully at each other. "When is she due?" Summer asked.

"Late July," Betty told them, and Jordan found his heart pounding.

"We don't know whether we'll have a girl, of course," Curtis reminded them.

"Congratulations, whatever the case!" Jordan exclaimed, and champagne flutes were clinked again. Then Summer put hers down and went over to extend a warm hug to Betty.

"We haven't told the boys yet," Curtis explained. "We've hardly told anyone."

"Smart," said Summer as she and Betty finished their hug. "Your dad knows?"

"That's why he's in town—we're making plans."

"How nice," Summer commented, sitting back down, "to have your dad's support now—something I'll never know. Though I'll have Arman and Mariana's when the time comes."

Jordan suddenly felt great pressure to produce this child, to catch up with Curtis in every way. He'd been imagining their daughter as Lucy, thinking they might name her after his grandmother, Luciana. Or Lucien, if they had a son: Cool-hand Luke.

"Do your folks know you're trying?" Betty asked, and Jordan shook his head no.

"Well, they might," Summer informed him. "I mentioned it to Robin. She's excited about Shoshana."

"Shoshana?" asked Jordan.

"Don't you love that name?"

"Yeah," he said, draining the last of his champagne. "Actually, I do."

Robin never liked Jordan's girlfriends and had played the bratty, chauvinistic sister numerous times on his behalf. Downright dreadful to Molly, Robin had set off an especially fierce lover's quarrel between Jordan and her. But Robin hovered around Summer like a honeybee around marigold. She implicitly trusted Summer's interest in her brother and loved their music together. Robin had taken off November from her job in London and over the next three weeks became Jordan and Summer's music manager. Even with modest recognition came a new stream of obligations for them: Return this call from a local radio station, get back to that reviewer for *Time Out*! Robin kept up with everything because Summer was overwhelmed, Jordan was teaching at the boys' school, and Z was booking holiday parties galore.

Robin stayed nearby with a friend in the East Village, which was a godsend since they needed not only a manager, but also a babysitter for Rashad. Now that Betty was pregnant, Summer hesitated to casually leave him at the Wilcoxes. After her good review resounded through the internet, Susquehanna gave them an extra evening that month and Summer was hired to sing at a club Sunday nights until Christmas. Even more excitingly, she would accompany Shazan White, a well-known trumpeter, in his seasonal New York appearance. That booking entailed rehearsals, and it added up to lots of time away from her son.

They wanted to wrap up the CD but could handle only so much at once. Z was laying in drum tracks; Summer was redoing "A Lot I Don't Know" and working hard to finish "That Kind of Friend." They would include four standards from her previous demo so she'd have nine songs in all. Robin would design the CD package before she left for London after Thanksgiving. Arman and Mariana were going with her.

"What will we do without them?" Summer asked, and Jordan had no answer. Betty was not feeling well as Thanksgiving drew near, and they often found themselves fending not only for Rashad but getting the twins to school and back. In a pinch, Robin was always there. If they needed her, she came by with dinner for the three little boys. She'd play video games and watch TV with them while Summer and Jordan were at gigs or rehearsals and Betty slept. Sometimes a friend accompanied Robin to help out with the boys, and sometimes Arman and Mariana came along.

"What'll we ever do when they're gone?" Summer kept asking. "Rashad is so happy, and Betty is so collapsed. Any way you can talk them into staying longer?"

"Look, Robin's already taken a long break from work. And my folks…they do what they do. But I'll ask everyone at Thanksgiving."

They planned turkey sandwiches on rye from the deli for their holiday feast, capped off with prosecco and cannoli. Arman and Mariana would stay all week in the Morningside Heights apartment.

During those precious days, there were always phone calls and plans. There was food, music, and heated conversations about many matters, including Robin's crushes on elusive men.

"Your taste is unfortunate," Arman advised his daughter.

"It's not taste—it's my crazy heart!" Robin justified herself.

"It's their crazy *lack of* heart," Summer interjected. Now a third voice counterbalanced the father-daughter dialogue Jordan knew so well.

After dinner, Jordan thanked Robin for all her help with Rashad and with their business. "We're actually scared we won't get by without you," he admitted. "And we're wondering"—he looked around at his parents and his sister—"is there *any* way you guys can hang out a bit longer? Like 'til Christmas? All of you?"

Robin tilted her head and pouted. "Aw," she said.

"You've been doing a terrific job," Arman agreed. "You underestimate your capabilities, Robbie." He had more of a pedantic way with her than with Jordan.

"Maybe I can stretch it out 'til the New Year," she said. "It's different in Europe and the U.K. They expect you to take sprawling vacations."

"But we may not be able to change our tickets," Mariana pointed out. "Prices get exorbitant around now."

"We're all on the same flight," Arman added. "Now, we could look into it. But I make no promises."

Summer cleared her throat. "Um, Robin and Rashad already know this," she began, and then announced: "Jordan and I are trying to have a baby."

"Now?" Mariana's eyes popped wide open.

"Really?" asked Arman with a smile.

"Will you be able, with everything else you've got going?" Mariana continued.

"May not be easy," said Summer. "But I'm a little older than Jordan. So I'm kind of under the gun because...we want this."

They hadn't been going at it with the usual fervor lately because they were exhausted after long musical days. But during ovulation Summer would wink at Jordan, pointing to her crotch—which he always found arousing.

"A lot's happening," Jordan agreed. "And we've got to do it all."

"It's a special time," said Arman in a fatherly tone that Jordan could tell had touched Summer. She managed to repeat, in barely a whisper, "It's a special time."

"Are you planning to get married?" asked Mariana.

"Once she's pregnant," Jordan said.

"Then here's what we'll do," Arman suggested. "Right now, we hope to be back here in May. If Summer gets pregnant before then, we'll come back sooner—at least Mariana and I. Can't speak for Robin."

"Oh, I'll be at the wedding," Robin declared.

"You've got to be," said Summer. "You're our maid of honor."

"It will probably be simple—town hall and all that," said Jordan.

"We'll all be there," Mariana promised.

But it still hurt like hell when they took off the next week.

The winds grew unbearably harsh, trees in all the parks now bare and craggy. When they were alone, Summer was snippy and despondent. Other times, she couldn't stop crying and slammed the bedroom door, not wanting Rashad and Jordan to see her dissolve. In fact, they couldn't even hear her because she kept it quiet. But she always emerged with raw, wet eyes.

"Oh, honey," Jordan would moan.

"It was nice to have a mom and dad and sister again," she'd say.

"Look, they'll be back."

But now they were gone. Betty, who slept poorly and awoke groggy, was often napping when Summer and Jordan brought the twins home from school for her. The burden of the twins' lives before Curtis got home fell heavily upon Summer and Jordan.

Without Robin's help, it was challenge enough to find good sitters for only Rashad. Summer tried teaming up with the mom of a two-year-old girl in the building, and Rashad hated it—at four, he already found the little girl a nuisance. From abroad, Mariana asked her cousin Amalia to come in one night. But she was drab and gray, and Rashad didn't relate to her. "I want Robin," he whined. "I want Betty."

The next time they desperately needed someone to look after Rashad, Z showed up with a set of Chinese checkers and Parcheesi, proclaiming, "Time for something beside video games." Surprisingly, Rashad enjoyed the novelty. But Z, who was often out gigging or teching, was not a long-term solution for them. Jordan was grateful when the Wilcoxes took Rashad one night, like old times.

"Sorry I've been out of sorts," Betty apologized when they dropped him off.

"I'm sorry you've not been feeling well," said Summer, and they embraced.

"Hope I'm getting over this trimester hump," said Betty. "I miss you guys. Miss my life."

Rashad slept at the Wilcoxes', and the next morning Jordan and Summer tried again to draw Lucien or Shoshana from the ineffable universe. Jordan felt it was a good shot, literally, but wondered if it was a good idea. The last thing Summer needed was morning sickness like Betty's and other hormonal changes. "Everyone loves a pregnant singer," she insisted—but he wasn't convinced. Maybe they should hold off until they achieved more acclaim and security.

But he kept quiet because Summer would surely veto that agenda. She wanted to beat the biological clock and bind herself into his clan. She seemed hungry for family, thrilled to tape photos of Thanksgiving and his birthday party to the fridge one afternoon, exclaiming, "Wow. This feels so…normal."

Jordan shrugged with faint annoyance. "Arman and Mariana are not normal."

He remembered how they'd walk around the house half-naked, in that European way, embarrassing him if he had friends over. Sometimes his mother got high and spent three hours washing dishes, making them shine. He remembered Arman grumbling at her to never leave pieces of paper in her pockets, because he always mistook them for money. And now Summer was telling him how normal they were.

"Sometimes my folks didn't have a dollar between them and had to go out on a weed-selling rampage." As he recounted such memories, Jordan felt he wasn't getting through to her. In Summer's world, people were quintessentially ideal, like Betty or Gus—and now his family—or they were quintessentially evil, like her parents.

"I have extended family," she claimed, "such as Betty and everyone else."

"Family should extend in both directions."

"You know that in our case it can't."

"What about those photos of you and Deb in a sandbox?"

"What photos?"

"You showed them to me a while back."

He knew they weren't the happiest photos of Summer, but he hadn't been the most appealing child either. Until adolescence, Jordan had been runty, with big teeth and shaggy hair. It had taken him a while to grow into his face. Since she'd taped one of his runty photos to the fridge, they should have a funny kid picture of her too.

"I don't want Rashad asking questions about my sister," she parried. "What can I possibly say? I had a built-in best friend for thirty years. And I turned on her—I nearly destroyed her marriage..."

"So you were a typical kid sister. Robin nearly busted up all my relationships before you."

"Yes," she said, looking fondly at a photo of her and Robin. "We talked about that. Never thought I'd end up having a kid sister myself. And I never thought she'd be better at managing my life than I am. I always relied on Deb that way—I stopped paying taxes because I didn't even understand how to do it without her."

"Can't you make it up with her?"

Jordan remembered the kindly tone of Deb's card from last summer.

"Not so long as she's married to Stewart Richardson. See, she didn't marry him because she loved him. She married him because she loved someone else, and she was terrified of love. That's a big difference between Deb and me. She can't bear to lose control, and I live out of control.

"It was disappointing to see this shallowness in her, and I told her she was a coward, controlling things behind the scenes, like our parents did. She felt so guilty about not really loving her husband that she let him dominate her life, and when it came time for him to cut me out of the picture, that's what happened."

"But it was years ago, right?"

"Love isn't for everyone," Summer said, turning to the stove and grabbing a pot to make tea. "It isn't for most people. What I'm doing, hanging with a hot guy whose got a good heart and plays a mean tenor—well, that would break most women's hearts, and it will probably break mine someday. But my sister's heart will never be broken. She's got that all worked out."

Whenever Jordan saw Eliot Waxmann at the Tribeca pub to play blues, he'd get an earful about his father. "Conservative in sheep's clothing," Eliot insisted as he tuned his guitar. "Kind of guy the system loves. Intellectual who supports the state."

Jordan found himself defending Arman. "He was just telling you not to burn out on a wild goose chase. Look, he was in France on 9/11, and he saw Muslims cheering in a bar, and they thought he and my mom were Muslims too. From what they said…well, I can tell you they weren't cheering because they thought Bush and Cheney's men had pulled a fast one."

But Eliot clammed up as Jordan spoke. He had his version of the world and didn't want it tampered with.

People seemed defensive and provocative as the days grew short and bitter cold. The only chance for relief was playing music together. Get Eliot to shut up about conspiracy theories and slide his fingers down the fret, and the night was good. Summer sang with such force that she received standing ovations at the Susquehanna. Downcast as she often was at home, she was calm and happy onstage. She cracked witty jokes and made the audience hoot. And when she glowed in that halo of spotlight, Jordan remembered what he adored about her and felt it all over again.

Fuck real life: Being onstage was king.

Robin had been kind enough to devote an hour every weekday to email correspondence for them. While he savored the help, Jordan felt it was unfair to keep asking it of her.

"She has her own life, you know," he would remind Summer.

"She said she doesn't mind," Summer would object.

"Let's talk to your publicist friend, Sue," he kept suggesting.

She would shrug like she didn't care. "I hardly know her. And when I did it was twenty years ago."

"We can't keep depending on Robin," Jordan insisted. "She's in a whole other time zone. And she doesn't know the industry. We need someone who can build on your success and take you forward now. This is your time, baby."

"It's my time to *have* a baby," she replied.

When they next played at Susquehanna, she unveiled "That Kind of Friend," the song she'd been kneading for weeks, "dimpling and rolling it like dough under the baking pin," she explained to the audience. "And then I realized it didn't have to do with words so much as rhythm. So I asked our drummer, Z Saintcroix, over here to just start his shuffle beat and take it away with Bruce. Let the beat come and Jordan's riff, then I find the words…"

Cymbals thrashed, and Jordan's horn poked its way through them. Fred was pounding on the keys. Her voice sailed above, full as a moon over rippling waters.

"*Lip service to our kisses,*
That's what you're good for now, baby,
Lip service to our kisses,
That, and a check now and then, maybe.
But he's your son too, and it wasn't an immaculate conception.
Not to instruct your illusions, but only to lay bare the misperception.
Two lines from a post office box and you're good for the year,
No brush of his fingertips, no little voice in your ear
Oh I shoulda known it would all come to this in the end
You…being that kind of friend.

Lip service to our kisses,

That's what you're good for now, baby,
Lip service to our kisses,
That, and a check now and then, maybe.
When your woman loves another girl and she's not even gay, it's a killer.
Happens to the best of men, including but not limited to Henry Miller.
So he stalks those Crazy Cock *streets to find traces of Eugenia*
And what led her to say, 'Well, kid, I'll be seein' ya.'
Oh he shoulda known it would all come to this in the end
She being that kind of friend."

People clapped and whistled, though no one knew what the song was about except Summer and him, and maybe Z. Slinking across the stage in her sequined emerald gown from the thrift shop, she spoke into the mic as Z and Bruce continued their shuffle. "You ever heard of the Urban Dictionary? They define *Eugenia* as 'simply the most amazing woman ever, probably the best woman you will ever meet.'"

"Eugenia!" chorused Z, storming a short solo on the drums.

"Lip service, lip service to our kisses, baby...and Cathy, well, she's your best friend, partner in crime, flat-out awesome, they say. Hey now, he's giving that saxophone some lip service, right on the reed...old panty bandit Jordan there."

And she shot him a wink like they hadn't exchanged grumpy insults just that morning. He winked back.

After the show Jordan sauntered over to the creep who was eyeing Summer and chatting her up. "I should know all about falling in love again," he was rasping in one of those cocaine-hoarse voices you hear in movies, so slimy it could shine in the dark. "I'm getting married a third time in February. Hey, maybe you can play that song at the rehearsal dinner. We already got a band for the wedding, but I gotta have that song somewhere, doll...and the one about Brooklyn, 'cause I'm a Brooklyn boy myself."

Naturally, you greasehole, Jordan thought. And can you take your eyes off my girlfriend's breasts for even two seconds? Jordan stood beside Summer, his hand on her hip. She slipped a warm arm around him too.

"So, uh, how many dead presidents you gonna need?"

Before Summer could undersell them, Jordan asked, "How many players you want?"

"Oh, I don't care," the greaseball answered. "Enough to make music. You know, just the two of yous. You together or something?"

"Engaged. You don't want drums?"

"Nah, don't need 'em at the rehearsal dinner. Ya know, I been married twice before. Like I need to rehearse…"

"How many hours?"

The guy looked put out by the specifics Jordan wanted of him.

"I dunno, like three. You can just do some quiet background stuff and then, you know, sing it up. Sing that song about a Brooklyn boy. 'Cause that'd be me!"

"We'll need two grand," said Jordan.

"Deal," said the guy. "By the way, I'm Albert Pico."

He reached into his jacket for a business card, and Jordan did likewise, adding, "We'll need a down payment once you book."

"Deal," repeated Albert.

"We'll see about that," muttered Jordan as Albert slinked off.

"Oh, he won't call," Summer scoffed. "At least we won't have to sell our souls at his sham wedding."

Then Teddy, their point person at Susquehanna, appeared with a bundle of envelopes. Ever since the *La-B* review, Summer received mail at the hotel, mostly junk from pseudomanagers and voice coaches, and some legitimate audition requests. She sent it all to Robin, trusting her to follow up or not. So far, Robin had chosen well.

Glancing through it, Summer picked out a handwritten envelope: *Cathy Summers, aka Summer Vale* was virtually stabbed on it with blue pen. Her face froze. She stood for a moment in her emerald sequined gown, then looked at Jordan. "Could you do something?"

"Sure."

"Write *Return to Sender*," she said, quickly handing the envelope to him. "In pen, not pencil. Take it to Teddy and tell him to get it to the mail room, and make sure it's sent back unopened."

Jordan trotted off, glancing at the return address: Geoff Ahlstrom in Toms River, New Jersey. The name seemed familiar, but he couldn't recall where he'd seen it. He found Teddy at the reception desk and relayed Summer's wishes, which Teddy seemed glad to oblige. Jordan made sure that he wrote *Return to Sender* in pen, underlining it twice.

When he returned to the cabaret, Summer was sitting at a round table, head in her hands, while Bruce and Z crouched over the string bass that lay onstage amid mic stands and wires. When Jordan got closer, he saw that the head had snapped off. This happened once with a bass at Oberlin, and Jordan remembered that the necks were not bound by glue but by dovetail bracing.

"Get it to the Bass Place," Z was saying. "Or better yet, to Nathaniel's."

"I'm working tomorrow," Bruce said quietly. Jordan knew him well enough to see how upset he was.

"Such a fucking klutz!" Summer erupted from her table.

"She dropped a mic on it by accident," Z told Jordan under his breath.

"Shit," said Jordan, and then to Bruce: "I'll take care of it."

"We have some insurance," Z reminded him.

That next day Jordan stopped by the Susquehanna after teaching his afternoon class at the boys' school. Bruce's bass was zipped up in its case, and in a separate bag the head was swathed in bubble wrap and newspapers. With a bag in one hand, Jordan wheeled the bass down Central Park West through needles of hail that lightly pelted his face. His other arm rested on the instrument's headless shoulder.

Nathaniel, the luthier, lived in Staten Island but availed himself of a student's workshop in the West 50s. Jordan had been there once before with Eliot Waxmann for a guitar "fret job," which they'd joked about. There was an alley entrance that insiders knew—local jazz and folk musicians, Juilliard kids. As he pushed open the metal door, fumes of glue and lacquer assured him he was in the right place. He wheeled the bass down the corridor, following the muted horns of the Paul Whiteman Band.

By the half-open door he saw a wing tip tapping to the beat of "Doo Wacka Doo" on a threadbare rug. Recalling that Skip was working for Nathaniel now, Jordan stopped in his tracks. But why should he feel antsy when he was to Skip what Eugenia had been to him: the obstacle to happiness, a symbol of everything he'd lost? Jordan wasn't used to being the winner.

According to rumors, Skip's childhood had been so ghastly that he'd relinquished his own chronology and placed himself in another time: "Let's just say that I came to an end in 1968 with the rest of culture," he'd once put forth. "And I began at the turn of the last century, with Armstrong, Bix Beiderbecke, and Fats Waller. I walk on cobblestone, not asphalt. I watch moving pictures, not video. John Coltrane and Jackson Pollock were the last artists of note, and telephones are too heavy to carry in a pocket."

To complement his finger-wave haircut, Skip wore double-breasted suits with silk handkerchiefs and hand-painted ties, fashioning himself as more of an iconic ghost than a person—until he'd met Summer Vale and suddenly yearned to open his heart to a kindred soul. He fell hard and rhapsodized around town: "I have found her."

But he'd failed to captivate her. He'd failed to elicit from her what Jordan had managed effortlessly. Trying to conjure Eugenia's self-assurance and winner's indemnity, Jordan pushed open the door and wheeled the bass into Nathaniel's shop, barely mumbling "Hey" as he approached Skip.

"What you got there, my friend? Decapitated bass? Couldn't've been a brawl with Bruce Roman, who's got no more fight in him than a cricket."

"Mic stand fell on it after the show last night."

"Susquehanna Cabaret in the Lounge or the Victorian Ballroom?"

Jordan nodded. He'd forgotten Skip's ultra-marine blue eyes, which had the same Technicolor density as Mel Gibson's and stood out against latte-brown skin. "Who'm I billing?" he asked.

"Jordan Radfar Trio."

"How's your name spelled again?"

"Guess you haven't seen it lately in Leandro Gomez's column?"

Jordan delivered the counterpunch before reciting his name letter by letter. Despite himself, Skip cringed as he wrote up the ticket, his script filled with old-fashioned flourishes just as he played sax with that overly controlled syncopation that drove Jordan nuts. Beneath his vest, he wore a silk shirt with rolled-up sleeves; it was shocking to see him without cufflinks. Behind him stood the pegboard with its rulers and shells of instrument bodies—violins, violas, mandolins, and guitars—all curvy as women.

Skip wound the tag around the headless bass neck and handed a copy of the ticket to Jordan. "Your vocalist received the most mention," he commented. "Par for the course."

"We're lucky to have a vocalist worth mentioning," replied Jordan, pocketing the ticket.

"Look," said Skip, his hand on the counter with its various clamps and his head tilted like a dog getting his ears scratched. "I'm happy she's found someone willing to walk her walk. I tend to run hypochondriac, you know. You're a braver man than I. May be to your credit that she's still around."

Jordan affected a noncommittal shrug.

"You have no idea what I'm talking about, do you?" Skip persisted.

"I don't think you know what the hell you're talking about."

But Jordan was losing ground. Skip blinked his eerie blue eyes upward for a moment. "So you never asked yourself what makes a man change his will three weeks before he takes leave of this world, awarding his entire estate to a woman he's not even boning?"

"No," said Jordan steadily.

"Funny, ole Z looked into it once he got wind of her interest in his, um, skin tone, and decided that scene wasn't for him. But you're the perfect gimp for Summer Vale. 'Where ignorance is bliss, 'tis folly to be wise.' There's your epitaph. I just feel bad for the little boy. He was born okay, you know. But nursing from a woman in that condition…"

Jordan began walking out, leaving Skip and the muted cornets behind him.

"Call Nathaniel tomorrow about the bass," Skip bellowed after him. "He'll probably need a week. The number's on your ticket."

As Jordan marched to the subway, images flickered before him of Summer's trapdoor moods and sensitive tummy…and the spider bite. Jordan felt seized by his own heart—there were no recluse spiders in Vermont. Maybe what he'd seen on her leg was something else, like lesions or skin cancer. Now he remembered that she wouldn't let him buy the medication.

Then there were those roses in the urn near the photo of her and Gus—so brittle and colorless, but when Jordan had suggested he throw them out, she got hysterical. "Don't touch them—they're the last flowers he saw." Why would she care so much if she hadn't been Gus' lover? Recently she'd even received mail for "Catherine Granato."

But she would never take such risks with nursing Rashad. She didn't even drink wine during his first three years. Or so she said. But in all the time Jordan had lived there, Rashad never got sick, so it couldn't be, he told himself. The spider bite had gone away. Lesions didn't. Still, HIV could hibernate for long, asymptomatic periods. And if she'd been bereft over losing Khalil, she could have thrown herself into Gus' arms. Hadn't she herself said, "I live out of control"? The bit about Z retracting interest also seemed vaguely familiar, and now Jordan recalled that Ahlstrom was the name of her high school boyfriend.

When he walked into the apartment, she was eating big cookies, happy to see him. A Mildred Bailey CD played "Please Be Kind" as if the 1930s Jordan had left back with Skip was still happening.

If you love me, honey, please be kind…

"Just had a crazy rehearsal…some newbie called Tillie showed up at the studio begging to audition with Shazan. He said no, but she didn't let up. She even got down on her knees." Summer giggled and held out the bag of Pepperidge Farm Chocolate Chunk cookies to Jordan. He shook his head. "Finally, his manager threatened to call building security, but Shazan said, 'I see some passion here. Let's give it a whirl.' And damned if she wasn't top-notch, this kid from the U.K. via Nashville. Weirdest damn accent, except when she sings and it's Judy Garland America. We stayed an extra hour, worked out some harmony lines…"

"Are you out of your mind? Why would you give up your limelight to a kid?"

"Not giving it up—sharing it! There's plenty go to 'round."

"Not in this business. You should be the vocalist associated with Shazan now."

"He works with many people, Jordan. And it's not my choice to make anyway. Gee, I wish you'd grow up."

He narrowed his eyes at her.

"Gee, I wish you'd come clean."

"Clean about what? Why're you looking at me like that?"

Jordan could feel his throat tighten.

"You've never looked at me that way," she repeated. "Foofie. What's going on?"

"If you and Roo are HIV positive, you should've told me."

He felt some relief as her face underwent a spectrum of expressions, from surprise to sorrow to rage.

"What are you talking about?"

"You and Gus were lovers, weren't you?" Summer was shocked beyond speech, and he took that as a sign that she was busted. "You know, you keep a lot of secrets…and you feel lousy all the time, too lousy. It's just not normal."

"Who ever said I was normal?" Summer threw the bag of cookies across the kitchen table and marched right over to him. "Jordan, get a grip! Gus was stone gay. He never slept with women, and he wasn't going to start on his deathbed. As for me, I was changing his diapers."

"Maybe you got sick doing that!" Jordan cried.

"Look, you know I'm unstable as the day is long. I have what's called 'mood disorders' or 'borderline-something-or-another.' But I don't have HIV."

She whipped around and before he knew it she was out of the kitchen, in the living room, attacking her locked file. "And neither does my son!" she called, giving the cabinet drawer a good yank. Then she tossed folder after folder on the floor, already piled as it was with clothes, newspapers, and instrument cases.

"I know who you saw today. I know who works at Nathaniel's...asshole!" She slammed another folder down. "Fucking men—hate you all. Wish I could find a hot sweetie like Eugenia to turn *me* around..."

Jordan lunged across the room, incensed. They collided and she shoved a paper at him, screaming for him to read it. He grabbed her arm, trying to push the paper away and learning that her grip outdid his. The sheet of paper danced before his face.

"I said *read* it, jackass, don't try to scrap it." Through his fury, Jordan read that Rashad Pierre Summers' blood type was B positive; he had no diseases, including HIV, syphilis, or hepatitis. The test results were dated a year ago. She handed it to him, and he read it twice, his pulse rate beginning to subside as Mildred Bailey's vocals caught his attention again.

"I have no idea where mine is," she snapped. "I keep better records for him. But maybe we should just go to the clinic and get it from the horse's mouth, or ass."

"I didn't know his middle name was Pierre."

"Because the moral of *Pierre* is care. Remember that book? The boy named Pierre just said, 'I don't care.'"

"Dr. Seuss?" asked Jordan.

"No, your Brooklyn neighbor Maurice Sendak. Come on, let's go to Chinatown. We can get results from the clinic in five days."

"Summer." He reached over and touched her arm. "You were right. I did see Skip today at Nathaniel's."

She blinked defiantly. "If each of us is going to trust what Skip Harrington says about the other we may as well *skip* this relationship."

He felt suddenly terrified that she'd break up. Women were just too good at that with him.

"But I will come out of the closet about something," she offered.

"You've got some girlfriend up your sleeve?"

"Frankly, my relationships with women are too spiritual to cheapen with sex. But I wanted to tell you that after we got back from Vermont in August, I ran into Skip. He was very spiteful, and he told me you were crazy, that you stalked Molly and Eugenia so fanatically that they got a restraining order against you."

"Crock of shit! I ran into them once on the street."

"Well, it seemed out of character. Molly doesn't exactly sound like the helpless damsel type. But I know how persuasive Skip can be. He's like my dad; he can gaslight. But I pulled back from you...just in case he was right. Remember, you noticed that?"

Jordan nodded sullenly.

"Not that I've been the model of self-possession," she admitted. "But the stalking thing flipped me out."

"Well, the HIV thing flipped *me* out."

At that moment both of their eyes fell upon an old headshot of Summer that had flown out of a folder on the floor. The black-and-white glossy portrayed a thinner, brittle version of her face with hair flounced in that eighties style. Her smile was locked and rigid, her eyes demonic. She looked altogether angrier and less humble than now. Beside it lay a folded pamphlet with white knockout type on green that read *Reelect George Summers County Treasurer*. Jordan stooped to retrieve it from the floor.

"So," she said, clearing her throat with discomfort, "now you know."

He was looking at another version of her face that was stretched to fit a man's head. Behind tortoise-shell glasses with his brown hair combed back, her dad looked intelligent, wily, and like he regarded blacks as shoeshiners and didn't want Jews in his country club. Jordan opened the pamphlet and glanced at the lengthy endorsements and list of his achievements in office. On the back flap was a nicer photograph of him "enjoying a stroll through Monmouth Battlefield State Park with wife Vivian and daughters Deborah and Cathy Jane"—the cutest little girls and most darling wife imaginable, in that sixties Kennedy mold.

"Dad worked his way up in county politics," she went on to say. "He wanted to be a state senator, but it didn't happen. He served as Republican chairman of the county for a while."

"Why didn't you ever tell me?"

"I dunno. Why haven't you given me Arman's vitae?"

Jordan pointed to three-year-old Summer in the photograph, held proudly in her dad's arms, and remembered Curtis saying how a daughter was "the apple of her father's eye like nothing else." Meanwhile, the older sister stood demurely with her mother, whose life she would one day save. Jordan tried to find a disturbing aspect in that lovely mother's face—anything "suicidal alcoholic." But he saw only perky, impish glamour and decided that he liked her.

"Your mom's a babe."

"Not when she was passed out and peeing on herself. Unfortunately, Deb and I inherited the big Summers bones. We always wished we had her petite frame. We felt like trolls around her."

Jordan handed her the pamphlet and declared, "Not a troll. And look, we don't have to do the clinic."

"Yes we do," she said. "We're trying to have a kid together. We should get the facts."

Signs of neither HIV nor pregnancy were found in her blood. Two days after their discussion, Summer left the test results for Jordan on the kitchen table when he got home from teaching. She was sitting beside Tillie at the piano rehearsing for Shazan's already sold-out Christmas gig. Jordan noticed that, just as Summer had described, the girl's cockney-inflected Southern drawl—"Eliza Dolittle gone Annie Oakley"—disappeared when she sang jazz standards, becoming "all Judy Garland and Ella, a caramel-throated American alto." Tillie took no offense and only giggled at Summer's description of her accents.

Tillie came by a lot that week. Jordan sometimes played sax as the women sang and rehearsed. Tillie's presence had thankfully lifted Summer out of the doldrums. Accustomed to a sisterly bond like Robin's, Summer thrived with a buddy around and even waxed motherly with Tillie, lending the girl coats and sweaters. Tillie had just arrived in September and stayed at a woman's boarding house that extracted every penny she earned transposing music and walking people's dogs. So Summer clued her in on Salvation Army shops, cheap but atmospheric diners, and the best bodegas to hock a Hostess Twinkie.

The kid was twenty-four, and Jordan felt old and staid around her. He enjoyed her swooning smile as he embellished their duets while Summer played piano. Sometimes when she came by, Tillie brought a ukulele and mandolin, not exactly jazz instruments. "But I wanna make them so," she explained.

Her strange quest occasioned Jordan's invitation to Eliot one evening. "You'll love what he does with twelve bars on the Martin," he told Tillie, whose eyes lit up. Her Celtic coloring reminded him of Molly's dark hair and pale, tender skin. But Tillie's eyes didn't glow like Molly's did, and her face seemed a little too round. A porridge bowl haircut and fringe of bangs only furthered the cartoonish effect.

"She looks like a clock!" Rashad exclaimed once before Tillie came over, to which Summer quickly advised: "We don't tell her that." The eastern sky was dark before five, and Tillie showed up in Summer's yellow sweater from Betty, and scratchy-looking wool pants. Eliot arrived an hour later, raving about choro, a gypsy jazz style from Brazil: "You want to hear blues on the strings? This will knock your socks off."

Eliot taught Tillie mandolin parts as he played guitar on these upbeat blues. Summer's piano stood in for accordion, and Jordan improvised on the sax. Even Rashad jumped in with percussion on egg shakers until he got sleepy, and Summer made hot chocolate for him.

"Let's do this tomorrow again!" Tillie exclaimed, pronouncing it "a gain," inadvertently inviting Eliot over the next evening. But Summer and Jordan didn't mind, knowing no better way to pass winter nights than gathered around a piano, singing and strumming.

So the next night Eliot appeared with a bottle of cognac and several big *Inside*

Job buttons dangling from his cable-knit sweater. Summer served everyone left-over curry, and they played music until midnight, when Eliot uncorked his bottle.

"Now why'd'ya think 9/11 was a gov'ment scam?" Tillie asked him as they retired to the sofa. Summer produced four dusty, mismatched snifters.

"Oh," said Eliot, filling everyone's with his amber libation, "to get us into a war for oil and secure Halliburton contracts. All sorts of goodies."

"But the States have waged war before without destroying its own cities," Tillie objected with the kind of smile that a twenty-four-year-old reserves for someone who could be her grandfather. "Look at Vietnam," she pointed out. "Korea. No one flew planes into a building for any o' that."

"There was a draft then," Eliot replied with assurance. "Now they need an incentive to get our boys anywhere to bomb the daylights out of people. Or, I'm sorry. Guess it's called shock and awe."

"If this was a setup, why didn't they put Iraqis on the planes?" asked Tillie, examining the smudged surface of her glass and lifting it to her lips.

"Americans are too stupid to know the difference between Arab nationals," said Eliot.

Tillie sipped and winced as though the cognac tasted sharp. "Well, ya can't bloody count on ignorance with a swindle that big."

"In America you can," Summer interjected, coming to Eliot's defense.

"Are you kidding me?" Jordan shot back at her.

"Do you have any idea how ignorant most people in this country are?" she retorted.

"Aw, come now," protested Eliza Dolittle. "I see 'em reading the morning paper all the time in Starbucks, the subway…"

"This is New York," said Summer.

"Well, New York is *part of the States*," said Tillie, with the same patronizing smile she had for Eliot and a sprinkle of laughter that Jordan would have found maddening if he wasn't in agreement with her.

"Last I heard it's our biggest city," he said with a nod at her. "I mean Summer, Eliot—of course there are morons out there."

"Swaths of people whose ignorance and bigotry would stun you," Summer emphasized.

"But what Tillie's saying—and I agree with her—is that if you're going to pull off a worldwide charade, you're opening yourself to getting totally busted. There's just too much room for pushback."

"The son mimics the father," said Eliot to Summer, with an unwelcome confidence. "He parrots what his old man has to say about this."

"Not because he's my dad," grumbled Jordan. "He happens to be right."

Tillie glanced at him sympathetically, and it struck Jordan that neither his parents nor Tillie's were American-born, that maybe they shared an outsider's distaste for hyping half-digested truths. Eliot's socialist Jewish background couldn't differ more from Summer's parentage, but they were both gullible Yankees in Jordan's book.

Riled, he repeated another argument he'd heard from his father. "Look, if this administration wanted to recruit for an oil war, they could have installed a couple Iraqi snipers at a mall in Dallas. Kill ten innocent Americans. That would've done the trick. They didn't need to go all out with an attack on our financial capitol."

"And the Pentagon," Tillie added.

"Exactly," said Jordan. "I mean, the plane that crashed in Pennsylvania was headed for the fucking White House. Even a clod like our president wouldn't bomb his own home for propaganda."

"And they couldn't plan for guys on that plane to get up from their seats to stop it," Tillie observed.

"No way to count on that working out," Jordan confirmed. He added under his breath, "Let's roll."

Eliot did seem stumped by this particular argument, though he and Summer kept exchanging glances that bugged Jordan.

"Americans are special effects junkies," Summer finally said. "I follow your logic about Iraqi snipers at a mall. You'd think that would be convincing." She shook her head. "But it's too subtle. Americans need to be slammed over the head. Look at Pearl Harbor."

"Military attack on a military target," Jordan snapped at her. "Not a bunch of rogues hitting civilians."

"And certainly not the American president making it all up," chorused Tillie. "Who was the president back then, anyway?"

"Truman?" asked Summer, scrunching her face.

"FDR," Jordan and Eliot said in unison.

"Do you remember it?" Jordan asked Eliot.

The white-haired man nodded. "I was just a little tyke," he said, deferring to Tillie's British slang. "Younger than Rashad. Don't remember much about Pearl Harbor. What I do remember very well is how the government lied to us about Nam. We wouldn't have known the half of it without Daniel Ellsberg."

"Lying about a war overseas is one thing," Jordan granted him. "Staging an attack on our own Capitol is going a little far."

He planned to talk with Summer about Eliot's presumptions the next afternoon, when he got home from teaching and Rashad was still in after-school group. They'd have a moment to speak privately. He was surprised by how much her naivety annoyed him.

At first when he walked into the apartment, pulling off his wool cap, Jordan didn't see her by the window. "Summer?" he queried the silence. Although she didn't answer, he felt where she was standing. He flicked on a lamp and walked over to her, nearly tripping over the stray wires and pairs of shoes on the rug.

When he reached her, she said to him: "Betty miscarried."

"You're kidding."

"If I was, I'd have a pretty sick sense of humor."

She looked back out the window.

"Is Betty okay?"

"At the clinic with her OBGYN. Curtis is…"

She didn't have to say more. Outside, steam rose slowly from generators into the gray, dusky sky. Colored Christmas lights winked in people's windows and on terraces, echoing the more distant lights on barges and the bridge.

"I said we'd take Ian and Archer for the weekend. They've always been there in our times of need." She spoke in a coarse whisper, fighting tears.

"I know," Jordan whispered back.

But having Ian and Archer in their messy home with haphazard food and a small TV was not exactly the treat that it was for Rashad to be at their lovely place.

Suddenly their phone rang from the kitchen, shrill against grief. Tillie spoke over the answering machine: "Hello, hello? Anyone there? Summah?"

"Could you talk to her?" Summer asked. "I just can't sing today."

Jordan squeezed her arm and bounded over to the phone.

On Friday afternoon Summer began worrying that the twins might want to play on the terrace when they came over the next day. "We can't risk *that*," she kept repeating. "They're not used to being up so high."

"Why would they want to be out on a crappy day like tomorrow's supposed to be?"

"Boys will be boys. And if anything happened to them, I'd never forgive myself."

"You're really overreacting. We can just lock the terrace door."

But she insisted that wasn't enough, that they should take everything they couldn't stand looking at in the living room and put it out on the terrace. "You know, we'll make more room inside—and a bulwark out there."

So saying, she dragged crates of Gus' books and records, and Jordan helped her build towers of them on the terrace along with rusting file cabinets, Gus' broken office chair and some empty plant pots. Before long, their terrace looked like the town dump, and Summer seemed somewhat consoled.

Curtis brought the twins over the next morning with a small suitcase. He looked like a truck had hit him, with his hair uncharacteristically unkempt and circles beneath his eyes like small bruises. Upon seeing him, Summer fell into his arms, and the children solemnly watched their rather long embrace. Jordan was not one to hug another man, but when Curtis reached out to him, they exchanged a pat on the back.

"Betty and I haven't slept for two nights," Curtis said under his breath. "We just need to collapse and be alone together. You guys..." He looked from Summer to Jordan. "You're doing the best favor anyone could."

"Nothing you haven't done for me a million times," said Summer.

Curtis reached into his pocket and passed her a clump of bills.

"Oh, we don't need all that," she said.

Curtis pushed it into her hand. Then he looked at his two sons.

"Now, you be good for Summer and Jordan. Understand?"

The boys nodded without enthusiasm.

"Do what they tell you to—no nonsense and no smart talk. Got it?"

He looked back to Jordan, like a swimmer surfacing for air.

"Call me if there's any trouble."

Summer took the boys to the playground at Tompkins Square Park, even though it was a dull, chilly day. Then they saw *Dinotopia* at the cinema on 14th Street while Jordan and Z played at a Christmas party. After that he met up with them at Union Square for sliders and macaroni at a diner, and they came home to ice cream, TV, and video games.

When they got restless after hours in front of screens, Summer dressed up in her fur coat and Gus' huge Russian bear hat from Berlin. She chased them around, pretending to be a grizzly. "Grrr!" she cried. "I'm hungry! I want to catch some little boys for dinner."

Rashad and the twins shrieked with glee, zipping around the apartment, diving into closets and under the sofa—clearly, this was the high point of their day. "Grrrr!" Summer stomped around like Frankenstein, her gloved hands clawing the air. "I want some...french fried fingers! Ear calamari...belly button escargot. And tushy burgers!"

The boys squealed from their various hideaways, and even Jordan guffawed.

"I smell hair! Sweet and savory little boy hair."

She bent down, and Archer shot out from under the sofa, straight to the terrace door, which he proceeded to unlock and open.

A piercing cry ripped the night, like something out of Hitchcock.

"Get him, Jordan!"

Eager not to become a grizzly's dinner, the boy was stepping into darkness. Ian and Rashad laughed, thinking Summer's scream was part of the game. Jordan charged across the room to retrieve Archer—which was easy enough. The terrace was so packed with junk that there wasn't far for the boy to walk. Summer's premonition had proven strangely justified. As if she knew, she plopped onto the couch in her coat, the big furry bear hat falling over her eyes.

"Grrr!" Ian barked into her face. Then he screamed, horror-style, as she had. But Summer didn't respond.

"Okay," announced Jordan. "It's pajama time, gang. No more grizzly bear."

"But I *want* grizzly bear!" wailed Ian, pulling at Summer's coat.

When she still didn't respond, Ian started bawling that he missed his mommy and wanted to go home. "Your mommy's resting," Summer told him in a monotone that almost didn't sound like her. "You're staying with us, Ian. Your mommy's resting." Jordan sensed that Summer must have been told "your mommy's resting" many times as a child.

"I want Maaahhhh!" Ian hollered. "I wanna go home nowwww!"

Archer started blubbering too, in a milder way.

Rashad looked at Jordan and shrugged. "Maybe they should call Betty?" he suggested. Summer continued to sit with her mouth slightly open and the bear hat tipped over her eyes.

"Hey," Jordan stroked her furry arm. "You've been going, going, going all day, Summertime. You must be zonked. Go take a hot bath, and I'll deal with this."

"Are you calling Betty?" she asked in a voice that sounded more like hers.

"I'll see if they're up, so Ian and Archer can say good night."

Betty was apparently "out like a light," and Curtis overflowed with gratitude as Jordan filled him in on what they'd done all day. Then Curtis spoke to each of the twins as Jordan set up the Parcheesi board on Rashad's bed, where the young guests would be sleeping. Placated by his father's voice, Ian stuck his thumb in his mouth and nodded off as Archer, Rashad, and Jordan played a couple of rounds. Once they finished, Jordan and Rashad tiptoed into the big bedroom to find Summer fast asleep, face to the wall and long hair streaming over her shoulders. Jordan put his finger to his lips as he and Rashad climbed carefully into bed beside her.

Around 5 a.m. Jordan awoke to find Summer gone. The apartment was cold at that hour, so he put on a sweatshirt and got out of bed, blinking dizzily, to look for her.

She sat on the piano bench like an apparition in her bulky blue bathrobe. A carton of Rocky Road ice cream was on her lap and a spoon in her hand.

"Holy shit," Jordan whispered, sitting beside her. Half the ice cream in the carton was gone. "You better stop that." He put his hand on top of her hand that held the spoon. She flicked his hand away, digging into the ice cream and sliding the spoon into her mouth.

"Trapdoor, baby?"

"I'm trying so hard," she said after swallowing the ice cream. "How can I do that to you and Betty?"

"Summer, just quit eating. You'll make yourself sick."

"I don't feel so hot," she confirmed, dropping the spoon on the floor.

"You want a joint?"

"I'll take you up on it this time."

When Jordan stood up, she handed him the ice cream carton.

"Put it out on the terrace," she said. "So I won't think about it."

As he opened the squeaky door, he gazed over the files and boxes at the sun rising over the river. That blush of light reminded him of violins simmering in the first movement of Beethoven's Ninth, just before the full orchestra sets in—like the world recovering its form from darkness.

He returned to Summer with a joint that he lit on a stove burner. She drew upon it in her staccato gasps.

"This business with Betty is killing you, isn't it?" he whispered.

She nodded reluctantly, exhaling through her nose.

"We'll have our lives back tomorrow," he consoled her. "Curtis said Betty rested and hung out, and she feels much better. Been a shit of a day, but we did the right thing."

"Just what I need—kids screaming because suddenly their mama's wiped out."

"She'll be okay. Her doctor says she doesn't have any infections. She just needs to take it easy."

"She'll be okay. She'll be okay," Summer mimicked. "That's what people said about my mother, and she sure wasn't." She drew again on the joint and passed it to Jordan.

"Did something happen that changed her?" Jordan asked, taking his turn with the joint before it fizzled. "Wasn't it just the way she was? 'Cause Betty's not like that."

Summer spoke softly, to not awaken the sleeping boys. "Sanity is frail for everyone but more so for depressives. Still Jordan, sometimes she was so wonderful. When we were little…"

He held up the expired joint, but she declined it with a shake of her head, her eyes averted from him. "'Til I was four and Deb was six, we had a great time. She was such a little girl herself that she loved having little girls. She'd climb into bed with us and read *Winnie the Pooh* in funny voices. Once at this shindig for my dad and his cronies, Mom took off her heels and ran around with me and Deb in the grass. She made us feel more important than anyone. You know, she wasn't a politician's wife who'd stand around schmoozing imbeciles—she preferred playing with her kids. And she didn't care what anyone thought."

Jordan knew that he'd liked the pretty woman in that photograph on the flier.

He reached over to drop the joint, with its burnt tip, into an ashtray on the piano behind them.

"When I was three she took us down to Cape May with her sister, Aunt Maegan. We lived in this yellow house. My first memory is pine needles in sand, salty air, and Mom in a white bathing suit holding me in the waves. I traced all the droplets on her skin. And I said the sunsets made sea foam look like mashed potatoes with yellow butter. Deb remembers me saying that."

"Writing songs already."

"Years later, I learned that Maegan was separating from her husband and my parents were hitting their first rough patch. That's why we weren't with Dad too. I dunno...maybe Mom and Maegan should've run off with us. It was the best summer of my life, the summer I always think of when I say my name.

"Mom was"—Summer shrugged, now looking directly at Jordan—"completely normal and cheerful back then. But she probably would've started drinking anyway. She had it in her, and I can't blame Dad for all of that. She'd had 'trouble' in adolescence. He knew what he was getting into, and I think it turned him on. Crazy women are sexy. Isn't that why you like me?"

Jordan fidgeted and didn't answer. He had to admit that—while perplexing—Summer's strange moods held some allure. Still, he'd been drawn to Molly for the reverse reason: She seemed more stable than he.

"You kissed me the night I stole our dinner at Eddystone Light. I'm no bathing beauty. My thighs are thicker than potato sacks, and I'm not as pretty as my mom or Deb. But guys have a thing for me."

"So I've noticed."

"It's the loose screw I got from her, in my own way. Still, I wonder how much more you'll take. Not like I've produced offspring for us, or anything."

"Honey, we've been trying for just three months."

"Yeah," she whispered, "but we fuck at the right place at the right time and I don't think you're firing blanks. It's me and my soggy old eggs."

Jordan shrugged. "How do you know it's not me? You've been pregnant...but I've never made a woman pregnant."

"You could be with someone young, like Tillie. You're all of thirty. You could find a twenty-four-year-old—easy. And she liked you."

"Who? Beach-Ball Face?"

Summer laughed.

"I'm not in this for offspring," he said, sliding his hand onto her leg, under her bathrobe. He liked her fleshy thighs. "That was your idea."

"Don't you want a cute little dark-haired, brown-eyed Jordan kid?"

"Well, sure, but it's not a deal breaker. Look honey, I'm happy with you and Rashad and our music. Really. Sometimes I don't even think we can afford another kid. It's not like *I* make a killing, like Curtis."

He removed his hand from her leg. Beaming through their crooked Venetian blinds, morning light striped itself onto lamps, tables, and the sofa. He thought he heard a faint sigh from Rashad's room, where the twins were.

"Jordan," she whispered, "there's something in this apartment that we can pawn off if I get pregnant and we need to get by."

"Something from Gus?"

She shook her head no.

"From my mother. A family heirloom—and my mother's from quite the family. It's a necklace with stones from East Africa that change color in different kinds of light. Very valuable. Deb has one too. We recovered them from the Victoria and Albert Museum in London."

"Someone stole them?"

"Not exactly stole. My dad sold them off. Don't want to get into all that right now—the point being, I have a valuable necklace hidden here, and if we need to trade it in sometime..." Her voice trailed off.

Jordan stared at her. This entire story was so unlike anything in his own life that he felt like he was watching a Disney film.

"Where is it?" he asked.

"Not telling," she said. "Not until we absolutely need it. And if we do...well, it would be the least she could do for her grandchildren." For the first time since he'd known her, it seemed to Jordan that Summer felt wistful about her mother.

A week later Betty was back on her feet, but Summer remained out of sorts. Dress and tech rehearsals for Shazan went well, but on opening night Summer locked herself in the bedroom and declared she wasn't going.

"Tell them I'm sick!" she called out to Jordan. "Tillie can go it alone!"

"No way. Open that door!" He kicked it. "Come on, Summer, Z will be downstairs in the van for you in half an hour. We're all going!"

Rashad emerged from his room with a pinched little brow.

"Mama!" he called. "I told Miss Donna you're singing at the town hall."

"I'm sick, Roo."

"No you're not. You're faking it!"

"Cathy Summers-Vale-Granato-Radfar!" Jordan, pounded on the door again. "Come on, honey!" He and Rashad looked at each other with consternation.

"I don't *feel* like it," she groaned.

"Well, you know what? You're being amateur," Jordan scolded. "Professionals get onstage no matter how they're *feeling*."

Those words got her to crack open the door. With his weight, Jordan pushed into the room, and Rashad followed.

"Now get out of your bathrobe and into the gown."

"I should shower."

Jordan shook his head, livid. "Too late."

"But I stink!"

"You don't. Now get dressed, baby."

Rashad ran over and threw his arms around her. Jordan restrained himself as mother and son cuddled for two minutes.

"Roo, please go outside so your mom can get dressed," he finally said.

Rashad obediently took leave, glancing back over his shoulder at her.

"Come on," Jordan whispered in her ear. "What the hell's wrong with you?"

Jordan peeled off her bathrobe, helped her into a bra, stockings, and her gown, which he zipped up the back like he always did, careful not to catch her hair. "We have no time," he went on. "I'll brush your hair while you do your face."

As she applied lipstick and eyeliner, Jordan ran a brush gently through her fine hair, trying not to jiggle her head and fudge the makeup. They made it downstairs just in time to meet Z on East Broadway and drive uptown.

To his great relief—Jordan sweated through the opening band—the show went splendidly. Subdued because it wasn't her own act like Susquehanna, Summer didn't joke or engage with the audience, but she sang with relish, lapping up the spotlight as it spilled over her like a kitten laps up milk in a saucer. When Tillie came out and harmonized with her, Jordan remembered Summer describing Tillie's vocals as "a drop shadow that makes my high notes pop."

"Let's have a hand for this extremely special lady, Summer Vale!" Shazan roared at the end of the set. "And for our new star on the horizon, Tillie Mack!" Rashad reached up to Jordan and whispered, "Beach-Ball Face" into his ear. The audience clapped and whistled, and Jordan felt it like the flutter of a million dove wings. "She'll get Choice Cabaret," he told Z, who smiled as he continued to applaud.

Second set was no letdown, and afterward Summer lingered politely, speaking to press agents and reviewers. She was a politician's daughter when she needed to be. She could hobnob even when she'd barely made it out the door. With startling pride, Jordan noted his own sense of accomplishment in having helped her rise to this occasion.

"Hey there!" Tillie exclaimed when she saw Jordan, Rashad, and Z in the wings.

She dashed over, and Jordan kissed her on the cheek. "Congratulations, Tillie."

"Can I tell you? The most amazing thing happened. I auditioned with a swing band and got hired on the spot. Been in rehearsal almost every night for a bunch of Christmas gigs."

"Not Skip Harrington, is it?" asked Jordan.

"Do you know him?" Tillie's eyes widened. "Isn't he magical, kind of like no one you've ever met before?"

"He's one of a kind," conceded Jordan.

Summer then flew across the floor and stopped behind Tillie, placing both hands on the younger woman's shoulders. "Guess what?" she said. "We're going to New Orleans and Miami in February with Shazan."

They spent the Christmas season wondering what to call Summer's CD. Gershwin's "Summertime" was one standard from her original demo that they'd included, but Summer felt that *Summer Vale: Summertime* was "overkill cute" and preferred *A Lot I Don't Know*. Z felt that title was too abstract and recommended *Brooklyn Boy* as "more catchy and sexy." Robin agreed, and Jordan admitted, "I may be biased along those lines, but I like it." Meanwhile, Betty and Curtis favored *Summer Vale: That Kind of Friend*. "It's different and intriguing," said Curtis. "It hooks you."

They agreed upon *Brooklyn Boy*, but the title song didn't hit the streets first. Despite Curtis' misgivings, the world loves a sad song that touches raw nerves. "Short Stick" was the one that began circulating over YouTube. Summer's high school friends had posted their video of it with an article for the *Monmouth Gazette*, titled: "Our Cathy Summers Is Summer Vale."

"Well," she said, "there goes any lingering mythology about my dad and our lovely family," implying that her friends should have asked permission. Jordan reminded her that she'd been approached several times and had given the nod, claiming she didn't care. "'The moral of Pierre is care,'" he said, quoting her Maurice Sendak story to which she wrinkled her nose.

As it circled the globe, the song about her mother—"my dirge," Summer called it—found favor in Twelve Step groups. Fans wrote to her about their own struggles with addiction, their absentee mothers, suicidal brothers, or drunken friends. Summer was asked about her faith and invited to perform at AA conferences and roundups.

Sue, her publicist friend, asked her pointedly: "What do you want to do with this, Cathy? You could really take off."

"I don't want to go around the world playing for recovered drunks," she said.

But she also didn't want to sing with the respectable ensembles that were soliciting her. To Jordan's chagrin, she told everyone that she wanted to "scale down," doing only the Susquehanna and a couple of modest gigs downtown. She'd be good for the small February tour with Shazan but generally pleaded, "I want to keep it simple."

"Maybe 'simple' is a luxury you can't afford now," Jordan argued when they were alone.

"Look Jordan, if I wanted a control freak husband, like my sister's—or like my dad—I would have found some variety of rich jerk. Not our thing, so cool it."

"I'm not controlling you—I want to see you shine, and if it means pushing you out of your comfort zone, well, I've done it before."

"Oh, spare me clichés about comfort zones. I've never had one in my life.⊠

"Because life tends to give artists short shrift. So you've got to take life up on those rare times it doesn't."

She stomped away as though he'd insulted her, although she couldn't really argue with him.

But after they heard the rough mix of her CD, she found the perfect excuse to resent him. Jordan begged her to remove the name *Eugenia* from *That Kind of Friend* because he felt it violated Molly's privacy.

"So *her* privacy is important, but mine isn't?" Summer screamed at him.

"It's different," he screamed back. "You chose your lyrics. Molly has no choice here. It's just gossip."

"The name Eugenia has personality. And it rhymes with 'kid, I'll be seein' ya.' It's the whole song—my intellectual property now."

"Your intellectual property—whose life is it? Who told you I read *Crazy Cock* and tried to trace Henry Miller's steps in the Village?"

"It's my song! I copped those details from your life."

Z agreed with Jordan—that a life held more weight than a song—and told Summer that he wouldn't release his drum tracks unless she changed Eugenia's name to Sabina.

"Why's it such a big deal?" he asked Summer.

"It's a big deal to you guys," she protested. "To me it's nothing."

"If it's nothing, then let's just change it. I don't think Molly is 'out' with her family, and Jordan's right. Even though the chance is slim that this song could blow her cover, let's not go there."

"Guess neither of you got over Molly," she huffed, "which is what Skip said last August: 'Oh, Jordan will never be over her.'"

"It's not about Jordan being 'over her,'" Z charged. "That happened a while ago. It's about both of us not wanting to compromise her, as friends. Can't you get that?"

So Summer sang the song again, substituting the name Sabina for Eugenia. But over the next month, she turned only a cold shoulder to Jordan in their daily and nightly life.

By the time Summer's CD came out in mid-January, only Robin was excited about it. Jordan and Summer were "joined at the hip at loggerheads," as Z said; Curtis and Betty were healing the wounds of their miscarriage with a couples counselor. For the CD cover, Robin had montaged the Brooklyn Bridge behind a fetching shot of Summer in a garnet gown holding a pink rose to her lips. It sold easily at the Susquehanna. Z also registered it online and sent review copies to radio stations and magazines. Most of them didn't reply, but Robin faithfully kept a record of the media hits that did come in—all of which Summer dismissed as "college blog rot" or "not exactly the *New York Times*."

"How do you stay steady when she so disses you?" Jordan asked his sister privately on the phone.

"I don't feel dissed," said Robin. "I just think she's processing a lot. She wasn't writing songs a year ago. Now she's got a CD and a tour with Shazan White."

"It's called having a career," Jordan asserted. After years of Robin harassing his girlfriends because she felt he was too good for them, here she was standing up for Summer when she "turned down opportunities that other singers would sell their lungs for."

"I've crafted an open-ended response to those opportunities," Robin explained. "I tell them 'Summer's delighted with your interest, but she's booked for the season. We'd love to speak in the fall.'"

"Well, you got the touch, Robbie," said Jordan with relief. "I love you for knowing to do that without me telling you, and then her calling me a 'control freak'—which is what she thinks I am, by the way." Relieved that Robin was not blowing cold air on hot contacts, Jordan got off Summer's case about bookings. But then came the call from Albert Pico that nobody expected.

"Hey, remember me from the hotel? The Brooklyn Boy." Albert laughed into the phone like someone wheezing. "Well, I got the big bills for you, like you wanted," he told Jordan. "So how 'bout you and your wife talk music for my rehearsal dinner?"

When Jordan mentioned the gig to Summer, she said, "Oh, yuck. I've turned down much more reputable fare. Why should I go with that slimeball?"

"Because unlike reputable fare, Slimeball's paying us two grand for one night, and beggars can't be choosers. Two grand could send Roo to camp all summer," Jordan pointed out, knowing that she felt bad about having been short with Rashad lately. Unlike Jordan, who could be counted on for a comeback, her four-year-old son was open game for her guff. So on his behalf, Summer decided to go through with the high-paying gig, just before Valentine's Day and her tour with Shazan.

This concession came as a relief to Jordan. Work had tapered off since Christmas, and their cash flow was drying up again. He wanted to start repaying Curtis' investment in the CD. Even though Curtis never mentioned it, Jordan felt like a cad.

But he was heartened by a call from Z in early February: "Get ready for this. Five hundred CDs—a third of inventory—shipped out this morning, in one pop."

"Who bought so many?" Jordan asked skeptically.

"This will interest you," Z answered. "The woman said it was for her boss' gift baskets at a League of Women Voters fundraiser in California. Name on the credit card: Deborah Richardson, middle initial S. Big sister, right?"

"Oh yeah," said Jordan.

"Even at a discount rate, we banked as much as we ever have."

"I hear that. So you spoke to Deb?"

"No, to her assistant. The underling. You gonna tell Summer?"

"I don't know," Jordan said with a sigh. "I'd like to think she'd appreciate it, but she's always got some weird, counterintuitive interpretation of good luck."

Still, sometime around New Years', photos of Deb had appeared on the fridge—high school photos of the two sisters wearing reindeer ski sweaters in a snowy wood, laughing together like rosy-faced nymphs. Jordan figured that his referring to Deb was permissible, so he told Summer exactly who'd helped them cut the first big check for Curtis.

"I could've guessed," Summer said. "Well, it's time to break my silence. I must thank her—and tell her not to send a copy to our parents. God, I hope she hasn't."

"I thought she wasn't in touch with them either." Jordan played uninformed, though he remembered from the card last summer that Deb was back in touch with them.

"She's getting suckered back in. She writes me from time to time. I've just never answered. My dad's health is failing, and Deb seems to feel some duty toward him that I certainly don't. I just hope she doesn't send them a copy of 'Brooklyn Boy.'"

"Maybe they'll be proud of you."

"It will never be left at that. You don't know my family, Jordan."

Later that evening, Summer paced through the apartment clutching her cell phone when Jordan came in with Rashad and a load of groceries.

"Look, if I'd do it for *anyone*, I'd do it for you," she wailed, whisking by Jordan as though he weren't there and into the bathroom, slamming the door. A couple minutes later she bolted out again, still on the phone. "Best not to pull corpses out of the ground and expect a conversation. We said our goodbyes…no, no, that's okay. Listen, Jordan just came in with him." And then she shut herself into the bedroom.

Rashad and Jordan exchanged a shrug, but to Jordan it was clear that she was speaking to Deb—and that the "corpse pulled from the ground" was a prospective visit to her ailing father.

♫

Before Albert's gig, Summer sat for an hour in the bathroom groaning with menstrual cramps. When she came out she couldn't decide what to wear and threw piles of baubled and sequin-scaled gowns across the bed—velvet, silk, strappy, or layered tutus; 1940s cocktail dresses; prom gowns from a huge coat rack that she'd supposedly stolen from a hotel.

"I so fucking don't feel like this," she snarled. "Why did you have to wheedle me into doing these damn gigs?"

"Fucking this and damn that. You sound really hostile, and remember: we're bringing in two grand in one evening so Roo can go to camp. Can you step out of yourself for two seconds?"

In her bulky blue bathrobe with hair sticking out in different directions, she straddled that line between erotic and disturbing.

"Art isn't stepping out of yourself; it's going deeper inside."

"Well, it's both," he mumbled as he went into the living room to gather mic stands. She called after him. "It's neither. Great art dissolves the illusion of self."

They then proceeded to give one of their best performances, rekindling the old magic. Some fifty guests showed up at a hotel lounge in midtown for a catered meal that didn't look too appetizing. The bride's overweight family, from Pennsylvania, was entirely undistinguished dishwater blond, while the groom's friends included Brooklyn boys whom Jordan would not have enjoyed meeting under the boardwalk. The nicest crowd were the seniors, including Albert's short, thick-lipped mother, who kept shaking her head at Summer and repeating, "Isn't she something?"

"I never thought of slimeballs as having cute little moms who like jazz," Jordan whispered to Summer between songs, his lips brushing her hair. She giggled and he whispered even more softly, "Hey. You know I love you."

"Thought I was hostile and unruly and you hate me these days.'"

"You're the one who hates me—that's why you're hostile."

"It's not hate," she said. "I've just felt really hurt and betrayed. You find creative ways to break my heart every day."

"Oh, I find ways to break *your* heart?"

He prayed that they'd go home, talk about all this, and make love after the gig. They could fall into that pile of dresses on the bed, their bare skin scraping against tulle and rayon. It would be the first time in a while, and it was, after all, Valentine's Day.

Then Albert's mother approached the mic, cooing: "Such talent! I tell you, I'm just loving you kids. Listen, can you indulge me and my friends a Frank Sinatra?"

"Sure," Summer said. "What would you like to hear?"

"'Summer Wind.'" She leaned in, and her words produced a whiff of lipstick and nicotine: "Love is for the young and you alone. Don't let anyone tell you otherwise. For people my age"—her thick lips ballooned into a frown—"going through the motions, if you're lucky. But don't tell my son—he's such a romantic." The older woman winked, and Summer pursed her lips to keep from giggling.

"What's your name?" she managed to ask.

"Rose, dear. Call me Rose."

"We have a request from Rose," Summer said into the mic. "A tribute to the evanescence of love—and my wish, for this bride and groom, that the summer wind always blows balmy along your path."

Cheers and applause rang from the guests. Rose blushed deeply, her eyes bulging as Summer sang her heart out and Jordan teased the tune slowly on his sax, shadowing her lead.

They'd brought along some *Summer Vale: Brooklyn Boy* CDs that they gave to Albert and Connie, his enhanced-blonde bride with skin paler than Ajax.

"You should be signing with real labels," Albert told Summer after most of the guests left. He still fixed her cleavage in the crosshairs of his gaze, though both Jordan and Connie were present. Jordan couldn't comprehend guys who could do that, at their own rehearsal dinners with their mothers skulking around tipping caterers. "I can make introductions, if you'd like. I know some people. You know I own clubs and franchises. What you really need is a manager."

"True," said Jordan. "Listen, if you know anyone who'd be a good match for her sound, we'd appreciate the opening."

"This is nice. I mean, sure—why not?" Albert said, holding their CD. "But you could go beyond scrappy, know what I mean?"

"I like scrappy!" Summer protested, and Connie smiled at her. Brick-orange lipstick made her skin seem even more cadaverous.

In the cab home, Summer speculated that Connie had been Albert's domme. "She's at least fifteen years younger, maybe twenty."

"Too sweet to be a domme. She seems more like a setup or a dating-site find."

"Most dommes are nice girls showing their different stripes, Jordan."

"Claudia did it for a while. She had to pee on guys' faces sometimes."

Summer suddenly looked stricken. "Stop the cab," she said to the driver. "Please."

"I'm sorry," Jordan began, wondering if this reference to Claudia's antics had brought on her nausea. As Jordan paid the driver, Summer shoved her fur coat at him, dashed out to a garbage can at the corner, and leaned over the side.

Jordan shuttled their equipment out of the trunk and onto the street corner, hoping her sickness would pass quickly. They'd get another cab home, and she'd take a hot bath and some Motrin for her cramps. But her torso vibrated like she was in a voodoo trance, and then a group of grubby kids passed by, jeering at her.

"Leave her alone, fuck holes!" Jordan barked at them.

"Fuck holes!" one guy mocked him.

Jordan considered pushing the guy over, but they went on their merry way as Summer collapsed on the street like a marionette whose strings had suddenly snapped.

He ran over to her and—trying not to gag from the visceral smell—managed to ask, "You okay? Hey, Sum, you okay?" Propped up by the garbage can, she shook her head, which was bowed like a wilted flower. Passers-by asked Jordan if he needed help. He took out his cell phone and called 9-1-1.

"My girlfriend's violently ill and passing out on the corner of Seventh Street and Cooper Square," he said. "We need an ambulance." The bystanders echoed him and were still speaking into phones as EMS arrived, with sirens and circling red and blue lights. Two young medics lifted Summer onto a gurney and slid her into their truck. Jordan followed, carting his sax, her fur coat, their mic stands and amp along with him. He was grateful that one of the young medics helped him pack the equipment, the guy mentioning that he'd been in a band back in high school.

As they made their way to Beth Israel Medical Center, Jordan scribbled the name *Catherine Granato*, her age, and their address on a form he'd been handed on a clipboard. His parents had always used fake names when they went to the E.R. so they wouldn't be billed.

Had she been using drugs? No. Drinking? Jordan remembered a glass of good champagne; he'd had some too. So he wrote: a glass of Dom Perignon. Chronic health problems? Sensitive stomach, menstrual cramps, and "spiraling mood disorders." Medication? Lots of Motrin. Allergies? Insurance? By the time she was admitted to the hospital, Summer had passed out.

"Your wife didn't test positive for allergies or food poisoning," the young Indian nurse explained when Jordan returned the next afternoon with tampons and a clean outfit for Summer. "She's doing fine now. She can go home with you." They shuffled passed other patients' beds until they reached Summer's, where the nurse drew back a curtain. Jordan was startled to find Summer in a blue hospital gown, her hair frenzied over the pillow.

"Did you explain my condition to him, Pranati?" Summer asked the nurse.

In response, Jordan held up the report she'd given him.

"Rest for a while," Pranati urged Summer. "Then we'll discharge you."

As she walked away, Jordan settled at the foot of her bed.

"How you feeling?" he asked.

"I think I'm allergic to fame," she answered, breathless and blinking. "It's making me ill, 'cause nothing else is. Read the test: no problem with my food, or any environmental allergen—even dust. I'm not allergic to mold spores either." She showed him a quadrant of tiny scabs on her arm where she'd been tested. "But I am allergic to reviews and fan letters, and you and Robin planning a website, and Albert Pico talking about managers, all of whom are scum, you know. Deb buying stacks of CDs…for what? I've written five fucking songs in my life, and I hate two of them. I hate the one about Mom and 'Sabina.' I never want to sing them again."

"Summer," he pleaded, but she spoke over him.

"I've been pushing myself so hard, to make everyone else happy. Especially *you*. But I just enjoy our little gig at the hotel—really, I love Gershwin, Porter. I don't need all the other hoopla.

"You remember my headshot from the locked file? Well, that molten bitch wanted fame and fortune. The person you're seeing here shed her like an old skin. This person lying here"—Summer pointed to herself—"has shed many skins and is peeling down to her essence, which is really simple: 'freedom from all ambition.' Remember that one, Jordan? Poe. Freedom from all ambition. And then, creation."

"Success doesn't mean selling out," he contended. "It can be fun. Like our Susquehanna gig."

"Maybe for you. Hey, do you know how many songs Tillie has written?"

"Summer, I don't care about—"

"Sixty-eight! And she's fourteen years younger than I am. Let her out into the world with Skip to make it big. She's in her prime, she loves writing songs—she left London for Nashville. That's commitment to songwriting if ever there was."

"What does she have to write sixty-eight songs about? She's barely past infancy."

"Her songs are good, Jordan."

"Well, yours are awesome."

Summer cranked her head back and pointed at him.

"You're saying that because they're about you."

"No," he said, leaning in closer to her. "You can't cop out so easily. Don't you read what people write in those fan letters? Your songs are healing their hearts."

"It will take more than songs to heal those booze-soaked hearts. Speaking of which, Deb's planning to visit my parents. We've been talking a lot—more than I've even let on to you and Rashad. Our dad's been given about three months. Deb's whole thing is, let's take this chance for closure so he doesn't haunt us all our lives. But for once I actually agree with her husband, who said: 'I've had all the closure I need with your dad.'"

"Easy for him to say," Jordan commented. "Not his father."

"But he's right, Jordan. I accepted long ago that my old man's a dick, and there's such a thing as leaving unwell enough alone. So anyway, Deb and Stewart are on the outs about it, 'cause over Presidents' Day break she's bringing her three kids across the country to meet their grandparents...and everyone's asking if we'll come."

"I would do it," said Jordan. Summer shook her head vehemently. "But he's dying, and he's your dad."

"He's not like your father, or Betty's father. Not a nice man. He'd humiliate my son, in a room with his white grandkids. I know exactly what he'll do, and I'm not subjecting Roo to his sarcasm and favoritism...I want to keep it simple. No more hotshot gigs and reviews and, in the name of the god I don't believe in, no more songwriting. And no more George and Vivian Summers. I've survived my lifetime quota of them.

"You and Roo are my family, and I vote for a happy, simple life with music when we want it. Are you in?"

"I always want music," he said evasively and took her hand in his.

The morning Summer was to leave for Miami, Jordan awoke to hear her raging in the other room. He leapt out of bed to what he thought would be Rashad's defense but found her on the phone. Rashad looked up gratefully from his video game play station and beckoned to him.

"She's yelling 'cause she thinks Aunt Deb sent *Brooklyn Boy* to my grandmother," he whispered to Jordan, his warm breath smelling milky.

Jordan put a hand on the child's shoulder. "You brush your teeth?"

He nodded. All week, since Summer had recontacted her sister, they'd been inseparable on the phone. Because she was so distracted, Jordan had overtaken duties like making sure they had coffee and cereal and that Rashad brushed his teeth after breakfast.

"Your loyalty to her is pure Stockholm syndrome!" Summer cried to Deb, rushing past Jordan and Rashad, then circling back. "Like the American people and this psycho government that killed thousands of our own citizens to get us into Iraq."

Deb was responding so loudly that Jordan could hear her as though she were on a transistor radio: "Cathy, people from home told Mom about your CD—it wasn't me."

Jordan grabbed Summer's arm and stopped her from racing around further.

"Cathy," he began, knowing that when she spoke to Deb she wouldn't respond to the name Summer. "Cathy, go easy. You've got to get off the phone and get dressed. The limo will be here in an hour."

"I haven't even packed," she confessed.

"Well, I have."

Jordan grabbed the phone from Summer and pointed to the scuffed, powder-blue suitcase by the door. Last night he'd carefully folded in her gowns, stockings and slips, eight pairs of panties, shoes and socks, and some jeans and sweaters for "downtime." He put makeup and toiletries in the carry-on bag beside it.

"I helped too!" Rashad piped, rushing over to them. Rashad had folded her slips.

Summer smiled fondly at both of them, and Jordan noticed that he'd snapped the phone off. "Oh, sorry…I accidentally hung up on Deb. Please apologize to her."

Summer shrugged. "Let her see how it feels when Mister Man cuts off the conversation. Nothing her husband hasn't done to me a million times." She cocked her head and winked at Jordan. Earlier that morning she'd wound herself around him, rousing him from sleep into a delicious and long overdue sexual reunion. Now she asked, "Would you be a honey and please run a bath for me? Promise I'll be out in ten minutes."

By the time the limo called to say it was downstairs, Summer was bathed, coiffed, dressed, and back on the phone with Deb. Now she sounded sweet and conciliatory with her sister. Jordan and Rashad escorted her downstairs, Jordan toting the powder-blue suitcase and Rashad the carry-on bag.

"I'm not running from anything," she insisted to Deb. "I'm just staying clear of the undergrowth, with its thorns and poison ivy. And those ticks, vicious little soul-suckers." Their talk was always hyperbolic and filled with strange metaphors. Jordan understood why Deb's husband had put his foot down about it and felt gratified when Summer got into the elevator and off the phone.

"Will Beach-Ball Face be in the limo?" Rashad asked as they rode down, and they laughed together.

"Yep," said Summer. "They picked Tillie up first."

"I'm glad she'll be with you," said Jordan as they got out of the elevator. "Wish we could be."

The tour would start in Miami, then proceed to Tallahassee and end up in New Orleans around the same time as Mardi Gras. "Call me every day," said Summer, suddenly vulnerable as it seemed to hit her that she was leaving. "You guys are the best, you know that? You're my A-Team. I've been crazy all week with Deb back in my life and this tour…when I come home, I'll be a better mommy and sweetie." She looked beguilingly from Rashad to Jordan, her sensual lips in a pout, her brow knit.

"You're fine as you are," Jordan said, handing her the blue suitcase.

"I've been rude. Self-absorbed." She looked at them again. "And we three's a team. The A-Team—Roo, Dew, and Foo Boy."

When she trundled off with her suitcases and got into the limo, Rashad buried his face in Jordan's hip. "She'll be back in a week," Jordan consoled him, stroking his back. "And tomorrow we'll see dinosaurs at the Museum of Natural History with Curtis and the twins." Then his cell phone rang. She was calling from the limo.

"I don't want you seeing Molly when I'm away."

"Since when do I see Molly? It's been…how many years?"

"I suddenly felt her think about you."

"Well I suddenly got afraid you'll run off with the slide trombone player."

"He's more ancient that Shazan—besides, I'm engaged."

"That makes two of us."

They'd imagined their wedding that morning as they lay in each other's arms: how they'd say vows in the botanical gardens or by the sea in Fair Harbor, how Rashad would be the ring bearer, and their sisters would be the two maids of honor.

"I'm as engaged as you are, Dew Drop," he said. "Not chasing after Molly."

Two nights later she called with delight about the Florida shows, the audiences ready to stand up, clap, and swing their big hips to the music. "All very Latin," she described. "We could've gone all night. Shazan says I'd love South America, that women grow their white hair really long, and old people go out late at night to tango."

Jordan was overjoyed to hear her happy about travel and singing for people. Maybe, he thought, their hard times were over and they could get on with it. Maybe their dreams were not so divergent as he'd feared.

But in her next call, Summer stormed about Deb's pilgrimage to their parents. She'd learned that her father was receiving home hospice care, "lying around with tubes in him while Mom runs the show. Big role reversal! She's now quite the managerial wife after having checked out for three decades. And the old man is as irascible and bigoted as ever—of course he's suing the hospital where he got an infection. My father can't even die without running a racket." Summer mentioned that her family was obsessed with the *Brooklyn Boy* CD and "always talking about it, though I asked Deb not to tell me what they say."

Jordan burned with curiosity. "Must be weird to hear all this from Deb, like a fly on your own family's wall."

"Yeah, and it kinda sucks that she's there with our parents and her kids but no one in our generation—her husband and I both flaked on her. I said she could always call, but in a way I don't want to hear that Mom takes Deb's kids horseback riding and buys them stuff. Meanwhile, Deb is ready to burst with rage. Of course she's glad our mother's been sober for years and in Twelve Step programs and psychiatry. But where was she when we needed her? You know?"

Later on, another call cut through Jordan's desperately needed sleep. Rashad had been grumpy all day, demanding that Jordan buy him an inflatable plastic Spider-Man doll. Summer allowed Rashad one toy a month, and Rashad already had his February toy, so Jordan upheld the limit. The kid whined and frowned and reminded him of Summer, and Jordan exhausted himself by exerting authority that he barely felt.

"Great show again tonight," she breathed into the phone. "Nothing in the world like being onstage—except maybe sex with you."

"I miss you," he whispered.

"Oh, sweet fool. I just lost it today. Deb called me racking with sobs over a confrontation she had with my mother. I can't take much more of this…almost didn't get onstage. Good thing Tillie was there."

"Well, what happened?" Jordan asked, as curious as he was sleepy.

"When they were alone, Mom said she could see anger in Deb's eyes and told her something like 'You can let it out. I'm not going to break.' Well, my generally very gracious sister gave our mother hell about being the worst piece of irresponsible failure shit for not getting help earlier and depriving us of a childhood." Summer was losing her breath as she spoke.

"Honey, are you okay with all this?"

"Actually," she began, "I'm not, really."

"Can you maybe talk to Deb after the tour's all done?...Summer? Hello?" Jordan thought he'd lost the connection but then heard her sobbing.

"Yeah, sure...I can tell my sister, 'Hey, my career's more important than you. I'll get to you in my good time, not when you need me...'" Her voice broke.

"Oh, don't listen to me. I'm half-asleep. I didn't mean that you should be dismissive." But she'd hung up on him.

He tried calling back and got only voice mail. The next morning, she didn't answer her phone or call him. By afternoon Jordan was frantic, so he called Tillie.

"I just got her to breathe, you know," Tillie told him. "We looked at the sky and sang one note. I told her my mum does things I don't like either. But you can't let it get to you. Anyway, me and Shazan are trying to get her off this 9/11 kick, 'cause I don't think it's helping her at all. Shazan says it's just—same old, same old—giving white people in power more credit than they're due. He said: 'If there are any imperialistic lies in all this, that's the worst one to believe. If there are CIA cover-ups, it's that this government fucked up on 9/11 and didn't see it coming.'"

A Susquehanna cabaret was scheduled in Summer's absence. Neither Bruce nor Fred could make it either, so Jordan and Z carried the house. They each wore tight black jeans; Jordan wore a silk shirt with a golden scorpion pendant, and Z a Hawaiian shirt decorated with orange and yellow fish. "Welcome to the Witching Hour...with Mr. Scorpio and Mr. Pisces," Z announced into the mic, eliciting chuckles from the audience. "Our leading lady, Summer Vale, is in New Orleans singing at Mardi Gras with Shazan White." Applause rang out from her fans. "But sit tight and enjoy your cocktail. We'll give you plenty to talk about, even without her."

It felt funny to do her usual tunes without her voice, without even Fred's keyboard. Instead, Jordan's raspy saxophone took over the melody, rambling deliriously as it did, the lights hotter and brighter on his cheeks now that he was center stage. Z worked his drums, striving for varied effects as he held the rhythm without Bruce's bass. Since Jordan and Z had played on the streets for years, they easily found each other's groove. At one point Z even grabbed the mic and sang "Betty" in a growly, Nat King Cole vein that the audience loved, then "Summertime." His finale was "Short Stick"…"another original, by our own Summer Vale—her ode to a mother with drinking problems."

"Now you see her, now you don't;
She loves me, loves me no-o-otttt…
The short end of the stick is what I got."

How different when Z sang it, bringing to mind some aunt of his who'd been found nearly dead on Rockaway Beach with an empty bottle of whiskey, or even Z's "loves me/loves me not" girlfriends—but not Summer's doe-like mother with her haunted suburban glamour.

When the house lights went up after the second set, two dark-haired women waved from a back table. Excitedly, Jordan realized it was Molly and Claudia, and he clambered to meet them, stumbling over stray chairs as patrons took leave. The three friends managed a group hug and cavorted arm in arm to the stage that Z was clearing.

"Aw, hell!" Z exclaimed, beaming at Molly. "So great to see you."

"Amazing show, you guys! Would you care for a nightcap?"

Under the fine and discreet aroma of Molly's perfume Jordan fell back into another time, when someone else shouldered the burdens and he was along for the ride. Rashad was with the Wilcoxes, so he could party with impunity. After Z packed his drums, they headed to one of the two restaurants in the hotel, Yucat-ana, which served Mexican food and fancy cocktails: the perfect place for Molly to buy him three.

"Think I'm in the market for a double mojito," he told Molly as they were seated at a round table perusing cocktail menus that were laminated onto wooden slabs.

"And you, Mr. Pisces?" Molly turned a munificent face to Z.

"I'll go with coconut rum punch."

"Where are Dustin and Eugenia?" Jordan asked with his first sweet and cooling swallow of Hemingway's signature highball.

"Not a good night for either of our beloveds to come out and play," Molly explained, looking so stunning in a satin kimono-like tunic. "Too bad Summer wasn't here the night I could make it. I was looking forward to meeting her."

"Me too," said Claudia.

"Here's a little taste of her in absentia." Jordan handed them each a CD.

"*Brooklyn Boy*! I love the name," cooed Claudia.

"Wait 'til you hear the song," Z told her.

"The video online is wonderful," said Molly, turning the CD over in her hands. On the back cover was a photo of Summer in a filmy black minidress with fishnet stockings, her knee lodged in Jordan's waist as he stood grinning with her hair in his face.

"Sexy!" Molly commented. She nodded to Jordan and repeated, "She's sexy."

"Yes, and a handful these days," Jordan confided with a longer gulp of mojito.

"How so?" asked Claudia, never ashamed to pry.

"Well, if life with this one"—he turned to Molly, seated beside him, and slid his finger down her cheek to her collarbone—"was like a Ferris wheel, with panoramic vistas and sickening descents, my days with Summer Vale are like a power dive."

"Try the fun house," interjected Z.

"That bad?" asked Claudia, smiling archly as Jordan removed his finger from Molly's collarbone.

"That good," said Jordan. It was strange, he was thinking now, that Summer had asked him not to see Molly in her absence. Her radar for the future was uncanny at times.

"What's her beef?" persisted Claudia.

"Real ambivalence about success," Z ventured. "She hates how she loves it."

"Chronic indecision that gives me career blue balls," griped Jordan, and they all laughed. "With a little conspiracy theory thrown into the mix. Really," he said, grateful to be out drinking with old friends and his former muse. "Her four-year-old son is easier to hang with. He has his moments—he's a kid. But her drama's in higher gear. Our last phone call was like …" He tried to remember. First she'd told him that only sex with him could compete with the thrill of resounding applause—a suspect statement, given her ambivalence about life upon the wicked stage. Not five minutes later, she'd hung up on him because his advice about her sister was less than perfect. "I can't follow it anymore!" he fumed. "I'm great. I'm terrible. We're up. We're down…"

"Hmmm," said Molly, "sounds like someone I know."

"Eugenia?"

"No."

Molly reached out and drew her index finger down Jordan's cheek to his collarbone. They both burst out laughing and stared at each other with playful shock.

"No way, Molly."

"Jo-Jo, listen to her," said Z, grinning.

"I never knew what I'd come home to," Molly elaborated. "Great appreciation. Deference. Or…resentment. Insolence! Mutiny behind my back."

"And Eugenia's so predictable?"

"Hardly. But I would say your moods were horizontal." She stretched her arms out, satin sleeves billowing. "Topographic. Like moors by a turbulent sea. Eugenia's moods are vertical, Paleolithic. You excavate them strata by strata—in other words, when the going gets tough, you got loud and she gets…quiet."

Jordan would have liked to pursue this tangent, but Teddy burst through the doors of Yucatana as though he were looking for someone and caught Jordan's eye. With a sinking feeling, Jordan excused himself from the table.

"This…I think this is for her." Teddy handed Jordan an envelope. He hoped it wouldn't be from Geoff Ahlstrom again, and it didn't seem to be. At first glance it looked like a wedding invitation on creamy stationery. A halting script had addressed it to *Cathy Jane Summers, c/o The Susquehanna Hotel Cabaret*. The envelope flap, in engraved letterpress, read *Mrs. Vivian H. Summers*, at some cushy-sounding address like Ashley Glen in North Carolina.

Jordan shut his eyes for a moment, fighting the stress. If Summer heard that her mother now knew how to contact her at the Susquehanna cabaret, she might stop singing there. And it was their special gig, where they'd met, too precious to sacrifice.

"'Ey, Mr. Pisces," he called to Z, and his friend arose.

"Mom." Jordan flicked the envelope at Z. "I'm going to make an executive decision." Then he turned to Teddy. "Could you give us a moment please?"

The man stood back as Jordan huddled with Z, explaining his concerns and procuring a pen. He hesitated for a moment but then realized that Deb would tell Summer anything really important about their parents now. So he scrawled *Return to Sender* on her mother's envelope and advised Z, "All of this"—he flapped the stiff envelope, then nodded toward Molly and Claudia at the table—"didn't happen. Okay?"

"Your call," said Mr. Pisces.

"But do you agree with me?"

"You're the expert," said Z.

His belt buckle dug into his leg as their hips rocked so much pleasure from inside her on the hardwood floor. She'd just gotten back from New Orleans bearing hot sauce and Mardi Gras beads. It was 2:30 p.m., almost time to pick up Rashad at school, and they were enjoying a quickie. Their definition of quickie was "in clothes, in less than ten minutes, not in bed."

"You're beautiful," he cried, his head banging the wall behind him as he heard her familiar and throaty moan. There he throbbed indistinguishably between pain and rapture as her warm body ebbed away from his.

"We'd better get going," he said reluctantly, his open pants edged down to his ankles. She stood up, regaled in fake fur coat and blouse, without any pants.

"After I shower. Just got off an airplane and fucked my brains out."

She shed her coat and blouse on her way to the bathroom. In the shower she ran chromatic scales, not sounding forced or squeaky. It was kind of a miracle. Head still reeling, he stood up and tucking himself into his pants.

"Wish you hadn't hung up on me!" he called.

She stopped trilling her scales and called back, "What?"

"On the phone the other night. You just hung up on me!"

She burst from the steamy bathroom saying, "Okay, here I am—let's go. We're late for him."

But Jordan charged into the bathroom to wash his hands and splash water on his face. Steam cleared from the mirror, revealing his raggy hair that needed to be cut and the unshaven cheeks she had kissed, asking if he planned to grow a beard or just didn't trouble himself to shave when she was away.

On East Broadway they held hands as cold air tickled their cheeks. "I wish you hadn't hung up the phone on me," he repeated. "It messes me up."

"Yeah, those tough times with my sister kicking up old dust. But I loved the tour. Didn't think I would. I couldn't even pack."

"So I remember."

"Well, you did it for me."

She could express gratitude but not remorse. He held her hand tighter.

"Singing for people..." She shook her head. "Not the problem. I could live like that forever, hanging out all day in different cities, getting onstage at night."

"Sounds fun," said Jordan wistfully.

"And I learn from Shazan. He says I'm best in major keys. He's right, isn't he?"

"Come to think of it."

"Funny to go through so much professionally and not notice, but that's what I love about him. He might get us to Eastern Europe this summer."

"Really?"

"I mean me and Tillie."

Jordan tried not to look disappointed, though he knew Shazan worked with top saxophonists and didn't need him. Summer guided him to the curb where she tended to jaywalk to Rashad's public school a block away. "Please don't be hurt by what I'm going to say, because I don't really mean what you'll hear."

"What?" He already felt defensive.

"Being away from you and Roo made everything easier."

He was glad he'd seen Molly. Nothing had transpired between them beyond drinks and banter. But keeping his own little secret was armor against Summer's scathing and out-of-the-blue comments.

"Not that I didn't miss the hell out of you both," she added. "Tillie knows, I bawled like a banshee I got so homesick. But it was good to have the pressure off."

"What pressure?" Jordan asked, dropping her hand. "I help you do everything."

"I know. And you're fantastic. But *that* is pressure. You're too good, and now I'm hooked. Rashad is a wonderful kid. Deb's a great sister. Look at her. She bought—what? Five hundred CDs? And what have I done for her? Almost wrecked her marriage, years back."

She walked briskly to the curb, her heels smacking the damp concrete.

In the school playground Jordan noticed the Wilcox twins with some older boys.

"Barney and Betty are in counseling today," Summer commented. Their friends had suddenly become Barney and Betty, and the twins Bam and Bam. "I guess my poor son is standing around wondering where the hell we are. I'm a derelict, crappy mother…a demanding girlfriend, delinquent daughter. Really, all I can do is sing and fuck. And granted, I do both well. But that's all I do. Can't keep house worth a damn. I can hardly wake up and get my kid to school.

"On tour I was so free, people even cleaned my hotel room every day. But then I felt pangs of guilt and no—I didn't deal well with you or Deb on the phone. I'm just surrounded by too many perfect people."

"Then start talking to your parents again," Jordan suggested. "You'll have some imperfect people in your life."

"Deb said my father called you a 'little squirt.'"

"What?" cried Jordan. "When has he ever seen me?"

"In our videos, and on the CD cover."

Jordan hadn't wanted to react. Glancing at Summer, he saw that she looked almost pleased.

"Hey," she said, giggling, "he's a rotting old vegetable on life support. Who's he to talk? Besides, considering what he's called Stewart, 'little squirt' is flattering."

"What did he call Stewart?"

Summer stopped walking to shriek with laughter. "The 'union thug rat'— you know that awful, big rat they pump up by any hotel that dares hire nonunion contractors to fix a leaky roof or a botched elevator?" She started walking again. "Well, with Stewart's overbite and his mother being a progressive Democratic assemblywoman..."

"Your father really is a dick."

"Have I ever said otherwise? According to Deb, Mom rushed to your defense, claiming that you strike her as a 'talented and handsome young man.'"

"I prefer that opinion." He jammed both hands into his pockets as they approached Rashad's school. And he waited outside while she went in to retrieve her son.

♫

On March first, the Choice Cabaret awards for last year were posted online for "exceptional musical variety shows with vintage flavor." Summer and the trio were at Z's eating gingerbread with anisette to celebrate Z's birthday, which was later that week. Looking over Bruce's shoulder at the screen, Jordan read that the Skip Harrington Swing Band won first prize. "Fuck," he cried, in the middle of chewing gingerbread that he now couldn't swallow. Skip's mastery of swing and his nod to Dixieland were lauded and "new vocalist Tillie Mack adds a unique note of charm and command."

Second prize went to a barbershop quartet of brothers—Sean, Shane, John and Don—who sang doo-wop and Bing Crosby. Summer Vale and the Jordan Radfar Trio took third prize for their Susquehanna revue of "Beloved blues from the twenties through the seventies." The two honorable mentions went to a female vocalist slightly younger than Summer—by that time Jordan was too depressed to read her name—and another woman in her sixties who seemed to think she was Andrea Marcovicci.

Summer laughed it off: "Didn't I always say this was in Skip's pocket? He knows too many people, and he lets them think they're wiping the floor with him." When Jordan stared plaintively at her, she said, "Oh, get over it."

Z and Bruce respectively chimed in with "Hey, we're on the scoreboard, Jo-Jo," and "We can pick up mileage from this."

But their voices collapsed into gibberish for Jordan as he imagined Skip's triumph. Arman had called it correctly the night of his thirtieth birthday: Jordan was a first-prize-or-nothing sort who "didn't know the meaning of compromise." And it now seemed that the world was Tillie and Skip's oyster when it should have been his and Summer's.

"Are they, like, seeing each other or something?" Jordan asked when he and Summer left Z's for the subway.

"Not if I can help it. Tillie's got a crush ten miles wide and deeper than the sea. But since we roomed together, I've learned a tidbit about her that wouldn't augur well, given what I know about Skip. Without sounding cruel, I tried to warn her."

"Oh, you never sound cruel."

They sniggered at each other.

"So," he probed, "can you let me in on this tasty tidbit?"

She didn't until they emerged from the subway in Manhattan, climbing the steep stairway to Essex Street. "He's a tit man and our girl Tillie has no tits."

"Tit man?"

"Obsessed with mammary glands, preferably large and bulbous."

"Aren't we all?"

"Not to sound horribly vulgar…"

"Who, you?"

They were out on the street now, so she grabbed his arm and leaned in to whisper: "There are T-men, P-men or B-men: tit, pussy, or butt. Butt men are the worst. Probably gay, but they'd rather not be."

"So did you and Deb come up with these categories?"

She nodded. "And other girls with whom I've compared notes."

"We're that formulaic, are we?"

"Not entirely. But you tend to have your sweet spots…pussy man."

Jordan could feel the blush temper his face and glanced down at a puddle on the sidewalk. Summer took his hand as they ran across Delancey Street, trying to beat a fickle traffic light. "Tillie's actually built like a schoolboy with a vagina. She wears these ninty-nine-cent foam bras—you know, the kind cool ghetto girls find. She calls them her 'white lies' because they give her some shape. But I don't think Skip would find that punch line too funny."

"How do you know so much about Skip?"

"Well, we had our little thing."

"You said you just made out with him once," Jordan muttered as they hit the sidewalk before the light changed. To his left, the Williamsburg Bridge stood silhouetted by twilight, its string of pearly lights dotting the cables. The sky was musty but not yet dark.

"Where do you think his hands went when we made out?"

"Must you always be explicit?"

"Must you always ask? He was bereft that he never got to actually see them. I don't take my clothes off for just anyone, you know. I've conducted entire affairs without undoing a button."

She'd told Jordan that he was the fifth man with whom she'd spent time entirely naked. Molly's head count was much higher and, Jordan thought, more typical of young women after feminism's second wave and before the sobriety of

AIDS.

"I've given hand jobs in a winter coat and gloves."

"Ugh…hey, you didn't give Skip a hand job, did you?"

She crossed her eyes and stuck out her tongue. In a better mood, he would have laughed with her.

After their Susquehanna gig the next night, he watched her wrap her microphone cable. She had reached gloriously high notes that, as she described it, gave her own head a massage. Still not recovered from Skip's victory, Jordan appreciated their music and love. He didn't agree that all she "can do is sing and fuck," and yet, maybe that's what he also did best.

Inevitably, Teddy appeared with her clump of mail, including a flat UPS package. Jordan came up and read over Summer's shoulder as she leafed through it murmuring, "Yeah, yeah, voice coaches, modeling agency—right! Old heifer hips here will ignite the runway." Then she held up the UPS package, flashing the name *Vivian H. Summers*. Jordan girded himself for whatever was coming.

"Oh?" she said. "No 'George and Vivian' anymore—is she a widow already?" Summer tore into the cardboard. Horrified, Jordan saw the same creamy envelope on which he'd scrawled *Return to Sender* last time. But Summer barely seemed to notice that and simply ripped it open. In the middle of the folded page sat two sentences, written like an earnest third grader who was just learning cursive, with barely any punctuation: *Cathy Jane I heard your song. Will you forgive me?* After that, came several phone numbers.

Summer threw it across the stage, her face turned pink and nostrils flaring. "What part of 'goodbye' do we not understand, Vivian?" She then muttered, "Master work of passive aggression that you are."

"This doesn't seem too passive," Jordan remarked, retrieving it from the floor. Summer fought to grab it from him, and when he gave it up, she crumpled her mother's short letter in her hand.

"Now don't you get all suckered in here," she scolded. "That would be the last thing I need. And no, I'm not cruel. The many times I did forgive her she just took it as license to do the same damn thing again. So I learned not to bother."

Packing their amps, Z and Bruce were trying not to appear interested. Jordan didn't dare volunteer a word, because anything that came out of his mouth would be chastised. So Summer continued, half to herself and half to him and everyone else.

"Suppose I did a set completely off-key and kept forgetting lyrics. Would I ask the audience for another chance? The whole idea is to do it right the first time. If you need to ask forgiveness, you inherently don't deserve it." She frowned sharply. "Forgivenenss is such a wash…which is why Christianity hasn't solved any problems for two thousand years. 'Forgive them, they know not.' Of course they fucking know. They know damn well."

At least she wasn't refusing to sing at the Susquehanna. Their next gig fell on Saint Patrick's Day, but the trio wasn't playing with her that night, as jazz was just not an Irish idiom. Fred's piano was admitted, Tillie would sing backup with mandolin, and another friend accompanied them on penny whistle.

In an olive pullover and army pants, Jordan sat beside Z in his bright green tam. Tillie and Summer both wore green dresses with turquoise carnations tucked into their hair. Jordan tried to assess Tillie's figure but couldn't distinguish anything through the crowds and stage lights. Her face looked particularly sweet, her eyes large and guileless.

"Tillie and I are both a quarter Irish," Summer explained to the cheering audience. Then she turned to Tillie. "Where does your family come from?"

"Limerick," she said. "They were called Tierny."

"In Sligo, my father's family was called Ó Somacháin, which became Summers here. And so we dedicate these songs to them." They had practiced for this during their tour; they sang one or two numbers in Gaelic and then classics such as "Galway Bay," "Whisky in the Jar" and "Curragh of Kildare."

"No 'Molly Malone'?" Z whispered, and Jordan snorted so loudly that a woman at the next table turned and shushed him.

Before they left home, Summer had said, "I'll sing 'Nancy Spain' and 'Nancy

Whisky' and 'Peggy Gordon,' but no 'Irish Molly O.'" Now Jordan felt glad that she was singing anything. He hoped to keep the peace by keeping his mouth shut. And when she sang "If This Isn't Love" and "Look to the Rainbow" as their encore, with Tillie's tinkling mandolin and the warbly penny whistle, not an eye in the house was dry—including his.

"*Follow the fellow…who follows a dream.*"

She sang it just slowly enough.

"Thank you, everyone," Summer said several times into the mic before the rowdy clapping eased up. "Thank you so much. Now, I have an announcement. Which will come as a surprise to my boyfriend and his band, so I hope he doesn't throw me out on the street. If you see me jingling a cup, you'll know what happened."

Z and Jordan glanced at each other.

"Tonight will be my last performance here for a while," she continued. "I'm taking a leave of absence. The trio will continue with Fred, as far as I know, and if you're lucky, they'll ask Tillie to sing a set or two. So the show will go on. Just not with me."

There was an almost audible sigh of dismay from the group.

"What the fuck?" Z whispered to Jordan.

"News to me," he grumbled back.

"Every performer needs a break sometimes, so you're not just standing at the mic 'like some parrot chained to his stand night after night,' as Leonard Cohen put it—back when he had tour fatigue in the early nineteen seventies," Summer continued. "He actually went backstage and shaved, he was so tense. Maybe I should go tweeze my eyebrows."

"This act just won third prize for Cabaret—is she crazy?" Z pleaded into Jordan's ear.

"Welcome to my life."

Jordan began to rip the cocktail napkin he was holding into tiny bits.

As the weather grew warm, she sang for hours in parks and subway stations—for a fifth of what she earned onstage. Jordan didn't get it, but he went along and helped with his horn. Crowds gathered. People clapped as she sang blues and show tunes.

"Why can't you just do this at the hotel?" he asked under his breath one evening.

"I'll go back around my birthday. How does that sound?"

Jordan shrugged. Maybe that would happen and maybe not. He was learning.

Meanwhile, she'd embarked on a project that involved guitar lessons from Eliot after weekly 9/11 Truth meetings that she'd started attending with him. She wanted to sing "Where Have All the Flowers Gone?" in twenty-five languages, "to protest war in a less prosaic way." Online she found the lyrics in Spanish, French, and German. She offered a Polish waitress at the diner five dollars to translate and teach her to pronounce it in Polish. Some old friend of hers provided a Romanian translation. A stroll up East Broadway produced renditions in Hebrew, Yiddish, and Mandarin, between the Jewish agencies and Chinese restaurants. She posted a sign where she sang in Union Square Park: *Cash welcome, but translating "Where Have All the Flowers Gone" into a foreign language is even better.*

Jordan admired the project, though it consumed too much of her energy. She sat for hours in her blue bathrobe listening to recordings on the Dictaphone Eliot had leant her and mimicking foreign phrases. On her days off from waitressing, she boarded subways to Queens or Brooklyn and decamped in immigrant neighborhoods, coming back with translations into Korean or Greek. Along with the recordings she made of people's voices, she scrawled phonetic pronunciations in the notebook Jordan had given her for her own songs—overgrown now with *fleurs, flores, blumen.*

And Eliot buzzed around her like a horsefly, teaching her chords and lending her his prized Martin with its fancy tuner that cost more than his rent. He'd stopped playing at the Tribeca pub with Jordan—"Too much going on," he'd explained, though he had time to rage about the Bilderberg Group with every other activist on Medicare.

At one point Summer asked whether Eliot owned more than one shirt.

"I don't know or care," Jordan told her.

"He has a problem with body odor, doesn't he?"

"I'd say it's the least of his problems. But you're the one who hangs with him."

Summer had indeed become a card-carrying member of the elite that spoke of 'planned demolition' and how 'there was no plane,' as they hoodwinked each other with "insider knowledge that escapes most of us," Betty phrased it, when Jordan came by for Rashad one evening.

"Did you hear the latest?" Curtis asked him. "Flight seventy-seven didn't hit the Pentagon? It was all retouched footage—"

"Curtis, please," Betty interrupted. "Didn't she say some French guy claimed it was an American missile?"

"Eyewitnesses and fuselage be damned."

"Passengers be damned! Wedding rings and driver's licenses were found, but these people didn't exist."

"Ah," said Curtis. "Those items could have been planted."

"Her frigging opinion's been planted," grumbled Jordan.

"But by whom?" asked Betty. "We were wondering…" She looked to Curtis for confirmation that she should say it. "Is this coming from her sister? Seems the hysteria's ramped up since they've been back in touch."

"Not at all. Deb says she's 'off her rocker,'" said Jordan. "Deb's with us. Not that I've spoken to her myself. Summer won't let me. She put Rashad on the phone a couple of times with her but never me."

"Well, why?" asked Betty. "You're her fiancé. Deb's her sister."

"Summer's afraid we'll gang up on her."

"Look, I'll allow that more is going on in this world than meets the eye," said Curtis. "I have my own theory—Iraq's the weaponry trade show for the Lukewarm War. But that's not to say this administration pulled some sleight of hand.

Summer's bright enough to see the loopholes in that rant. So if it's not her sister, then who's cheerleading for it?"

"Eliot…the fat old guy you saw play blues guitar with me."

Curtis and Betty looked sadly at each other.

"She's always been so shrewd," Betty observed. "The girl who screamed, 'Yes, you're drunk' when her mother denied it. You heard that story, right? Summer told us she damaged her vocal nodes by screaming at her mom when she was sixteen. She's a whistle-blower at heart, not a lemming."

"Well," said Jordan, "maybe she's found a new whistle to blow. And maybe these days whistle-blowers are the worst lemmings."

"Have you talked to her about therapy or counseling?" Curtis asked. His hesitant tone undermined the question's inevitability.

"She says, 'Been there done that,' and that the medication makes you fat and asexual. I told her we could go back to my former therapist, Barbara, and just talk. But she never seems to have time. And then she accuses me of wanting to brainwash her into being a 'mainstream zombie' who doesn't care that the government is fooling us all."

"Go to your shrink with her," advised Curtis.

"Especially since her dad's dying," added Betty. "She told me they were close when she was a kid. Even though they're estranged now, I'm sure she's feeling it."

Whatever she was feeling, Jordan couldn't guess. She'd grown cryptic and, despite her sexy affection with him, somehow listless. When he mentioned their wedding, she'd smile remotely as though it no longer mattered, and Jordan didn't push her. Women were supposed to talk about guest lists and menus. If they preferred researching every translation of "Where Have All the Flowers Gone" to discussing their bridal flower arrangements, something was off.

He had no proof, but it dawned on him one spring day that she could be seeing another man. He ransacked her purse when she was sleeping and didn't find anything, like condoms or phone numbers. She also wasn't getting dolled up; much to the contrary, she wore wrinkled dresses and sometimes didn't brush her hair before leaving the apartment.

And then one day, after she'd slugged her aloe vera juice—"Tillie says it's good for our mucus membranes"—threw on a sweater, and went out in search of an Egyptian translation of "Where Have All the Flowers Gone," Jordan found a folded, scribbled-on paper in her coat pocket. Since she wouldn't return for a while, he took it out and unfolded it.

He was relieved to read *Dear Mom* penciled on top. That was crossed out, and she'd written *Dear Vivian*. Then she'd simply written *Mother*. He tried to read through more erasures and scribbles:

I'm sure you don't remember our last conversation. You were less cognizant than a pet rock, so it was pretty much my soliloquy. Now you're telling Deb that all those years you 'had a disease.' Sorry, Mother. What you had was no disease. Parkinson's is a disease. Alzheimer's, M.S., and cancer are diseases. People can't cure them in a Twelve Step group.

What you had was a really bad habit, a weakness. I would have empathized with your weakness had you, for example, grown up on a farm in Darfur and seen your family shot. Or if you were dying in an Iraqi hospital or returning to America without an arm. Or living in Kandahar with a husband who flogged you. I understand why such people might drink heavily, and I know why women in Afghanistan set fire to themselves, though I dread to imagine what happens to their daughters.

But you grew up riding horses and sipping tea, heiress to the Van Haarlan spoils, educated in French and Latin, so popular that even your brother wrote you love letters. Frankly Mother, you had no excuse.

Sometimes, when I remember how you and Aunt Maegan gave all that money to UNICEF to help children—not telling Dad 'cause you knew he'd…

The rest of the letter was unreadable, completely scribbled over and partly erased.

Only one paragraph remained untouched: *Mother, I've said everything I need to say through my song. It's yours forever. Please do not contact me again.*

Jordan had no idea whether any version of this letter was actually sent.

The next weeks produced no evidence of trysts with secret lovers. Perhaps nothing about Summer's apathy could be explained so logically. Or else the ghosts of boyfriends past were simply plying the illusion.

"I don't like that bloke," Tillie whispered to Jordan one evening when she sang with them at the Susquehanna.

Jordan too had noticed a character in a visor hat and denim shirt in back of the room, stopping at intervals to watch them through binoculars.

At the end of the set, a short, stocky guy with a shaved head and thick brown beard approached Jordan and asked under his breath: "Where's Cathy?" Jordan felt too affronted to answer.

"She's on tour," Z said.

"When will she be back?"

"None o' your business!" Tillie retorted to the guy.

"Look, miss, keep out of this."

"Look, mister, don't speak to our vocalist that way," said Z. "Now if you have any message you want us to relay to Cathy, I'll get you a pen and some paper."

The guy trudged away. They watched him meet his pal in the visor hat and exit the venue with him.

When Jordan described everything to Summer at home later, she instantly said, "That was Geoff. He stalked me for years, with binoculars and cameras. Real sicko. Lives by the bay in Toms River with a bunch of kids and a long-suffering wife. Glad I wasn't there tonight. See why I had to get away from the Susquehanna?"

"What does he want of you?"

She shrugged. "He still probably has some twisted idea that we'll end up together. He can dream on. I suppose he has nothing better to do."

"Why didn't he talk to us himself?"

"He always gets other guys to do his bidding. He formed the habit when I had a restraining order on him—until I made the judge change the wording so no one could pester me on his behalf. He finally blew off, but I knew he'd come around again, like stink in the wind. Him or my mother. "

As much as Geoff's appearance was no particular surprise to her, the letter from Khalil a week later came as a blow. Jordan found her smoldering at the kitchen table on which a series of identical envelopes lay fanned. He picked one up. Behind the glassine, he saw the address to Catherine J. Summers, in care of a post office box in Marina Del Rey, California. The return address was the Internal Revenue Service.

When Jordan looked at her for an explanation, she pushed a short, meticulously written note on mint green paper across the table at him, mouthing, "Asshole."

Jordan leaned over to read it.

> *Dear Cathy,*
>
> *Under the circumstances, I must discontinue the use of this post office box. I will be in touch with you again once Rashad is old enough to know about me. Sorry I can't be more helpful, but I received a call from someone saying I was 'listed as a reference' for you, and I will not endanger my family more than I already have. We both know that your family has the means to help if you're really desperate, if you can overcome your pride for Rashad's sake.*
>
> *I wish the best for you and him,*
> *Khalil*

Wrath streaking her cheeks pink, she seemed more upset than she'd been about Geoff at the hotel—which Jordan found much more creepy. Khalil's letter, unfortunately, was reasonable, and Jordan asked her: "How much do you owe the feds?"

"Tens of thousands by now. You know, they wanted to tax what I earned from performing. Wasn't like I had a steady salary or something—they wanted a huge cut. But it was years ago. They should move on already."

"They could find you. They could seize your bank account."

"They won't."

"Why? Because you don't want them to?"

He stood with a fist on one hip, his other hand on the gritty tabletop.

"Stop condescending," she muttered, eyeing him up and down. "What you don't get is that 'Catherine Jane Summers' died six years ago."

"Excuse me?"

"I'm dead."

Jordan nearly stumbled forward, balancing himself by gripping the table. He mouthed, "WTF?"

"Khalil registered a death certificate, claiming that he thought I committed suicide when I got pregnant. I don't think they accepted it, though."

Summer then slid over an open package of Archway oatmeal cookies. She grabbed a cookie, took a large bite, and held the bag out to Jordan.

"Are you kidding me?" He didn't even bother to decline a cookie.

"No, no—I asked him to. It was his last favor. You know, like Molly doing your CD and finding you that job. People love to help out when they're dumping you. Makes them feel better." She glanced up at him as she swallowed her cookie with a coquettish pout. "Those kinds of friends." She pushed the cookie bag away from her.

"Isn't your bank account in your name—or at least under your soc?"

"This is the beauty of it. When my aunt died…"

"Aunt Maegan?"

Summer nodded. Jordan took his hand off his hip and stood back from the table, as if to see her more fully.

"…my parents never registered her DMF in New Jersey because they didn't want her estranged husband to know she'd kicked the bucket. Long story."

"What's a DMF?"

"Death master file. So she's still alive on the social security database…though I think she's dead in some other state records." Summer shrugged. "It's kind of, well, misty: I'm dead in some databases; Aunt Meg's alive. I can't pay taxes as a cadaver, but she's still using credit…" Summer giggled fiendishly. "The banks are nuts. You can get a credit card in your cat's name. Seriously. I know someone who did."

"I'm sure you do," Jordan said under his breath.

"But it was my dad," she went on. "He suggested they keep Aunt Meg's credit card, like, an extra card for them. Mom was too upset about losing her sister to stop him. But a couple of years later, she got scared her brother would find out about it—you know, my uncle Nick. He manages the family holdings. Maegan was his sister too.

"So they stopped using her card. But when I first ran away from home, I knew to take it with me. And I always paid it back. You know, a hundred bucks here, twenty there. Sometimes I didn't use it for years. But I had enough credit to open up a bank account under that soc. So after my dad disowned me for being the unwed mother of a black man's child, I figured it was a good time for Catherine Jane Summers to croak and reemerge as some other person."

"Like Summer Vale? Or are you Aunt Maegan?"

"No," she said. "Neither. That's enough for now."

"Well, you've got to be Maegan…"

"I just use money from the account. I don't use her name for anything else. That would be identity theft."

"But wait. Your blood test—you got it under Cathy Summers. And your bank statements."

"That's enough," she said, standing up.

"So that's why you don't want to marry me," he suggested. "You no longer exist. You're not—legally recognizable?"

"Who said I don't want to marry you? It's *all* I want to do."

"You can't get away with this," he persisted.

"Well, I sure can't pay the piper." She looked at the envelopes on the table, then back at him. "Can you?"

"What about—do you think you should cash in your heirloom necklace and just come clean? Cut all the crap…"

"That necklace," she said slowly, "will not go to waste on taxes for Homeland

Security or the Department of State. That necklace is for our daughter, from her grandmother and great-grandmothers before her."

"We don't have a daughter," Jordan reminded her.

"But we will. One day." She flashed him an angry smile and grabbed the stash of envelopes from the table. Before he knew it, she was throwing them into a pot in the sink.

"What the hell are you doing?" Jordan stood behind her.

"What's called cooking the books. They'll send more dumb collection letters to Khalil's P.O. box. He's supposed to write *return to sender/recipient deceased*, but I guess the collectors are catching on.

"Meanwhile, I'll tell my high school chums to scotch me from that stupid website. I'll just say Geoff is bugging me. No one could stand him. Damn, that site has given me grief—the only way the feds could possibly connect me with the Catherine Jane Summers who supposedly croaked, and disappeared from public record. Why on earth did you look into me, anyway? Everything was better when we left my past in the vault."

She struck a match and Jordan cried, "Hey wait. Let's just cut 'em up."

She shook her head. "I might be tempted to read them."

And she set the sealed envelopes on fire, opening the kitchen window wide so the smoke detector wouldn't squall. Once flames caught and burned the envelopes sufficiently, she cranked on the water faucet, producing a smoke so foul that Jordan stormed out of the apartment, hacking as he did over a bad joint.

Rashad's fifth birthday was Cinco de Mayo, and Summer threw a high-decibel party with sixteen kids screaming, pointing neon Nerf guns and plastic swords at each other, charging through rooms, tripping over wires, picking themselves up and carrying on.

Grown-ups clustered in corners, drinking beer or wine to blunt the assault on their senses. Some busied themselves with Summer and the huge rectangular cake from Carvel's. "Chocolate with yellow and blue roses," she said as she placed five big candles in it. "Like yellow and blue diamonds."

Betty squeezed her way into the kitchen to help, scolding Ian as he butted right into her. When she realized she wasn't needed in the crowded kitchen, Betty edged over to Jordan. Yet more little boys jostled her in their pursuit of big plastic spoons that Summer and another mom were handing out.

"Curtis and I want to meet with you sometime," she said.

"Sure," agreed Jordan, assuming they'd be finalizing summer camp plans. "We'll find a night when we're all free."

"Just you," Betty stipulated, with a quick, odd glance at Summer.

At that moment the lights went out, and pale sky beamed through the windows. Summer held the A major on "*Haaahhhhhhhh…*" Then everyone sang with her: "*-py birthday to you. Happy Birthday, dear Rashad!*"

Wielding their big plastic spoons, kids swarmed around Summer as she and another mom ceremoniously placed the cake on the piano bench. While Summer began counting guests with her finger, the other mom assembled a stack of blue and orange bowls.

But a couple of kids stabbed their spoons right into the cake and slurped off the icing.

"Okay," Summer said lyrically. "So much for bowls."

The children held spoons high in the air and slammed them joyfully into that carcass of chocolate cake, pushing each other aside for more. One thoughtful little girl cordoned off a section especially for Rashad, and kissed his cheek. Some grown-ups whipped out digital cameras to capture the pillage. Others reached for more wine or Scotch.

"No cake for the grown-ups?" asked Betty.

"Just grab a spoon and dig in," Summer invited her. "I've always believed in anarchy."

"No thanks."

"Not your style, eh?" Summer chided.

Betty whispered to Jordan, "Behold the Destruction of the Temple." But Rashad seemed jubilant with his chocolate frosting and guillotined roses. His expression suddenly recalled Summer's dad on that political pamphlet from the locked file. Unmistakably, Jordan thought, the child bore his grandfather's air of dominion.

Summer then appeared with an overloaded spoon and a wink. "Open your mouth, and shut your eyes." When Jordan did, she guided the spoon into his mouth. As he closed it around its gooey sweetness she swept her other hand down his arm and then his thigh, murmuring, "Yummy."

The next evening Jordan met Curtis at a pub nestled below street level and down a couple of steps. Though it wasn't crowded, Curtis had reserved a stool by throwing his linen jacket over it. A frothy-topped beer appeared in a dimpled stein for Jordan.

"I'm not going to shit around with you." Curtis slugged a hit of the brew himself as Jordan took a seat. "Betty saw something disturbing last week. We talked it over and decided you should know." Nervously, Jordan tasted his own tinny and bitter ale.

"You've heard that we might open up a yarn and knitting shop, right?" Jordan recognized the fruit of counseling sessions and a suggestion from Betty's mother. "Well, Betty was checking out a couple of storefronts with a commercial broker. So they're walking, like right around here." Curtis indicated the street outside. "Suddenly Betty recognizes Summer and what's-his-face—you know, Mr. 9/11 Truth."

"Eliot?"

"I guess. And they were huddled together in the doorway of an abandoned building, kind of..." Curtis averted his face, cutting a sudden profile against the dark wall to say "smooching."

Jordan placed his beer stein on the wooden bar, fighting a pang like barbed wire in his chest, a spooky "I knew it" echo.

"Eliot?" he repeated.

Curtis looked back at him. His brown eyes seemed to waver.

"Betty couldn't believe it."

"When you say smooching…"

"Holding each other. Embracing."

In that barb, Jordan tipped back into another place and season, when Molly told him "I'm madly in love with someone." In that same spooky way, he'd realized the word *someone* hadn't referred to him, and he'd snapped in two like a stale biscuit.

Someone I know?

No…and I shouldn't have slept with you last week.

How can you say that?

She'd placed her hand on his as though she knew the only cure for the disease was a shot of it. He could still see her translucent green eyes and cranberry-red sweater—as if his life had skittered on that beat like a needle on vinyl replaying over and over. For two seconds he forgot where he was and the name of this brown-haired friend in a white shirt who said, "Did you hear me?"

What had happened since that over-and-over-and-over? Where exactly did he live? It had all seemed urgent; there was a child…and the name Rashad configured him back into what had become his life.

Curtis stared as though he'd start to cry. "God, I hope I didn't do the wrong thing by telling you. If you were saying it about Betty, I'd be on the floor."

"I'm there." Jordan realized he was stunned silly.

"We thought maybe it wasn't our business, so we just let it go for a couple of days. Then we both admitted that it didn't feel right to keep this from you."

"She saw them together just once?"

Curtis nodded.

"Could I—could I talk to…" he blanked briefly on the wife's name. "Betty? I wanna know exactly what she saw."

Jordan reached for the copper beer and poured it down his throat as if to salve the sting of wire cutting his heart open. Curtis dialed, handed him his phone, and ordered them both another on tap. Betty's voice bled, roseate, into his eardrum.

"I'm completely certain. I recognized her striped dress. And him. If it's consolation to hear this from another female, I see nothing attractive about—"

"Were they kissing?" Jordan interrupted her.

"Just hugging. He was rocking her in his arms."

"So it was a…really sexual hug?"

"Well no, but it was more than friendly."

Instead of going home, Jordan got on the subway and headed out to Z's, to let him in on the breaking news.

"Oh, don't feed her red meat" was his old friend's first recommendation, as he packed up for an audio gig that evening. "Don't get all crazy and start making accusations. Could have been a momentary thing, seen out of context. I can practically promise you they're not fucking."

"You're saying that to console me, aren't you?"

Z stopped packing his amps. "You know comfort's not my style, Jo-Jo. I just think if they were seriously fucking, they wouldn't play kissy-face in doorways. Hey, when I was seeing gorgeous Sabina, who was married to a diplomat—remember her? Funny that we used her name in that song, 'Lip Service.' Oh, we guarded that secret with our lives. Wouldn't even take the same elevator down from her apartment. You follow?"

"Yeah, but why was she in Eliot's arms?"

Z shook his head with disgust. "Who the fuck knows? Sounds like a father thing to me. If I were you, I'd cut out of there for a while. She's been driving you batshit for weeks."

Jordan shook his head. "She's my fiancée. I'm not bowing out so easily."

"Then put your foot down. You can't be hearing this shit."

Jordan closed his eyes. Z continued to assemble equipment and load the truck. As he took leave, Z welcomed Jordan to crash in the basement as long as he needed to—a few hours, a few days, a few years.

By dusk, Jordan noticed calls from Summer on his phone. She asked where he was, and eventually he called back to say he'd be staying at Z's for a while.

"What do you mean 'for a while'?"

"I don't know. I need some time to think," he said.

"Think about what?"

"Jordan stuff."

A taut silence followed.

"Who is she? *Are you with Molly?*"

"No, I'm with Tillie. We're smooching in doorways on the Lower East Side and—actually, I'm writing a song. My first song with lyrics." He howled hoarsely, "*I'm a one-woman man, and I'm looking for a one-man woman! Toodle-loodle loo, no two-timing will do for me and you.*' What do you think? You stopped writing songs. Someone's got to keep those fires burning."

All she did was snap the phone off.

Jordan chortled cynically. "You got that right, baby," he said to the silence and went to turn on Coltrane and drink another beer. He felt thirsty, like he was swallowing sandpaper as he settled back on Z's pillows. He'd spoken to her from those very pillows when she'd been in Vermont and said she missed him so much that she couldn't hear music in the birdsong or her son's voice.

"So fucking unfair to Rashad," he said aloud. "If you could 'overcome your pride for him.' Hey, Khalil. She should overcome her insanity for him."

He shut his eyes and saw only her face.

Around 10 p.m. the buzzer rang. Jordan answered the door, and there she stood in an old leather jacket, lumpy dress, and scuffed, secondhand boots. Wind blew hair across her eyes and brow. She pouted endearingly with that lower lip he'd always adored.

"Are you leaving me?" she asked, her voice dithering. "Please…please…why didn't you come home? You're not leaving us. Please."

"What's going on with Eliot?" he asked, arms over his chest.

"Oh, Eliot. Is that what this is about?"

"What's going on?" Jordan repeated.

"Did he tell you about his dappy crush on me?"

"No. But someone did."

"Who?" She looked appalled and stepped forward. "Jordan, please…don't leave us."

He beckoned for her to come in, and she followed him into Z's kitchen with its lacquered brick wall and shelves of pottery.

"Where's Roo?" he asked.

"With Barney and Betty. I said it was an emergency, and they were great."

"You want some tea? I think he has some mint or green."

"Green," she said.

Jordan plunked two of Mariana's ceramic mugs on the picnic table that Z had found on a deserted campground, taken home, stripped, and shellacked.

"Did your mom make these?" Summer looked to the bottom of the mug for a signature.

Jordan said, "Uh-huh" as he poured water into the kettle and turned on the gas. Unlike their stove at home, which was splattered with coffee, grease, and tomato sauce, Z's range was shiny and spotless.

"I want some honesty," he said, when the water had come to a boil. Carrying the kettle to the table, he recalled Z's advice: no red meat, foot down. He poured hot water over the tea bags in a hiss and perceived that she was cowering, that for once he had power. He slid onto the bench across from her.

"You're having an affair with Eliot. Yes or no?"

"No! He wants to. He's been pursuing me. But I don't feel physical desire—I told you, he has body odor. But my ego is slurping it up."

"Have you kissed him?"

"No."

"Touched his dick?"

"Oh, god no."

"Promise?"

"On my sister's life, I promise I haven't done anything with Eliot Waxmann but hold his hand, let him stroke my hair, and hug me, fully vertical and fully clothed."

"Well, what the fuck is that about? You're my girlfriend, my fiancée!"

Summer sighed and looked penitent. Her description of their activities coincided with Betty's citing and Z's theory, but it crushed Jordan nevertheless.

"When did this start?" he persisted.

"Okay," she said faintly, trying to sip tea that was still too hot. "I've gone to his apartment a couple of times for guitar lessons. You know he lives in artist housing with a roommate who never leaves."

Jordan nodded, remembering the small, smelly room with old green shades.

"Just saying we've never been there alone. About a month ago we're singing Woody Guthrie songs and suddenly Eliot confesses that he's 'fallen head-over-heels in love' with me, that he knows his cause is doomed but that I 'epitomize his female ideal of beauty, brains, and talent' and that he loves being in my presence—he called me a goddess. And he begged to kiss me, just once. I said I couldn't. But I did find it…flattering—to be so wanted, and approved-of. It soothed me. You're very tough on me, you know."

Jordan took a sip of tea that was too hot to taste.

"Tough on you," he muttered. "If I was nicer I'd be a punching bag."

"Eliot didn't drop it, when we met after that—he'd say stuff like 'I know I'm too old for you, but you're too old for Jordan.' He said by the time you hit thirty-five you'll want a younger woman. Guys always do." She gazed across the table. "I've wondered if we'll be the kind of couple that marries and then divorces eight months later, ready to tear each other's limbs off."

"I think Eliot can shut up about us."

"Sometimes we fight so hard—and can you really, Jordan, can you really imagine still being with me in seven years? When you're thirty-seven and I'm forty-five? I just don't see it. You're too cute and good. There's got to be a catch. Like those stretches when my mother was normal again…and sometimes she actually was. But the minute I thought, 'Wow, we have a mom like other kids,' she was on a bender. I've never known a time when the other shoe hasn't dropped. Why should this be different?"

Her questions were fair, and there were no immediate answers.

"And hell," she muttered, "'her boyfriend left her' sounds so much better than 'her husband dumped her.' Doesn't it?"

Summer's face was flushed, as though she couldn't breathe. Jordan began to feel guilty about upsetting her and then remembered that she was betraying him for a conspiracy theorist crank with body odor—to whom he'd introduced her.

He realized how pathetic their dilemma was, how it could completely unravel their engagement if he allowed it to get to him. "Remember," he began, "both of our parents are still married. Your mom sounds like she's doing better. You idealize Arman and Mariana, but they've had their troubles. When we were kids Arman disappeared for a year. We were told he was abroad with his family, and I remember asking when he'd be back. Years later, we learned they were having a trial separation. But they missed each other. People get over stuff. We will too."

Summer sipped her tea, hair falling over her face.

"I fuck things up." She glanced at him, brushing the hair away with her fingers. "I've warned you many times. Yes, my parents are still married, and by all reports my mom's sober. But they're both stark raving mad, so…does it even matter? Why do you want to risk marrying this Molotov cocktail of DNA? You could find someone easier, younger, pretty…"

"Young and pretty," he scoffed. "Hussies. I'd rather be with a seasoned woman."

"Seasoned? That your latest euphemism for *old*? Speaking of which," she said, "now I have a question: have you seen Molly since you moved in with me?"

Jordan blew on his tea. His head throbbed from the beers he'd had with Curtis and later with Z. "Seen her?" he asked. "*As in seeing* someone? Not that way. I just hung out with her once."

Summer looked horrified, nearly shattering her teacup by slamming it on the table.

"Don't pivot." Jordan's anger returned. "We're talking about you and Eliot. I wasn't hugging on Molly, stroking her hair, and calling her a goddess. She took me and Z and Claudia out for cocktails one night. They came to the Susquehanna when you were on tour with Shazan. I wasn't even expecting them."

"It's become quite the mecca for our exes, hasn't it?" she snarled. "Geoff Ahlstrom skulking around with binoculars, Molly buying drinks for the gang…"

"Z ran into her and Eugenia last summer. They're friends too. Look, we've had very little contact. She doesn't call or email me, she doesn't seek me out."

"But you never told me you even saw her."

"Well, you never told me about Eliot. Hey, we haven't fucking talked to each other, Summer! This is our most open conversation in months."

Summer pushed her teacup aside and sank her head into her hands. She remained that way for a minute or two, rocking slightly as Jordan studied the uneven part in her hair with its pale hints of scalp as he sipped his own tea with a resentful heart pounding. What a clever little play, to discuss Molly now.

"He's dying." Her voice creaked out. "I'll never see him again. Deb got to say goodbye. Even though she hates him. He didn't even walk her down the aisle—prick."

Jordan brought his tea to the other side of the table. Uneasily, he sat beside her. He wasn't sure if she was crying, she seemed so hidden.

"He could be odious," she continued. "Biggest jerk you'd ever meet. But not a phony moment. Even when he lied, and he lied plenty—he was a fucking Republican—he wasn't phony…it was who he was."

"He called me a little squirt."

"He was just being my dad. Not a good dad. But Dad."

She rolled her head onto Jordan's shoulder and sighed. Consoled by the scent of her skin and shampoo, he put his arm around her.

"Still love me?" she asked.

He nodded, his stubble brushing her forehead.

"And you're not leaving us?"

He shook his head no.

"Let's set a date for the wedding," he said softly. "Tonight. Let's figure it out. You stick with it, and I stick with it. No bullshit." Jordan hoped this was what Z meant by putting his foot down, but somehow he doubted it.

"Who told you about Eliot? It must have been my sister, wasn't it? She's the only one who knows—she and Eliot's slob roommate. Did she call you? She was furious with me. Said I was being a shithead to both of you."

"She's right. But it wasn't Deb," said Jordan. "It was someone here in New York who saw you two cuddling on the street."

"Z," she guessed defiantly, raising her head from his shoulder. "That's why you're here, isn't it?"

"Not saying. What's important is that it happened, and it's got to stop."

"It will stop. I'll call him now if you want."

"We'll talk to him together," said Jordan. "In person. And he's gonna get a piece of my mind, if not a fist in his sorry mug. But listen, when we get married—Summer, I don't want this 'open marriage, polyamory' crap. I want loyalty."

"Me too. I've just never let myself hope for that."

"What about with Khalil?"

"The minute I started believing he'd stay with me, he said goodbye. I've trained myself…"

"…not to trust."

She blinked simply, as though to say, "That's right. And that's me." And when you marry someone, you take that "me" for better or worse.

"You wouldn't have forgiven me if I hadn't come out here tonight and made my case. Would you?" she asked.

"Maybe not," he admitted. She looked forlorn, and he didn't want to remind her that she didn't believe in forgiveness.

"We know each other pretty well, don't we?"

As she snuggled back against him, he felt her nose and wet lips on his shoulder, heard her moan with sorrow and relief. His right hand found her left and he whispered: "Cathy Summers. This finger needs a ring."

"Please don't worry about that." Her breath fell sweetly on his neck. "Diamonds come from racism, slavery, and exploitation. I just—I wanna be like we are now."

Several hours later, they had collapsed on Z's pile of pillows in the basement. Jordan stirred when Z came in, shutting the door with a hearty thwack. He must have thought Jordan was awake, because lights were on.

"Hey Jo-Jo Mojo," he called. Then he stopped short, probably seeing their faces side-by-side on the pillows with closed eyes. Jordan heard Z exclaim under his breath: "Oohhhh, shit."

PART TWO

Hiding the hurt or fighting and bickering
Thinking that we've had our fill
If the lies don't do it then the honesty will
But I am a fool and I water you every day.
　　　　　　　　—Dean Friedman, "Solitaire"

AUGUST 2006

The morning was clammy but not hot enough to warrant air-conditioning. They had to save pennies now, not only for their wedding in October, but also for medical and legal expenses that might never be reimbursed. In the full heat of summer, when work and cash were low, they'd taken the hit. As if desperate to recover some normalcy, Summer coaxed Rashad into shorts and a shirt for day camp.

"What about you?" she asked Jordan. "Will you see the sun today?"

"I'm waiting to hear from the D.A.'s office and Lydia."

"Lydia?"

"Lydia Pomerantz, that attorney from Curtis. Think I'll stay put."

"Are you scared?" asked Rashad, and Jordan shook his head no.

"I'll be all right."

"But, will they come again for you?"

"No. The police have 'em. We're safe, Roo."

They hugged and Jordan said, "See you tonight" with a premonition that he might not.

Summer leaned in for a kiss before she took her son to camp and continued to her lunch shift across town. "Don't stay in all day," she begged Jordan. "Or else they'll really have won. Like the terrorists."

"But there were no terrorists, Summer. Remember? All smoke and mirrors. Government magic show of thermite and controlled demolition."

"I'll clobber those scumwads for how they've hurt you and my son."

"We'll let the law handle this."

"Like they will."

She'd been spewing threats all morning, like "I'll set his fucking house in Toms River on fire" or "I'll do a drive-by." Jordan knew she felt helpless. Still, he reminded her that Z said their chances sounded good for multi-count felony charges of gang assault, and aggravated assault, possibly even deeming them hate crimes, with all those words about Rashad's background.

"We gotta nab these jerks on as many counts as possible," he said as she shuffled toward the door.

Lydia had advised him to press civil and criminal charges, and to proceed with the criminal case first. The D.A.'s office was already pursuing prosecution. She'd told him to write out exactly what happened while it was fresh in his mind. Then she'd get him the names, with photographs, of each defendant.

After Summer left with Roo, Jordan rolled a joint and found part of the sofa where no newspapers and bags were piled up. On a yellow legal pad he began to scribble his recollections in ballpoint pen.

On Clinton Street between Broome and Delancey the evening of August 16 with Rashad Pierre Summers, the son of my fiancée.

He crossed that out and started at the beginning.

I'm Jordan Radfar, 30 years old and a lifelong resident of NY State. For a year and 8 months, I've lived in Manhattan with my fiancée, Cathy Summers, and her 5-year-old son, Rashad, who I plan to adopt when we marry. I'm a musician and met Cathy when my band auditioned to back her vocals.

Last April an ex-boyfriend of Cathy's, Geoff Ahlstrom, showed up at a gig. Cathy wasn't there. He watched my band and me through binoculars and didn't speak to any of us. But on the evening of August 16, Ahlstrom's brother, Frank, and four other guys with shaved heads and tattoos jumped Rashad and me when we were walking home from his day camp at the Pitt Street pool.

Jordan drew on the joint, savoring its pungent tang. He wished he could say he'd sensed the predators' approach, but he hadn't. He and Rashad had been talking about the beach, and suddenly he'd heard the shuffle of footfalls and felt himself down in the rubble. Absently, he now rubbed his sore chin before drawing on the joint again so good and hard that it scorched his throat and he coughed forcefully.

Then the phone rang, and he figured it might be Lydia. But a warm, familiar voice cried: "Jordan! Are you okay?" The caller ID also seemed mysteriously familiar.

"Who is this?"

After a brief silence, during which he coughed a bit more, she said, "Molly. Calling from *your* cell phone."

"And how do you have *my* cell phone?"

"Some guy called this morning and said he found it under the Williamsburg Bridge. My number was the last one dialed. I did have a call from you on Wednesday. Shit, Jordan. I thought you were murdered."

"Almost—I was assaulted, with Summer's kid."

Molly sounded shocked and spoke slowly. "What the hell happened?"

"I'm just writing up my felony complaint. Bunch of skinheads jumped us in a lot."

"No way."

"Oh, believe it. They ran off with the kid, and my sax."

"Were they caught?"

"Cops got' em in the holding pen, 'cause it seems most of them have a string of priors. There are eyewitnesses—a mom from Rashad's day camp, and three cops."

"Is the kid okay?"

"Doing better than I am now."

"Well, that's helpful. You'll have a slam-dunk indictment with cops as witnesses. Shouldn't I get your phone to you? Can I take you for coffee or something?"

"Honestly…" Jordan sighed. "I don't even want to go out the door."

"Don't you need your phone?"

"Probably."

"Well, I was planning to drive downtown anyway. Genie and I have guests at her place in the West Village, and I was going over there. I could swing by you first, if you'd like."

"Yeah, sure," he said.

☆

Not wanting to look like a basket case, he had thrown on a gray T-shirt and tight, faded jeans. Since the attack he hadn't eaten much, and even his Adam's apple looked sharper. They stood in front of the big living room window, gazing down at East Broadway where Molly had parked her navy-blue Fiat, she explaining that it always netted her a parking space into which no other vehicle could fit. "Gene and I call it 'Parking Jigsaw Puzzles.'"

But of course, the little Fiat was their "city car." They drove out of town in the vintage Starfire convertible that Molly had gotten Eugenia two years ago for her "big 4-0." Such details stoked painful references, not only to the lover for whom Molly had abandoned him, but to the painfully elusive ease of their wealth—compared with his ongoing struggle.

"I love East Broadway," Molly commented. "It probably looked the same in 1936 and 1963. Like my street. We need places that don't change, or everything will become one big strip mall in cellophane. Speaking of—" She proceeded in that maternal tone Jordan remembered from their days together, "Why do you have all that junk on your terrace?"

Glancing left with her, Jordan noticed that Gus' file cabinets had rusted over the months they had been out there, and the cartons of books looked soggy and jaundiced. "You've got a great view," Molly continued. "Southeastern light. This could be a really nice place." Turning back to the room, she appraised the throng of amps, mics and dollies, instrument cases, mountains of newspapers that Summer intended to read one day, dirty plates, old takeout tins streaked with sauce, stray and muddy socks from Rashad. "You never were one for housekeeping," she concluded, "but you've hit a new low."

"You know me. Whenever I try to get organized, monkeys fly out of my butt."

Molly smirked and he felt wistful and relaxed, just looking at her in an apple-green blouse that echoed her hazel eyes. By appealing contrast, her cheeks were pink from days in the sun, her little nose peeling.

"Truth is, we're both really stressed," he explained, his eyes still enjoying the palette of Molly's presence. "Summer's a waitress four days a week, she sings a little, I run around gigging, giving lessons—when I'm home I want to chill, not put myself to work."

Molly strolled through the living room. "Maybe," she remarked, "you could build a wall unit." She pointed to the wall across from the long window over the sofa. "Store all the amps and equipment at floor level, and install your speakers in the shelves. You'd still have room for books. And think of the floor space…"

"Jesus, I don't need your feng shui," he barked. "I was just fucking beaten up."

Molly bit her lip. "I know, Jordan. But we're beyond feng shui. Your apartment is a health hazard. I, uh, I even think you have carpet beetles."

"We do not."

"I'm pretty sure I saw a couple."

"You didn't."

"This place is a tinderbox waiting for a match."

Jordan rolled his eyes and repeated "wall unit" with disdain, much as Summer would. Molly looked insulted and it struck him that form, light, and color were her art, that she was naturally visual in a way that he and Summer were not. Their lack of decor grated on Molly the way his students' lack of musical phrasing grated on him.

"Feel it!" he'd implore at their lessons. "Modulate. Hold some notes longer, play some louder, look at how the composer wrote the dynamics." Maybe that was all she meant to say now.

So he conceded: "Guess a wall unit's not a bad idea. We just don't have the cash."

"Doesn't Z do carpentry? And aren't you having a big birthday this year? If you're interested, we could work something out."

"I already had that big birthday," he said, miffed again. "Last year."

Molly looked perplexed. "You weren't born in seventy-six?"

"Seventy-five," he corrected her.

"My bad. Well, I owe you a present. You decide what."

"Cash?" he begged, trying not to sound frantic. "I gotta go to the dentist, get my teeth checked out. The scrumbags pushed me down pretty hard. I'll probably get reimbursed, but not for a while."

Concern swept Molly's face as she reached for her purse—which, unlike Summer's, was not scratched up and crumbling but looked as shiny as though she'd just purchased it. Everything about Molly radiated taste and coordination, even the flyaway strands of her dark hair, which always looked sexy and hinted at her wildness, her "flickery hair" she called it.

First she took his cell phone from her purse—for which he thanked her—and then her checkbook. She scribbled on a check and tore it out for him.

"I like to remember milestone birthdays. Sorry I let this one pass."

Jordan looked at the turquoise check in his hands for two thousand dollars, relief coursing through him. He thought, ironically, that he could now buy Summer an engagement ring.

"Molly, you're an angel. Could I trouble you…" he began. "Could you write it to the Jordan Radfar Trio rather than to me personally? That way, she won't have to know about it, and she won't kill me."

Molly took the check back, and he watched her add 'the' and 'Trio' around his name. "Why would she kill you?"

"She gets jealous if I even say a word that begins with *M*. She's crazy that way—not that *she* didn't cheat on me with this seventy-year-old creep whose gut is so big I doubt he's seen his dick in thirteen years, and I told him so in those words."

"Excuse me?" Molly asked, slightly alarmed.

"They didn't actually fuck. It was just ego balm for her."

"Jordan," she began, "are you sure you should marry her? From what you've told me she sounds troubled, and the trench of marriage can be tough to dig out of. I see what my brother and sister-in-law go through—"

"Non-negotiable," he interrupted her. "She's not always easy, but we need each other. We're like a family with her son. I mean, look, is Eugenia totally cool that you're here with me?" To emphasize that point, he stood beside her as seductively as possible, hands hitched at his small hips.

"She might be a little upset when I mention this," Molly admitted. "But I wouldn't say she'd kill me."

"Are you even gonna tell her?"

"Of course," replied Molly. "We don't keep secrets. She knows I have your cell phone and wondered why you called me on Wednesday. I had no answer. Why did you, by the way?"

"I needed someone to prove I'm not a conspiracy nut. Remember, we used to talk about all that, back when we were dating?"

"Kind of."

"Well, Summer has beliefs about the government, you know: not only did they stage 9/11, but they unleashed the AIDS virus, they seeded the clouds to create Katrina, they even make sure that fire engines in New York sound super loud so intellectuals can't properly think, they knock off anyone who 'tells the truth…'"

"She seems to have survived intact," Molly commented.

"Intact enough to piss off these so-called patriotic skinheads."

At that moment her phone jingled and Molly groaned.

"This guy is unrelenting. I've ignored his last five calls, so I'd better take this one. Pardon me, please." Then she said, "How are you, Saul?" into the phone as Jordan watched with fascination. "Yes, I'm sorry. I'm a couple of days out from a new ad campaign." She was silent for a while.

Jordan went to bury her check in his wallet. He'd have time to deposit it before Summer got home from her waitressing shift. If she knew about it, she'd claim Molly was trying to "buy him." That was how she thought.

"I understand," Molly said to the unrelenting guy on the phone. "But as I mentioned, I don't want to be the go-between, the messenger everyone kills."

Quiet again, Molly picked up a napkin with a smear of soy sauce on it, made a dismayed face, found the trash can beneath the sink, and plinked the napkin into it, phone at her ear.

"Yes, I know," she kept saying as she paced around Jordan's living room. "But it's not my place to tell Dahlia what to do. I've let her know that you and I have been in touch, and I'll tell her that we spoke again today."

Molly walked by the urn with parched, browning roses for Gus that Summer refused to discard and did a double take. Jordan steered her away, his hands on her unthinkably soft arms.

"I'm sure you'll hear from her, but I can't say when. I can't make it happen, Saul." Jordan heard her exhale as she did when she was exasperated. Finally, the call ended. Pushing aside a pile of books and a paper bag with stale donuts from last week, Molly wiggled her shapely butt onto the sofa, which was filled with crumbs.

"You know, I feel bad for this guy," she began, shutting her phone. "He's married, lives in a suburb of Chicago, manages a shopping mall. He has three teenagers and a perfunctory marriage, but for six years he's been having a secret, passionate affair with Tamara's sister. You remember my sister-in-law, Tamara?"

"Of course. She's gorgeous."

"So is her sister, Dahlia, who's single."

Jordan sat tenuously on a pile of Summer's old *New York Times* op-eds as though it were a stool.

"He was talking about leaving his wife for her."

"Don't they all?" Jordan asked.

"They planned a trip for Dahlia's birthday two weeks ago. But the day before they were supposed to leave, Saul's daughter got into an accident at gymnastics camp. Poor girl has a brain contusion."

"Shit, that's bad." Jordan didn't know exactly what a brain contusion was, but he felt glad that neither he nor Rashad had suffered anything so serious at the hands of the skinheads.

"Dahlia, of course, understood the change of plans, but she didn't understand why he called me the day it happened, and not her."

"Because it sounds like the guy's got a thing for *you*." Jordan pointed at her.

"He doesn't," protested Molly, shaking her head. "I'm just his lifeline to Dahlia now. She refuses to speak to him—she cut him off, cold turkey, after six years."

"You're just too irresistible, Molly. You don't mean to, but you make trouble."

"No!" She smiled and blushed. "He actually was in crisis—he thought his daughter was going to die, or lose her brain function. Thank goodness she's okay, but it was chancy for a while."

Just then he heard scratching at the door, like someone playing with the lock.

"Goddamn it!" screamed the man who had been attacked two days ago, bounding across the room to lock the chain into its catch on the door. "Get the fuck away, or I'll call the cops!"

"It's just me," he heard Summer call back. Why was she home so early? He opened the door and there she stood, in the dress that looked like faded wallpaper in which she'd left this morning, her hair in a messy bun with strands falling in her eyes and sandals held together by duct tape.

"Jesus, Jordan," she said, plunging her hands onto his shoulders. "They've made a jumpy old man out of you." Then she stepped into the foyer, proclaiming: "I will personally carve their guts into linguine and graffiti their scrotums—" She stopped when she noticed Molly chuckling on the sofa. Suddenly Summer's expression changed from playful woman to guileless little girl.

"Lydia?" she asked Jordan. She walked across the living room, Jordan at her heels. "Are you Lydia the Litigator? Or sorry, I mean Petra the Prosecutor?"

Molly stood up and extended her hand.

"I'm Molly," she said. "Nice to finally meet you."

Summer couldn't have looked more shocked if a layer of skin had been steamed off her face. Not only did she refuse Molly's hand, but she turned to Jordan with an expression he'd never seen on anyone.

He quickly grabbed the cell phone from his pocket.

"Look what's back," he volunteered. "Some guy found it and called Molly. She was just dropping it off."

Apparently this was the worst thing to say. Summer scrunched up her mouth, puffed her cheeks, and squinted first at Jordan then at Molly. Misinterpreting the expression as a joke, Molly giggled and said rather warmly, "You're hilarious. I love your songs."

Through anger-slanted eyes, Summer took in Molly.

"Those lyrics," Molly continued. "What was it?" She put a hand to her forehead, and Jordan peeked at Summer. Her face was purple and her cheeks ballooning. "*When your girlfriend loves another girl and she's not even gay it's a killer…happens to the best of men, including but not limited to Henry Miller.* Oh, you nailed me." Molly laughed. "Perturbed my girlfriend for a while, but she came around. At first she was kind of like, 'Why should the world know our little history?' But then she said, 'Hell, why not?'" Molly looked from Summer to Jordan, her eyes shining. "We appreciate that you made her 'Sabina.' That was thoughtful. And, oh my goodness, your songs about Jordan are marvelous."

Summer's lips began to curl like a rabid dog's.

"Could you please stop being catatonic?" Jordan begged her.

"I lost my job," she announced into his face, as though Molly weren't there. "Mike just canned me. For no reason. And I never got a callback from the audition. Even that half-assed manager from Albert Pico that you forced me to sign with doesn't return my calls."

She about-faced, stomped into the bedroom, and slammed the door.

"I'd better get going," said Molly, collecting her purse and sweater.

Jordan walked her to the door and mumbled, "Sorry 'bout the outburst."

She looked at him sympathetically. "Seems like—an emotional breaking point?"

He whispered again, "I'm sorry."

"Gene hasn't shown you her best side either."

"She's been snarky to me but not sociopathic."

They stood outside the apartment with the door partly ajar.

"Listen, if you need help," Molly offered him, "don't be a stranger."

"Thanks," he said, drawing her into a grateful hug, recalling how she was slight, like a bird—not as voluptuous as Summer. Her fresh, floral perfume smelled like paradise.

"Stay out of trouble," she said before walking down the hallway. He lifted his fingers to wave, and she lifted hers back before boarding the elevator.

When he looked around, Summer glared at him with raw, glassy eyes.

"What?" he barked. "I don't have a right to thank her and say goodbye?"

She shook her head and snapped, "Asshole—you've been carrying on with her all along, haven't you?" Her lower lip quivered.

"Oh stop it." He let the door bang shut as he stepped inside. "I've seen her twice in three years."

"All this time…" she repeated, starting to cry, covering her face with her hand.

"All this time"—Jordan marched into the living room, kicking aside an empty pizza box—"while your ex-boyfriend was plotting how to jump me and your kid, while Skip was gossiping about you having HIV and Eliot was stroking your mermaid hair, I had no contact with Molly. At all! She came here today to return my phone that your ex's henchmen grabbed from me."

"Why did she have your phone?" Summer wailed at him.

"Someone found her number on it."

"You must call her all the time."

"No way! Just check for yourself." He quickly handed his phone to her. "You just look at the record of my outgoing calls and texts."

"You probably erased them."

"Believe what you want," he retorted. The facts clearly were no competition for her fantasies about what was happening. "I promise you I called Molly once this year—on Wednesday, 'cause I thought she'd fucking help when we were under attack."

"Help how? What would she do?" Summer looked at the phone in her shaking hand, clearly too upset to figure out how to access his records, and tossed it onto the sofa.

"You didn't tell me she was pretty," she stammered through her tears. "I thought she was some schoolmarmish, chubby dyke you admired—not a hot little Irish-looking icon, so stylishly thin and feminine."

"I never said she was schoolmarmish."

"But you didn't say she was prettier than me. Oh, of course you still love her.

She's adorable, filthy rich, not neurotic…"

"And she's with Eugenia, and she's plenty quirky when you know her well."

Summer rushed to the terrace, wiping her eyes, and threw open the door. Horrified that she might jump off, Jordan followed her out to the piles of rotting books and vinyls, the crusty file cabinets. She stooped to rummage through a crate of videocassettes and eventually produced *A Place in the Sun*, his mother's favorite old movie. From the corner of his eye, Jordan noted that Molly's little blue Fiat, sixteen floors below them, was angling out of its parking space on East Broadway and Montgomery.

"Do you know this?" Summer asked, holding a VHS cassette to his nose. "About a man and two women?"

"Yeah. With Monty Clift."

"So handsome you can inhale him. He was just thirty in this film. Your age. In love with this rich, dark-haired chick played by Elizabeth Taylor, but he's got a ball-and-chain factory girl who he's knocked up and has to marry."

The cover showed Clift and Taylor in various shades of yellow and sepia against a sunset.

"Remind you of someone, Jordan?"

"Oh for fuck's sake."

"That woman is so not gay!" Summer screamed, throwing the cassette inside the apartment. "She didn't look at me the way gay women look at me, and she didn't look at you the way gay women look at you."

"You know she's not *gay*—you wrote a song about it."

"The two of you would've shagged right here on Gus' sofa, wouldn't you?"

Jordan grabbed her arm, guiding her back into the living room. He didn't want her to know he was worried that she would jump sixteen stories from the terrace, or that he'd watched Molly's car merge with westbound traffic. She shook his hand off her arm like a bratty child but came back inside.

"I wasn't born yesterday." She bent down to pick up the cassette and wag it at him again. "I know this kind of thing happens. He led a totally double life, this George…George," she repeated the character's name, her father's name.

"She just told me how messy our apartment is and raved about Eugenia," Jordan reported angrily. "And some guy called from Chicago who's in love with a friend of hers."

"It still bugs you that she talks about Eugenia, doesn't it?"

"You know what really bugs me, Summer? That we rush to Fourteenth Street with our little busking dimes to pay off Con Ed before they kill our juice. But she and Eugenia can pop into their convertible or fly anywhere in the world without worrying if they can afford it."

"That's not what bugs you. You envy her 'cause she's not depressive like we are."

"We? Excuse me, *we*? I'm not depressive."

"Just listen to you." And she imitated him expertly: "'I'm not depressive.' You sure as shit are or you wouldn't put up with me."

"I fight you on it all the time," he reminded her.

"I envy people like her," she said, squinting at him. "It's not money that gives her freedom. It's her stability. She's so normal she probably even thinks she's weird. But hey"—Summer imitated Molly with a coy wink—"if you need help, don't be a stranger."

"Well, I don't plan to be—'cause we may *need* her help. We're fucking in trouble, Summer."

There's always a diner scene in American films where someone like Jack Nicholson upends a table. But Jordan had never witnessed it offscreen, until Summer bent down and pushed the coffee table over, shattering several glasses and a dish—though not Jordan's ashtray with his joint.

"I'll find that bitch, and I will blind her with my hairspray!" she cried, charging into the bedroom to scoop up coins and dollar bills from her dresser top, packing her purse with a bottle of hairspray, a plastic comb, and a box of tampons. Jordan trailed her like a goalie trying to block her.

"I damn hate her...I hate her..."

"You're not leaving home in this shape."

"I'll do what I want...I'll go have a cozy chat with Eugenia."

Jordan grabbed her as she tried to bolt and held her against the bedroom wall, his arm cutting into her soft, round belly. She grunted, knocked her head against his, and tried to bite his earlobes.

"Let's fuck," he whispered, and swiveled her to the bed. They bounced onto the mattress with its scrambled sheets. As he lay on top of her, her legs parted and she shook off her sandals, which were broken and easily shed. There they found peace for a moment, their hearts beating together.

"It's sad," she murmured, clearing her throat. "She's been here, in this apartment. Our spell is broken."

"Our spell isn't broken."

"You know it is."

Beneath Summer's dress, he found her panties soaked at the crotch.

"Gotta change my tampon," she whispered. "So bloody bloody."

He closed his eyes, imagining her wet and molten, and undid his fly. She grabbed his cock with exciting aggression.

"George Eastman, are you thinking about Angela Vickers?"

Jordan laughed, shivered in the heat, and then the phone rang from the kitchen.

"Oh shit. It's probably Lydia or the D.A.'s office."

Sighing, he got up and hobbled to the kitchen, pants around his calves and his "erection at half-mast," as Molly used to say.

"Hi everyone," Betty called breezily over voice mail. "We've got tickets to Cirque du Soleil tonight. Could we invite Rashad along? I'll try Summer's cell..."

Thinking it provident to keep Rashad out of the house later, Jordan picked up and gasped, "Betty. Hey. That sounds great."

Meanwhile, Summer stepped into a pair of high-top sneakers, threw her crumbling purse over her shoulder and raced out the front door, which banged after her.

Jordan cleaned all afternoon, now perceiving their apartment as the pigsty Molly had seen. He kicked the rug aside and swept shards and grains of the broken dishes from the overturned table. He dusted, scrubbed floors of their entrenched coffee and ice cream stains, threw out bags of old food, stacked all the newspapers in one corner, and lined the amps and instrument cases against the wall. Most important, he rolled up the big, grimy rug with its mud and jelly stains. As he lugged it to the compactor room, he noticed tiny white bugs crawling in it and wondered if those were carpet beetles.

When he returned, the living room looked bigger and brighter.

Half-undressed, he'd been in no shape to chase Summer when she'd dashed out earlier. But once he'd pulled up his pants, put on shoes and ventured out, he couldn't find her anywhere. He'd cruised up and down East Broadway, around to Grand Street, to the doughnut shop and liquor store. He went into the bank and deposited Molly's check. Then he bought mops, sponges, and Ajax for his cleanup effort.

He called Summer's phone all afternoon but never got an answer. "I'm sorry, honey," he kept saying. "Come home and we'll talk, okay?" He added in the last message: "Our spell isn't broken. Let's continue where we left off."

But she neither called nor showed up at the door.

He knew Molly had been the last straw in her agonizing week. Summer clearly had imagined her predecessor as less attractive, more glum and dumpy—anything to make Molly manageable, because Molly would always be dear to him. He simply wished Summer would understand that Molly's destiny with him was so different from hers. Sometimes her radar for adult nuance was uncanny; other times she oversimplified to the point of sounding ludicrous. He glanced at the Liz Taylor videocassette on the floor and the *Summer Vale Was an Inside Job* poster on the wall. He tore it down and ripped it up, shoving the scraps into a garbage bag.

When his cell phone rang he jumped. But it was his mother, confirming their plans for Fire Island. They'd come out next weekend and stay through Labor Day, making it a nine-day getaway.

"We must talk about the wedding plans, Jordie," she said.

The sky had softened to pale lavender—that eastern sky, a supporting actor in the drama of sunset, reflecting the world's loss without blazing it. He sat drinking beer in the darkness that followed. Eventually he called Betty, who was walking home from Cirque du Soleil with Curtis and the boys. Jordan felt overjoyed to hear that Rashad had loved the jugglers and acrobatic flyers and that he hadn't spoken about the assault.

But they hadn't heard from Summer either.

"I hope nothing's wrong. She left here in such a huff," he confided.

"She'll be fine," said Betty. "She's been high-strung for weeks."

But Betty called back an hour later with a different take.

"We heard from her. You'd better come over, Jordan. It's bad."

"Is she—is she hurt?"

"She's in jail. She vandalized a car."

Jordan fought a fishy stench, like an unwashed body, on every street the next morning. Only the cooler winds of autumn could dissipate New York City's filth in August. He'd barely slept all night and woke up when he started to dream. His brain felt clammy, his entire body ached from his topple in the vacant lot, and he nearly stepped into a sunburst of fresh barf by the subway entrance.

The address was scribbled on his hand in ballpoint pen, and he soon found himself at Eugenia's Cajun—where "the Big Easy meets the Big Apple" as the review read in the window. "We go light on fat, heavy on flavor, says founder Eugenia Drury. "If you care to be adventurous, our Hot Tamale Pie and Crawfish Étouffée will not disappoint."

Jordan sought neither adventure nor disappointment as he checked the door to see that Eugenia's Cajun was open for business. Among credit card insignias, he read: *We honor food stamps. Speak to our hostess.* A poster on the glass revealed that a Cajun ensemble was playing live that night and that the Skip Harrington Swing Band with Tillie Mack was billed for the next evening—new lovebirds Skip and Tillie had become New York's prime duet.

He shoved the door open, relieved by a blast of air-conditioning and happier aromas. Stencils of New Orleans grillwork lined one wall, and on the other hung Mardi-Gras masks and beads. From the jukebox, a vocalist wailed in Creole to accordion. At the register by the bar, Eugenia chatted with a tan, muscular guy in a T-shirt and bandana. She was even taller than Jordan remembered, her long legs in embroidered leather boots and tight, faded jeans like his own. Jordan took a seat at the bar and peered at the door and his phone. He speed-dialed Molly again.

"I'm at Eugenia's Cajun," he whined. "Really gotta talk to you."

The muscular guy walked away. Eugenia slammed the register drawer shut and spun around on her boot heels. With clear aggravation, she strutted behind the bar and planted herself before Jordan, leaning on the wooden counter with double-jointed arms to stare him down. She was gorgeous, in a "you've got to be kidding" way, with high cheekbones and eyes so grippingly blue they seemed illuminated from behind. Soft, natural blonde hair fell to her shoulders, and strands of it dangled over her forehead. Her lips were a masterpiece of flourish. But no lipstick, blush, or eyeliner for this raw beauty, unsweetened.

"She's not here." The voice issued delicately, like a muted clarinet.

"I need to talk to her."

Eugenia tipped her head toward his phone, which lay faceup on the bar.

"Not answering," he explained.

"Then have some patience."

She stood back behind the bar, one hand on her hip. Damn, was she smoking. A simple, black tank top showcased her long torso, elegant breasts, and smooth, toned arms with a lone tattoo. He had never run miles to nowhere on a treadmill or lifted weights that had no meaning besides what they weighed. He couldn't see doing anything so pointless and exhausting, but she seemed the Miss America of it.

"Did my fiancée come by yesterday and try to talk to you?" he asked.

Eugenia shrugged like she thought he was nuts. "Not that I know of."

"I've got a crisis on my hands," Jordan continued. "She's in jail."

"And you'll be wanting Molly to post bail."

Not only was she hotter than tamale pie, she was painful.

"One of our friends already took care of that. I just want to talk to Molly, if that's okay with you."

"Gotta be okay with her." Eugenia put her other hand on her hip. "If I may ask, what did your fiancée do to land herself behind bars? In this city, that takes work."

"She was caught in a parking lot keying a car."

"Who's car?"

"It belongs to one of the douchebags that pushed me down on the street. Still got a scar." He raised his chin to Eugenia. The tan, muscular guy in the bandana reappeared and looked over her shoulder at Jordan.

"Street brawl," Eugenia explained, removing her hands from her hips.

"Just walking along with our five-year-old, minding my own business, picking him up from day camp, and before you know it…"

"They tossed his phone into the gutter," Eugenia explained further to the guy, who appeared to be her bartender. "After he called Molly."

The bartender asked Jordan, "Do you know them?"

"My fiancée does. They're white supremacists from Queens, or something— she dated one of 'em in high school."

Summer had scraped *fucKKKyou!* on the door of Frank Ahlstrom's Volkswagon. Not that he didn't deserve it, but her vandalism could compromise Jordan's case.

"See, she believes Bush and Cheney's men plotted 9/11 and are framing poor, innocent jihadists. But the motherfuckers who attacked me would string up any old Muslim, like the guy who owns a deli on my block and had nothing to do with 9/11. Personally—if anyone cared to ask—I think it boils down to the same human trash on both sides. Different gods, same shit."

With a tinge of empathy, Eugenia asked him, "You want a shot of bourbon?"

"I'd love one," he said.

"How about some breakfast?" she continued.

"On the house?"

"Where else would it be?"

"I'm starving," said Jordan. "All I had yesterday was cheese doodles and beer."

Eugenia looked faintly disgusted. She slid a menu over to him, and the bartender produced bourbon and a glass of ice water. The phone rang at the bar, and the bartender called over to Eugenia: "Molly!"

With resentful interest Jordan watched her take the receiver and say, "Hey, baby doll." She strolled down the bar, probably so he wouldn't hear more of their conversation. Jordan sipped the smooth, warm bourbon, studying Eugenia's lanky profile, conjuring Bob Dylan against the Cajun tune from the jukebox: "*Curves, just like a woman, yes and verve, just like a woman, yes, and you've got nerve just like a woman…but you're reserved like a fucking guy.*"

Eugenia wandered back to him, saying on the phone to Molly, "Whatever you work out is fine. I'll put him on." Eyeing Jordan, she held the receiver to her long thigh. "Well, guess what? You've got a chance to do Molly a favor." Then she tossed the phone—which he, of course, failed to catch.

"Hello?" Speaking to Molly at last, he wobbled between exhaustion and bourbon.

"Hey," she said. "So sorry to hear about Summer. I apologize if I upset her."

"Oh, she just flipped out yesterday. You know, the assault, her job…"

"I heard your messages. She went at someone's car with a key?"

"Can I, like, meet you somewhere and talk?"

Molly sighed. "I can see you Tuesday. There's something you can do for us, but you've got to be discreet about it."

"Yeah?"

"And I'll pay you."

He perked up.

"My friend David, who's dating Tamara's sister, was going to pose in a photo shoot for us. But now it looks like he and Dahlia are off to the Hamptons. Gene just told me they're out of here tomorrow, driving against traffic. Would you have a couple of hours Tuesday afternoon?"

"I've got nothing but hours and Tuesday afternoons. Is it, like, a nude photo shoot or something?"

Eugenia whispered to the bartender, who snickered.

"You'll be wearing an Armani suit. I'll text you the address of the studio."

"Awesome."

Jordan drained his whiskey and glanced at his untouched glass of water.

"But we don't go telling our volatile girlfriend about this, okay?"

"Fine, Molly."

"Promise?"

Before he knew it, a plate with scrambled eggs and cornbread was placed before him, and Eugenia had completely disappeared.

As he staggered home Betty called to say that Rashad was doing well. He'd spent the night with the twins after Cirque du Soleil. Meanwhile, a colleague of Lydia's was hoping to get Summer an ACD: "She's being released on her own recognizance," Betty explained.

"I have no idea what that means," Jordan told her. In the elevator, he swiped at the button that said 16, missed it and hit 14 by mistake, then tried again. He was weary of words like *arraigned* and *recognizance* when he'd hardly slept and had whiskey before breakfast.

Betty's voice formed solemn phrases like "adjournment in contemplation of dismissal" that Jordan could hear only as iambic pentameter, and he longed for simpler times with Summer, when all they did was play tunes on the street and steal an occasional fancy dinner or a roll of toilet paper.

"She may have to pay damages."

That much he understood. Jordan sighed as he unlocked the door and walked into the empty apartment. The air hadn't moved since he'd run out that morning. Thank goodness Molly had hired him for the photo shoot. He could begin to repay Curtis for bail and attorney fees. And they'd now owe damages to Frank Ahlstrom, one of the guys he himself was prosecuting. At least the living room floor was clean and the stained rug swirling with tiny insects was gone.

An hour later the kitchen phone awoke him from a stupor on the sofa, and Jordan heard their jingly, outgoing message. "You've reached Summer, Jordan, and Rashad," his voice recited. "Please leave a message after the—" and Summer hit her high C that melded with the electronic tone.

"Cathy." An unknown basso profundo weighed in.

Jordan sat up, worried that it was one of their goons out on bail.

"Cathy, are you at home? I have tried you many times and nobody answers. It is Khalil. I didn't speak before on your tape because I don't know how private it is, but I must take that risk because collection agents are calling my family. And you know—if they can reach me, they'll reach your mother and your sister. I'm sure you don't want that."

Rashad's father spoke like a prince, his rich bass like vats of dark chocolate to the milk chocolate of Jordan's baritone. Women would swoon over that deep, resonant voice like they swooned over Eugenia's magnetic blue eyes.

"Oh fuck me," Jordan mumbled. He was not going to pick up the phone.

"I've written to you, sent all the mail from the IRS. So here's the eight-hundred number," Khalil continued. "Call them and set up a payment plan. Just do it, Cathy. In the name of the Almighty, you know what your mother wrote when Rashad was born…look, I won't say more because you know it already. Don't be foolish. Don't hurt yourself or the child. Make that call."

He hung up, and Jordan started screeching the Allman Brothers: "*Lord, I was born a rambling man…*" In some kind of time blur, he was screeching to Summer: "Why didn't you call me? Why did you call Curtis?"

"Because he could actually do something," she shot back, a towel wrapped around her as she stepped out of the bathroom. "I was allowed only one call, and I didn't want to risk it on *your* useless panic."

She'd spent the night in the crypt beneath Center Street "on a sheet of aluminum," she described it, "listening to fire sirens wail outside and a crazy old bird in the next cell shriek every hour while I bled through tampon after tampon."

"'Subterranean Blood Bath.' A Dylan tune?"

"Don't fucking patronize me!"

She slammed the bedroom door on him, just as she had the day before when Molly had tried to shake her hand.

"Yo!" he hollered. "Patronize? You totally blew our case."

"Nothing I did changes what Gemma's mother and the cops saw."

"Frank Ahlstrom can countersue us now."

She flew back out in black pants and a T-shirt, stopping to look around the living room and run a hand through her wet hair.

"They could always countersue. Hey! What happened to our rug? What's gone on here?"

"Do you have any idea what a mess you are?" he cried. "Identity fraud, tax evasion, vandalism?"

"You can't accuse me of false advertising."

"How can you testify about these assholes with your record? You're not even…alive! You fucking faked your own death."

"Which is not illegal," she growled at him through gritted teeth. "Unless you try to cash in an insurance policy, or defraud the courts. Which I have never done," she reported proudly.

"Thank God for small perks."

"They found Nazi literature in Frank's car!" she screamed above him. "You think I'm out of control—you think I'm an idiot! You don't trust me, but I knew what I was doing. I was trying to help your case because I know I can't testify. But I owe something to you and my son. Now you can prove Frank's bias in court—and you'd better believe that black cop reacted when he saw the KKK shit in Frank's trunk. He kept one of the pamphlets. See, I did something your lipstick lesbian wouldn't dare think of."

"Khalil called about your fucking taxes."

"What? Did you talk to him?"

Jordan shook his head.

"Liar," she charged.

Jordan marched across the room and punched on the answering machine, turning up the volume. "Message one. Two fifty p.m. 'Cathy. Cathy, are you at home? I have tried you many times—'"

"Fuck, turn that off!" she screamed.

"No!" he screamed back. "Own up already!"

"Fuck you, Jordan!"

"Why fuck me? Did Curtis just shuck out a grand on my bail? Do I owe the thousands to the feds?"

"Scared little squirt."

"Will you shut up and listen to him?"

"I've written to you, sent all the mail from the IRS," Kalil continued.

"Turn that shit off now!"

Soprano, baritone, and bass collided as Khalil recited the toll-free number, which Summer refused to write down and Jordan memorized, before she completely erased the message.

On Tuesday morning Jordan submitted his felony complaint to Lydia. He'd hated looking at photos of the five lowlifes who had attacked him a week ago, trying to remember who'd said or done what: the lizard, the tatted wonder, the jerk who'd called him a "sand nigger," Frankie, and the guy in the ripped leather vest. He just felt glad the ones with records were behind bars—for the moment and, if he had any say in it, for a while.

Afterward, he arrived at a studio in Tribeca with shiny wooden floorboards, white bricks, white window shades, and white umbrellas, with people adjusting tripods and reading light on meters. The embossed tin ceiling was high, streaked with pipes and track lighting. He didn't see Molly until she surfaced from behind a white gauze curtain with a tanned woman in a periwinkle-blue dress and two little girls. Jordan then recognized Tamara, Molly's sister-in-law, whom he'd briefly met years ago and seen in many photos. The dark-haired girls must be Molly's nieces.

"You remember Tamara," Molly said, as Jordan approached them.

"Of course," he said with a smile whose impact he could see in Tamara's eyes.

"Hi," she said self-consciously.

"And this is Mira, and this is Kayla," Molly continued, indicating the girls.

"Nice to meet you." Jordan bent down to extend his hand to each of them. He was, by now, quite accustomed to children that age, and they seemed to feel it. "Your aunt Molly told me about you when you were born. How old are you now, Mira?" he asked.

The girl splayed all five fingers of her right hand and held up the index finger of her left, in such a Molly-ish, earnest way that if Molly had her own daughter, she couldn't have seemed more like her.

"Next week," she explained. "I'll be this age."

He counted the fingers: "One, two, three, four, five, six. My boy's five."

"And I'm three!" Kayla stated, throwing back her head with a grin.

"I didn't know you were married," remarked Tamara.

He stood up again, leaned in, and whispered to her, "I'm not yet."

His eye dropped to her finger, with its nice-sized diamond ring—from Molly's brother. Neither of them hid the flirtation, and Molly didn't hide her observation of it. When her phone serenaded her, she promptly shut it off.

"Saul?" asked Tamara.

"No, just some solicitor. Saul's actually let up on me."

"Oh, I don't believe that," jeered Tamara. "He'll be back."

"I've said everything I can possibly say to him."

"Maybe *she's* speaking to him again."

"Hardly. She and David are off to the Hamptons."

Tamara turned to Jordan and said, "Sorry for all this inside chatter."

But she'd said it: *Sorry*, the word he'd wanted to hear from Summer for months —just some acknowledgment that she hurt him.

"No apology needed," he assured Tamara, taking in her warm brown eyes and full lips with a shiny hint of gloss. "I actually know a little about this situation."

"About my sister's discombobulated love life?" she asked with a giggle.

"Time to get into your costume," Molly said sternly to Jordan. "Nadine, could you get Jordan his suit? And the release form?"

A trendy-looking woman with short brown hair nodded and pranced off.

Molly turned to Tamara and her nieces.

"I'll walk you to the elevator."

Mira slipped her hand into Aunt Molly's, and they went off chatting about Mira's sixth birthday party next week, swinging hands. Nadine clicked back across the wooden floor holding two long, black zippered bags. She slipped one with a white sticker that said *Evan* onto a rack. She handed Jordan the one with his name on it.

He looked toward the door in time to catch Tamara's brief, sweet wave goodbye, and to wave back to her.

In the dressing room he inspected himself contentedly, soothed by this airy, white atmosphere, by the bustle of purpose and normal people around him. With a sartorial makeover, he didn't seem a man whose life was going down the tubes. A midnight-blue collar peeked out from the suit, accenting his tanned face and thick curls of black hair. He was sorry Tamara hadn't seen him in this getup—but glad that Molly would.

Summer was far from his thoughts, though he was essentially doing all of this for her. He stroked his soft, silk jacket sleeves, thinking that he'd ask Molly if he could wear it to testify before the grand jury in late September.

"You ready?" Molly called.

He strutted out, in leather shoes they'd given him, to the lights, camera, and action.

"We'll tell you how to pose," Molly explained, as Nadine handed him a cup of water from the cooler across the room. This was the life. When he finished drinking, Nadine took his paper cup.

"Get behind him, Bill," Molly commanded one of the photographers. She wore silk pants, a tight, sleeveless top, and studs of earrings that were flecked with small jewels. Her "flickery" dark hair straddled the day's humidity.

"Okay, Jordan—just take a step forward please, extend your right arm. Try it...perfect. Now do it again."

Shutters clicked like a chorus of scissors snipping away. Lights were rearranged and different positions requested. Click, click, snip, snip, flash, flash.

At one point a wedding band was fitted upon the finger of his left hand, and he was photographed holding a credit card, then holding a sheaf of hundred-dollar bills. Molly directed it all, chanting, "One, two, three," like they did before starting a musical number. She seemed happy with his work and, at the end of the shoot, lauded him with an excitingly thin envelope. Inside was a check for three big ones, authorized to the Jordan Radfar Trio. Bail.

"Keep the shirt, suit, and shoes too," she said.

"Molly!" He sighed. "I...I seriously love you."

"Well, I'm 'that kind of friend,' aren't I?"

He kissed her dark hair, inhaling the aroma of paradise.

"I seriously love you," he repeated.

"Use it all in good health."

"So what exactly are you gonna do with all these photos of my shoulders and arms in a suit?" he asked.

"Don't ask, don't tell, don't wonder," she said firmly.

"Oh, come on. I haven't said a word to Summer."

"We're flying under the radar here. Loose lips sink ships."

"Hey, Molly..." He was hoping to phrase his request gracefully. While she'd given him five thousand dollars in the last week, he needed so much more. They were drowning in debt and expenses from Summer's skirmishes, and he wouldn't have his teaching salary for another month. And who knew when she would get another job?

"Um, I was wondering if you had any more work for me. August is really slow for us, and now that she's lost her job and gotten into legal trouble...I know you have a couple of businesses. Do you have any part-time stuff I could take on after Labor Day, when we're back from Fire Island? Like, I could be a messenger or something."

"Maybe," said Molly, tilting her head with consideration. "I'll talk it over with Genie, and we can speak after Labor Day."

"Think she'd mind?"

"She understands. Her ex from Colombia was deported for faking a U.S. passport and driver's license."

Jordan chuckled. "Shit. Sounds like something Summer would do."

"Gene said she would've found your story appalling if she hadn't lived through it herself several times."

In the warm, salty air Jordan felt like he was being coated with a layer of chalk. Rashad had a new haircut for the trip to Fair Harbor. He scuttled around the ferry deck in Jordan's sunglasses as Jordan chased him, crying, "Who stole my shades, man? This sun is bright!"

Summer wore a flat-topped straw hat and large sunglasses that covered half her cheeks. She sat stoically, wind in her hair, a guitar case by her side. Other passengers tried not to stare at them, the white couple who had, they probably thought, adopted a black boy—maybe saving him from starvation in Ethiopia or abuse by some Ugandan warlord. Jordan was now accustomed to these subtle and not-so-subtle gawkers.

Midway into the gray Atlantic, he took out his sax, sat beside Summer, and played cheerful tunes about lost love: "Foolish Things," "Georgia on My Mind," and "Do You Know What It Means." Fellow passengers clapped after each number. Summer didn't sing. At one point he lowered her sunglasses and found her eyes red and glistening.

"Look," he whispered so Rashad wouldn't hear as he knelt by the railing to watch waves slap the ferry's hull. "Let's have a good time, can we?" He reminded her that they'd agreed not to talk with his parents about her night in jail, the skinheads, the prosecution. "We'll leave that rot behind for now."

She didn't say anything. But he appreciated that before they docked, she went to the ladies room to wash her face.

When his mother caught sight of them on the gangplank, she waved her arm back and forth like a slow windshield wiper, the white tunic sleeve contrasting her tan. Her hair was pulled back, and two dark ovals of sunglasses sat on her face.

"Look, there's Mona," Jordan said to Rashad, who jumped up and down. Standing behind her in an unbuttoned blue-and-white Hawaiian shirt, Arman held up a colorful beach ball and Rashad ran to him, weaving through other descending passengers. Summer and Jordan trailed behind with their suitcases.

And suddenly they were reunited at the pier, as though no time had passed since they'd all stayed together in the cottage last October. Hugs were exchanged, sunglasses removed, cheeks were kissed, and Arman tossed the ball to a squealing Rashad. Then he helped Summer and Jordan place their bags in the red wagon beside him, which would serve as their transportation on the island with no cars. Arman began dragging it along the boardwalk, and they all followed him.

"We love your CD. We play it all the time," Mariana said.

"But you don't have a grandchild from us yet," Summer responded.

"That's my family," Arman consoled her. "Late bloomers. Mother didn't give birth until she was thirty-five. And we wanted another child right after Jordie, but it was four years 'til Robin came along. The Radfars are taciturn. No one jumps into this crazy life, not my sister or my daughter—and so, now my grandchild."

"He's being fanciful," Mariana said to Summer, "but of course I worried when we didn't conceive all those years. And then, just like that, poof. It will happen to you too."

"You really think so?" asked Summer.

Mariana nodded and Arman said, "Give it half a year."

Jordan put his arm around her shoulders and felt a tender response as she extended her arm around him. A proud blue broke through the hazy sky, and in this briny, piney air their spell came back.

He was glad that cell phone access was spotty in Fair Harbor, that the cottage had no Wi-Fi. He needed to get away, even from the good news that Lydia felt his case, as a post-9/11 hate crime, might warrant interest in the state. But Rashad was the only witness, besides Jordan, to the assailants' racial slurs. Would a five-year-old's testimony be taken seriously? And if so, what effect might it have on him? Would the evidence from Frank Ahlstrom's vandalized car serve the case—did Summer actually have a point about that?

Jordan was glad enough to table such concerns, to vegetate in the sun all day and play music at night while Summer sang along. They'd have beer with barbecued chicken, corn on the cob, and brownies spiked with tasty Mexican pot for dessert. Mariana forever made potato salad or egg salad with onions and cilantro, as dinner was repurposed into the next day's lunch and back to dinner again. Everything was served on her ceramic plates and bowls or sipped in her goblets.

"So let's talk about the wedding," Arman announced one night after dinner as they distributed themselves in sundry rocking chairs and futons around the living room. The sliding doors were wide open. Mariana insisted on burning the bug torch, but Jordan was prepared for another night of flies and mosquitoes. To him, the fresh sea air was worth it.

"So who's coming?" Arman asked, finding a piece of scrap paper and a pen, sipping beer from one of Mariana's glazed chalices. "You two, of course. The two of us and Robin—with an escort. Probably just a friend; as you know she's having romantic turmoils. So that's six, and Rashad is seven."

"My sister," said Summer, "and her husband and three kids."

"Their names?" asked Arman.

"Deb and Stewart. The kids are Graham, Becca and Maxwell. Maxie is a year older than Rashad. They've never met before."

Arman nodded. Mariana drew on the water pipe before passing it to Jordan. Summer declined.

"Up to twelve," said Arman.

"Sixteen with Curtis, Betty, and their twins."

"Ah yes, Curtis and Betty," said Arman. "They hosted the surprise birthday party. Nice people."

"They've been dear friends." Summer swooned. "Real friends. They've seen the best of me and the worst of me, and they love me anyway."

Jordan knew the remark was a test for him and sat still as wax.

"The worst of me is pretty bad," continued Summer. "Worse than most people's."

"Same here," piped Arman. "It's a sign of intelligence."

Mariana laughed knowingly.

"I've lost friends and family to it," Summer elaborated.

"It's one way to separate wheat from the chaff," Arman replied.

Rashad had fallen asleep on a futon, breath whistling through his nostrils as his little chest rose and fell. Mariana draped a blanket over him. Outside, crickets chorused consolingly.

"Your father and mother." Arman tapped his pen on the paper.

"My father's almost dead," said Summer. "Literally. In-home hospice care… dying slower than Mimì in *La bohème*, but I doubt he'll make it to October twenty-second."

Arman looked somber. "So he'll miss your wedding."

"Yup," Summer said. "But it's okay. He didn't even walk my sister down the aisle."

"Why?" asked Mariana.

"Couldn't bear to see his daughter marry a Democrat."

"Has he any idea of the iconoclasts you're marrying into?" Arman asked.

Summer shook her head. "We don't really talk. We…"

"Where is he now?"

"They retired in North Carolina. Middle of the state. My mother loves horses. I think she wants to buy a horse farm there or something."

Neither of Jordan's parents had a word to say, as "buying a horse farm" was nothing they'd ever contemplated.

"We should have this wedding as soon as possible," concluded Arman, "and hold it in North Carolina so your parents can make it."

"Well, wait a minute," said Jordan. "We've already invited people here…"

"So we'll have two ceremonies," decided Arman. "One down South, just for family in September, and the other in New York for friends too, in October."

Doubtlessly, Jordan mused, Arman considered his insistence a courtesy to Summer's family and didn't realize he was dominating everyone. But even if he had a point about the bride's parents, Jordan couldn't leave town before his court date.

"Let's not plan anything around my father's death," Summer asserted.

"Of course not," agreed Mariana, who was sky high—Jordan could hear.

"But we must," Arman said with a convinced laugh. "What's a wedding without the bride's family?"

"He won't make it," said Summer. "Mom told Deb his wick is burning down."

"Will your mother be in any shape to come?" asked Mariana.

Summer shrugged. "We can't hold the presses. She'll come if she can."

This was news to Jordan. So far as he'd heard, Summer was determined to have nothing more to do with her mother. That seemed one principle to which she was fully committed. But when it came to changing her mind, Summer had proven her skills.

"My mom's family footed the whole bill for Deb's wedding," she explained to his parents. "Dad didn't lay down a cent. Our dashing uncle Nicholas—Mom's brother—walked my sister down the aisle. It was the third time in our lives we'd seen Uncle Nick. He lives in Cape Town and Antwerp."

"What does he do there?" Arman asked.

"Everything."

"Must be one busy man."

"Busy and mysterious," said Summer. "There are family rumors that he and my mother were in love, as teenagers. He never married. Came to Deb's wedding with an exotic girl from Guam." She lifted a bottle of Rolling Rock to her lips, swallowed, and continued. "When he was young he looked like Leslie Howard…you know, Ashley in *Gone With the Wind*."

Jordan knew exactly what was coming next. He could say the words right along with Arman, as though they'd been scripted: "You know Leslie Howard was Jewish?"

Then his mother's response, equally predictable: "Leslie Howard? No way."

After which Arman would name other WASPy-looking stars of old Hollywood who were actually Jewish, or part Jewish: "Lauren Bacall, Kirk Douglas…"

"But my friend Molly Douglas is totally Scotch Irish," Jordan inserted into this familiar banter.

At this point Summer announced that she was going to sleep.

When she left, Jordan made sure that Rashad got into pajamas and brushed his teeth. Then he opened the door to a darkened room and climbed into the squeaky bed beside Summer. She rolled over and snuggled her head onto his chest.

"You forgive me for saying her name?" he whispered. She kissed his collarbone. For a while they lay in each other's arms as crickets serenaded and a breeze flicked the curtain by a window above them.

"I want you to know something," she murmured, "and I'll say it now but never again: whenever I'm an asshole to you, I'm aware of it."

"Do you think you were an asshole downstairs just now?"

"Sort of…I've been worse."

"You really have." They laughed softly. "Do you think you could…not be an asshole a little more often?"

She shifted her weight on him and sighed. "I have no control over it."

"Doesn't that bug you?"

She nodded, her head moving against his chest.

"You scare me sometimes," he whispered.

"I scare myself."

"So…when will you tell me your actual name?"

"You know my name, silly."

"Not your legal name. We are getting married, you know."

They both laughed, inexplicably. He'd never felt closer to her.

"I'll be entitled to know such things," he reminded her.

"Ummmm."

He had thought he was too sleepy for sex, but when she sighed in his ear and whispered his name, edging her warm legs up his thigh, he felt her desire create his.

"There's something more," she breathed choppily in his ear. "A damn cliché, but it's true. You're the best thing that ever happened to me. Ever. That's *why* I'm such a bitch…I can't believe we're actually still together and going to get—"

His lips stopped hers from saying more. Slowly, the rhythm of waves flitting beneath his eyelids, he climbed on top of her. They didn't even think about birth control. Regardless of what his parents had prophesized, they pretty much knew they wouldn't conceive a child.

But that early September night by the sea, they were wrong.

He knew it was Labor Day by the influx of people along the path to the beach the next morning. Weekenders greeted Jordan and his father genially, stepping aside to permit each other's passage on foot or bikes, or pulling children in wagons. Arman carried a big umbrella, and Jordan had rolled a blanket and towels under his arm.

"We like her," Arman said decidedly. "She speaks her mind, and she's a lot of fun. You'll grow with her. She keeps you thinking and feeling. I wish your sister could find someone like that—who returns her affection. Robin's waiting for some Titan to descend from the sky and sweep her away."

"Summer and I have had our ups and downs," Jordan told his father.

"That means you're breathing."

Jordan glanced at the wooden slats that ribbed the sand and brambles beneath him, at his own narrow, brown feet in flip-flops and his father's broader feet in sandals. This could have been a time to speak about her flirtation with

Eliot and her tax evasion, about the defaced car and overturned coffee table. But Jordan wouldn't break his promise to leave all that behind. Last night in her arms had been precious. He didn't want to gossip, even with his own father. So he spoke generically.

"Intimacy can be really intense. I mean, a lot to handle."

"Then don't try to handle it. Be intense yourself."

"Do you think I'm depressive?"

"No," the older man said quickly. "You brood and obsess, when something's in your craw. But that's different."

"Summer's depressed."

"Says who?"

Jordan looked over at Arman in his dark glasses and sun hat.

"Whoever says these things: shrinks, psychologists…"

"Ach," said his father. "Depression is an affliction that has caught America's fancy. But it's a way of life for Europeans. When I grew up after the war, everyone was depressed. If you weren't, you'd have been considered mad."

They stood aside to permit a wet-haired family wrapped in towels to pass.

"Frankly," Arman continued as they walked on, "I see nothing depressed about a woman who kicks a ball down the beach with her son and sings her heart out no matter who's listening. Didn't she do 'Que Sera' beautifully this morning?"

"She did," said Jordan.

She'd been singing on the porch, to the pine trees and sky.

"And I see a woman who clearly comes from money who helps us wash dishes every night. Hey, she washes more dishes than you do, Jordie. She doesn't have airs, and her breeding and talent could easily give her airs."

"All true. But there are other sides of her."

"What counts?" asked his father. "Which side counts most?"

They shuffled along as the slatted walkway ceded to mounds of sand. Picket fences bent into the dunes, as though wind and waves had crushed them there. Beyond the sandy buttresses and swales, an expanse of beach welcomed them.

"And if you wouldn't mind my saying, you should get her a ring by now."

"She says she doesn't want one. Look, Mariana just wears a band."

"Working with clay, your mother wouldn't wear a diamond. But I think Summer's the kind of woman who'd appreciate a ring. Just a feeling I have."

"Not what she says."

Striped, weather-worn umbrellas were propped, and blankets laid over the jagged sand. Salty wind rushed into Jordan's face and through his hair as they stopped to plant their own umbrella. The sea was opal, almost waxy in the sun, and deep blue out by the horizon. Long, shiny waves crested slowly, pummeling their white froth to shore, splashing some of it skyward while children darted around in bright bathing suits.

"We have debts," said Jordan. "She lost a job…"

"Don't stress about that now," said Arman. "Enjoy the day. You'll take care of it when you get back home."

The one reason he could take care of it, and he knew with the certainty of each tumbling wave, was Molly. She wouldn't say "You'll take care of it," as if everything would magically happen. She'd say "I'll take care of it" or "I'll help you." He needed that kind of friend more than ever, as he didn't have that kind of family.

"I wish we could stay here forever," Summer lamented, walking in a breeze that twirled the sand. "Maybe I should sell the apartment and we can live like your parents—everywhere and nowhere. I could so do that."

"It wouldn't be fair to Rashad," Jordan pointed out. They ambled on, behind the dunes toward the walkway to their cottage. It was their last day of vacation, and dread about returning home virtually raked the air between them. "Do you think you should sell Gus' place?" Jordan asked. "We could pay off a bunch of debts, put money away, and maybe rent in the neighborhood?"

She shook her head, shutting eyes against the raggedy sea breeze.

"Well then…how do we get out of our pickle?" he asked, stopping in his tracks.

"Curtis isn't busting the door down," she pointed out, stopping with him, combing long, fine hair from her eyes. "My sister bought all those CDs last winter. You threw him some cash. It's not like we just keep taking and don't give back."

"Yeah, but we owe beyond what we can keep borrowing. He has his own family, and Betty's starting a business. And he's not the only one you owe."

"I keep telling you," she grumbled, "the IRS won't track me down. They haven't succeeded yet, have they?" Her skin was raw pink from the sun, her hair lighter than it was all year. She shaded her squinting eyes with a cupped hand.

"They found Khalil," he said.

"Not the same thing as finding me. Khalil's not dead."

"How do you know he won't point them in your direction?"

"Because he hasn't. He's the father of my kid. He's that kind of friend."

"Well, what about our September bills? On top of your attorney fees and the settlement with Frank Ahlstrom…"

"Can we not say horrible names like that here, on this perfect day? Can you forget about money for five seconds, Jordan?"

"Well, we're heading back to that crap. And there's something I want you to know." He recalled Molly's sincere words about herself and Eugenia: "We don't keep secrets." Now Summer stared at him from below her cupped hand, her shoulders streaked with sunburn where the lotion hadn't reached.

"I've arranged to speak with Molly about maybe taking on some work, like for one of her businesses. You know, like maybe being a messenger."

Summer dropped her hand and popped her eyes open in shock. Everything about her love of the open air left her face.

"It's temporary. Like 'til New Year's or something, to help us catch up."

"You just want to be around her."

"Oh Summer, please don't. You know we're fucking desperate."

"So I see. This time she'll save not only you but me too."

"It's not about saving."

"Of course it is. Why don't you trust me?"

"What?"

Suddenly she pushed him, with a kind of grunt, and then dashed off.

He ran after her. "Don't do this," he cried. "I'm just…I'm looking out for us…"

They ran through humps of sand and high grass to the wooden walkway. Because she wore shoes and he was barefoot, she picked up speed.

On the boardwalk a splinter gashed Jordan's right foot, and he stopped abruptly, shrieking with a pain that she apparently mistook for his usual annoyance with her. She ran down to the cottage as Jordan sat on a rock and pulled the wood chip from his foot. He wasn't sure if he'd gotten all of it; he was sore and bleeding. Just as a week of salt water had healed his scuffed chin, along came a new wound.

"What happened?" asked Mariana when he finally limped through the door.

"Bad fucking splinter."

"Let me see." Mariana left the kitchen, and Arman, who'd been cleaning the grill, followed her.

"I don't know if there's still wood under my skin."

"Here, sit down."

Both of his parents put on reading glasses and examined his foot. Molding it gently, as if it were clay, his mother's fingers found the tender spot. Jordan looked up to see Summer standing in the shadows by the pantry, stroking Rashad's hair and watching Jordan's parents care for him.

When Labor Day ended, kindergarten began. Jordan walked Rashad to school, and the child said that cars on the street were like waves and the sidewalk like a beach.

"Except you can't swim in the cars," said Jordan.

"I can't swim in the big waves either," Rashad replied sensibly.

Summer complained of "feeling crummy" and spent the first days back home lying down with a damp washcloth on her forehead. "Think I have sunstroke. I miss Mariana. I want her to take care of me," she groaned at one point.

"Well you have me—her son," said Jordan.

"Sometimes a girl needs her mom."

She seemed jittery, quick to snap or cry. So when Jordan paid off September's bills with the money from Molly's photo shoot, he didn't divulge the source. So much for not keeping secrets. If Summer saw red, he figured it best not to wave the cape—the money, he told her, was "from a trio gig last spring."

"Thank god it came in now," she muttered.

"Thing is…we don't have much left."

Summer had been granted her ACD and now owed Frank Ahlstrom, on whose Volkswagen door she'd scratched *fucKKyou* with her keys, two thousand dollars for reparation. If she didn't pay, owners of the parking lot would be liable and come after her for much more. So there was no further argument about where they'd get money. They needed it too badly, "which was always my point," Jordan assured her. He would talk to Molly about work, and Summer would resume singing at the Susquehanna. She would also talk to Betty, who'd signed a lease for a storefront on Rivington Street. Maybe Summer could work for her.

Summer took off with Betty to Vermont for a couple of days to help her pack inventory from her mother's antique shop in the Champlain Valley. She'd feel better in the fresh air, Jordan forecast. She left town after a tussle with Tillie, who'd begged to bring Skip to their wedding as an escort, and with Deb, who was under orders from her husband not to spend so much time on the phone.

"Control freaks," she'd groused to Jordan. "But the women permit it. Now *you* never treat me like that. And I wouldn't let you. We're more equals." Then she'd thrown her arms around Jordan and squeezed him.

In her absence he received a check in the mail for seven hundred and fifty dollars from a folk-singer in Minneapolis called Danny Perkins. Inspired by the "Short Stick" video, he'd rendered his own version on acoustic guitar with a Don McLean, folky edge. Twelve Step groups had invited him to perform, and he'd developed a small following.

Danny Perkins had written to her:

Your song is brilliant, Ms. Vale. It brings tears to people's eyes and makes them want to hug each other. I should have gotten permission before I recorded your song but couldn't find a number for you. So I spoke with Zikomo at the Jordan Radfar Trio. Please accept this check for the moment. Going forward, I will draft a licensing contract for your consideration.

Jordan had written Perkins a thank-you note. In normal times, he reflected, they'd be doing damn well. Z was booking a bunch of big parties for the fall. But with legal fees and damages to pay off, they were still on the treadmill. So he mailed the thank-you letter to Danny Perkins on his way to meet Molly near her office in the Flatiron district. Today they would speak about whatever kind of work he might do for her.

He waited outside the small cast-iron office building, which was painted the color of lobster bisque. With typical promptness, Molly burst out the door. Jordan was surprised by how she bustled down the street, not even greeting him.

"You okay?" he asked as they headed east, toward Madison Square Park.

She shook her head no.

For a strange moment Jordan's heart jumped. She and Eugenia were finally having trouble.

"What's going on?" He tried not to sound exultant.

"Meet me in the park at the southeast entrance," she said. "And don't turn your head, but I'm being followed."

"Waddaya mean?"

"I'll explain later. Cross the street, don't walk with me."

Jordan crossed the street and glanced back for a moment. Absolutely no one was behind her on the sidewalk. When she showed up at the Madison Avenue entrance to the park, she seemed more distressed than he'd ever seen her.

"Are you in trouble?" he asked.

"I don't know. Let's find a bench with no pigeon shit on it."

He suddenly remembered meeting her and Z in that same park six years ago, looking for a bench with no pigeon shit, as Molly always did, and eating onion bagels that gushed cream cheese all over the napkins and tin foil in their laps.

"If you look at Twenty-third Street," she said, sitting beside him on the bench spot they nabbed, "you'll see an ugly white limo that's shaped like a Humvee. Two long windows and one short: dash, dash, dot. Dot is kind of ear-shaped. It's been trailing me for three days."

Jordan craned his head. "Think I see it. Um, Molly…there are many cars like that in Manhattan. Are you sure you're not imagining this?"

"I just said, they've been following me since Tuesday. They park across from home in the morning, and when I get to the office, they're waiting for me. If I meet a client for lunch, as I did yesterday, they park outside the restaurant. They follow me everywhere, except to Eugenia's Cajun. Do you know anything about this?"

"Shit no," he said. "How would I?" Jordan revered her level-headedness and now marveled at this lapse into paranoia. "What does Eugenia say?"

"She brought it to my attention. We call it 'the Milk Truck.' She thinks her ex from Colombia is behind this. Drug money. But I think it's Saul."

"The married guy from Chicago who keeps calling you?"

"*Kept* calling me," said Molly. "Suddenly he stopped. And then came…the Milk Truck."

"But why would he do this?"

"To try and find Dahlia, his love. He might figure that if he follows me, or hires someone to follow me, I'm bound to cross paths with her."

"You have a great imagination, you know."

"That's what I told Genie. I thought she was overreacting to a coincidence… until I kept seeing the damn thing everywhere I went. Dash, dash, dot." Molly smiled fiercely at him. "You don't believe me, do you?"

He shook his head. "You're wound up about nothing."

Molly pulled out her BlackBerry and showed him a list that included Saul, Claudia, his own name, and several he didn't know.

"Suspects," she said.

"What the? Why am I a suspect?"

"Because Eugenia pointed out that the appearance of this vehicle coincides with my seeing more of you." Molly's limpid green eyes were inescapable. Jordan wanted to scream "Fuck her!" but didn't, as he was going to ask a favor.

"Have I sufficiently proved that I'm not driving that limo and sitting here at the same time? Unless…maybe it's the body-snatched me." Jordan made nasal, sci-fi sound effects that didn't seem to amuse Molly, so he asked, "Have you thought of going up and asking what they want?"

"They could pull a weapon, or push me into the car. Though Gene says if they were up to something really nefarious, they wouldn't be so…prominent. And I pointed out they could be a distraction, like a decoy. There might be someone else in on it. In any event, we concluded that we should keep our distance. Hopefully, they'll just go away."

"You're really stressing over this, aren't you?"

"People are crazy," she declared. "Alessandra warned me that there's a dark side to having lots of money."

"Do you want to go somewhere else to chat?" *Chat* was his word for hitting her up for work.

"Doesn't matter," she said. "If we go to a café, they'll follow me. Maybe let's stroll. Best to be a moving target. So…"

She stood and he followed.

"How's your court case?" she asked.

"Getting complicated. You know, five guys attacked us, but only three are felons. The accomplices will be handled separately."

Molly looked preoccupied, as though she'd barely heard him. Jordan squinted back through bushes that lined the park. He saw the squared-off shape of the white limo: two long windows, and one short and ear-shaped—dash, dash, dot. They continued toward Fifth Avenue, walking against a ubiquitous scent of urine, topsoil, and lousy "skunk weed" dope.

"I spoke with Gene about odd jobs for you. Trouble is, we have only grubby ones, and it didn't feel right. You were my boyfriend. I don't want you scraping grease for my girlfriend's chefs."

"Molly, I'll do what you need—just 'til Christmas or whatever. We're so behind, and money evaporates when you have a kid, a couple of law suits, and a wedding."

"I want to help you," she said, her eyes soft and clear. "But I'd rather just give you a loan."

"Well…that I would appreciate."

"How much do you need?"

"Ten grand?"

"Okay," she said.

"I always paid you back. Remember?"

She looked at him with raised eyebrows. "I remember how my apartment became your headquarters *behind my back.*"

"But I paid off the loan."

His own ironic plea reminded him of Summer's rationales. He added, "This time I'll win clean in court—I lost two weeks of work because my chin was messed up. I can sue for psychological damage…for me and Rashad."

Thinking of Rashad, Jordan glanced at his phone. "Gotta pick him up at school, 'cause Summer's in Vermont. Hey," he said suddenly, "wanna come with me and meet him? Rashad's such a great little guy. He's about your godson's age."

"Can't," said Molly. "Too much to do. Walk me back to the office?"

As they crossed Fifth Avenue at 25th Street, they spoke about his paying her back in two years, little by little and with no interest. Molly scanned the street, and just before Jordan opened his mouth to call her paranoid, he flinched involuntarily as a man with a shaved head, like his assailants', walked by them.

"Guys suck," he muttered, surprised at his own agitation. "I really understand being a lesbian. Maybe I am one."

"Well, I'm not," said Molly. "My preference isn't billions of people, like 'men' or 'women.' I'm too picky. My sexual preference is Eugenia. When I was seeing you, my sexual preference was Jordan." She leaned in and added in a whisper,

"Beautiful day in the neighborhood…"

At first Jordan thought she meant the schlocky, yellowing paintings outside the antiques warehouses. Then he saw the white limo slinking behind them, as though scavenging for a parking space. Its fender was so low it nearly grazed the asphalt. Cars tried to pass it, some honking aggressively.

Jordan was still not convinced it all wasn't a coincidence.

"Where's Rashad's school?" Molly asked, appearing to shiver for a moment.

"A block from me, down on East Broadway."

"Maybe I should go with you…just to shake 'em."

At the corner, they about-faced and walked down Sixth Avenue toward the F train station on 23rd Street.

"Perfect," Molly mouthed, pointing out that Sixth Avenue traffic moved uptown, so the Milk Truck couldn't keep trailing her.

As they waited for the F train, Molly told Jordan that she'd met Saul because he accidentally left his phone at Dahlia's apartment, and she'd found it on the floor. He wasn't comfortable meeting Dahlia with his daughters, so Molly had stood in to return the phone to him.

"Always returning cell phones," he commented.

"And no good deed goes unpunished. Though I'm not without empathy for this man." Gazing down the tunnel with its small, static lights, Jordan sensed the train would take its time. He was sure that only New Yorkers understood that particular stillness. "He and Dahlia were close," Molly continued, "physically and emotionally, for years. Her silence must kill him."

"I know that feeling."

Molly grimaced.

"I credit Saul for taking more emotional risk than most married businessmen. But this…" She turned back toward the exit to the street. "Over the top. I guess he was frustrated that I didn't do more for him."

"So he doesn't know that Dahlia's dating that other guy?"

Molly shook her head.

"All a mystery to him. And you know that mystery is worse than truth."

Jordan saw part of the dark tracks shudder and become a rat that darted off. The air cooled and headlights ignited the parallel rails that curled back through the tunnel. Then came rumbling, two bright headlights, and a breeze as the train squeaked into the station. He and Molly walked into the air-conditioned car and took a seat.

"Eugenia's brother got a private detective when her nephew first disappeared last fall. But they think he's in Israel now…and if they had any doubt, they'd follow Eugenia—not me. Whoever's doing this," Molly suggested as the train stopped at 14th Street, gently bumping their arms together, "is making it clear that they've got it in for me. When Genie and I bifurcate, they follow me. Not her."

"Could it be someone you'd never guess?" Jordan asked.

"That's why I'm fixating on Saul—he's among the more innocent prospects."

"What do you mean?"

The train rumbled on, paused briefly in the tunnel, and continued.

"You know, Jordan," she said, as they pulled into West Fourth Street, "I made a pact with fate when I got all that money six years ago—that I would help the vulnerable and oppressed, however I could. That's what our photo shoot was about the other day. But when you have friends…you have enemies. When you help one group, say, a class of abused people, you hurt the exploiters. This could be their way of saying 'Back off.'"

"Ladies and gentlemen," a voice then announced over the loudspeaker, "we're being held momentarily by the train's dispatcher. Please be patient."

"Do I have a choice?" Jordan glanced at his phone. He'd be in time for Rashad and the twins—who were also in his charge, with Betty in Vermont and Curtis at work.

"The other possibility," Molly suggested when the train moved again, "is that someone has her eye or his eye on Eugenia…and wants me out of the picture."

Jordan said into her ear, "You're just as hot as she is."

She smiled back, with distant gratitude.

"Not how the world construes it. She's tall, naturally blonde…"

As the train wended its way east, to Broadway-Lafayette, Molly continued rhapsodically: "She's a stunning, athletic, sexual woman who's great fun to be with. And not only that—now she's got some money."

They climbed the steps at East Broadway to a sky fringed with leaves from Seward Park. "I'm proud of Rashad," Jordan said. "He's a nice kid. Not a brat."

"I'm sure you've had a hand in shaping his character."

"Oh, I don't know."

"Jordan Radfar." Molly stepped up from the stairwell. "Who would've predicted you'd be great with kids? I hear only rave reviews about your music teaching from my neighbors."

He felt relieved they were discussing something beside her mystery stalker, though she still seemed on edge. Molly was beginning to chat about her godson, Andy, and how she and Eugenia had decided not to adopt a Guatemalan boy. "Not because we aren't parental—setting limits comes easily to each of us," she explained. "We could be hard to take as a team and may actually give our best to children that aren't ours."

Then he saw it. Across the street, parked at the corner of Rutgers and Canal Streets, between a Chinese grocer and the Golden Sun Buddhist Temple: dash, dash, dot. On the grocer's yellow canopy, Mandarin characters blurred into red butterflies.

"Shit," he moaned. "Shit, Molly. Over there. Look. You're right."

She swiftly surveyed the street and turned back to him, her eyes now crystal gray and narrowed. To his shock, she said, "You must be in on this."

He shook his head helplessly. "I'm as flabbergasted as you are."

"You're the only person who knows we're here—unless you told someone."

"When would I tell someone? I haven't been on my phone since we met. Here…" He handed his phone to her, as he'd handed it last month to Summer, when she'd insisted that he was contacting Molly on the sly. "Look at all my texts today," he invited her, weary of proving his innocence to women.

Unlike Summer, who'd been too upset to cross-examine the evidence, Molly scrolled through his texts as they walked slowly to Seward Park. The playground gates were chained, so they walked along to a semicircular stone bench just outside of it. There they took a seat, hidden from the Milk Truck by trees and the glaring windshields of cars parked along Essex Street.

She handed his phone back briskly, saying, "I didn't see anything. But how did they know to trail us here?"

"Maybe they stopped at each F train station and waited for a while?"

"No good, Jordan. They didn't even see us go into the subway on Twenty-third. Either you're in on this or someone wants to make it *look* like you are. Got any theories as to who that might be?"

"For shit's sake, Summer's in Vermont. I told you that."

"When did she leave?"

"Couple of days ago."

"Well, that's when this started—you sure she's in Vermont and not in that car?"

"Totally," said Jordan. He raised his index finger. "I'll call her. You know the area code for Vermont?"

"Eight, zero, two," said Molly.

"Good. Because here." He fiddled with his phone and found Eli and Marjorie Wolff's number in the Champlain Valley. "Here's where Summer is staying. I won't speed-dial. You. Dial. Eight, zero, two...we are calling the state of Vermont."

"Could be a cell phone number," she suggested.

"Well, it isn't."

Jordan put his phone on speaker, and Betty's mom answered.

"Hi, it's Jordan calling from New York," he said.

"Oh, hi there," she said pleasantly. "Too bad you couldn't come up with Summer."

"Next time, I hope."

"You're always welcome. Looks like you've got some nice days downstate."

"Yeah, the humidity's let up. How 'bout you?"

"Bit chilly at night but no frost yet."

"Marjorie, can I trouble you to get Summer to the phone? I haven't been able to reach her all day."

"She's in the barn with Betty. They've been hard at work," said Marjorie, and Jordan nodded defiantly at Molly. "Please give me a second." And then she went off, calling, "Summer! Jordan's on the phone."

In the interval it took for Summer to get on, with a listless: "Hey, what up?" Jordan harshly whispered to Molly that she was vindicated.

"Wondering how everything's going, how you're feeling…" he said to Summer.

"You're so sweet. I'm okay, but last night I had a migraine. Betty thinks I might have mono, but I say it's stress—hey, you'd better get your butt to school for Rashad and the twins, mister."

"Where do you think I am?"

They spoke more about his evening with the boys and when she and Betty planned to return. Then, satisfied, Jordan got off the phone.

"She's not behind this," he declared to Molly. "I think Eugenia's more suspect."

"Sure, Eugenia really knows where your kid goes to school."

"Maybe she put a sensor on you."

"You mean a location sensor? Wouldn't we think I'd have noticed?"

"Maybe she snuck it in your cell phone."

"Way too farfetched, Jordan. That's a '9/11 was an inside job' explanation."

Jordan could have left it at that, but he felt tantalized by a rare, defensive vulnerability that Molly exuded now. "Maybe she's in it with her ex," he suggested. "Maybe she's tired of you and she wants to cut out with some other chick."

Molly looked like she'd been stun-gunned. "If that were the case, she'd tell me. Gene wouldn't haul up this indirect rigmarole."

"Maybe she doesn't want to hurt your feelings or piss you off. Maybe she wants some kind of huge settlement."

"Maybe you and Summer want a bigger loan," quipped Molly, regaining her composure. "A tad more likely, isn't it?"

"Me and Summer don't know a damn thing about all of this."

Molly didn't answer but reflected aloud: "If someone put a sensor on me, it could be in my purse or phone. I've been carrying them these last few days. Maybe one of my employees…maybe even Larry. Damn. Everyone becomes a suspect."

"Including Eugenia."

Molly shook her head firmly. "Exempt."

"Why? I bet she's trying to frame me."

"Not her style."

"'Friends last forever. Girlfriends tend not to.'" He quoted Eugenia's words that had gotten back to him through Claudia years ago.

"We're way past that point…fucking Claudia," Molly said under her breath.

"The lady doth protest."

"Jordan, she's my love." As she leaned in, Molly's hazel pupils turned almost golden. "No one's ever been closer to me, and I trust she wouldn't do this. But you may be onto something with this sensor theory." She glanced around. "Let's try something. I'm going back into the subway, to Brooklyn. If these jerks are following me by sensor, they'll go downtown, or at least hang a U-ie for the Manhattan Bridge. But if they're using logic, they'll turn right and go uptown to my office. Watch and text me what they do. Okay?"

Jordan walked her to the subway entrance at Straus Square, which didn't say uptown or downtown. The Milk Truck had remained on Canal, between the grocer and the Golden Sun Buddhist Temple. Jordan suffered a prickly sensation of being watched as the two of them came back into its view.

"Give me a hug," Molly commanded. "Don't show them we're upset with each other. That may be their aim."

When Molly threw her arms around him, he remembered how strong she was for a petite woman. They embraced with zest. She slid her lips quickly over his unshaven cheek and then ran down the subway steps.

Almost immediately, blinkers went on in the big white car across the street. Astonished, Jordan saw it pull out of the parking space, turn right, and head uptown on Essex Street. It stopped at the traffic light by Hester, which enabled Jordan to sneak up and watch them continue straight uptown. They didn't turn on Grand Street.

Uptown, he texted Molly. Then he added: *Nix sensor theory.*

He didn't hear back from her and stuck the phone into his pocket. As he sauntered toward East Broadway, he admitted to himself that he didn't believe Eugenia was the culprit. She seemed devoted and protective of Molly. Nor did he feel Summer could pull off anything so elaborate in her afflicted state. Jordan also doubted it was the lovelorn man from Chicago. It probably was some asshole that wanted Molly out of his way because she was foiling his scams and schemes. And he shuddered for her integrity in a crooked world.

As he crossed Montgomery Street, Jordan became aware of someone too close behind him and swiveled backward, ready to kick. There stood Molly.

"You fell for it," she said, with an incongruous sparkle.

"What now?" he asked.

She explained, as they walked toward Rashad's school: "I sat in the station for five minutes, then came upstairs. Never got on a train. So they're not tracking me by sensor or they would've stuck around. That's the kind of thing they clearly like to do—intimidate me by knowing my every move.

"If you were working with them, you'd have told them to go to Brooklyn and make it appear like they were following me by sensor. But you didn't."

"I'm not part of this," he pleaded. "For whatever it's worth, I promise. And I'm worried for you."

"You're worried for me," she said. "That's good. I figured it all out, and I'm actually relieved. But *you* should be worried as hell."

They were standing at the chain-link fence by the schoolyard where other parents milled around. Rashad, Ian, and Archer would appear any minute. Molly received a text, and reported: "From Dahlia. She says, 'Not Saul. Learned the hard way.' I could've spared her, now that we know exactly whose racket this is."

He shrugged. "We do?"

"Someone who can't stand me, who even hates your saying a word that begins with *M*. Someone who knows exactly where you'd be going at two thirty this afternoon, someone with a sci-fi view of politics, and a penchant for vandalizing cars—"

"Jesus, Molly!" he interrupted her, raising his voice. "I just proved she's in Vermont."

"She's not necessarily the driver."

"It would take cash to get someone to trail you in a car like that. She's broke."

"Someone posted her bail, didn't they?"

"Are you kidding me? Curtis and Betty wouldn't do this. They're more sane than you are."

"Maybe they have no idea. Maybe she borrowed money and lied to them."

"She's not even well enough to scheme. You heard, migraines and nausea…"

"Pregnant," said Molly, her eyes sharpening. "Raging hormones upping her already volatile ante."

Jordan felt squeezed, like he would choke. He was ready to spit flames at her. "Quit dissing her! Quit talking about my fiancée like that."

"And you didn't diss Gene," Molly snapped back, her face flushing. "You didn't just imply that she wants to 'cut out with another chick' and shake me for as much as she could get?"

"I shouldn't have said that."

"And there's a lot I *should* say."

"Unless you see Summer at that wheel, you have no proof of *anything*. It's a real '9/11 was an inside job' explanation, Molly. You told me in the subway that you have enemies, that you take risks."

"Which is precisely why her ploy is hurting me."

"Can we agree to disagree about her role in this?" Jordan demanded.

"You know…that bromide always comes from some corporate bully defending his right to poison rivers. If we're worth our salt, Jordan, we have an opinion because it corresponds to some facts. So let's not 'agree to disagree.' All day you've been calling me crazy and paranoid—until you saw you had no grounds."

She shut her eyes in exasperation, and he thought: Bitch.

He was better off with Summer, who infuriated him in a parental way, like a bad girl would. But she could admit when she was wrong, or nuts. Molly managed to one-up him and make him feel like he'd never amount to anything, like he was dumb and expendable. Summer needed him.

"Let's quit talking about this," he said. "Neither of us knows what's going on. I'll email you the loan contract later."

"You'll email me the contract," she repeated, before crossing East Broadway to head north. Clearly, she had decided not to meet Rashad.

Jordan suffered every heartbeat as she walked away. Then he checked the school's steps for the boys. Rashad was dashing out, his red shirt half-tucked into his pants and knapsack slung over his shoulder. Archer followed close behind.

"Daddy, could we get ices?" Rashad begged, once he found Jordan. "Please?"

Ian, who was in another class, sauntered over, pushing a boy away from him.

"My dad's getting us ices," Rashad said as he approached.

"He's not *really* your dad," Ian sneered.

"He is too!" Archer defended, and Ian raised his arm at his twin brother.

"Is not!"

Rashad eyed Jordan for reassurance, too smart to overlook Ian's charge.

"Ian!" Jordan knelt down to grab the boy's raised arm. "Enough." He looked Ian in the eye and repeated: "Enough." He realized how easy it would be to dump rage and distress onto this child, and made sure that he didn't. "I'm Rashad's adoptive father," he explained. "I'll be adopting him in October, when Summer and I get married."

"That's not real," Ian insisted.

"It's plenty real," asserted Jordan, standing up again. "Rashad and Archie, let's get you some ices. None for you today, Ian. I don't like your attitude."

The little boy stamped his feet. Jordan took Rashad's hand in one of his, and Archer's in the other.

On line by the Italian ice truck, Jordan recognized Gemma's mom. She called herself Mel, and he forgot whether she was Melissa, Melinda, or Melanie, but it was something like that. She wore a Yankees cap backward over her long, copper hair.

"Oh, hi!" she said to Jordan. "I didn't realize Rashad goes to school here too."

"He's in kindergarten," said Jordan. Gemma, still in preschool, stood beside her mother with the arched spine and distracted gaze of a limber little girl.

"Listen," said Mel, "I've been working on my deposition—or whatever they call grand jury testimony."

"Thanks so much. I owe you, Mel. Big-time."

"Wish we could've been quicker to help you. But I wanted to get photos and write down the license plate number before calling the cops."

"License plate?"

"Yeah, of that big white car they got out of before chasing you guys. I took a photo of the license plate. It was from pretty far away, but I figured I could enlarge it later, on the computer. I was shooting in raw format."

He said nothing to Molly, Summer, Z, Betty, or Curtis. The bombshell went straight to his attorney, who agreed that the story was "getting more and more bizarre."

Blinds were raised and her office windows open on that warm morning. A corner fan hummed softly, and Jordan sat in the leather chair across from her desk, clasping both armrests. He was grateful she'd made time for him that day.

"We have no evidence that it was the same white car," the prosecutor commented, pushing glasses up the bridge of her nose. "Though the coincidence is striking. And there's certainly no hard evidence that Cathy has been trailing your former girlfriend, or was present the evening of the crime."

"She wasn't," said Jordan, thinking sourly of Molly's pronouncements. "When we were attacked Cathy was auditioning for a TV commercial. She didn't make the cut, but she's got an alibi. People saw her there. Anyway, why would *she* want to hurt me or Rashad?"

"It doesn't make sense," agreed Lydia. "The license plate Melissa gave us, by the way, is registered with a livery company called Pluto Cabs. They have an office in White Plains and Newark. Seem to make a lot of runs to the airports."

Then Jordan remembered that when the trio had first rehearsed with Summer at Z's, she'd place those "Cinderella calls," always saying: "This is Cathy. I need a car." Her friends owned cabs that went to the airports. He must ask her about them before mentioning anything more, even to Lydia.

Summer and Betty drove back from Vermont in a U-Haul stuffed with quilts, yarn, woven blankets, and small antiques. Jordan, Curtis, and the boys helped carry bags and boxes into the basement of the new storefront. Betty's plan was to paint the walls before setting everything up.

"I'll help you tomorrow," Summer offered. She was pink again from sunburn, and her blue eyes looked shifty. She gazed at Jordan, then away from him.

"We're calling the shop Ball of Yarn," Betty announced. "Summer's idea."

Curtis asked Summer, "Anyone ever tell you you're a genius?"

"Someone just did," she answered, with a wink at him.

As they walked home from Ball of Yarn with Rashad, Jordan described running into Mel at school. "I've never been clear on how these imbeciles knew where Rashad went to camp," he said casually to Summer. "Like, how did they know where to jump us?"

"Those imbeciles and I have friends in common," she said quickly. "So-called friends. From high school."

"You mean the guys with the cab company in Newark?"

"Exactly. Geoff and I were their pals, back when we were dating." Jordan sensed that Rashad was trying to understand this conversation, but couldn't quite. Still, he slipped his hand into Jordan's as though he knew they were talking about the assailants. "Years before they started the car service," Summer was saying. "Once Geoff and I went our separate ways, we both kept up with them… loosely. They betrayed me last year. All except one of them."

"How did they betray you?" Jordan tried not to sound too interested as they turned onto Straus. He glanced at the subway entrance where he'd hugged Molly two days ago, before she'd brushed her lips over his cheek and disappeared downstairs on her ruse.

"Well, when Geoff bribed them, they violated my restraining order. They told him where they dropped me off on Essex Street, at Betty's. It's where they thought I lived. They probably saw me take Roo to camp one morning. Refugees from Ceausescu's Romania—those whores would do anything for cash."

Break in the Milk Truck case, Jordan texted Molly the next morning. *They were following ME.*

At my apartment and office every day?

May have been a cover.

For what? She quickly followed up with: *Now it's Tom Sawyer painting the fence white: everyone wants in.*

Can't disclose details, he replied. *My atty traced their license plate to a car service linked to my case.*

What link? How does your attorney have a license for them?

Then he thought better of answering.

Jordan's last words to Eliot had been "If you still had balls, I'd kick the shit out of them." Their rule was that Summer could see him in the thrall of other 9/11 Truthers but not alone. The anniversary of the terrorist attack fell on a Monday, and on that overcast morning Summer trekked out with Eliot and other crusaders to Ground Zero. There they would circulate pamphlets and urge tourists and mourners to "question the mainstream interpretation" and "do your own research" about the events—research that they anticipated would lead everyone to the same conclusions as their own.

Other than that spate of activism, she'd taken to lying around in her blue bathrobe, watching *A Place in the Sun* or Hitchcock's *The Man Who Knew Too Much*, again and again. She claimed she was waiting for "the paint to dry and the dust to settle" before working at Betty's store, because even the water-based paint fumes made her nauseous.

"I saw this on TV at Aunt Maegan's when I was nine," she said, staring dreamily at Doris Day behind a grand piano, surrounded by lilies and scarlet drapery. "Then we sang 'Que Sera, Sera.' My first song." Jordan stood beside her, riveted by Doris Day's charm and beauty onscreen. "I was nine," Summer repeated. "I wanna do it at the hotel."

"You should, honey. My parents loved when you sang it in Fire Island."

"Aunt Maegan and Mom kind of look like Doris—their family's Belgian, hers is German. Same part of the world."

Jimmy Stewart then appeared onscreen, in a suit and striped silk tie, surveying the room with a cryptic nod.

"Daddy." Summer's head fell into her hands.

Your attorney's right about the car service, Molly emailed Jordan the next day. *They showed up again yesterday, after a hiatus. We disguised Gene in a cap and trench coat so she could get close enough to see the license plate.*

That must have been erotic for you, Jordan replied.

What do you know about this?

Not much.

You're playing close to the vest.

Let's talk about the loan. Things are tight here.

Jordan didn't approve of his own tactic but felt he had no choice. If he mentioned Summer's acquaintance with Pluto Cabs, Molly would jump to the most incriminating conclusion. She was on a tear against Summer, as though some jealousy or resentment were getting the better of her. Either that, or she was clinging the simplest resolution to this mystery. So he emailed her a loan agreement and suggested that they notarize it, as they had done in the past.

"Who are you writing to? Let me guess." Summer sneered from the sofa, fiddling with the remote. That morning she was back from Doris Day to the three-way machinations of Monty Clift, Shelley Winters, and Liz Taylor. "Why do you even need me to earn money with your lucky shamrock lending you a life savings?"

"My lucky shamrock's been dragging her feet," muttered Jordan, quickly closing his email window.

"Ms. Perfect is sometimes imperfect. Radical." Before Jordan could respond, Summer arose and stomped across the bare floor, crying, "God in heaven and hell, what is wrong with me?" She slammed the bathroom door, and Jordan turned up the volume so he wouldn't hear her heaving again. It had sounded particularly wrenching lately. He'd rather hear Elizabeth Taylor say to Monty Clift, "Are you blue? Exclusive? Do I make you nervous?" Molly's hunch that Summer was pregnant peeved him. Next week, when her period was due, he would know.

♩

The young woman in Abingdon Square Park sang on pitch but couldn't support her high notes with Summer's power, squeaking them out as she struggled nobly with Leonard Cohen's "Hallelujah." A guy beside her at the base of the statue tapped along on a wooden conga drum. They were college kids; Jordan felt much older as he stuck his hand in his pocket, his fingers around a crumpled five-dollar bill. It was okay to let it fly into their frayed guitar case—they'd be so happy. They might even be able to afford dinner. He could be generous because Molly was going to meet him with the loan check after she saw a client nearby.

He sat on an empty bench with no pigeon shit on it, took out his phone, and revisited their last text exchange. A tall, fair young man in sunglasses sat beside him, also checking a phone. He hummed "Hallelujah" along with the buskers, and Jordan watched him jiggle his long legs in blue jeans.

Then a strikingly beautiful woman with cascades of dark hair sat on his other side. Jordan tried not to stare but felt he recognized her—maybe she was a TV actress. She unwrapped a mozzarella sandwich from waxed paper and began eating it with a sensual familiarity that flustered him. Realizing that he hadn't eaten all day, Jordan found himself asking, "Excuse me, could you tell me where you got that sandwich?"

"When you tell us who's driving the weird limo over there, Jordan," said the blond young man in a soft, steady voice with a Southern accent. Jordan's first thought, as he turned to look at him, was that he was connected to the skinheads.

The guy removed his sunglasses and revealed eyes so brightly blue they seemed lit from inside his head. Sunlight dabbed his hair and glowed orange through the shafts of his ears. "I'm Evan Drury, Eugenia's nephew. And that's Dahlia."

Jordan turned back to her.

"What's the deal here?" he grumbled.

"We're hoping you'll tell us," she said. Her large, dark eyes were like Tamara's, which was why she'd seemed so familiar to Jordan. But instead of appearing to be taken with him, like her younger sister had, Dahlia looked pissed and scornful.

"Who's driving that car?" Evan repeated. "Who's Aunt Molly's new best friend?"

Sure enough, Jordan saw the Milk Truck parked diagonally across the street.

"I can tell you what little I know."

"Or maybe a good lie, so you can confuse us some more," goaded Evan. Though cut from the same cloth as Aunt Eugenia, he wasn't nearly so miraculous a creation; the kid's features didn't configure deliciously as his aunt's high cheekbones and flourished lips; his face lost cohesion beneath the eyes. Yet his lanky angularity lent him a strong presence.

"It's guys from Romania that my fiancée knows. They run a car service."

"Why're they parked here?" asked Evan.

"I'm really not sure."

"Maybe since they're expecting Molly?" Dahlia suggested.

"Maybe."

"Will she be here?" Evan's feigned curiosity was hardly convincing.

"She just texted me," said Jordan.

"You mean like this?" Dahlia put her sandwich down and produced a cell phone from her purse with the exact text in it that he'd just received from Molly.

Jordan stared, not quite comprehending that Dahlia had overtaken Molly's phone and must have texted him herself.

"Molly and my aunt Gene left town last night," said Evan. "For Maui."

"They told me Ireland," refuted Dahlia. "Molly's ancestral voyage."

"Come to think of it," Evan said with a laugh, "they decided on Tahiti at the last minute."

"No, it was the Upper Peninsula of Michigan," said Dahlia. "They're taking the trip that never happened for me and Saul."

"Wherever she is, your driver'll get bummed waiting around for her. *Hallelujah*," Evan sang, again with the kids at the base of the statue. "*Hallelu...u...jah.*"

"What could they want from Molly, anyway?" asked Dahlia.

Jordan stared at her, then at Evan, too discombobulated to speak.

"Blackmail in a white car?" Evan offered. "That's what Aunt Gene calls it."

"How clever," Jordan mumbled.

"We all thought it was Saul, my ex," interjected Dahlia. "So I finally called him. Four hours of grief and rage. Thanks so much."

"Well, maybe it was time you talked to him," Jordan suggested.

Evan and Dahlia glanced at each other.

"That is so none of your beeswax," rejoined Evan, like the teenager he was.

"Look, these jerks were following me too," said Jordan. "I'm not part of this."

"And you're not willfully ignoring anything?" Dahlia prodded.

"No, I'm not," he snapped. "I'm looking into it with my attorney...someone qualified to press charges."

"Well, now." Evan sat back on the bench, his shoulders broad in a pricy-looking polo shirt. "You charged my aunt of running out on Molly with another chick for a bundle of cash."

"Sticking sensors on her," Dahlia reminded him.

"Just a theory," retorted Jordan. "And you know," he said to the kid, "your aunt prematurely indicted me, as a matter of fact."

"The big difference," said Evan, "is that Aunt Gene had a point."

"You had no business accusing her of betraying Molly," Dahlia scolded.

"Really upset her." Evan's eyes softened. "She couldn't believe you'd say something so fucked up, when they were trying to help you. Well, read for yourself."

Dahlia handed Jordan a thick, white envelope with his name on it in Molly's unmistakable cursive.

"Time to moon the shitheads," said Evan, and Dahlia smiled.

She and Evan got up from the bench.

"I know a little Romanian," she said.

"Molly was nervous about provoking these guys," Jordan warned. "We don't know them. They could be armed or something."

Dahlia glanced at Evan protectively. He scowled, raised his hand high, and shot the Milk Truck his bird before he and Dahlia walked off.

Jordan ripped the envelope open and counted ten fifty-dollar bills paper-clipped to a note:

Jordan,

If I'd met Rashad last week, my heart would have opened to a child my godson's age. That's why I walked away—after your ugly words about Genie, on top of Summer's little ploy.

Seemed we were finally burying hatchets and able to hang out and have fun together. You know I treasure your music and your wit. But sadly, I've learned that I'm not among friends with you and Summer, and I must retract my loan offer. Because a child is not accountable for the malfeasance of those around him, you'll find some cash here for Rashad's needs. Please do not worry about repaying me.

Gene and I are leaving town for a while to recover from the strain we've undergone. It will take me a while to get over this betrayal, Jordan. And if you can't figure out what I mean, then only gravity can drop that apple on your head.

—Molly

Jordan kicked himself now for giving the college buskers five dollars. He was going to be strapped.

Later on, he didn't tell Summer what had happened in Abingdon Square Park. Crushed by the loss of a ten-thousand-dollar subvention, he couldn't bear to think that she might have occasioned it—to say the least for occasioning this painful rupture with Molly—who would need "a while" to get over his betrayal? He couldn't begin to wrap his mind around her backing out of the loan and fooling him with texts, and then that guillotine letter.

Meanwhile, Summer's cost to his life was escalating.

When they sat together on the sofa after dinner, he showed her Mel's photos from the day of the attack.

"From what she saw, it seems that Frank Ahlstrom pushed me over."

"That figures," Summer scoffed, pushing the photos away. "They think you're Muslim and fair game for persecution."

"Dad's Jewish, mother's Catholic. Which makes me Muslim *how*?"

"Facts never rated highly for the Ahlstrom brothers."

Jordan fished through the printouts of Mel's photos and found one of the white car. It was blurry in the long angle, but recognizable. He held it up before Summer. "They're all getting out of this weird white car. I think it's one of your friends' cabs."

"Why do you think that?"

He tried to find her gaze but couldn't. Her eyes were icy, unfocused, trying not to see the photo he was holding.

"They're not my friends," she said. "Not after this."

♫

He was afraid at the Susquehanna the next night when Summer held the mic close to her lips, announcing a number that had special meaning for her. Her head drooped and her voice sounded more sultry and intimate than her usual microphone manner. He was afraid she would talk about 9/11 and the "New World Order," completely embarrassing them. He didn't dare look behind him at Z, on whom Summer's caprices were wearing thin.

"When I was nine," she began, "my mother had a nervous breakdown, and my sister and I lived for a year with our aunt, a concert pianist who taught music. That was how I started singing. And this was the first song I learned."

The room sat hushed and spellbound for her "Que Sera, Sera." Fred chimed in softly on piano, and Jordan provided accents on the horn. Applause thundered at the end, and in the darkness, people stood at their small tables with flickering candles and shouted, "More!" and "Another!" and "Sing 'Brooklyn Boy'!"

Summer bowed several times and said, "Thank you. Thank you so much. No encore tonight…thank you."

After the set, Jordan spoke to people in a whirlwind, exchanging business cards and enthusiasms while Z and Bruce packed up. Clasping a wad of bills from CD sales that they desperately needed now, Jordan was too thrilled to notice that Summer had vanished.

Curtis and Betty went to the precinct with him early the next morning, and he faxed Summer's letter to Lydia. But none of that or their calls to detectives, shelters, and hospitals all over the city yielded clues to her whereabouts.

Summer had left her cell phone at home, on the bed. There were only two saved messages—one from a year ago, when Jordan had first played his "Brooklyn Boy" refrain on the sax, and a recent call from her sister. When they'd listened to the latter, Betty and Curtis at first thought they were hearing Summer.

"Her sister's a little more alto," Jordan had observed.

"And less emotional," Betty added.

Less constantly on the brink, Jordan thought, of a seething outburst.

"Hey Cath," Deb had begun. "He's going fast. If you want to call, this is the time. He told Mom that we're the only people he loved worth a damn…that's how he put it: 'Vivian, you and the girls.' She says he's dipping into dementia. He asked her, 'Who's that man in black across the room?' Can you believe Dad said that?"

That message had been left the day before. Curtis, Betty, and Jordan played it again after the boys had gone to bed—a full twenty-four hours after Summer's disappearance.

"Tell me once more," said Curtis, "exactly what happened last night?"

So Jordan described the candle-lit room and the scent of Chanel in a brandy swirl of people raving to meet Summer or have her sign their CD. "I didn't see her anywhere, so I figured she went to the girls room. She's been feeling so lousy."

Betty nodded. "She was in bed half the time, in Vermont."

"Then Teddy came with the envelope, saying that Summer had rushed out and given it to him for me. I read it with Z, and we asked Teddy if he had any idea where she'd gone. He thought she was heading home.

"Z drove me back and came upstairs. We looked all over, I mean, under beds, in closets. We thought about going to the cops but figured I should wait until morning, in case she showed up. When she didn't, I called you guys."

Betty shut her eyes and Curtis shrugged sadly. They hadn't been much help.

Jordan told Rashad that Summer was on tour with Tillie and Shazan again and that they were staying with the Wilcoxes because their own apartment was being fumigated while she was away. Rashad seemed to accept that was why Jordan slept on the sofa in Curtis and Betty's study, and Jordan badly wished it were all true. But in fact, he couldn't bear to be alone with Rashad at their apartment and not know where Summer was.

After saying good night to Betty and Curtis, he pulled out Summer's long letter again. How many times now had he scoured those lines of jangled script? In the last three days he'd been handed two letters—one from each of the women he'd loved most, and each of them saying, "Goodbye, and don't look for me."

Dear Jordan,

I know you've read all sorts of private correspondences, like cards from Deb to me or my letter to Mom. So here, finally, is something intended for you. You'll prob-

ably show it to others, maybe even law enforcement (who you seem to trust more than you trust me). But it will be too late because I'm out of here.

Ever since we met (and you must remember this) I told you I was way too much for you to handle. I said that I'd fuck up. As time went on, I questioned whether we should marry. But you always insisted (not to plagiarize Lennon and McCartney) that we could work it out. You reassured me that even our parents raked through the thickest tangles. As usual, just as I started to believe it, the door slammed in my face. When you started hanging with Molly again, showing more allegiance to her than to me, I knew our marriage was doomed.

Tonight, before I take leave, I will sing like nothing matters but whatever will be will be, and a beautiful boy. I want to leave you with something extraordinary because the ugly stuff will surface. I think you know what I mean because of your expression when you showed me Mel's photos of the boxy white limo.

That stupid car, and two others just like it, were donations from Geoff and Frank Ahlstrom to Pluto Cabs. The Ahlstroms got them through this Aryan Brotherhood copycat group they belong to. For their extravagant donation, Bogdan, the Romanian refugee who owns Pluto Cabs, performed favors for Geoff and Frank.

I always believed Bogdan was my old friend and that he gave me free cab rides to help me out. But he backstabbed me, funneling info to Geoff—restraining order be damned. Remember how they thought I lived on Essex Street and could never find me?

So between that cussed high school reunion website and my activism against the 9/11 lies, they zeroed in on me. After eluding him for 8 years, I had Geoff on my trail again: at Susquehanna that night you saw him, at antiwar rallies, and when I sang in Union Square—always in the creepy white car. I had no idea why this damn car was up my ass, on every street sometimes and at Rashad's school and camp. I thought it might have been the fucking CIA or someone who knew my dad. Once or twice it even followed you and me. You had no idea and thought I was acting crazy.

Then one of the guys who works with Bogdan—another high school friend from Romania, named Vali—told me the truth. Geoff was following me around in that white car, whenever he could, and he was furious to learn I have a half-black kid. Remember, I was with Geoff only for a year, when we were 17. You know how I'm a sucker for male flattery (I was even worse then).

But we also know how men are suckers for their own pasts, Jordan. Vali told me that Geoff wanted to hurt Rashad. He has this thing about "the white race being diluted" by kids like Rashad, all this symbolic hate. They were planning to kidnap him! Get you out of the way, then take my son. Vali warned me. For his loyalty I gave him the last ring I had left from my mother.

The day you and Rashad were attacked, Vali texted and called me in a frenzy. But I was in that TV audition and didn't get his messages until I came home, and the damage was done. And I tell you, it could have been much fucking worse. If Mel hadn't gotten the cops on those sick fucks, Geoff would have come around in the white car again and taken both you and Rashad where the sun don't shine. That was the plan.

I'm sure you're wondering whether Vali will testify for you. He's still deciding. He's a little scared of Geoff. But he did confide to me that he and his wife plan to leave the country soon. So he may break ranks with Bogdan and this whole mess. In which case, he'll contact you about being a witness before the grand jury. No question that his testimony about Geoff and Frank Ahlstrom would seal your deal.

It was Vali who told me where Frank's car was parked when I went to key it, and the kind of Neo-Nazi shit that was in it. He even said he'd break into the trunk with me. But I knew that burden was mine, that I've hurt enough innocent people. And I'd asked more than enough of Vali, who was driving the white car you and Molly saw.

Because your sham of a lucky shamrock is NOT innocent. I was just so fucking pissed at Bogdan for betraying me and so fucking pissed at HER for seducing you with money—your Achilles' heel—that I figured I'd sic 'em on each other. Figured she'd be sharp enough to bust Pluto Cabs; either that or they'd rock her world. Either way, I could gloat.

Vali agreed to stalk her in the white car during his week off, because of our bond from adolescence and because I handed him the last of Mom's rings and it was the nicest thing he ever gave his wife. He wasn't comfortable following

Molly, but I said SHE was ruining our marriage plans. Vali's also very Catholic and conservative about gay stuff, so I convinced him to just follow her around and wig her out. Maybe now you see that she's not so invincible. In fact, she was weak and ridiculous.

Still, she's not dark. She's not a destroyer, like I am. That's why you're drawn to her, and maybe it's healthy. We both know I am not healthy. And so I must absent myself and go where I will never hurt anyone again.

Anyway, we can agree that you're a better parent to my son than I am. You two are bonding in a special way. My mother and Deb have their special bond. I'm not needed anymore. The rest of you can take over with each other. I'm so happy that Rashad has Mona and Capitano to love him, and Betty and Curtis.

Please tell Curtis I'm glad he produced my songs. Tell Betty I'm sorry about bugging out on the shop. Maybe Mel needs a PT job. Any single mom would welcome the chance to work for someone as great as our Betty. I'm glad she'll always have her song. Remember when I first played it on the piano? Our good times will live in my heart until it breaks for good, my sweet Jordan.

You alone gave me life in the open air, the love of another being, and Creation. But we had no freedom from ambition. By that, we were ruined.

You might mourn our separation at first, but one day you'll realize what I'm doing is for the best. I've craved true love and friends, but with me darkness always comes, sooner or later. Even in a white car. Do not look for me. You'll never find me. I'm no good for you, or anyone else.

> *Your love,*
> *Summer*

Another day went by. The detectives told him to start notifying people who knew her. Jordan called Robin in London, asking if she'd heard from Summer. She hadn't. He didn't want to alarm Deb or Summer's mother, with the father at death's door—he felt like a jerk at the thought of it. Besides, if Deb knew anything, why would she keep calling Summer's cell phone about their father's decline?

He didn't want to contact Pluto Cabs or Skip and Tillie, and certainly not

Eliot or the other 9/11 Truth fanatics. What could they know, and how could he find the words to ask them?

He begged everyone to give it one more day.

A week had now passed since the 9/11 Anniversary, and this Monday night brought dreams of alpine trees and waterfalls. Doris Day appeared in the gray skirt suit she wore when she sang "Que Sera, Sera" to her kidnapped son in the film. As he awoke, Jordan felt wrenched from her, expelled from a forestial dreamland.

Before emerging from the covers, he lit a joint and sat up to smoke.

Exhaling, he conjured a clammy summer day in Flatbush, where he'd mulled around in hand-me-down jeans and a stained shirt, his hair still so long in the mid-eighties that people called him "a little girl," or worse.

"Where's Arman?" he remembered whining to his mother. "Why isn't he here?" Mariana must have been forty, thin and retro-hip with her long, black Joan Baez hair. She didn't answer him. Robin, at four, had been on the floor playing noisily with blocks. Her hair was also long and tangled, but people thought she was a boy sometimes, with those unisex names his parents had preferred.

"Where's Arman!" Jordan had screamed, as though his mother couldn't understand language. All she had done was march swiftly out of the room.

The weed was drying his mouth, but Jordan nipped at it again, coughing gently, as he envisioned Summer around that same age of nine. She'd be wearing seersucker shorts and a clean, pressed blouse with a lapel and asking her father, "Where's Mom? Why are we going to Aunt Maegan's?" The politician, in his suit and tie, might have told his daughter, "Mom must go to the doctor's." Summer had probably said something sharp like, "Not for that long," and her dad might have said, "Yes, for that long. But don't tell other people. Don't say anything to the kids at school, Cathy."

Meanwhile, Molly at age nine, unlike him and Summer, always knew when dinner was and who would be at the table. Jordan exhaled through his nose. Father, mother, sister, brother, white picket fence. The great crisis of their dinner table would be "Mom, tell Matthew to quit kicking my legs," and her brother squealing back, "She started it!"

"Children. Behave." That's what Molly's parents would have said, words that he and Summer hadn't heard. For different reasons, neither of them had been "children."

He inhaled hard, furious that Molly had been right about everything that day in Seward Park, disgusted with her retracted loan, the "cutting out of here" with Eugenia, and getting Dahlia to text him. She knew how miserably he needed money, and had faked a meeting with him at Abingdon Park. She'd been a hypocrite, asking him to lie about the photo shoot to Summer—she, who "didn't keep secrets" from her own lover.

He stood up, putting the half-smoked joint between pages of a paperback for later, and decided to really fumigate their apartment. He didn't want to keep lying about that to Rashad. Later, while Rashad was in school, Jordan secured plans with the building management at East Broadway. After giving the super a set of keys, he picked up their mail, which was mostly for Gus Granato. Then he left fast—too upset, even in the lobby, to think that Summer might never be there again.

On his way to help Betty finish painting shelves at the store, Jordan answered his phone. "Any word from Cathy?" his attorney asked.

There hadn't been. Lydia then told him the grand jury hearing might be postponed until October because of a "new, related case in New Jersey. Maybe you've heard?" Jordan hadn't. "It appears that one of the defendant's brothers was arrested this morning. He'd been driving the white car when you were accosted."

"Geoff Ahlstrom."

Jordan wondered why that creep had suddenly come clean.

"The name hasn't yet been released," Lydia said. "But I'll get back to you."

As he hung up, Jordan felt a surge of optimism, a "ding-dong, the witch is dead" kind of hope that Geoff Ahlstrom's sudden arrest might lure Summer back to them.

The door to Ball of Yarn was propped open, and, to his surprise, Summer's songs emanated from the CD player inside, making him miss her even more.

Betty emerged from the back room, her dark hair pulled back in a ponytail and blue eyes wide.

She told Jordan eagerly, "I just called the precinct."

"About Geoff Ahlstrom's arrest?"

She shook her head. "Don't know that name. I called about Summer. Just had a feeling they'd found something."

Jordan grabbed Betty's slender wrist. "Have they?"

He realized that his hand was shaking and quickly released Betty's wrist.

"The Susquehanna is a far cry from the hospitals or shelters we expected. Nothing definite, but…the detective who has her photo says that they got a call from the hotel. Seems she may have spent Saturday and Sunday night in a room there, under the name Maegan Haarlan. I wrote it down. An unusual spelling of *Maegan*, and *Haarlan*, with two *a*'s. According to their description, the woman was wearing the yellow sweater I knitted for her."

"Aunt Maegan." Jordan nearly chuckled.

As if to underscore their relief, Summer's voice sang melodiously from the stereo, "*I remember when Aunt Maegan said 'You're scaring everyone.'*"

Jubilant, Jordan and Betty embraced. Even in her exuberance, Betty felt so much more placid in his arms than flinty Summer, or Molly. Jordan knew he would never be intimate with a calm, modest woman like Betty—ever.

"Her mom," Jordan cried, stepping back from Betty. "Vivian H. Summers. I remember the middle initial. *H* for Haarlan."

He thought of mentioning the credit card but quickly decided to honor Summer's secrets.

"It must have been Summer," Betty agreed excitedly. "She apparently paid for the room with a VISA in her aunt's name. I could swear she said this aunt passed away, but there's a line of credit and an address in Burlington County, New Jersey. The cops said a Maegan Haarlan had lived there eighteen years ago. They think she may have left the country. I didn't mention she might be deceased." Betty shrugged.

"When did Summer check out of the hotel?" Jordan asked.

"Guess it would have been Monday morning. Yesterday."

Monday, Monday; yesterday morning.

Summer was hiding out in a maze of lyrics.

That evening, Jordan sat on Betty and Curtis' terrace with a bottle of Heineken, letting her songs cycle through him. The sky darkened earlier now, as the calendar tipped toward the autumn equinox. In a month, he and Summer were supposed to marry. They had liked that date, October 22. "One two for me," she'd said, "and one for you."

So far, everyone who'd been named in her songs had figured in her sudden fadeout: Betty, the yellow sweater, Jordan himself, and Molly; even the late Aunt Maegan. But not Deb or her mother, who figured strongly in "Short Stick." Jordan assumed, as he swigged from the green bottle, they would be next.

It made sense for Summer to hide with her soon-to-be widowed mother, whom she claimed she'd never forgive. No one would look for her there, as in: "You'll never find me." Or maybe she went to Deb's and was hitching across the country now. It was time to call people who knew her mother and Deb.

Jordan fiddled in his jacket for Summer's cell phone and remembered that one new call had come in that morning. He hadn't yet listened to it; he didn't recognize the number, and the name was unavailable. At his ear, the phone hummed now with a hoarse voice, a Romanian accent mangled by adolescence in New Jersey.

"Cathy, hi. Listen, I know it's right to testify. Not to sound uncompassionate, but some people never change…and we both know where Geoff belongs.

"Bogdan says Geoff's flipping out about the grand jury investigation and taking off tonight to hide with those rats in the Midwest. I'm gonna call the cops in Tom's River about his racket in the cellar. Like, now. Listen, call me when you can."

Clearly, Vali's police report had led to Ahlstrom's arrest that day. Now Geoff was in the clinker, squirming with the other worms like the dashes and dots they all were. As Jordan took another swig of beer, the glass door to the deck swished open and Rashad popped out.

"Is dinner ready, Roo?" Jordan asked him.

"C'we call Mom?" Rashad asked back, his dark eyes searching Jordan.

"She left her phone here," Jordan replied, holding up Summer's cell phone. "Remember? She didn't take it on the tour."

The child stared back, his brow scrunched.

"When is she coming home?"

"In a while."

"But when? How many days?"

Jordan thought of how he'd asked his mother that question about Arman years ago, when Robin had been slamming toy blocks on the floor. Now he understood why Mariana couldn't answer, though he'd hated her walking out on him.

"I don't know," Jordan said, not doing much better than his mother had.

"But how *come* you don't know?"

"Because she might visit your aunt Deb."

"Well...well, Aunt Deb will be at the wedding," Rashad protested. "And I'm gonna hold the ring with Cousin Max, who's in first grade."

Jordan glanced away, to the soft lights from windows of other buildings, and Rashad stepped back into the world inside.

Behind the glass doors a big TV screen flickered bright colors. Jordan watched Betty set the table for six, as though it were part of the show. Curtis brought out a bottle of wine and a corkscrew. He placed the bottle on the table, sank the corkscrew into the top, and drew the cork from the bottle. Betty placed a pan on the trivet. Jordan remembered his thirtieth birthday party, the surprise on this very roof deck, like it was part of a fanciful Fellini film with people celebrating—including him.

Clouds grazed the moon slowly, as it beamed like a single headlight in the broken sky. "*Now you see her, now you don't. She loves me, loves me not...*"

He sang the lyric for a moment, then hit redial on her phone.

Vali answered breathlessly. "Cathy! Where the hell've you been? You know what's going on?"

"Vali? This is Jordan."

After a brief silence, Vali said, "How do I know that?"

"Well, for starters, I was wearing a white shirt on Friday the eighth when you followed me and Molly Douglas to East Broadway and parked by the Golden Sun Buddhist Temple."

The man said nothing, so Jordan continued: "I wore a blue button-down shirt when you drove to Abingdon Square Park last Thursday when Molly didn't show up, but two other people did—a blond guy and a dark-haired woman."

"You're not supposed to know who I am," said Vali. "What happened?"

"Cathy disappeared."

"What?"

"She's gone. No one's seen her since late Saturday night. We notified the cops."

"Are you telling the truth?" Vali sounded alarmed.

"Why the fuck else would I call you?"

"Look…she said she'd drown herself unless I scared Molly off. Said she'd take the Staten Island Ferry and…you know about her mother, right? I mean, I had to do this. I felt horrible enough about Geoff, like I coulda done more to stop him."

"Well, you probably could've."

"Does Deborah know she's missing?"

"I don't think so. She keeps calling about their dad. He's dying."

"Yeah, yeah," said Vali. "You must speak to Deborah. If Deborah doesn't know anything, this is very serious."

Jordan slept fitfully, awakening every few hours in a cold sweat.

"*When I go to hell, he'll get on the J train. When I go to hell, he'll get on the J train.*" The lyric plagued him.

Yes, the J traversed Brooklyn, though not in neighborhoods where he'd lived. It paralleled the Z line, and they always ran together, J and Z. While she'd been tormented, he'd been on track with Z and the trio, and he'd cast Molly as their savior. What self-respecting man would obsess about cash flow with his woman, even if she cost him more than anything else? Maybe two women, like Molly and Eugenia, could discuss each other's balance sheets in good faith, especially when the news tended to be as upbeat as theirs. But it did not befit a penniless man and a woman of privilege. And so he'd deserved Summer's desertion.

He woke again an hour later, his throat parched from wine and weed, in a paroxysm to dissect the local variations of hell: Hell's Angels, Hell's Kitchen, Spuyten Duyvil. No. He didn't want to think about what Vali had said about the Staten Island Ferry, or the precinct detectives asking him: "What does she mean by 'You'll mourn our separation,' and 'You'll never find me'? Could this be construed as a suicide note?"

Jordan had quickly said no, but Betty had told them about Summer's mother.

"She never talked about suicide," Jordan argued. "Just about how she's not good for me, and we shouldn't get married, and she's weak. She didn't admire her mother."

But now he remembered her nausea and wondered if she'd been taking something. He tossed over again and lost consciousness until warm fingertips slid over his cheek, and he heard someone whisper, "No, honey. Let him sleep." He opened an eye to see Betty, in a long, sage green robe, escort Rashad out of the room.

Would a seagull circle over Central Park, blinking shadows against its own white breast as it flew? Would a gull, like those he saw in Fair Harbor, fly so far inland, or was this actually a pigeon's wing glinting against an azure sky so perfectly quiet it was like its own halo? After forcing himself to teach two sections of band at the boys' school, Jordan stole into Central Park to smoke a joint. He emerged from the bushes with his saxophone case and noticed the gull, or pigeon, circling overhead.

Settling on grass beneath a tree near the reservoir, he hoped no joggers sniffed his cannabis as they loped weightlessly by, women's ponytails jiggling a half second behind their heads. He took out his own cell phone and Summer's to perform his review beneath the oblivious and perfect September sky.

On his phone, Lydia bore news about Geoff Ahlstrom's counterfeit stamp business in his cellar being seized. "They'd been using infrared ink for years," she said. The story felt creepy and surreal, like everything about Geoff Ahlstrom. Then Vali had called wondering if Jordan had "heard from Cathy."

Jordan took in the sun-drenched greenery around him, the ambitious joggers in neon-colored t-shirts. Then he went to Summer's phone, where a new voice message from Deb had come in while he'd been teaching. "Whoa," the sister of his betrothed began. "Cathy, what the…? Your message from this morning sounded really…I don't believe for two seconds that Jordan threw you out on the street. Not for two seconds. Why would he? Even if he wanted to, the deed is in your name, isn't it? Come on, Cath. You're talking to me, not some dupe."

Jordan shut his eyes and moaned softly with relief. If Deb had received such a message this morning, Summer was alive and telling her usual lies. The air felt suddenly sweeter.

"I know a lot's going on," Deb was saying. "Losing a father, gaining a husband. But it's time you speak to Mom. Cath, you've really got to. Some collectors from the IRS got ahold of her, and she was great. Said if they could prove the amount of your debt, she'll pay them." Then Deb drew in her breath and murmured, "Stewart's working at home today and driving me to the office. If he sees me on the phone with you, he'll have a fit. Let's try to talk later." The message abruptly ended. Jordan watched a red Frisbee arch above the reservoir fence and into the sky.

Immediately, he called Deb's number back. Across the United States a phone rang, and a voice answered so faintly that Jordan wasn't sure it had happened. "Hello, Deb?" he hazarded.

"This is Deborah's husband," said the voice. "Who might you be?" The systems engineer, or whatever Stewart was, sounded terse and defensive.

"Stewart?"

"Who is this?"

"Um, actually, I'm Cathy's fiancé, Jordan. Calling from New York."

"Oh," said Stewart, after a seemingly startled moment. "You play music or something, don't you? My kids think you're a rock star."

"I'm glad someone does."

"Deborah's not here. She's at work. How did you get this number?"

Not wanting to betray Deb, Jordan quickly said, "Your mother-in-law."

"Vivian called you?"

"She called Cathy," Jordan said quickly. "But Cathy's, like, gone. She disappeared."

Stewart paused. "Describe 'disappeared.'"

Jordan confessed, "I didn't want to alarm you guys, but it's been four days. No one's seen her since Saturday night—and she left me a pretty disturbing letter."

"She's done this before," said Stewart evenly. "I hope you didn't get worked up."

"I've been out of my fucking mind."

The man on the other line sighed. "How long have you known her?"

"Two years."

"And you're tying the knot?"

"If I can find her."

"You will. When Cathy goes off to lick her wounds, everyone trembles because of the family history. But Cathy's not like her mother, who's-the-real-deal desperate and impulsive. Have you met Vivian yet?"

"No."

"Welcome to the weirdest family in Hubble's deep space sphere." Stewart laughed quietly.

"Thank you," said Jordan. "So…you say Cathy's done this before?"

"She left Deborah a missive when our first child was born about how she was too dark and troubled to be around us at our time of joy. Then she hid out in Cineplexes in L.A., you know, going from screen to screen all day. Meanwhile, my poor wife called every precinct, the fire department, and our congressman.

"Another time Cathy went AWOL after a big fight with her dad, she popped up at my mother's in Scotch Plains, New Jersey."

"Your mother's?" Summer had never told him that.

"My mother does animal rescue, so I suppose Cathy figured she'd take in any stray. Which she did. All by way of saying—and I'll cut to the chase—that she's too self-centered for suicide. Like her father. Look at how that old dog is holding on in the face of multiple organ failure. People like this have no taste for death, really.

"But the great victory here, of course, is that Vivian will outlive him. Nobody thought she would, given her…um, predilections. But she's twelve years younger than George, sober for six years, and in remarkable shape, considering the hit her body has taken from booze, nicotine, and lithium.

"She's finally found a psychiatrist who possesses some sense about how to rehabilitate her with a minimum of medication, and she's in Twelve Step groups that George would never let her join when he was in politics. So now, after the high jinx he pulled with her inheritance, the marital property reverts to her." Stewart emphasized: "All of it."

"All of what?"

"You don't know?"

"I don't even know where Cathy fucking is. Sorry," Jordan said quickly. "Didn't mean to bark at you."

"I didn't mean to be sarcastic," said Jordan's erstwhile brother-in-law. "But Cathy has her way of keeping people in the dark when the sun is rising. It's not my role to overstep here. But if you're marrying her…oh, okay. Okay. That's probably why Vivian was calling her. Do you have a minute?"

"Of course."

"You might be able to help us."

"With what?"

"A long, messy matter of estate law. Sheesh…where can I even begin? In Cape Town, over a century ago, an aristocratic Belgian family called Van Haarlan were powerful merchants until the Brits came along, elbowing them out of the way—but not without an intermarriage that bears on both of our circumstances today."

The voice that had been guarded and surly when he picked up the phone had now grown lively. And it sounded like a good story about the rest of Jordan's life was about to be relayed.

"A variation on the old Romeo and Juliet saga," Stewart began. "Around 1868 one Giliam Van Haarlan fell madly in love—probably opening the madness vein of that family—with a British girl named Margaret. He changed his name to William Harlan and became, for all purposes, British. Does that sleight of hand bring anyone to mind?"

"Sure does," Jordan agreed.

"So, once he 'became' British, William married Margaret. Meanwhile, his brother, Nicolaas, emigrated to the United States, to Delaware and then to New Jersey, where he too dropped the *Van* and changed his family name to Haarlan, keeping the two *a*'s. And so, with one emigrating and one marrying a Brit, these clever boys—the forebears of Deborah and Cathy—spared themselves the fate of other European colonists, who were quashed in Africa by the Brits.

"William's in-laws were mining magnates, and Nicolaas raised capital in the Americas for the metal trade in South Africa. You see how they played it: Nicolaas helped fund his brother's mines, which boomed in the late 1800s, and his so-called British brother cut him in on the profits. You never heard this?"

"Not at all," said Jordan, riveted by the implications. "Please go on."

"In their declining years, these shrewd brothers willed to their male heirs shares of the land where the mines operate—they're thriving today, incidentally. Meanwhile, their female descendants would inherit—how can I put it?—a highly appraised booty of mine-cut gems and court jewelry."

"That I've heard a little about."

Jordan remembered Summer in her blue bathrobe eating ice cream at sunrise when the twins stayed with them after Betty's miscarriage. She'd hinted that a valuable necklace was hidden in their apartment. Jordan had since wondered whether that was even true.

"You may not know that this illustrious family didn't multiply so fruitfully," Stewart went on. "William's descendants, the British Harlans, pretty much vanished in the forties during the war. There are one or two scions in South Africa, some second cousins in Antwerp, but that's it. And most of the American Haarlans didn't have children, for various reasons—one being that a lot of them were screwy, like Vivian. And the ones that weren't, understood that wealthy people take risks when they marry. Which may be why Nick never did. He's had more than enough women to choose from. You've heard of Uncle Nick?"

"You mean Ashley?" Stewart erupted into laughter that surpassed Jordan's ideas about how a systems engineer could laugh. Jordan found himself laughing too, because in his gut he knew Summer was okay, that this episode was like a loop on those childhood board games he'd played, with moving pieces, booby traps—and prizes.

Finally Stewart said, "Uncle Nick does bear a resemblance to Leslie Howard. He plays it up—wears his hair the same way. And I'm sure she mentioned that there apparently was progressed adolescent nooky between him and Vivian. Initiated by her, the rumor goes, and it's easy to believe. In wealthy families, or very poor ones, I guess, brothers and sisters go at it. I have no idea...I'm an only child." But the lore seemed to hold some fascination for him. Deb's husband probably didn't get to speak with many people like this.

"The original Nicolaas, who came to New Jersey, had only sons," he continued, "so his granddaughter, Vivienne—Deborah and Cathy's great aunt—inherited the gemstones. She was a classicist who taught at the Sorbonne. In the fifties, she tracked down two former apprentices of Alphonse Mucha. One was in Paris and the other in Vienna. She commissioned art nouveau necklaces with themes from Greek mythology—all pertaining to the sea, 'cause that was her thing.

"The most magnificent of them replicates Botticelli's *The Birth of Venus*, you know, on the shell. She had the craftsmen embed her garnets and diamonds. I think she did about seven of these necklaces in all. It was rumored that she and one of Mucha's apprentices had a torrid love affair. When it ended, so did most of the art nouveau necklace production.

"Vivienne never married, and the next in line to inherit these treasures when she died in 1969 were her nieces, Maegan and Vivian—the latter being her namesake and our eccentric mother-in-law."

"Awesome." Jordan watched the red Frisbee catapult across the reservoir fence again as he sat beneath his tree. Runners continued to trudge by, their skin slick with sweat.

"After their aunt passed away and they came into this sudden inheritance, Vivian and Maegan ran off to Cape May with the girls—who were all of five and three years old in the summer of 1970."

"Oh yeah," said Jordan. "I've heard about Cape May, and the yellow house."

"What did Cathy tell you?"

"That her mom was normal back then."

"Normal…and suddenly heiress to a fortune that both her own mother and her husband, George, coveted. That's why she and Maegan ran off…the young heiresses needed to talk about how to handle their husbands, and their mother, Martine—who wasn't a direct descendant, and not entitled to any of it, per the wording of the will. So George Summers and Maegan's jerk husband bonded with Martine to try and declare the jewelry marital property, rather than an heirloom.

"In typical George Summers style, he denounced the inheritance practice as 'archaic' and 'un-American.' You can imagine, in 1970, how this Republican prick was hailed as a feminist, of all things—people saw him as supporting his mother-in-law against sexist European traditions." Stewart laughed again, disarmingly.

"But he had no standing in court. 'Marital property' is basically a divorce concept. And the jewelry wasn't in a trust. So: too bad for Martine, who had always been jealous of her daughters. And too bad for Maegan's husband, who was an abusive scoundrel. They had no children, so Aunt Maegan solved her husband problem by separating from him and living in South Africa with Nick for a while.

"Vivian solved her husband problem by drinking. She was appalled that George would deprive his daughters of what she considered their birthright. Guess she was starting to realize whom she'd married. But she didn't want to divorce George, with his emerging stature in politics and their two lovely daughters, of whom we're so fond."

"Mmm," agreed Jordan.

"Not being the independent cuss that Maegan was, Vivian capitulated to George's wishes and agreed to declare the jewelry their joint property—all the while suffering guilt about her forebears and her mother and also about her girls. So she kept a secret stash of rings for them, while George put the more valuable, elaborate necklaces and other spoils into a bank safe. Except for Venus, who's on long-term loan to the Louvre.

"Fast-forward to 1971: after two years of grueling probate, paperwork, and guilt, Vivian—being Vivian—is ready to hang herself. George is horrified by her first attempt. He's really thin-skinned about all that and gets her to a private facility.

"Before she's carted off, in a panic she throws a stash of rings into a paper bag and tells six-year-old Deborah, 'I'm going away and may never come back.' Sweet words for a little girl, aren't they? Then she says, 'Please keep this for you and Cathy Jane, because I love you more than anything and always will.' With a kiss on her head, and a stroke on her cheek, their mother disappears for a while. You might know the rest of the story."

"Yeah, I do. But Cathy says that apart from the rings, which she pretty much pawned off over the years, there's a necklace somewhere in our apartment."

"One of Great Aunt Vivienne's most sensational pieces, with color-change garnets from Kenya—you've never seen it?"

"I think she keeps it in a locked file." That was Jordan's hunch.

"You've got to check it out. In daylight those garnets are blue or green, but they turn pink in brighter light. George had originally sold it and the companion necklace that Deborah now has to the Victoria and Albert Museum in London. You know about the trouble he got into back in the nineties. Cathy must have told you."

"No," said Jordan.

"What do you talk about with her, if you don't mind my asking?"

"What key to play a song in. Who's gonna pick the kid up from school…"

"All right," said Stewart. "I don't want to spill every bean in the jar here. Suffice it to say that when he got into a pinch with the law over receiving bribes and needed hush money, George sold two necklaces from his marital property. I'm not sure if he had her on suicide watch yet, but Vivian was heavily sedated and not terribly focused. George didn't tell her about the transaction, and she didn't notice.

"But some years later, Nick was alerted—or, Ashley, the lovebug brother—and he purchased the necklaces back from the V and A Museum. Appreciate that Nick Haarlan, heir to the Van Haarlan mines, has that kind of cash at hand."

"I appreciate it," said Jordan.

"You know, George refused to escort Deborah down the aisle when she married me because he loathed my mother's liberal politics. Couldn't stand to see his daughter marry a Democrat! So Uncle Nick performed that rite at our wedding, and we've kept in touch with him. We weren't surprised when he called us six years back—but we were shocked by the story about how George sold the necklaces behind Vivian's back. Deborah, long a veteran of her father's shenanigans, burst into tears.

"Seems Nick had descended, unannounced, with both of the necklaces he'd recovered, upon George and Vivian when they were still in New Jersey. That's when he saw, firsthand, what a drunk his beautiful sister had become. He really gave it to George. Said that if Vivian didn't get help, he would seize their family assets. You better believe George Summers copped to that threat. You know about him—son of a pediatrician. Not exactly poverty-stricken. But not so well situated as his wife. He married up and knew it.

"Vivian was so shaken when she heard what George had done without her consent that she resolved to get sober and insisted that Nick entrust a garnet necklace to each of her daughters for safekeeping. They all agreed that once Nick saw she was doing better—and he wanted a doctor's letter—the necklaces would be restored to her and George and no assets would be taken from them.

"So that's the necklace Cathy's talking about. It has mermaids. Deborah's centerpiece is Poseidon. Drawn by Mucha's former apprentice, plated with white gold and sterling silver. They're easily worth a quarter of a mil each."

"Which couldn't come a day too soon for us," said Jordan.

"Yeah, but Nick doesn't want them sold out of the family again. He wants to start a museum in Cape Town. Everything's changing now. George is on his way out. Nick and Vivian, the surviving Haarlans, call the shots. They plan to change the inheritance structure so male and female heirs receive equal amounts of capital, and the jewelry will go into this family collection. Considering his wealth, Nick is refreshingly principled, and Vivian's repenting her fallen ways. So if you ever worried about how you're going to retire, or pay for the higher education of Cathy's son..."

"Hell, we worry about keeping our lights on. We're musicians."

Jordan watched two girls roll down a hill across the jogging path. Both arms stretched over their heads, they held hands until their tumbles separated them. Once they made it to the bottom of the slope, they raced up again and started over.

"But look, here's the wrinkle you might help us with, which is probably why Vivian called: Cathy changed her name legally—not to her stage name, which we know is Summer Vale. We have no idea what her new name is. And she's adamant about not trusting her mom, and not wanting anything to do with her."

"*I'm* not even sure of her legal name."

"Even though you're marrying her?"

Jordan just sighed, and Stewart continued.

"This could delay all sorts of paperwork. Possibly for years. But even if we never learn her legal name, you can count on Deborah making sure Cathy gets her due, even if she has to fly to New York and uncurl her sister's fists and stuff every bill into her hands. Cathy has this rap about how it's tarnished money, from slave labor."

"I'll talk her out of that," said Jordan. "If I find her."

"Look, if Vivian calls again, it's a call you want to take. It would behoove you to lock everything in with her now that she's sober and focused—and in atonement mode, big-time. You know how they work Twelve Step programs? You're supposed to make amends with people who were hurt by the addictions. She's very eager to help her daughters."

"Awesome," repeated Jordan, too astonished to say anything else.

"And while we believe she's here to stay, Vivian remains a bit of a variable. Recovered alcoholics tend to fall off the wagon. Or, for all we know, she may find another George Summers. According to Deborah, any number of snakes in their retirement community already have their roving eyes on this attractive, wealthy, almost-widow."

"I appreciate your leveling with me," said Jordan, still taking it all in and not quite believing any of it.

"All by way of saying, go long on that short stick while you can."

"Stewart, I'm getting another call. I better take it."

"You'd better. We know who it is."

"Jawdon," said a familiar voice when Jordan switched to his call waiting line. "Tillie Mack here."

"Hey, Tillie." After tales of African mines and necklaces with precious metals, Jordan felt disoriented. He recalled singing choro music with Eliot and drinking tea with port on winter nights. He assumed Tillie was calling about the wedding invitation, but she sounded somber.

"Can you talk now?"

"Yeah."

"I've seen Summer."

"Where?" He gripped the phone.

"Look, she's"—Tillie began with such tension in her voice that Jordan felt the happily-ever-after version of their life slide like wet mud—"she's in the hospital."

"Was there an accident?"

Tillie didn't answer immediately.

"Psych ward. Here, in the city."

When Jordan could find nothing to say, Tillie continued. "I was with her at intake—"

"*Intake?*"

"Listen, she needs her blood test. She needs you to bring it to the hospital tomorrow, during visiting hours. Remember, you both took an HIV test last winter?"

"Tillie, what the fuck is going on?"

"They did a presumptive toxicology test. And you know Summer. She's not a drinker or user. It was fine. But she wants to show them that her blood was good even when she wasn't planning to check into a psych ward."

"What is going on?" Jordan repeated.

"Jawdon," Tillie said, almost too quietly for him to hear, "she's pregnant."

The psychiatric nurse led Jordan through a corridor with men in wheelchairs who somehow couldn't keep their tongues in their mouths, and puffy women with hooded turtle eyes. One had gnarly gray hair like his grandmother's and might have looked cozy had the nurse not mentioned that some acute inpatients were violent.

Summer would meet him in the visitor's room.

"I can't believe she didn't tell you about me," Jordan said to the nurse.

"We have only Tillie Mack listed as her contact."

Whatever, Jordan thought scornfully. He had given the nurse Summer's blood test, which he had retrieved from the locked file. Tillie had told him where to find the key, in an old jar of jellybeans in the kitchen cabinet. In another mood, he might have ravaged Summer's locked file, but not that morning; he'd barely been able to walk out the door.

The nurse led him to a lounge, where a few other patients and guests sat around low tables. A Latina woman with her family seemed briefly annoyed by new people walking in, and a middle-aged woman feeding an older woman in a wheelchair didn't notice. Summer would enter, with a security guard, from a door across the room.

"Take a seat," the nurse said to Jordan. "She'll be here shortly."

"I didn't know we could bring food," he said, watching the Hispanic woman distribute rice, beans, and chips from a plaid picnic sack to the others with her.

"You can bring food, books, games, and magazines," said the nurse. "No electronic devices." Jordan had already surrendered his phone to security downstairs.

The nurse left and he sat, at some distance from the other groups, on a chair with a small slit in the vinyl cushion. All the chair cushions were stained or ripped; some were repaired with shiny green tape. In the otherwise antiseptic hospital, this room seemed shabby. He thought of the Victorian Ballroom at the Susquehanna, where he'd first seen Summer, and stuck his hand inside his jacket. The little velvet box was there. When he'd given over his cell phone, which they'd placed in a drawer with a small padlock—he kept this. He'd found the ring at a pawnshop in Chinatown with rivers of jewelry gleaming in the window.

The group to his left spoke heatedly in Spanish and worked on a jigsaw puzzle as they ate from plastic plates. Jordan couldn't tell who the patient was because they all wore street clothes. He assumed, of the two women across the room, that the one in the wheelchair was a patient.

Then the door opened, and a stocky security guard escorted Summer inside. Her hair was clipped up on her head with one thick strand that dangled to her neck. Her blue eyes were wide and watchful. Unlike the other patients, she wore a hospital gown, knee socks, and slippers.

She said something to the guard, who nodded and left.

"They're still watching us," she mentioned as she sat in a chair beside Jordan, barely looking at him.

"Who is?"

"Staff." She tipped her head toward a pane of translucent glass. It was her typical, quasi-paranoid gesture that could have happened on the ferry to Fire Island or onstage. But there she was—her familiar arms with their fading sunburn, her rounded legs.

"Guess you know this room well, from Tillie's visits."

"Jesus, Jordan. I've just been here two days. And I want to get the fuck out—but I don't know where I belong." She said it fast, as though she was afraid someone could hear.

As if on cue, the woman in the wheelchair across the room selected that moment to start screeching like a baboon. The Hispanic group looked over at her.

"She'll be okay!" the younger woman called.

"Did you give the blood test to my psychiatrist?" Summer asked Jordan.

"I gave it to the nurse. She didn't even know about me. Here we are, getting married, and you didn't think to—"

"My personal life isn't their business. I came here for an evaluation of my psyche. So, are you really pissed?" A crack in her voice betrayed more vulnerability than he saw on her stoical face.

"I'm concerned," he said carefully. He wondered how she could possibly not know where she belonged but didn't want to push that point too hard.

Now she seemed able to look at him. She reached tentatively for his hand, which he accepted in his.

"How's Roo?"

"Starting to wonder where you are. I told him you're on tour again with Shazan."

"That was resourceful. But, I mean, is he upset?"

"What do you think?"

"Well, it's only been four days," she said.

"That's a long time for a kid. It's a long time for me. What the hell happened?"

"I wasn't right." She removed her hand from his, folding it into her other hand on her lap. "Remember when you needed to go to Z's that night, after you heard about Eliot lusting after me? You said you needed 'time to think' because Z was saying all this negative shit about me. You didn't come home."

"I had my phone. You kept calling, and you knew where to find me."

"I didn't leave my phone at home on purpose."

"Yeah, but Summer, we didn't know what happened, where you were."

"I left you a note that explained it. Then I had Tillie contact you. You're acting like we haven't seen each other in five years and I left you high and dry."

How she could make that defense seem persuasive was beyond him.

"But why…" He looked around the shabby room, shrugging. "I mean, we could have gone to my old shrink, Barbara. You never wanted to."

"A transactional analyst?" Summer made a face.

"She was good."

"I need a more hard-nosed team." She bit her lip, looked away from him and then back. "Look, I know you don't want to believe this, but I'm really fucked up. Something's profoundly wrong with me."

"Is being here…making it right?"

She shook her head. "I should be an outpatient."

"What do you think I've been saying?"

"Now they feel they have to observe me." She rolled her eyes. "I just wanted to come in for a day or two, talk to some people. Get some kind of"—she shrugged—"feedback or guidance. Get out of my own head. But then I talked too much about my mother. I shouldn't have, but I needed to. Now they think I might be a danger to myself, and they want to keep me here a couple more days."

"Do you want that?"

"I hate it here, but my shrink is pretty smart. And you know me. I generally don't give such idiots the time of day." She laughed uneasily. "But this one's okay. I felt terrible leaving Roo. But I couldn't bring him where I was going, and I knew that you and Betty and Curtis would take great care of him."

"He misses you."

"Does he? Do you miss me? Or has Z poisoned your feelings?"

"Why're you saying this shit about Z?"

"Couldn't you feel it that last time at the Susquehanna? He hates me. Your best friend hates me, Jordan. He probably thinks you should too."

"He doesn't," Jordan said quietly. "You get on his nerves, but that isn't what counts. He also thinks you're brilliant."

She seemed eager to hear this, staring at him like a small, hunted rabbit.

Then he almost felt himself moving as though on camera, in a video he'd look at someday when he was older than his father, when he'd play the saxophone with a bent spine and arthritic fingers. He would remember sitting on that chair with its ripped vinyl cushion and taking the black velvet box from his jacket pocket, and how her entire face seemed to darken as she mouthed, "Are you out of your mind?"

"I wouldn't be the only one around here."

He tried to hand the box to her, but she shook her head adamantly.

"This is all wrong. Look. They're watching us. You're not supposed to give me anything."

"They said I could bring in food and books…"

She kept shaking her head. "They'll never let me keep it."

"Well, let's just see if it fits."

He remembered his father saying, "She seems like the kind of woman who'd want a ring."

"Here." Jordan moved closer and tried again to hand her the box.

"I can*not* do this to you," she said sharply. "I've done enough damage."

"It would give me great joy if you accept my ring. It would mean the fucking world."

"What's this?" she went on, a frenetic pitch rising in her voice. "Some cut from *Marnie*, where Tippi Hedren asks Sean Connery, 'Who's the crazy one?'"

"For better or worse," he said, opening the black velvet box to display her ironically small diamond. "And it won't get worse than now."

"So…you're, like, buying shares of a stock that's plummeted?"

"Nowhere to go but up."

Strangely, she caught his eye and almost smiled.

"We both know," she stammered, "that I'm not worth the carbon dioxide I emit or the turds that fall out of me."

"Summer." He extended the box to her again. "Let's see if it fits."

"Don't tempt me."

She fidgeted in her seat, her face turning strawberry pink, her shiny eyes pleading. Never had he felt older, or more stable.

"I'll get you out of here," he assured her gently. "I'm supposed to talk to your shrink tomorrow. We'll go to Barbara and work things out. It will be okay."

"And if it isn't?" She leaned in and whispered to him, so close that he could feel her body heat. "Suppose I keep having episodes? And I get old and fat, and we stop fucking? Summer Vale becomes the has-been of the world, and her handsome young husband a man-about-town? Let's spare ourselves the clichés, Jordan. We can still be friends and have the child. It will work better that way."

"No," he replied, shocked. "I'm not letting you off so easy...I'm not like Khalil. I won't abandon you with my child."

"Oh, be free, Jordan. Be free with my blessings."

She stared at him, ready to cry, and he wondered if that was what she had also said to Khalil.

"How will you explain this to Rashad?" he demanded. "I promised to adopt him."

"I don't expect you to stick around for him, or Shoshana."

"I'm not sticking. I'm choosing. You're my family, and I love you all."

"You're crazy too, aren't you? Bringing me an engagement ring in a loony bin!" She looked around, began to laugh, then stopped herself. "You're crazy too."

"Half-crazy," he said. "My better half. So, can I put it on your finger?"

Slowly, she buried her face in her own cleavage, clasping arms tightly over her head. Jordan cleared his throat.

"What you did to Molly sucked," he said to the top of her head, with its uneven part, like a path through brambles. "It was the sickest thing anyone I know has ever done...except maybe when Claudia and I dealt dope from her apartment, without telling her. I don't approve of everything you do because I love you."

"And I'm not asking for forgiveness," she mumbled into her cleavage, from beneath her arms. "I don't believe in it."

"Well, I'm not forgiving you. I'm marrying you."

Slowly, she raised her head with its horrified eyes, dropping her hands on her lap.

"Once you snag me, you'll regret it and try to get out."

"I don't even know how to break up with anyone."

"You'll learn. Maybe you should go now."

"I just got here!" He almost laughed. But he retracted the little velvet box, sat back in his chair, and held it in his hand. "So are you still sick in the mornings?"

She leaned in again, shushing him as she glanced around. Then she whispered in his ear, "SSRIs are supposedly low-risk for pregnancy, but I'm not taking *any* risks. And I don't want to miscarry."

"And you're—absolutely sure?"

"Fire Island," she said.

"Does Deb know?"

She shook her head. "Only Tillie. She saw the positive tests. We did it three times, when I was at the Susquehanna. Positive, positive, positive." Summer pointed to her belly. "She's here, Jordan. That's why I'm here. Do you understand?"

He said quickly, "We'll get you to a good ob-gyn, and a therapist. Maybe Deb can help us."

"Help us how?"

"With advice. And—" He couldn't quite say the word, but she knew.

"We're not taking money from my sister. Or my mother. Do you understand that, Jordan? And I'm sure my mother will come out of the clouds like the angel she thinks she is and offer it. Deb told me she's planning to do that. She can go to hell."

Jordan sat poker-faced.

"Why are you—hey, you didn't speak to my sister, did you?" she persisted. "Because if my father's gone…" She stopped speaking for a moment and pursed her lips. "I don't wanna know. That's why I didn't take my phone."

"He's still here."

"You spoke with Deb, then?"

"I tried," said Jordan. "Listened to her calls on your cell. But we didn't talk."

"I knew you'd do that. Ask my shrink. I predicted you'd listen to my messages and call the people who were trying to reach me."

"Well, what did you expect?" He tried to control his annoyance. "It was all I had left of you."

"Leave my family to me," she said. "Once they take over, we'll never see ourselves again. I'll get health coverage another way."

"Like how?"

"Could you please stop acting like we're helpless? I still have Aunt Maegan's credit card. I just have to get the hell out of here."

"So are you Maegan Haarlan here? Is that your legal name? Or are you Summer Vale?"

She looked surprised. "I never told you my legal name?"

"That's right. And I'm marrying you."

She smiled wanly, almost starting to flirt—but she seemed too sad and tired. "Cathy Summers. I just knocked out the Jane. Hide in plain sight, I always say."

Suddenly a scream blasted from across the room, hoarse and guttural: "Das what I am, mwatha fucka!"

"Oh, Delilah!" moaned the woman who sat with her. "Delilah…"

A teenage guy in the Hispanic group started laughing.

"Das what I am!" The woman was trying to roll herself across the floor in the wheelchair while the other one struggled to stop her. A man got up from the family's table, but the security guard who had accompanied Summer now dashed in to handle Delilah.

Summer suddenly grabbed the black velvet box from Jordan and stuck the ring on her left finger. It fit perfectly and looked as elegant as anything from Tiffany. She leaned over as though she would fall forward off the seat and then straightened herself, laughing as Delilah continued her diatribe.

"Mwatha fucka! Leave me alone, you assholes…das what I am!"

The security guard wheeled Delilah out of the visiting room.

Once he'd been a lightweight, living for music and sex, often stoned, selling plastic Baggies of weed to friends, listening to Coltrane and Davis. "Boy toy,"

Molly had called him. Now the toy had his own boy and a new baby on the way—no money, and a troubled fiancée, who was hell-bent on estranging the people who could help them most.

If he turned to them, it would amount to turning against her.

Why now, Shoshana?

On his second beer at a bar on First Avenue, he implored his yet-to-be-born daughter. Summer kept his diamond ring ("I'll hide it in my socks if I need to," she told him), but she'd returned the box to him. He hadn't found the pills inside it until he exited the hospital.

"We're officially engaged," he'd told Skip and Tillie in the hospital lobby. After he'd seen Summer, Tillie was planning her own visit. They all agreed that it wasn't a great idea for Skip to join her. Still, Skip shook Jordan's hand when he announced their engagement and said a heartfelt, "Congratulations."

"Wonderful!" Tillie chimed in, giving Jordan a hug. "But…is she okay?"

"Not so long as she's here," contended Skip.

"You weren't with her before," Tillie objected. "You didn't hear how she was talking."

Skip shut his eerie blue eyes. "There's something she knows, and I know, but the two of you don't," he murmured. Tillie and Jordan glanced apprehensively at each other. Skip had opened his eyes again. "I did pull strings to get first prize," he admitted. "In the cabaret contest." He looked dolefully at Jordan. "They really liked her song about you, 'There's a Lot About This World I Don't Know.' She deserved first prize…I'll make it up to you," he said. "Get her out of this dog crate. We'll all go on tour or something. She was pissed at me, really devastated."

Vexed by Skip's appraisal of his influence on Summer, Jordan had explained, "See, here's the deal. I had to borrow cash from Molly, my ex. I made too much of it, and that humiliated Summer. It really got to her. I was so fucking stupid."

"Both of you!" Tillie interrupted, more upset than Jordan had ever seen her. "This is about *her*. Summer feels out of control. She told me she always sabotages, and she doesn't know how not to. She knows she needs help—but this isn't about either of you, or cabaret prizes, or whatnot. It's something inside *her*."

"What's inside her is our child," Jordan had said.

Why now, Shoshana?

He opened the black velvet box and looked at the pills, their different shapes and colors. Most were round, but one was pointed at the top and looked hard to swallow. She must have kept them in her socks and transferred them when Delilah made her racket and the security guard wheeled her out of the lounge. Jordan remembered Summer leaning over as though she'd fall off the chair. She was probably grabbing the pills from inside her knee socks. Thrilled and relieved that she was simply accepting his marriage proposal, Jordan had assumed she was just acting awkward.

Why now, Shoshana?

He started to weep on the bar, aware that his shoulders were shaking, that the bartender and other customers were probably noticing. A glass of water was placed by his head as he moaned like an ailing coyote.

Why now, baby girl? What on earth can I do for you? he thought. Did Grandfather—oops, excuse me, Capitano—give you bright ideas about taking us by storm after you'd proven so taciturn? Or are you taking cues from the now-you-see-her, now-you-don't side of the family?

It would be shame enough for Rashad to contend with his mother's breakdown and Jordan's ineptitudes. But that resilient kid was bonding with other grown-ups. How would a tiny baby cope? How could they begin to dig themselves out of the debt accruing from Summer's stay in a private hospital, her fraudulent use of Aunt Maegan's credit card, the pending court case, and everything else?

Stewart's words about the necklace in their apartment then came to him: "Drawn by Mucha's former apprentice, plated with white gold and sterling silver. They're easily worth a quarter of a mil each."

Jordan stopped crying and lifted his head, seized by intuition.

He stared at the velvet box, remembering that jar of old jellybeans. Never in a million years would he have thought to find the key to her locked file there. He must have looked stunned because the bartender and another patron stared at him as though he'd erupt. In fact, the bartender stealthily procured a bucket. Jordan just cleared his throat and asked: "How much do I owe you?" He probably had that much in his pocket.

He sped home, ready to climb every stair to the sixteenth floor. Though he'd left all the windows open, he still detected traces of the poisonous fumes when he stepped into the apartment. He was relieved to find the crumbling roses in Gus' vase, the vase that Summer never allowed him to touch or—heaven forbid— empty of its flaking, withered contents: "The last flowers he saw."

Jordan jammed his hand into the vase. Sure enough, something bulky lay beneath the dry silt. He withdrew a heavy plastic sandwich bag streaked with grit and crumbled rose petals. Breathlessly, he opened the plastic bag and extracted a perfectly clean pouch of sage-green velvet with black tassels that was lined with black silk. From that, he removed the most astonishing necklace he'd ever seen: two symmetrical silver mermaids, their arms stretched to each other's, fingers touching like ballerinas', with plumes of bright golden hair flying around them. Their tails linked in an art nouveau spiral that, embedded with gems, became sea spray.

Jordan held it to the window, watching diamonds catch the light and the garnets change color, as Stewart said they would.

"Holy fucking shit," he said aloud, and he said it again and again as he stared at the precision of the metalwork depicting classic mermaid profiles with low- ered eyes, the garnets in their tail shifting from turquoise to pink.

It felt like Coltrane's "Olé," something beyond this world.

Before he put it down, he checked the reverse side, upon which type was embedded into one silver mermaid silhouette:

On the blue surface of thine airy surge
Like the bright hair uplifted from the head
Of some fierce Maenad...
        —P. B. Shelley

On the other mermaid's reverse side, the letters *V* and *F* had been incised by hand, enclosed in a heart. Jordan placed it on the sofa beside him as though it were a live creature, like a macaw or another tropical bird.

Indeed, Summer's father was the keeper of the Eddystone Light. And he had married a mermaid one fine night. But he'd sold her off, and it occurred to Jordan that right now he could disappear with this treasure, retail it to some collection, and live like a fugitive forever on a remote Pacific island, playing saxophone by himself. Just as swiftly, it occurred to him that he'd never do that.

He would marry his mermaid and let the wind blow free.

A small sheet of parchment was rolled in the green velvet pouch with black tassels, and Jordan unfurled monogrammed stationery. *Cathy* was scrawled in handwriting so stretched-out it seemed like Jordan was viewing it through super strong prescription lenses, *Please confirm your receipt*, it read. At the bottom of the parchment *Nicholas J. Haarlan IV* was engraved in gold script.

Jordan reflected on his own line of dirt-poor Basque farmers, Italian potters, and persecuted Jews. But his child also claimed the bloodline of Nicholas J. Haarlan IV. She lay in the belly of the man's niece, like a gem in the earth. Her grandmothers were Mariana and Vivian. He spoke their names aloud, hearing music in them, like a drumbeat: Mariana, Vivian. Mariana, Vivian. He began to hear a song.

Then he panicked—to think that he'd entrusted a key to the super and actually let fumigators into the apartment, unaccompanied. They'd have to change the lock. He'd never had to think about anything so valuable, even to imagine one close to him. Maybe he'd get it into a bank safe. Suppose someone jumped him on the way to the bank? He'd get Z to walk with him. Then he imagined Z turning on him, or Curtis demanding it as collateral on his loans.

Jesus. Where did these crazy thoughts come from? He remembered what Molly said on the F train: "Alessandra always warned of a dark side to having lots of money."

He needed Molly's help now. The first order of business, he decided, was to put the necklace back into its pouch and into the plastic bag in the vase. He'd know exactly where it was—and so would Summer. It wouldn't get lost. After that, he'd write an apology to Molly. She'd receive it upon her return from wherever she was, maybe in a tiki hut on some tropical beach with palms and almond trees. He imagined her and Eugenia dancing as other tourists nodded out at a bar. Those beautiful American girls who loved each other would turn every head and steal the night.

Dear Molly, he began to plan the letter. *Dear Molly. You knew she was volatile…and pregnant. You figured out she was behind the Milk Truck. You knew more than me. You always do. I wasn't willfully ignoring anything, like Dahlia accused me of. I'm just really dumb sometimes. I didn't mean to hurt you, and Summer didn't know what she was doing. We've had the fuckedest, most surreal month, and it's not over yet.*

While his words were humble and accurate, he found he was unburdening himself, once again, to Molly. Nothing would change. He felt stuck, silly, suddenly horrified about being such a buffoon to her. If he wanted to restore honor to this friendship, he needed a woman's guidance—but not Summer's.

He still had time before he'd need to pick up Rashad at school, so he booted up the computer. Google told him that Tamara Douglas had been promoted to associate editor at a children's book imprint and was just back from maternity leave. Google even yielded her email address at work, where normal people were on a weekday afternoon.

Hi Tamara, he quickly typed, remembering her sweet gaze from the photo shoot in August. Then he stopped, watching the cursor blink as he figured out how to say it. When he finished writing, the note read:

Hi Tamara,

We met years back with Molly on the street, and I saw you at the photo shoot in Tribeca in August. Molly said you have a new baby son. Congratulations.

After Labor Day, Molly and I had a bad falling out. I hope to make up with her but need a little help, 'cause when I try to fix stuff like this, I bungle it worse. Could

I buy you coffee sometime and ask your advice? If you don't feel up to this, I will understand. No pressure.

Thanks,

Jordan Radfar

He read the email over ten times, thought better of soliciting Tamara's input, and then promptly pressed *Send*. Ten minutes later, he was pleased by her reply in his inbox: *How's Monday?*

Monday would probably be Summer's last day in the hospital.

Great, he wrote back. *Thank you.*

I can't guarantee results, she responded. *Molly's her own person, famously tough to persuade. Happy to listen though.*

No miracles expected. Your kind ear is all I could ask.

SO curious about what happened.

Let's just say my fiancée and I rolled Molly through hell on wheels. Your sister hates me for it.

Dahlia? Why is she sticking her nose into it?

Shit finds your nose.

Tamara sent back a smiley face and wrote, *Dahlia's not exemplary. So is your fiancée jealous of Molly?*

Pathologically. Like Othello looks tame.

Well, my husband is too. Sibling rivalry in the worst way.

We have lots to talk about, Tamara.

Is it Monday yet?

Jordan caught himself laughing over a new friend who'd been there all along. Monday would be sweet.

When the phone rang, he wondered if it might even be Tamara. But he didn't recognize the area code or the soft, formal cadence that inquired, "Is this the correct number for Cathy Summers?"

The female voice didn't sound officious enough for a collection agent. Still, Jordan was guarded. "Yes," he said. "But she's not here now."

"Am I speaking with Jordan?"

"You are," he said uncertainly.

"Jordan." The sound of his name uttered in this faint cadence fell upon him like a snowflake and dissolved on his nose. "This morning, very early…my husband, George, passed away."

Shocked into a different mind-set from his email banter with Tamara, Jordan stared across the room. Of course people like Summer's parents could find her phone number. They'd probably had it for years. "I'm sorry," he managed to say.

"Thank you," she replied, her voice lyrical as a shy girl's and constricted as an older smoker's. "I hear myself telling this person and that, but I can't believe it. I was hoping to speak with my daughter. Do you know when she'll be home?"

"Wish I did. Mrs. Summers, Cathy's in the hospital."

He didn't need to indicate what kind of hospital. Her mother seemed to know and just clucked softly: "Oh, goodness. Goodness. When did that happen?"

"She checked herself in the day before yesterday."

There was no response, so Jordan continued. "I'm so sorry to bear bad news."

"That makes two of us today. Jordan, is she getting adequate attention?"

"She's in a unit for acute care. Private hospital here in the city. It seems okay. They recommend that she stay 'til Tuesday."

If Summer knew he was telling her mother these details, she'd be livid.

"It's most…unlike Cathy to undertake such measures. She was quite critical when I did. What—would you terribly mind my asking—what precipitated this?"

He didn't want to mention her pregnancy, the Ahlstrom brothers' attack, and certainly not the Milk Truck. Whatever Summer's mom needed to know would come out over time.

"Has she been drinking?" The woman prompted him with quiet dread.

"She's actually not a drinker, smoker, or pill popper—it was just emotions."

There was a pause at the other end. "You surely know that I had a devil of a time at Cathy's age. You've heard the song."

"I have."

"How is her son taking it?"

"He's not sure what's happening, but he gets that something's wrong."

"They always do," the woman confirmed. "I was hoping you and Cathy might bring him to the burial of his grandfather in Monmouth, where we're from. But it's not realistic to expect you, even for the memorial."

"We should try," Jordan volunteered.

"Uh…knowing what I do about case review and discharge, I won't ask that of you now, Jordan."

"We should be there for you."

"Oh, I'll be fine. Debbie will come, and my brother is flying in from Cape Town. Though George would have wanted Cathy Jane…" Jordan could not imagine this hypnotically gentle voice in tandem with heavy drinking or suicide. "He spoke warmly of Cathy," she continued, in flutelike speech that sounded more like breath than actual tone. "Always asked me to play her songs in the morning."

"I wish I'd met him."

"In a sense you have, living with Cathy. She's very much George's daughter, which is why her voluntary admission surprises me. Neither of them were fans of hospitals. Are you aware that George was suing for malpractice?" Mrs. Summers asked.

"Uh…she mentioned it. Back in March or something."

"Ironically, he won the suit three days ago. He said…" Jordan could hear the woman gulp softly. "He said—well, I confess, I coaxed him a bit. He said, give the proceeds to our girls and our grandkids. It was his last decision. I wanted it to be his best."

Before Summer's family came to town after the memorial, Jordan resolved to fix up the apartment. With Z's help, he'd toss out the junk on the terrace. In fact, he'd toss out every shitty-looking thing they owned. If he had time, he'd paint the kitchen and buy new rugs.

Z came by to take measurements for the wall unit he and a friend would build that weekend. Rimless glasses edging down his nose, Z scribbled numbers on a yellow legal pad. "You won't need to invite them here, you know," he mumbled to Jordan, as he popped the measuring tape out of its case, stretched it over a strip of wall, and snapped it back in. "People like Summer's family stay at posh hotels and take you to brunch."

Indeed, Mrs. Summers and Deb would share the penthouse at the Susquehanna, of all places. Uncle Nick had booked the Bentley Suite at the St. Regis. Mrs. Summers confided to Jordan that her brother never stayed at the Pierre or the Plaza when he visited New York because "he says Central Park should be seen but not sniffed." She, on the other hand, loved horses, and added, "I hope they have enough space in the city and turn out to pasture."

Jordan spoke on the phone to his future mother-in-law every day, sometimes more than once. He felt captivated by her nicotine-grazed voice, her charmingly inappropriate disclosures about loving the odors of horses, and other anomalies. The quirky benevolence reminded him of what he loved about Summer.

"They're not like your parents, looking to crash on a sofa," Z repeated didactically.

Jordan wondered if his friend resented how well Jordan could pay him for this job, and whether he might be jealous of Summer's inheritance from her father's malpractice suit. Jordan hadn't yet mentioned her pregnancy to Z; she'd suggested that they not let on until after their wedding, once they were past the first months. He certainly didn't want to tell Curtis and Betty after all they'd done for him. His good news might invoke memories of their miscarriage. Ironically, Skip and Tillie had become their confidantes about Shoshana.

"Hey, can I bum some weed? Got any more of that good Hawaiian shit?" Jordan asked Z suddenly.

Z looked up from his legal pad, took off his glasses and slipped them into his shirt pocket. "Go easy on weed. And beer."

"We do weed and beer all the time. C'mon, let's blaze."

"You're at three times your usual caliber. Just saying."

"What are you, my babysitter?"

"Friend," said Z. "We've been friends a long time. Generally, we keep out of each other's hair. Which I like. So maybe I'm a hypocrite to ask—when her brother-in-law says *w*, and her shrink on the ward says *x*—you're marrying her *why*?"

"Because, Z…"

Jordan recalled her warm breasts pressing through her hospital gown when they'd hugged goodbye and the diamond ring sparkling on her finger.

He saw her in a splash of colored lights onstage holding each note to full-bodied perfection. He saw her curled on the sofa in her blue bathrobe watching old movies with hair in her face. He saw her in her fake fur coat and Berlin bear hat pretending to be a grizzly for the boys, and in her bathing suit diving into Lake Champlain.

"She's my home," he answered.

"But she's not home. She's in a fucking psych ward. She's crazy, Jo-Jo."

"Half-crazy. There's another half."

"Would you eat something half-toxic?"

His tall friend walked over and sat on the sofa, tapping his kneecap nervously with his pen. "Marriage is sticky, you know, even with a good woman. But this one…stalking Molly? And the business with Eliot…what deranged shit she gonna pull next?"

Jordan repeated Tillie's prognosis: "She needs help, and she knows it."

"You said she's not even taking meds."

"Meds aren't the only help around."

"Then what are you talking about?"

"Counseling. She's found a shrink there who she actually respects. Her mother's coming and…"

"Won't *that* be lovely? More short ends of her stick. Does Summer even know about your daily chats with Mom?"

Jordan shook his head, jonesing for a joint. He could practically taste it on his tongue.

"You think she was ticked off when you hung with Molly? Wait 'til she hears who's your new best friend."

"Why are you being an asshole?"

"Why are you tying yourself to this crackpot and her family? Is it the money, Jo? You know what I'm saying."

"I love her," Jordan declared again. "I proposed to her before I knew about her family."

"Oysters *on* the Rockefellers—Republican chairman of Whatever County? You knew from the get-go where she comes from."

"That's not what did it. We make great love and great music."

"Unless she's vowing to never sing again, and running out on you…"

"You know she's fucking brilliant. There were times you defended her and thought I was overreacting." Jordan got up from the sofa and marched into the kitchen, calling, "I'm having beer, even if you're a pussy about it."

"One beer," Z called back.

"One beer," Jordan mocked him. Then he added, under his breath: "I make my own rules, and I'm not a drunk."

"Not yet," said Z.

Jordan walked back into the living room and coldly thrust a bottle of Heineken at his friend. The two men swigged together in silence, Jordan resenting this pressure to defend various choices but feeling compelled to keep doing so. He had privately wondered if he would have married Summer, after all their trouble, without the family wealth or her pregnancy. But that had always been his plan.

"You know how many great poets and musicians were messed up worse than her? Everyone from, like, Walt Whitman to Johnny Cash—so many of 'em. They found love. Someone loved them." Jordan guzzled more from his bottle. The tart beer quenched his thirst and made him thirstier. "Besides, I promised Rashad that I'll adopt him."

"Let me tell you about you and Rashad," said Z. "In ten years, he'll be fifteen, you'll be forty. He'll be out with girls and friends and want nothing to do with you and Summer. He'll probably be embarrassed by you."

"Sounds like a normal father and son," said Jordan. "Like me and Arman."

"It's your business," conceded Z. "But someone's got to put it to you before you meet her at the altar, now that Molly's voice has been conveniently silenced."

Jordan lowered his bottle of Heineken to the floor. Summer actually had a point about Z trying to persuade him not to marry her. "Molly dumped me. Summer is wearing my ring. Why are you on Molly's side, man?"

"Summer doesn't have 'a side,'" Z emphasized, staring back at Jordan.

"Come on. Summer didn't hurt a hair on Molly's head. She didn't stab her or poison her—didn't even intercept her mail. She had some idiot follow her in a car for a week. Wasn't great, but it's not the worst story I've heard. And then she felt crappy. Started beating up on herself. Committed herself, trying to get help…"

"Do you know what Molly does?" Z asked righteously.

"Like, yeah—ad agency, Cajun place with Eugenia. And she and her rich friends do some day trading. God, just wait 'til I'm richer than her. Summer's family blows Molly out of the water, with her measly couple of million—they make her look proletariat." Jordan stamped his foot and laughed stridently, a wave of triumph rising in his chest as he imagined running into Molly at the Four Seasons or the Rainbow Room. "Summer's mom's family—they're crazy rich. You know, diamonds, gold. I'll show Molly an Impala convertible—or was it a Starfire?" He tried to remember which vintage car Molly had mentioned buying Eugenia for her fortieth birthday.

"Molly busts human traffickers," Z interrupted. "She helps the victims get on their feet again. She does a lot that you may not know about, and she's been successful—like a guerilla philanthropist. Imagine how certain people hate her, without even knowing who she is. Imagine how terrified she was by that stalker car. I call it complete harassment. And what do you do? Marry the bitch."

"Don't go all moral on me. You've been with some out-there women in your time, John Saintcroix."

"Been with," said Z. "Not married."

"You're jealous," Jordan charged.

Z rolled his eyes upward. "It's your fun house. Cry if you want to."

"I did. In a bar."

Z brought the beer bottle to his lips for a swallow, then asked, "When?"

"Last week. First time after I saw her on the ward."

"Well…?"

Z motioned for him to say more, to fill in the blanks about why he'd wept in public. There was no anger in his eyes now, just curiosity. Jordan almost revealed that he'd be a father in eight months, that he expected to become the decorative young husband of an unstable heiress—and that it was a better future for himself than any other he could imagine.

"In my world, a promise matters more than saving my ass. Because what's my ass if I break promises, or break a kid's heart?"

Z nodded as though he knew this already about Jordan.

"I'm not deluded. She's very difficult, and it will be hell, sometimes. Hope you're not just gonna say 'Told you so.'"

Z shook his head. "No," he said. "No. You can always come to me and talk."

On Sunday night Jordan and Rashad moved back into the apartment on East Broadway. It felt like a different place, smelling of freshly sawed wood, varnish, and wall paint. Jordan had stored all their amps and instruments in the wall unit, as Molly had advised, and it did open up space in the living room. So he splurged on a bright Moroccan rug and convertible sofa. His future mother-in-law had welcomed him, in that gently hypnotic voice on the phone, to "get anything you need for your comfort and Cathy's." So he'd even ordered a huge flat-screen TV.

"Whaddaya think?" he asked Rashad as they stood in the foyer with their bags. "You like the wall unit?"

"It's okay."

"Think your mom will like it?"

The boy shrugged.

"She'll be back on Tuesday," Jordan reminded him, setting his saxophone case and knapsack on the floor.

"I know."

Summer had spoken to Rashad several times by phone, but her son seemed to have lost interest in her.

"Will I hold the ring?" he suddenly asked, looking up at Jordan and squinting slightly. "For my mom or for you?"

"Hmmm, I don't know how that works," said Jordan. "Never done it before."

"'Cause I like you better," Rashad announced.

"Oh no." Jordan flinched. "You don't have to like me better."

"But I do."

"It's not a contest. You can like us both."

Rashad seemed to consider the possibility without yielding.

"I know she's been gone a lot," Jordan began, "but it's not because—"

"She's *sick* a lot," Rashad interrupted with a frown. "And she says I'm not allowed to meet my grandma."

"Do you want to?"

Rashad nodded. "Most people have two grandmas," he said. As if remembering the new TV from her that was supposed to be even bigger than Ian and Archer's, he looked eagerly across the room.

"Is that—ours?"

"That's why it's here."

Rashad kicked off his shoes, ran across the floor, and jumped onto the new sofa. Like all five-year-olds, he knew exactly how to operate the remote control.

"I synched up the cable box today," Jordan told him.

Rashad suddenly turned and pointed the wand at Jordan, pretending to press the power button.

Jordan struck a pose, baring his teeth and stretching his fingers like talons. Rashad pretended to change the channels, and Jordan crossed his arms and stuck out his tongue. Giggling, Rashad changed the channels again, and Jordan placed his index fingers beneath his eyes and pulled them down, exposing the whites. His sister had hated that when they were kids, but Rashad shrieked with delight.

Then Jordan heard himself chuckle too, as though he were somebody else.

Poe and the four conditions for happiness.

(1) Life in the open air.

(2) The love of another being.

(3) Freedom from all ambition.

(4) Creation.

—the notebooks of Albert Camus

July 1939

About the Author

Half Crazy is Dara Lebrun's third novel in an
interconnected series called *Children Who Aren't Ours.*
The Bunny Hop (2014) and *Sub Rosa* (2016) are
the series' first two titles. Dara's writing has appeared
in *Honeysuckle Magazine,* epicfantasy.com and paleghosts.com.
In 2009 she was a finalist in a *Glimmer Train* short
fiction contest.

A native and longtime New Yorker, Dara now
makes her home on the West Coast.